BROKEN PATRIOTS

James C Edwards

Inquiries & Permissions: Vanguard Patriot Press | jamescedwards.auth or@gmail.com

ISBN (Paperback): 979-8-9898495-8-1
ISBN (Hardback): 979-8-9898495-9-8

I dedicate this book, "Broken Patriots," to the sources of my inspiration and strength.

I wanted to thank God, the maker of the universe, for granting me the gift of a creative mind. Your boundless imagination and creativity have illuminated the path of my storytelling journey. With every twist and turn of the narrative, I am reminded of the wondrous tapestry of creation that you have woven through Jesus. While this book is not religious, it was created with that gift in mind.

Finally, I want to thank my wife Amber, your unwavering support and encouragement have been my guiding light throughout this creative endeavor. Your belief in me and my stories has been a constant source of inspiration. You are my greatest ally. Thank you for being the steady hand that guides me through the labyrinth of creativity.

1

CEDAR HILL STILL HAD a July Fourth parade. Most towns had canceled theirs after the Missouri Capitol bombing, but in Cedar Hill, they marched anyway. Tattered American flags fluttered above cracked sidewalks while old men in American Legion caps saluted from folding chairs. Children tossed candy from the backs of antique pickups, their laughter straining against the silence of a country cracking apart.

Seventeen-year-old Jonah McAllister marched with the high school band, his tuba slung across his chest like a weight from another lifetime. His mother had begged him not to go. His older brother, Caleb, had been conscripted by the new Federal Draft and shipped off six months ago; that was another world before Troy Thomason's assassination, before all of this.

"This country's not yours anymore, Jonah," Caleb had warned him before leaving for a war no one wanted, save for the politicians and the weapon manufacturers. "Stop pretending it is."

Jonah wanted one more day of normal. He got twenty-three minutes. It started with the phones buzzing in unison, screens flashing SOS. A hush fell across Main

Street as parents checked black glass. The drumline faltered; the brass section went quiet.

A low rumble rose in the distance. The first plane crested the sky like a storm front: a gray C-130 flanked by two F-35s. They bore the unmistakable insignias of the Air Force stars and stripes. The feeling in Jonah's chest wasn't pride. It was dread.

People clapped at first, until the back of the C-130 opened and the paratroopers began to fall. Screams rose before the first chute even touched the ground. Soldiers in Federal blues choked the sky, their chutes snapping open in white bursts that blotted out the sun as they dropped into the soy fields west of town. Gunfire peppered the air as locals armed themselves and ran toward the tree line.

The tuba slipped. The brass bell crumpled against the asphalt with a discordant ring swallowed by the first scream. Jonah didn't reach for it; that life was already gone.

"We're under martial law!" someone shouted.

"No, we're under attack!"

Deputy Hamilton ran up the street, gun drawn, yelling over the panic. "GO HOME! GET INSIDE! This is a Federal operation targeting Great Plains Militia! MOVE!"

Militia? Jonah's stomach dropped. Caleb had joked about Missouri being a "Free State" now, but they had never officially seceded. Had they? He pressed the power button on his phone to call home, but the screen read: No Signal.

The air changed again with a scream that split the heavens. Two jets soared in low from the south, painted in bold yellow and red with a blue charging bison on the tails. Jonah recognized the "Buffalo Patch" from the viral resignation videos on Vyber.

The jets unleashed fire. Missiles streaked from underwing pylons, striking a paratrooper cluster mid-air. Chutes incinerated. A Federal jet peeled hard right, trying to climb, but the second GPN fighter clipped its wing with cannon fire. It spiraled behind the tree line and exploded with a violent roar.

Jonah ducked as shrapnel rained across the street, a telephone pole splitting in half ten feet from where he stood. Children screamed and cars swerved into ditches while, somewhere, someone began praying aloud.

The C-130 banked sharply, trying to abort, but a missile struck its tail. The giant craft spun, vomiting fire and bodies before slamming into the hills beyond the river. The explosion was deafening. Then, silence. Smoke rose over the valley like a funeral pyre.

Jonah staggered to his feet, ears ringing. Blood trickled down the side of his head. His tuba lay in the street, twisted beyond recognition. His screen flickered, a high-priority override forcing its way through the jammer. A single emergency message scrolled in stark, red text:

Missouri is now a sovereign state under the protection of the Great Plains Pact. All Federal forces will be considered hostile. Shelter in place. Secure weapons if available. DO NOT COMPLY with Federal orders. This is not a drill.

Jonah read it twice. Like millions of others across the fractured heart of the continent, he realized the truth: The United States of America was at war with its own corpse.

Great Plains Presidential Office — 7.4.26

Jeremiah looked up from the intelligence report and reached for his coffee, but the cup remained halfway to his lips as he stared at the casualty projections. The friction with the Confederation had already pushed him to the edge of his capacity; now, he faced a looming conflict with the United States. The weight of it was etched in the red-rimmed lines across his brow.

Miranda paced a tight circuit in front of his desk, one hand pressed white-knuckled to her chest. "It's just so devastating, Jeremiah," she whispered, her voice barely carrying across the room. "We've lost so much already. This war is swallowing everything we have left."

Jeremiah stood, his joints popping in the silence. He walked to her and wrapped an arm around her shoulders, pulling her into the solid heat of his side. His face was a mask of grief, but he offered her a thin, fleeting smile that didn't quite reach his eyes. "I know, sweetheart," he murmured against her temple. "I know."

The heavy oak door was thrown open as a short, wiry aide stepped inside. His hair was frayed at the edges and his suit jacket hung crookedly, as if he'd dressed in a dead sprint. He held a red-stamped folder in both hands, his fingers trembling against the cardstock. "Mr. President," he said, his voice dry. "Cedar Hill. Civilians attacked."

The words landed like a hammer. Jeremiah released Miranda and stepped forward, reaching for the folder with a hand that remained perfectly steady despite the shock. He didn't open it; the classified designation on the cover told him everything he needed to fear. He turned to the window and set the folder on the desk behind him. "I want General Marcus Ross and the rest of the Cabinet. Forthwith," he commanded, his voice hardening into the steel he used for the public. His gaze was fixed on the distant Montana horizon.

"Right away, sir. Yes, sir." The aide disappeared as quickly as he'd arrived.

Jeremiah turned back to Miranda, the presidential mask slipping just enough to show the man underneath. "Sweetheart, I want you to head back to the Big Sky Ranch. It's quiet there. You can breathe." His voice softened, thick with the knowledge that she was still reeling from Jake's death. Every fresh tragedy felt like a hand pushing her closer to a breaking point.

Miranda nodded slowly, but the hesitation in her eyes was sharp. She didn't want to leave him, even though she knew he could carry the weight. But Jeremiah needed her safe, especially if the war reached as far north as Helena. "But Samantha's still out there," Miranda said, her voice finally breaking into a tremble. "I can't lose her too."

Tears tracked through the blush on her cheeks, and Jeremiah pulled her back into his arms. He held her tightly, breathing in the faint, grounding scent of her hair. "We're lucky to have her," he said into the silence. "As a frontline commander, there's no one better. I can't promise the war won't touch her, but I can promise nothing will happen to you."

He gently released her and turned toward the door. The same aide reappeared, breathless. "Sir, the Situation Room is ready. General Ross is waiting."

Jeremiah nodded once, then turned back to his wife. "Please, go home. Big Sky is safe for now. If it isn't, the bunker is ready."

Miranda wiped her eyes and stepped back, a final, lingering kiss on his cheek her only goodbye. "I'll wait for word from Samantha," she said, her voice steadying. "When you see Marcus, tell him not to treat her like a pawn."

Jeremiah forced a soft smile. "She's more than that. She's hope." He lowered his head and turned to leave.

The Situation Room was a reinforced concrete box buried beneath the old state capitol, a Cold War relic hastily renovated into the nerve center of a new republic. Thirteen people sat around the polished steel table: ministers, governors, and generals. A giant screen glowed at the far end of the room, flanked by satellite feeds, decrypted comms chatter, and live drone footage from Missouri.

General Marcus Ross stood at the head, arms crossed over a dark tactical jacket. His expression was tight, his jaw clenched. "Mr. President," he said as Jeremiah entered. "It's worse than we thought."

Jeremiah nodded. "Give me the overview."

Ross clicked a remote. The screen shifted to overhead drone footage: smoke rising from Cedar Hill and plumes of fire in the hills. "Paratroopers dropped at 10:27 Central. Civilian casualties unknown, likely dozens. Our intercept team neutralized two F-35s and a C-130, but not before a full platoon made landfall. The Buffalo Patch wing out of Sioux City confirmed a defensive strike, but it's already going viral as a 'Great Plains Aggression.'"

"Where did they launch from?" Jeremiah asked.

"Whiteman Air Force Base," Ross said grimly. "Still technically under Federal control. They've retaken Jefferson City, though most of Missouri never acknowledged Bennett's authority in the first place."

Governor Riley of Iowa leaned forward. "This wasn't an accident. This was a provocation. They wanted us to retaliate."

Jeremiah exhaled slowly, fingers steepled. "Do we have confirmation it was sanctioned by Washington?"

Ross hesitated. "Not direct confirmation. But we intercepted encrypted chatter out of the Pentagon regarding Operation Foothold. It's an active push to reclaim noncompliant territories under Federal emergency powers."

"So it's begun," Jeremiah said quietly. "The Second War for the Union. What's the status of our eastern defense line?"

"Intact, but strained. The garrison in Kansas City is holding, but any more Federal incursions and we'll have to call for reinforcements from the Dakota Corridor. Samantha's Bison Plains Regiment is closest; she's already en route to Jefferson County."

Jeremiah blinked. "She's already moving?"

Ross nodded. "She moved without waiting for orders. She saw the drop from twenty miles out and mobilized on her own. I figured you'd approve."

A small smile tugged at Jeremiah's mouth. "God help whoever stands in her way." He paused, eyes still fixed on the monitors. "Any word from the other secessionist states?"

The question hovered like smoke in a field after gunfire. Silence reigned until Governor Riley finally spoke. "I had a call this morning from Samuel Burris. He's not Governor anymore, not officially. He's calling himself President of the United Alliance of America."

Several heads turned. "UAA?" Ross asked.

Riley nodded. "Formed out of North Carolina and the northern half of South Carolina, now calling itself Carolina. The other states of Virginia, Jefferson, Florida, Alabama, and Georgia, all ratified entry last week. Their central government's operating out of Raleigh."

"Jefferson?" someone asked.

"New state designation made up of parts of the former South Carolina and Georgia, formally recognized within the UAA. Everything they're doing is by-the-book constitutional. Their book, anyway."

Jeremiah's brow furrowed. "What triggered them?"

Riley's voice dropped. "Three things, officially: the mobilization against the Great Plains Nation, the assassination of Troy Thomason of North Carolina, and the massacre in Congress. That was the last straw. They declared the Union dead. Said the Republic had 'ceased to function.'"

Ross leaned forward. "Are they siding with us?"

Riley shook his head. "They're not enemies, but they're not our subordinates either. Burris made that clear. Their statement was explicit: they've declared neutrality in the West. They will defend their own borders and they've denounced D.C.'s aggression against us."

"So we're allies, conditionally," Ross muttered.

"More like co-belligerents," Jeremiah said, his voice cold. "We have a common enemy, but they're not flying our banner."

The display shifted to a tactical map, UAA-controlled territory now glowing gold with naval assets blinking along the Atlantic. "Norfolk is fully under their control," Riley added. "According to our intelligence assets, the state guard took it without much resistance. Most Navy personnel either defected or were detained. They've absorbed the bulk of the East Coast fleet."

"Do we expect them to move inland?"

Riley shook his head again. "Not unless provoked. They've locked down major corridors: Savannah, Columbia, Richmond. But every statement they've issued is defensive. They're fortifying, not expanding."

Jeremiah exhaled through his nose and stood slowly. "So they'll hold the coasts. We hold the plains. And D.C. holds the crumbling bones of the old Republic. Fine. Let them govern their way. But if the Feds try to use them as a pincer..." He looked at Ross. "I want contingency plans drawn up. Quietly."

Ross nodded grimly. "Already underway."

"What of the other states?" Jeremiah asked, his voice steady but laced with fatigue.

"Samantha reported UAA forces assisting in Evanston, Wyoming. She also mentioned a group calling itself the Republic of Texas, and another group called the Bluegrass States Republic." Jeremiah looked to Riley, then Ross. "We just talked about the UAA. Who the hell are the rest of these factions?"

Ross tapped a control on the table. A new map flickered to life: irregular borders, new flags, and blinking unit positions like a patchwork of rebellion. "It's fragmented. Texas declared independence formally several months ago, within weeks of us seceding. They've secured Austin, Dallas, and most of the energy infrastructure. They're heavily armed, highly organized, and refusing Federal oversight of any kind."

Riley added, "They've also issued a formal statement recognizing the Great Plains Nation as a sovereign ally. Mutual defense clause and everything."

Jeremiah raised an eyebrow. "They declared a pact? Did we sign it and I missed the memo?"

"For now, they are," Ross replied. "But Texas is proud and insular. They declared a defense pact in absentia. When D.C. collapses, Texas won't take orders from anyone but Texas."

Riley turned a page in his folder. "As for the Bluegrass States Republic, that's Tennessee, Kentucky, West Virginia, Ohio, Indiana, Illinois, all the way up into Michigan. They moved fast after Thomason's assassination. Claimed moral authority to 'restore Constitutional order.' Their rhetoric's intense."

"Religious?" Jeremiah asked.

"Militant," Ross answered. "They're invoking God and guns in every speech. And while they've been targeting Federal forces, they're not exactly coordinating with us. Samantha's report from Evanston confirms they were in the area, but it wasn't a joint op. Looked more like a parallel ambush."

Jeremiah nodded slowly. He stepped toward the map, eyes scanning the expanding constellation of breakaway governments. "So the Republic is splintering not just into factions, but ideologies."

"Correct," Ross said. "We've got constitutionalists, nationalists, militias, and state guard coalitions, each carving out their piece of the dead Republic."

Jeremiah folded his arms, jaw tight. "And we're the glue. Whether they like it or not."

"Maybe. Or the accelerant."

"Back to Cedar Hill," Jeremiah said, his voice low but decisive. "How should we respond?"

The room fell still again. Beneath the hum of the monitors, the weight of the question settled like smoke. General Ross cleared his throat. "We already responded tactically. The Buffalo Patch wing scrambled from Sioux City. Ground teams swept the drop zone and confirmed most of the platoon is neutralized. But," he hesitated, "it's already online."

"I saw it," Jeremiah said. He turned toward one of the screens, paused on footage of fire in the hills and a boy ducking behind a crumpled band trailer as debris rained from the sky.

"Amateur recordings," Ross added. "Posted to Vyber and Telegraph. Probably a dozen angles already circulating. It hasn't hit mainstream feeds yet, but it will."

Governor Riley leaned forward. "The narrative's fractured. The raw clips make it look like an unprovoked strike. No context. The usual blue-check crowd's already calling it Great Plains terrorism."

"Even though it was a Federal drop," Ross muttered. "Even though we were defending our airspace."

Jeremiah nodded slowly. “The boy in that video... he’s not a soldier. He was in a marching band. That’s what people will remember. Not the strategic breakdown. Not the drone footage. That boy.” The silence deepened. “I want someone on the ground by nightfall. Independent press, verified militia. Document everything: testimony, damage, casualties. Get ahead of the lie before it calcifies.”

“But sir, it’s an active site,” someone in the room protested.

Ross looked at the speaker and then gave a firm nod toward Jeremiah. “We’ll pull someone from the Helena Bureau. Low profile. Boots on the ground by sundown.”

“And what about retaliation?” one of the governors asked. “If this was Operation Foothold, don’t we need to hit back?”

Jeremiah’s voice was calm but cold. “We hit back when it matters most. Not when they want us to. Let D.C. overextend. Let them bleed credibility.” He stepped away from the screen. “But Cedar Hill will not be forgotten. That footage is our Lexington. Make sure the world knows it.”

Samantha stared out the narrow, reinforced window of the armored personnel carrier as it rumbled south. Behind her, an Infantry Fighting Vehicle trailed closely, both carrying members of the Bison Plains Regiment.

She had twenty souls under her command and carried that weight like armor. She'd lost two of her regiment in Evanston, Wyoming, and nearly more in Skokie, Illinois, but today was a new day. News of the attack in Cedar Hill had left her no choice: she ordered the militia to hold the line in Skokie while she redeployed her core team south.

"Lieutenant Colonel Johnson! Comms from Helena!" The voice crackled through the loudspeaker, snapping Samantha out of her thousand-yard stare.

She leaned forward. "Play it, Private Martin."

A burst of static preceded the message: "Johnson, one of our primary munitions facilities is located in the Cedar Hill area is likely the target. Your orders: secure the site and repel all hostiles."

The transmission cut out. Samantha gave a short, steady nod. "Understood. Get me a channel to the IFV."

Private Martin tapped his headset. "You're live."

She pressed the comm button on her chest. "Bravo Vehicle, this is Johnson. We've got confirmation: the munitions facility near Cedar Hill is a high-value target. Possible infiltration. We're to secure and repel. Rules of engagement are active. Full combat posture. Acknowledge."

"Copy that, Colonel," came the reply. "Weapons hot."

Samantha leaned back and keyed in a local map on the tablet beside her. The convoy was five klicks out, but the signs of conflict were already unmistakable. Smoke rose in thick columns against the summer sky. One plume trailed from the hills where the C-130 had gone down; another curled black and oily above the town center, likely from torched vehicles. A scorched F-35 wing jutted from the treeline like a broken blade.

Too quiet, she thought, watching civilians flee the roads on foot. Some carried children while others waved makeshift flags of surrender. She turned to her second-in-command, Sergeant Owen Clay. "Get recon drones in the air. I want eyes on the town square, the munitions corridor, and that crash site. If someone's still alive out there, I want to know."

Clay nodded, already working the controls.

"And Sergeant," she added, her voice dropping. "If this turns out to be more than a Federal drop, I want the Bison ready to stampede. We don't lose this town."

"Ma'am, we came through Evanston and Skokie," he said with a sharp look. "We'll hold."

The first gutted buildings of Cedar Hill appeared beyond the tree line. Burned American flags still hung from some storefronts. "Then let's get to work."

Recon drones buzzed free from their launch bay, scattering into the sky like a swarm of hornets. "Eyes live," Clay reported as a dozen monitors flickered to life. The feeds came in one by one: grainy visuals panning over rooftops, tree lines, and scorched earth. The drones spread in a web formation, sweeping the area in concentric arcs.

"Not seeing anything, Colonel," Clay muttered, his fingers dancing over the controls.

Samantha leaned in, eyes narrowing at the static-laced images. "Switch to thermal. They're out there."

The screens shifted to infrared, showing harsh gradients of red, orange, and black. All they found were the heat signatures of fire: burning vehicles, smoldering rooftops, and a field still crackling from the downed jet.

"Nothing moving," Clay said. "No bodies. No patrols."

Samantha's jaw tightened. "Which means the area is either secure or..." One of the drone feeds crackled and went to static. A second dropped out right after it. She leaned in. "As I thought. They're wearing thermal camouflage."

She grabbed her mic without missing a beat. "This is Johnson. IFV team, deploy now. Sweep west of Main. Eyes up, safeties off. We are not alone out here."

The IFV hissed open, armored panels retracting as boots hit the pavement. Sergeant Koa Benoit motioned his fireteam forward. Three fanned left and three right, weapons raised, eyes scanning the perimeter. Samantha stepped out behind them, the acrid scent of burning plastic and scorched earth hitting her all at once. Smoke curled over Main Street where a shopfront still flickered with flames. A truck had flipped onto its side, its undercarriage charred beyond recognition.

She moved toward the center of the intersection, tracking the angles of windows, rooftops, and alleys.

"Drones five through nine are still online," Clay reported over comms. "Flanking both sides. No movement, but thermal interference is climbing."

"Jamming?" she asked.

"Possible. Or masking tech. Either way, something's not right."

She knelt beside a scorched curb, her fingers closing around a shard of twisted metal. It was smooth, black, and too precise to be civilian. It was military-grade. Federal, but not standard issue. She turned it over and paused. An emblem was etched into the alloy, faint but unmistakable.

It wasn't Federal. It wasn't Militia.

"I've seen this once before," Clay muttered. "Back at Camp Travis. We downed a black ops drone that was completely off-book. Same symbol on the guidance fin. Intel tagged it Project Eclipse. Contractors with no official footprint. Not even a paper trail."

"I don't recognize the seal," Samantha said quietly. "Looks like CIA, or something else." She tapped her mic. "All units, status orange. Unknown presence confirmed. Advance in squads. Sweep every block."

Smoke still curled from the hills where the C-130 went down. Whatever had started in Cedar Hill hadn't ended yet.

Phen knelt in the underbrush, his rifle slick with smeared mud to dampen its heat signature. Twelve crouched silently behind him, still as a statue, while Vannah and Jack faced the opposite direction. Their eyes scanned the tree line for the next wave of drones. One had already spotted them and hadn't lived long; Phen had dropped two from a distance. They were quick, but not quicker than him.

"Great job, honey," Vannah whispered, resting a hand lightly on Phen's back. He allowed himself a small smile.

"Militia's on the ground," Jack muttered as he slid up beside them, his face streaked with dark clay. "We need to eliminate the weapons facility. No delays."

The four moved as one, a silent phalanx cutting westward through the brush toward the Montana-Idaho Militia who had just begun securing the town. Twelve raised a fist, halting them. "The IFV's sweeping this way," she said, her voice clipped and sharp.

They dropped lower, bodies melting into the terrain. The sound of treads on pavement echoed through the trees, drawing closer. Twelve didn't flinch. Her eyes tracked the movement, calculating the sweep radius. "They're scanning every thirty degrees," she whispered. "Infrared, maybe LiDAR. But they haven't dialed in elevation."

"Means we've got a margin," Phen murmured. "Not much of one."

Jack adjusted the scope on his rifle. "We get one chance at this. If they get a thermal ping, we're blown."

"Then we don't give them one," Vannah said. She crawled forward on her elbows, each movement deliberate and practiced. "Keep low. Use the drainage ditch."

The team slipped into the shallow culvert, concealed by thick brush and runoff from the week's rain. The IFV rumbled past less than thirty yards from their position, close enough to see the outline of a gunner through the armored viewport. Phen waited until the last track clanked past before speaking again. "We break west behind the tree line. Facility's three clicks out according to satellite pass. Small footprint, mostly subterranean."

Jack clicked his radio once. "Take it quiet," Twelve added. "We breach, plant, exfiltrate. Leave nothing they can trace."

The four moved like shadows deeper into the timber. Behind them, the militia convoy fanned out across Cedar Hill, unaware that their true enemy was already inside the wire.

Voices drifted toward them. Twelve raised her hand again and motioned across her lips. They froze, breath held and bodies pressed low into the brush.

"Why the hell would the Feds hit a town like this?" one voice muttered from just over the ridge.

"Hell if I know. Cap said there's a munitions factory buried out here."

"Maybe. Still, they came in hot. Attacked us for defending our way of life."

The footsteps grew faint, crunching over dry leaves until they faded altogether. The underbrush rustled again. One of the militia men broke off from the path, muttering about needing to take a leak.

"Hold here," Twelve whispered. Her eyes tracked the lone figure stumbling toward the brush. He was careless, his rifle slung lazily. He stopped just ten feet from where she lay, unzipping with a grunt and tilting his head toward the trees.

That was when he saw her. Fiery red hair caught a shaft of filtered sunlight; emerald eyes locked with his. His mouth opened to shout, but it was too late.

Twelve surged forward. One gloved hand clamped over his mouth while the other drove her sidearm up beneath his jaw. A silenced shot cracked like a muffled cough. He slumped without a sound.

But the silence didn't last. "Hey! Cooper?" the second militia man called. "You good, man? Coop, quit screwin' around!"

Then came the static burst of a radio coming online. "Unit 3, this is Peters. I've got a man down. Cooper's gone dark. Repeat, we may have contact. Requesting back—"

Another silenced shot rang out. The radio dropped into the dirt, sputtering its half-finished call for backup.

Jack swore under his breath. "That's gonna wake up the whole damn hornet's nest."

"They're coming now," Phen muttered. "Clock just started ticking."

Vannah knelt beside the second body, pulling a map from his vest pocket. Her eyes flicked across the paper. "They were on patrol routes. They weren't guessing. They know about the factory too."

Twelve already had her weapon reloaded, her eyes fixed back on the ridge. "Then we need to move. Fast."

Sergeant Owen Clay leaned over the console inside the Infantry Fighting Vehicle, his eyes locked on the flickering thermal feed. His thumb held the transmit button down, his voice low but urgent. "Peters. Peters, copy."

Nothing but static answered him. A faint hiss, then silence. He exhaled sharply through his nose and switched to the broader comms channel. "Contact. Contact, eastern perimeter. Cooper and Peters are MIA."

Across the dim red glow of the interior cabin, the other operators snapped to alert. Weapons lifted and heads turned as the steady hum of the IFV's engine suddenly felt too loud. Clay keyed his mic again. "This is Clay. I want visual confirmation from Squad Two now. East quadrant, tree line by the creek bed."

Corporal Janis, seated near the rear hatch, tapped on her slate. "Drones are still compromised. We have no recon visual in that sector."

"Then we do it the old-fashioned way," Clay muttered. He pulled his rifle from the rack and slammed a fresh magazine into place.

A call came through from Private Hall at the forward scout position. "Sir, possible movement, low to the ground. I can't confirm if it's wildlife or hostile."

"Assume hostile," Clay growled. He turned toward the driver. "Advance twenty meters. Hold position. Deploy the cover team." He clicked his mic again, switching to Samantha's command channel. "Colonel, we've lost comms with our forward unit. No gunfire, no heat signatures. They're just gone."

"Investigate, Sergeant," her order came back.

The IFV rumbled forward, slow and deliberate, its treads crunching through scorched gravel and splintered asphalt. Smoke curled lazily from a burned-out storefront ahead, casting shifting shadows across the vehicle's viewport. Inside, Clay adjusted his earpiece, straining for any sign of Peters, Cooper, or anyone.

Still nothing. The vehicle halted with a hiss of compressed hydraulics. "Squad Two," Clay said into the mic, "dismount. Sweep the eastern approach. Assume stealth. Assume hostiles."

The rear hatch groaned open. Four soldiers moved out in a wedge, boots low and rifles ready, their steps muffled by ash and soot. Janis brought up the rear, her eyes darting between thermal readouts and the alleyways flanking Main Street. Clay stood in the hatchway now, half in and half out, scanning the tree line with binoculars. The world felt too quiet. It wasn't calm; it was muted, as if the air itself was holding its breath.

His headset crackled. "Sarge, this is Hall. I have movement roughly fifty meters east of our last ping. I've got heat: small, crouched. It's not a deer. No return fire yet."

“Do not engage unless confirmed hostile,” Clay said. “Mark your position. We’ll triangulate and close in.”

Suddenly, the comms popped, sharp and garbled. “... Janis, can’t see, oh God he’s...”

“Repeat!” Clay barked, yanking the headset tighter. “Janis, say again!”

Nothing followed but a new voice: hollow, crackling over an open mic. It was a whisper. “...they’re not milit ia...”

Static. A low thump. Then a dead channel.

Clay froze. He turned toward the interior of the IFV, his face grim. “I want flares in the sky. Sweep the alleys. We’ve got ghosts in the wire.” He flipped back to the command channel. “Colonel Johnson, we’ve got an unknown operator in the AO taking our people silently. They’re likely black-bag level trained.” His voice dropped a note. “This isn’t random. It’s a surgical strike.”

Jack and his team moved quickly out of the underbrush, taking advantage of the smoke still curling through the trees from the crash site. They kept low with rifles ready as they slipped into the skeleton of the town. Crouching behind a rusted dumpster, Jack tucked his rifle into his shoulder while his eyes swept the broken alley ahead. Brick walls were scorched black. A fire guttered from a tipped generator across the street, casting orange shadows against the smoke-streaked windows. The air reeked of burning rubber.

Jack tapped his comm twice. No words. Phen shifted beside him, already mapping their next route. His fingers moved across a rugged tablet, running thermal overlays and intercepting radio pulses on local bands.

"These aren't your average redneck LARPers," Phen muttered, his eyes still on the feed. "Montana-Idaho. Tactical spacing. Coordinated sweep patterns. This is real training."

"They'll be disciplined," Jack replied, "but predictable."

Behind them, Vannah and Twelve took up overwatch, covering rear and rooftop angles with quiet precision. Twelve's custom sight flicked briefly as it detected two heat signatures moving along the northern ridge. She made a low hand signal. Jack scanned forward. "Push west. Train yard's still our vector. Avoid direct contact until we find the target."

Vannah glanced toward the next building, a collapsed general store with faded signage and a bullet-riddled propane tank. "Movement northwest," she whispered. "Three-man patrol. No drones overhead. They're sweeping wide, probably looking for the team Peters called in."

Phen pocketed the tablet and shouldered his rifle. "I've got a disruption beacon set up along the northern corridor. It should buy us ten minutes of blackout, longer if they haven't figured out we're using thermoptic masking."

Jack gave a single nod. "Then we move. Low and quiet. If we're spotted, we leave no survivors."

The four moved in staggered formation, navigating through broken fences and between burned-out storefronts. Somewhere nearby, a GPN recon team shouted through a scratchy radio, the audio garbled by the localized comms jamming. The words were indistinct, but the urgency was clear.

Twelve's voice cut in softly over the shared channel. "Footsteps, southeast. Closing fast."

Jack raised his hand. They froze. A militia soldier rounded the corner ahead, alone, his rifle slung low as he mumbled about needing a cigarette. He stepped off the sidewalk and pulled out his lighter, puffing a few times while casually walking toward the shadowed wall where Twelve waited in silence.

The last thing he saw was a flash of red hair and green eyes. He didn't have time to scream. Twelve moved fast, her hand clamping over his mouth as the knife went in deep. He sagged, breath gurgling, and she dragged him into the darkness.

But a second soldier was already calling out. "Mick? You good? Mick?!" His voice tightened. He stepped forward with his weapon raised, but a short burst of suppressed fire caught him mid-step.

Thp-thp. He dropped instantly, hitting the concrete with a dull thud. The radio on his chest sparked to life: "Eastern patrol, report. Eastern patrol, do you copy?"

Phen moved fast, yanking the handset free and cutting the line before it could transmit their location. "They know something's off," he said. "They'll reroute drones next."

Jack turned to the rest of the team. "We go loud if we have to. Eyes sharp. We're inside their wire now."

2

"COLONEL, DRONES ARE PICKING up more movement. Eastern approach." Sergeant Clay's voice cut through the radio.

Samantha straightened. "Visuals up. Now."

Grainy thermal footage stabilized on the monitor. A single IFV rumbled into frame, its silhouette angular and reinforced with welded plating. There was no visible insignia. "One of ours?" she asked. When no response came, she leaned in. "Repeat: one of ours?"

An explosion cracked the silence from beyond the ridge. Smoke coiled into the sky while static jumped across the feed. Clay's voice returned, strained. "Not Federal. They're flying UAA colors. Wait, there's a second convoy just pulled in behind them."

Another feed popped online. A battered old jeep rolled into frame draped in Confederate-gray canvas. Bourbon barrels were lashed down with rope, and long rifles jutted between them like porcupine quills. The jeep was flanked by dirt bikes and ATVs.

Samantha stared hard at the screen. "I recognize those flags," she muttered. "Evanston. They got us out of a jam back there." She shook her head. "I still don't trust them."

"The IFV intercepted our transmission about hostiles east of town. Some guy on a motorcycle just launched a missile into the sector," Clay said, his eyes still glued to the monitors.

Samantha's radio crackled to life. "GPN, GPN!" a man's voice called, breathless. "We are UAA. Not hostile!"

Samantha grabbed her mic. "What are you boys doing so far away from home?"

The line went silent for a moment before a response came through. "We heard about the Federal strike on this town. Figured it couldn't wait. Missouri's too close to home to ignore."

Before Samantha could respond, another explosion shook the earth beneath the convoy, this one closer. The screen blinked with static as the feed struggled to recover. Clay cursed under his breath. "That one came from inside the perimeter."

Another missile veered off course. "Damn hillbillies are going to kill friendlies," the voice from the UAA IFV muttered.

"If they hit one of ours, I'm lighting up their whole convoy, flags or not!" Clay shouted into the radio.

"That came from one of the ATV riders near the jeep," the UAA operator chirped back.

"Keep your distance, UAA. The Bluegrass boys haven't established contact yet," Colonel Johnson shouted back. A brief pause crackled through the comms before the voice from the UAA IFV responded, calmer but edged with static. "Copy that, GPN. We'll hold the perimeter on the east ridge."

Clay leaned closer to Samantha. "Bluegrass States might not be so patient."

"I know," she muttered. "They're cavalry types. Fast to arrive, faster to shoot."

Before she could issue new orders, a series of dots appeared on the drone feed: bikes and trucks weaving through the trees. "No formation. No IFF signals," Clay observed. "But they're definitely headed this way."

Samantha tapped her mic. "Bluegrass Republic, you better announce yourselves or we'll take it as hostile."

The response came with a thick Appalachian drawl and a chuckle. "Easy, darlin'. We're here to kill Feds, not friends. Heard there was trouble brewin'... figured we'd stir the barrel."

Samantha frowned. "You show up uninvited, make a mess of my airspace, and call it help?"

"No offense meant, ma'am. Just figured Missouri was close enough to Tennessee and Kentucky to lend a neighborly hand."

Clay gave her a sidelong glance. "Sounds like they brought a jug and a gun."

Samantha allowed a faint smirk. "Let's just hope they can shoot straighter than they drive." She keyed her mic again. "UAA and Bluegrass, hold position. We've already lost contact with two men in the eastern sector.

That makes this an active combat zone. No freelance heroics."

"Roger that," both voices replied, nearly in sync.

Dust pelted the armor plating as the IFV roared down the cracked road. Inside, the atmosphere was tight: too hot for comfort and too quiet for peace. Viper stood near the front with a hand braced against the roof, his eyes locked on the viewing slit ahead. "Slow it down. I want to hear the damn town before it hears us."

"Aw, come on, Sarge," Joker drawled, his boot resting on an ammo crate. "You mean I shaved for this?"

Ghost didn't look away from his scope. "No one cares about your neck, Joker."

"I care," Joker said. "It's sensitive. Like my feelings."

Boom grunted. "The only thing sensitive is your trigger discipline."

"Allegedly," Joker muttered with a smirk.

Viper didn't take the bait. He gave a nod toward the comm panel. "Radar?"

"Signals are a mess. Either jamming or sloppy bandwidth. Could be local," Radar replied, his fingers working the keys.

"Or it's the Bluegrass boys drunk-dialing again," Specter muttered as he double-checked his satchel charges.

Joker perked up. "If they're drunk, does that mean it's a party? Because I didn't bring snacks, but I did bring high explosives."

"Shut it," Viper said without raising his voice. "If they're jumpy, your mouth is going to get one of us dead." Another low boom in the distance rattled the frame. Bricks looked up, his jaw tight.

"Just fireworks," Joker said. "You know, freedom-flavored fireworks."

Stitch, Bricks, and Chatter sat near the back. This was their three newer recruits' first op with Zero Company. Stitch looked like he might get sick; Chatter was already chewing on his tongue; Bricks, however, didn't blink. Viper turned to them. "When we drop, stay tight. No cowboys. You three stick to Boom or Ghost until I say otherwise."

They nodded, quick and nervous. The radio hissed as Colonel Johnson's voice cut through: "Keep your distance, UAA. The Bluegrass boys haven't established contact yet."

Radar tapped the mic. "Acknowledged. Friendly visual, no engagement."

Viper scanned through the slit. "Specter, ID that jeep."

"Old Willys. Confederate canvas. Barrels strapped down like moonshine runners. ATVs on both sides."

Joker leaned in. "I'm just saying, if those barrels don't have bourbon, I'm going to feel lied to."

Another explosion lit up the ridge ahead. “That came from the rider with the launcher,” Radar reported.

“Noted,” Viper said, his eyes narrowing. “And someone tell Joker if he opens his mouth again, he’s riding on the hood.”

“I’d look great up there,” Joker said. “Like a patriotic hood ornament.”

“Like a dead one,” Ghost replied.

Viper keyed his mic. “Zero Company ready. Waiting green.” The radio crackled to life with a “Yeeeeeehaw!” just before a third blast rattled the IFV’s frame. Bricks leaned forward, a grin tugging at the corner of his mouth. “Damn, those guys are nuts.”

Joker didn’t miss a beat. “More like a squirrel looking for a nut.” Even Viper cracked a half-smile.

Bullets began clanging off the armor plating. “Contact! Contact! Contact!” Viper yelled. “Get ready!”

The radio chatter spiked. Phen crouched atop a crumbling rooftop, his anti-armor rifle resting steady on a broken AC unit. He exhaled slowly and lined up the shot.

CRACK. A plume of smoke burst from the side of an approaching IFV, staggering its advance. He keyed his mic. “Jack, we’ve got a problem. This op’s going sideways fast. The town’s getting overrun and some lunatic civvies are launching missiles into our old LZ.”

Before Jack could respond, Twelve's voice cut through the static. "Chairman won't be happy," she said dryly.

"I know," Phen replied, adjusting his position. "But we're getting overrun."

Jack raised a fist, silencing the conversation. "Not up for debate," he said firmly. "We took the Consortium Liturgy. We swore the Oath. We don't back down."

Phen hesitated. "But—"

"No buts," Jack snapped. "From the satellite images, we're less than three hundred yards from the munitions facility. Our mission was to destroy it." He looked toward the smoke-choked skyline, where the faint silhouette of the facility was just visible through the haze. "We finish our mission."

After a long silence, Twelve's voice finally crackled back across the comms. "Understood. Repositioning to high ground."

Phen didn't respond at first as he adjusted his scope. Through the heat distortion, he could see the edge of the facility: a squat, reinforced concrete structure nestled behind a chain-link fence topped with rusting coils of razor wire. There were no markings and no signage. It was exactly the kind of place the world wasn't supposed to know existed.

"Vannah, on me," Jack said, slipping down a fire escape to the alley below.

"Already moving," she answered, cutting between two collapsed buildings without a sound.

The four converged near a crumpled brick laundromat. Shadows danced across its scorched walls as a flare arced overhead from the GPN lines. A chorus of distant gunfire echoed down Main Street, stitched with the irregular pop of suppressed rounds.

"Thermal masking still holding," Phen muttered, checking his slate. "But they're closing the net. Another patrol sweeps north, closer to the factory."

Jack crouched behind a pile of cinder blocks. "Then we punch through." He pulled a small satchel from his belt containing carefully packed thermite charges. Each one was stamped with a serial number that didn't exist in any inventory database. "Plant these on the intake vents and service hatch. Make it look like structural failure from the airstrike."

Twelve took two of the charges without hesitation.

"What if we're spotted?" Vannah asked.

Jack looked her dead in the eyes. "We're not spotted."

She gave a sharp nod, the ghost of a grin curling at the edge of her mouth. Phen exhaled slowly and stood. "We'll draw fire if we need to. Set the detonators on a staggered delay: ninety-second intervals."

Jack turned to Twelve. "Flank left. You're on perimeter breach. Ghost it in and out."

Twelve gave a two-fingered salute and melted into the shadows, her red hair vanishing under a hooded mesh veil. The others slipped through the back alleys like phantoms while the broken bones of Cedar Hill creaked around them. Above them, the faint thrum of another drone passed.

For the first time since landing in Missouri, Jack felt the clock ticking louder than the mission plan. If they failed now, it wouldn't just be the Chairman's wrath they'd face; it would be exposure. It was the kind of revelation that could bring the Consortium's entire war effort down around them, and Jack wasn't going to let that happen. Not in this town. Not tonight.

A private from the Bison Plains Regiment ducked behind a burned-out sedan as other militia scattered into position. Sweat streaked down Private Cole's face while his hands slipped on his rifle, peering through the iron sights.

"Four confirmed dead Feds," Sergeant Woo reported as they advanced.

"What's the sitrep?" Clay's voice buzzed over the radio from the IFV.

"Locals say twenty on the ground. We've only accounted for four," Cole answered, his voice tight.

"Copy. Keep pushing," Woo ordered, signaling with two fingers before darting across the street. The militia fanned out in staggered pairs, rifles sweeping doorways and shattered windows. A burst of automatic fire rattled from an alley ahead: three sharp pops, then silence.

"Contact front!" Private Jenkins called. "Alley, ten o'clock!"

Cole shifted behind the sedan, lining up on the narrow gap between two brick buildings. A figure in torn Federal camo slumped against a dumpster, a rifle slipping from limp fingers. The alley beyond was darker, cloaked in smoke.

"Can't see if there's more," Cole said into his mic.

"Don't guess," Woo replied. "Clear it."

Two militia members advanced, one covering while the other pushed forward. The stench of ozone and rot was stronger here. "Building's got a rear exit," one reported. "Could've slipped out."

Before Woo could respond, a heavier, deliberate crack of gunfire echoed from deeper in town. "That's not ours," Cole muttered.

On the comms, Clay's voice cut in, tense. "Eyes open. We've got unknown shooters in the AO."

Woo's jaw tightened. "Alright, boys, watch your six. I'm not sure how many Feds made it to the ground."

The men crouched low, moving methodically block by block. "Don't shoot!" a voice called from a block ahead.

"Come out with your hands up!" Woo shouted, rifles snapping toward the sound.

"Coming out! Throwing my rifle down!" A rifle clinked against the pavement, kicked forward by a boot. A man stepped into view: battered, bloody, and wearing Federal blue.

"Identify!" one of the militia barked.

"Private Wallace, U.S. Army." His hands stayed high as he stumbled closer. "Please, I've got a family in Lancaster. I don't want to fight this war." His voice cracked as tears came fast. "Please, I want to go home. I don't want to die!"

Woo stepped forward, keeping his rifle leveled. "We're not in the business of killing men who surrender. But you try anything..."

"I won't," Wallace blurted. "Swear to God, I won't."

From behind Woo, Private Hastings muttered, "Sir, he could be bait. I've seen it before. You drop your guard and the rest of his squad lights you up."

"He's bleeding," Jenkins countered. "Look at him. He's done."

Woo kept his tone even. "Search him. Now."

Hastings approached, his rifle trembling as adrenaline pumped through his system. Wallace flinched when Hastings grabbed his sleeve, and the sudden movement made the private's finger twitch. The shot cracked like a whip. Wallace's body jerked, a red bloom spreading across his chest as he crumpled to the pavement.

"What the hell, Hastings?!" Woo roared, shoving the private back.

For a heartbeat, no one moved. The street went still. Cole's knuckles whitened on his rifle while Jenkins' jaw hung open, his eyes locked on the spreading red stain. Even Hastings stood frozen, the barrel of his rifle still pointed at the spot where Wallace had stood, his finger rigid against the trigger guard.

"I—he moved! I thought—" Hastings stammered, eyes wide and chest heaving.

Blood spread across the pavement as Wallace's eyes filled with terror. He stared at Hastings, sputtered once, and his breathing shallowed. Then nothing.

"Hastings shot the Fed, Sergeant," Woo said into his radio.

"Contain him. We're coming," Clay responded.

High above on the ridge, the survivors of the C-130 didn't need the radio to understand what had just happened. They watched through the shimmer of heat as the boy in Federal blue was gunned down with his hands in the air.

"Jesus, did you see that?" one hissed, lowering his binoculars.

The other's face was hard, his jaw clenched. "They shot him. Hands in the air. Just gunned him down."

A third soldier, limping from shrapnel, spat into the dirt. "Then we don't take prisoners."

Voices rose in fury from their position as rifles snapped into ready positions. Anger spread through the group like dry brush catching flame.

Inside the factory, machinery loomed like rusting skeletons and conveyor belts sat frozen mid-cycle. Crates of unshipped ammunition were stacked shoulder-high alongside pallets of heavy artillery shells. Twelve knelt by a load-bearing column, pressing a block of C4 into place with cold precision. "Charge one set," she murmured into comms. "Moving to number two."

Across the floor, Vannah unspooled detonation cord with surgical neatness. Jack checked his watch, then the dim skylights above. "Three minutes to be ready for detonation," he ordered.

From his perch on an upper catwalk, Phen propped his rifle against the railing. His scope swept over the town as he adjusted the magnification, scanning through drifting smoke. His breath caught. Down the street, militia clustered around a single kneeling Federal soldier whose hands were raised and eyes wide. One of the militia lunged forward. A flash followed, and the man crumpled. The reaction from the surrounding troops was immediate: guns snapped up and bodies bristled with aggression.

Phen keyed his mic. "We've got a problem."

Jack didn't look up from his map. "Define problem."

"Your little parade out there just turned into a bloodbath," Phen said, his voice low and measured. "Looks like they executed a Fed. Every bluecoat in sight is about to lose their mind."

There was a pause before Jack's tone shifted. "Let them. The more chaos out there, the less they see us in here."

Twelve glanced up from her work. "And if they decide to push this way?"

"Then we blow the charges early," Jack said, his eyes narrowing. "Make sure to set some near the ammo and artillery. We'll turn this entire facility into a massive IED."

Through the glass, Phen saw the flicker of shock on the soldiers' faces collapse into pure rage as fingers tightened on triggers. No one was thinking anymore. He kept watching through his scope as the sounds of shouting and gunfire swelled in the distance. "Better hurry, then. The hornet's nest is open."

White House — West Wing, Early Morning

The rain came in thin, slanting sheets against the windows, tapping a restless rhythm on the glass. Inside the Roosevelt Room, the tension hung as heavy as the acrid scent of burnt coffee and cold pizza. A digital map dominated the far wall, glowing red where Federal forces were in contact, orange where frontlines were unstable, and a widening ring of yellow where Washington's authority had fractured completely.

President Hal Bennett sat at the head of the long table with his jacket off and sleeves rolled high. His hands were flat on the polished wood, his knuckles pale. He didn't look at the Joint Chiefs, National Security Council, or intel advisors arrayed before him; half were loyal to the flag, while the others served something else entirely. He stared instead at Missouri on the map, where fresh icons pulsed with incoming reports.

"Tell me that isn't another one," Bennett said, his voice low and edged like a blade.

The Army Chief of Staff cleared his throat. "Confirmed, sir. UAA armor entered contested territory before dawn. Bluegrass irregulars are operating in the same area, and our drone feeds suggest cooperation."

"Cooperation," Bennett repeated, slow and deliberate.

"Yes, sir. And there's more. Three more governors are in backchannel talks with the different rebel groups. Terms unknown."

Rain pattered harder against the glass. Bennett leaned back, folding his arms in a controlled, almost theatrical motion. "We are at war with the Confederation, an existential threat to this country. While our soldiers bleed to hold the line, states we fund and arm are negotiating with secessionists."

No one spoke. Some wouldn't meet his eyes while others met them too directly, sending coded signals back across the table.

"Sir, we weren't fighting that war against the Confederation. That's why we—" A low-level staffer had spoken without thinking, still holding a half-empty pizza box.

The room froze. President Bennett's fist slammed the table so hard the coffee cups rattled. "Who the hell are you?" he growled, spit catching in the corner of his mouth as his voice rose to a roar.

The staffer stammered, his eyes darting to the floor. "I... I was just—"

"You were just what?" Bennett's stare bored into him, the room suddenly smaller and hotter. "Finishing a thought you don't have the clearance to start?"

The young man swallowed, nodded mutely, and backed toward the door. Bennett let the silence linger before straightening his tie and looking back at the generals as if nothing had happened. Inside, he knew the truth the staffer had stumbled toward, but he also knew he couldn't let anyone else say it out loud.

The staffer disappeared through the door as a couple of Secret Service agents slipped out behind him. Bennett didn't look at them; he didn't have to. The edges of his lips curved into an imperceptible smile. Orders didn't need to be spoken.

Agents Reed and Williams followed the cue, slipping silently from the office to shadow the young man. He moved quickly, clutching his briefcase to his chest like a shield. He didn't notice the agents trailing him, but he'd heard the stories of aides who asked the wrong questions or challenged President Bennett in front of the wrong ears. Those people didn't get fired. They vanished.

Fresh from Harvard and only six months into the D.C. circuit, he felt his career ending before it began. He glanced over his shoulder. There was nothing but the hallway, lit in flashes of lightning. The green glow of the EXIT sign pulled him forward, his loafers clicking louder on the marble as his pace quickened.

"Excuse me, sir." Agent Reed stepped casually out of a side office, blocking his path.

The staffer froze, sweat prickling his hairline. Before he could speak, the air shifted. Agent Williams had closed in, his broad shoulders blocking the light from behind.

"You're needed for a quick follow-up," Reed said, his tone cordial but his eyes unblinking.

"I... I have another meeting," the staffer stammered, trying to step sideways. Reed mirrored the move perfectly.

"It won't take long."

Williams' hand settled lightly on the young man's shoulder. The grip was polite but left no doubt that resistance was useless. His breath quickened as he glanced toward the exit, now only a dozen steps away. "Where are we going?" he asked, forcing a nervous laugh.

"Service corridor," Reed said. "Easier than cutting back through the press gaggle."

They steered him toward a narrow side door painted the same cream color as the wall. He'd walked past it dozens of times and never noticed it led anywhere. Inside, the air turned cooler and the light dimmer. Marble gave way to bare concrete. The sound of the West Wing faded behind them. "This really necessary?" he asked, his voice cracking.

The agents didn't answer. They just kept walking, their eyes hidden behind dark lenses. The corridor bent sharply to the left, leading to a set of industrial double doors. Williams swiped a keycard and they opened with a muted hydraulic hiss. Beyond was an unmarked freight elevator. Reed gestured him inside. The staffer hesitated just long enough for Williams to apply gentle, immovable pressure to his back.

The doors slid shut. Reed pressed the button for the lowest level. No one spoke during the descent; the hum of the elevator motor was the only sound. When the doors finally opened, a small, windowless hallway stretched toward another unmarked door.

"This way," Reed said. Williams' hand never left the staffer's shoulder.

As they walked through the door, the soft sound of piano music began to play. The room beyond was a foyer of marble columns and polished floors, chandeliers glowing like captured sunlight. There was another green EXIT sign ahead. The agents walked him through, and suddenly, they were outside.

Washington, D.C. was gone. This place was different. The air was clean and the sky an impossible blue. Streets were immaculate, cars gliding in perfect harmony. Pedestrians moved with practiced order, smiling as if they'd rehearsed it.

"Where are we?" His voice cracked.

"President Bennett wanted you to see what you'll never be a part of," Reed said.

Williams raised a sleek black pistol, a weapon more advanced than any standard firearm. A pale bolt of light lanced out, striking the staffer in the chest. It felt cold at first, like ice blooming under his skin. Then it burned, searing through his veins and stealing his breath. He opened his mouth, but no scream came. His body dissolved into motes of light, scattering like fireflies into the air. When it was over, only his clothes remained.

The agents gathered the garments wordlessly and fed them into a wall-mounted incinerator. Reed tapped his earpiece. "Dealt with."

"Good. Well done. Did you show him Consortium City?" The voice was a whisper, yet it carried like a blade sliding free of its sheath.

"It was his last sight."

A pause followed. Then, almost warmly: "Excellent. Return to your post."

"Yes, Chairman."

Cedar Hill - Edge of Town

"Twelve planted the last charge," Vannah confirmed, her voice steady despite the distant rumble of 40mm cannons pounding the streets. The factory floor stank of oil and gunpowder. Jack gave a curt nod. "We're done now. Move."

They were running before the words left his mouth, boots pounding across the floor toward the rear exit. Outside, the air was thick with smoke and dust, hot and alive with the noise of war. Up the main road, an IFV hammered out another burst: the deep *thunk-thunk-thunk* of its autocannon followed by the wet thud of shrapnel finding flesh. Jagged screams carried through the haze. These weren't just soldiers; civilians were caught in the fracas.

"Sounds like the whole damn town's lit," Phen muttered, adjusting his rifle sling.

"Not our problem," Jack said flatly. "Stay on task."

They cut down an alley between a collapsed brick storefront and a burned-out pickup, moving low with weapons ready. Figures emerged from the thicker smoke ahead, running full-tilt. A mother clutched a bleeding child to her chest while an old man limped behind her, his head on a swivel. More followed, some barefoot, some crying, some clutching whatever belongings they could scavenge. They were all fleeing in the same direction.

"They're going to slow us down," Twelve warned.

"Cut left," Jack ordered, jerking his chin toward a narrow service lane.

They slipped through as another wave of gunfire erupted on the main road. Bullets smacked into brick and sheet metal. A man in the crowd dropped; the others screamed and fanned out in panic.

"Clock's ticking, Jack," Vannah said, scanning the rooftops. "We've got maybe two minutes before those charges cook off."

They moved faster, weaving between outbuildings toward the tree line. The air was clearer here, but the chaos followed behind them. The autocannon fired, the roar of something heavy collapsing intermingled with small arms fire. Phen glanced back. "If we don't get some distance before that place blows, we're eating steel for breakfast."

Jack didn't slow. "It won't blow until we say it does, but we gotta get out of here before we get caught."

They broke into the woods where the ground was soft with pine needles and the smoke gave way to damp earth. The helicopter was still a full klick out. Behind them, the first concussion rolled through the ground like thunder.

"Here it comes," Twelve said.

The second blast was larger. The shockwave ripped through the trees, flinging leaves and dust into the air. Seconds later, a metallic hail of jagged steel shards scythed through the woods. "Down!" Jack barked. They dove behind the nearest trunks as shrapnel tore through bark. When it passed, they were moving again, running hard toward the clearing. Jack veered around a cluster of pines and froze for half a second. Up ahead, half-hidden behind a fallen log, was a family. A man crouched low, his arms spread to shield his wife and a small girl who couldn't have been more than six. Her face was streaked with dirt and tears as she clutched a stuffed rabbit.

The father's eyes locked on Jack's. "Please!" he rasped. "They're shelling the town! Help us!"

For an instant, the team slowed. "Jack—" Twelve started.

"No," Jack snapped. "We don't break mission. Keep moving."

"They're not even armed," she pressed.

Jack's glare cut sideways. "We stop, we all die. That's the math. Move."

The family watched them pass, their fear giving way to something worse. They had just cleared the tree line when the final blast hit. The shockwave punched through the woods, carrying a storm of razor-edged steel. Twelve glanced back in time to see a shard slam into the fallen log. The man dropped instantly. The woman crumpled beside him. The girl's stuffed rabbit tumbled from her arms, vanishing in the rising dust.

Twelve's stomach clenched, but her feet didn't stop. The others didn't look back.

Mission before morals. Jack's words echoed in her mind. A small part of her recoiled, knowing what they had done was wrong, but the mantra held firm. *Mission before morals.*

Sergeant Woo and his militia ducked low as gunfire erupted from every direction, tracer rounds slicing the air. Hastings was yanked to the ground as Clay's IFV roared up, its 40mm cannon barking toward the advancing Federals.

"Get in! Get in!" Clay shouted. The side hatch slammed open and Woo's men scrambled inside, boots clanging against the metal floor. Almost all of them. Private Adams was five steps from the hatch when a round punched into his spine. He collapsed face-first onto the asphalt, a desperate cry tearing from his throat. "Momma!"

"We can't leave him!" Woo started forward, but Clay cut him off. "We'll come back for him. We can't stop now!"

The IFV lurched forward before Woo could answer, the hatch slamming shut. Clay kept his eyes on the viewport with his jaw set tight, but Woo caught the shame in his eyes. Rounds pinged off the armor as they tore down Main Street. Suddenly, an explosion cracked through the air. The blast punched through the noise, rattling the hull.

"What the hell was that?" Clay leaned toward the viewport just in time to see a column of fire roar into the sky. "Dammit! They hit the factory!"

A second detonation followed, deeper and meaner. The shockwave rolled through the street, carrying a hail of jagged steel. Shrapnel screamed through the air and clanged against the armor. One chunk the size of a brick slammed into the hatch, denting the steel.

"Hold on!" Clay barked, gripping the console as the driver swerved through debris.

Then came the third explosion. The earth convulsed beneath them, rattling the IFV so hard Clay's teeth clacked. Through the viewport, he saw a towering mushroom cloud, but unlike any he'd ever seen in training. Sickly greens and deep purples churned together while veins of lightning danced through the core.

"My God..." His voice was barely a whisper. "Heaven help us."

No one answered. In the cramped interior, every man felt it. Whatever had just gone off, this fight had changed. Clay's knuckles whitened on the controls as the shockwave hit, a wall of pressure that punched through the armor. The IFV swayed on its treads, groaning as rivets popped. A split-second later, the light hit. It was searing and unnatural, twisting shadows along the walls.

"Eyes down!" Clay barked, but some had already looked. The green-violet glare burned into their vision, the images pulsing with every blink.

Outside, Cedar Hill was coming apart. Storefronts folded inward. Roofs collapsed in clouds of glass and dust. Cars flipped like toys, fire blooming before they hit the ground. Then came the low rumble, followed by a strange groan like ground beneath them was dying, before rising into a tearing metallic howl that clawed at the ears. It wasn't just air being displaced; it was something deeper, as if the bomb was pulling heat and energy out of the world around it.

Private Mendoza spoke, his voice shaking. "Sir... the street." The alarm in the IFV began squelching with radioactive warnings as Clay glanced out. The asphalt had split into jagged plates, curling upward like blackened paper. Beneath, the ground glowed faintly with that same sickly green. The air shimmered above it in writhing tentacles off the asphalt.

"Keep moving," Clay ordered, his voice distant.

They rumbled past a collapsed diner where the neon sign sparked once before dying. A lone figure stumbled from the smoke with hair matted and skin pale with dust. He opened his mouth to shout, but the next pulse hit. He stopped, locked in place, then crumbled to ash.

Inside the IFV, no one spoke. The smell of ozone and burning metal filled their lungs. Clay knew that Cedar Hill wasn't just a target because of the munitions plant; it was a message, and it was being erased.

Jack was the last to haul himself into the chopper, his boots scraping on the diamond plating. He turned, one hand gripping the doorframe, to take in the towering mushroom cloud over Cedar Hill. Greens and purples churned inside it, lightning lacing the folds like veins of something alive.

The others were already buckled in with their heads down, checking gear. Phen's fingers moved over the screen on his tablet as the pilot throttled the engines up toward a roar.

"Sure is a beautiful sight," Jack said, snapping his harness into place. His tone was casual and admiring, as if he were watching fireworks instead of the death of a town. "That," he added with a faint smile, "will keep the GPN guessing for weeks. They'll blame the Confederation in no time."

Outside, the cloud swelled higher, covering the sun and casting its shadow far beyond the wreckage of the town. Twelve kept her gaze fixed on her rifle with her jaw tight. She loved him, but the glee in his eyes, and the eyes of the others, shook her resolve. She knew if he sensed it, or if any of them did, she would be thrown from this bird without hesitation.

Jack leaned over and kissed her. She kissed him back, letting the warmth push the doubts aside for a heartbeat. But as the helicopter lifted off and the cloud devoured the horizon, the truth settled in the back of her mind. It wasn't the mission that unsettled her; it was the joy they took in watching innocents die.

She wasn't innocent in the endeavor, nor was she feeling bad about the outcome. It was just how far they had come. But then her mind reassured her with Jack's words, *Mission before morals.*

Mission before morals.

3

HELENA, MONTANA - SITUATION Room

The crystal decanter of bourbon shattered against the mahogany-paneled wall, amber liquid splashing in an arc before raining to the floor. Shards spun across the hardwood, catching the light before settling in silence.

"What in the hell!" President Jeremiah Johnson roared, his voice rattling the framed maps. He was on his feet with his fists planted on the table, glaring at the Pact governors frozen in place. "Is that a neutronium bomb that was used in Cedar Hill!"

Governor Bradford Davidson tapped his tablet, his face pale in the glow of the screen. "Bison-13 satellite passes just confirmed the spectral signature, Mr. President. High-energy ionized particles and a localized gravitational spike. It's a match for the West Coast hits."

Johnson's chest pumped like a piston. "These damn monsters."

Governor Davison Carey of Wyoming broke the silence, leaning forward with a paper in hand. "Sir, reports say the remaining forces of the Bison Plains Regiment made it out, but the death toll could reach into the thousands. The munitions factory is gone."

"Can we get them on the line? I want a full report, now," Johnson demanded.

"Communications are down in the blast zone," Governor Roger Billings of Missouri said grimly. "State troopers are moving in to search for survivors, but it'll take time."

Johnson's hand slammed the tabletop, rattling coffee cups. "I don't give a damn if communications are down. Find me someone who can get through. Patch a signal through the State Guard net, a satphone, or use smoke signals if you have to. I will not sit here blind while Cedar Hill burns. Get me eyes and ears in that town before nightfall."

Carey's gaze tightened. "Sir, with your approval, I can have the 3rd Montana Armored cross the border and secure the area. They can provide immediate recon and relief."

Billings cut in sharply. "That could be seen as an incursion by the UAA. We don't even know for certain it was the Confederation."

Johnson's eyes narrowed. "Who else has neutronium?" His tone was clipped and certain.

Colonel Dana Trask, head of GPN Strategic Command, stepped forward from the wall. "Mr. President, with respect, the Confederation's been quiet for months. They've been fortifying the Great Wall along

Oregon and Washington with no inland activity. We have no intelligence suggesting a push eastward."

Johnson leaned on the table, his eyes fixed on the glowing operational map. "That's what worries me. They've been boxed in too long. Maybe they see the Secession Wars as their window to move. Cedar Hill could be the first shot in a new offensive. Neutronium isn't just meant to kill, it's meant to terrorize. You drop that in a town and you're telling the world nowhere is safe, just like the West Coast."

No one had a better explanation, and that was exactly what made the situation even more dangerous.

"Carey, your armor needs to stay where they are," Johnson said finally. "Get me contact with Lieutenant Colonel Johnson **and** get medevac on standby. Billings, put every trooper within two hundred miles on alert. Trask, I want solid proof before we call this Confederation aggression. But if it is," he straightened, his voice low and hard, "we'll hit them so hard they'll wish they'd stayed behind their damn wall."

Outside Cedar Hill – Zero Company

Zero Company had made it far enough outside Cedar Hill to avoid the worst of the blast, then the sky behind them bloomed green and purple. The shockwave rippled through the tree line and rattled the hull of their IFV.

"Turn us around!" Viper barked from the gunner's seat.

The driver didn't argue. The armored vehicle slewed hard with treads grinding against loose gravel and roared back toward town. The engine howled as they pushed the throttle beyond safe limits. Inside, the men were packed shoulder to shoulder, hunkered down under radiation-proof blankets.

"I hope you boys took a shower," Joker said, his voice muffled through the heavy fabric. "I don't like snuggling with the smell of ass and body odor."

No one laughed, but a couple of smirks tugged in the dark.

"Hold your breath," Ghost muttered. "You'll need it."

Specter's voice was barely audible under the rumble of the treads: a steady murmur of Hail Mary's and Our Fathers as the beads of his rosary clicked in his hands.

Boom shifted uneasily. "Don't start that, man. Gives me the creeps."

"It's not for you," Specter said without looking up.

Another tremor rolled under the IFV as they drew closer. The radiation blankets muffled the sound but not the smell of burned metal, scorched earth, and a chemical ozone drifting in through the vents. Reaper lifted a corner of the blanket and immediately wished he hadn't. "Jesus."

Through the narrow viewport, the outskirts of Cedar Hill were barely recognizable. A gas station lay flattened with its pumps twisted into molten spirals. Cars burned on the roadside, their glass shattered by the initial blast. Farther in, a dark column of smoke twisted upward beneath that unnatural green-and-purple glow.

"Driver, slow it down," Viper ordered. "We don't know what's still cooking up ahead."

The IFV eased forward, treads grinding over debris. Somewhere in the haze, distant pops of small-arms fire echoed. "Eyes open," Viper said. "We're going in."

Viper caught the movement first: a Federal soldier breaking from the smoke with his rifle popping. Rounds pinged harmlessly off the hull. Then, mid-stride, the man ignited. One heartbeat he was screaming and firing; the next, his flesh sloughed away in a burst of ash and flame.

"Scratch that! Move! Move! Move!" Viper snapped, yanking down the anti-radiation shades. "Stop for nothing. Push it. Now."

The IFV barreled forward, its engine screaming as the treads bit into torn asphalt. Chunks of concrete clanged off the hull like rain. They burst into the edge of town and found the streets unrecognizable: storefronts gutted, signs dangling by single chains, and light poles sheared in half. A burned-out sedan lay on its side, blocking half the street.

"Left!" Viper barked.

The driver spun the treads hard, clipping a mailbox and skidding past a collapsed building before a spray of shrapnel rattled across the armor. A figure stumbled into their path: a woman, barefoot, clutching a limp child.

"Can't stop!" the driver shouted.

Specter's grip tightened on his rosary. "God forgive us," he muttered.

The woman turned as they passed with eyes hollow and a mouth moving soundlessly. A deep boom followed, sending vibrations through the treads that thudded Joker's helmet against the wall.

"Viper," Radar's voice crackled. "Radiation's spiking. Every block we move in, it's worse."

"Then floor it," Viper said. "We stay here, we die."

The driver punched the throttle. Cedar Hill blurred past in jagged fragments and fleeting shapes of people who wouldn't survive long enough for rescue.

"Zero Company! Zero Company! You okay?" Colonel Samantha Johnson's voice burst through the radio.

Viper grabbed the handset. "We're intact. Took some heat, but we're moving. What's your status?"

"I'm fine, but word's already moving up the chain about that blast. If you're down, it turns into a diplomatic mess between the UAA and GPN, not to mention the Bluegrass States Republic."

Viper's jaw flexed. "We can handle ourselves. Don't let anyone think otherwise. Any word from the Moonshiners?"

"Nothing yet. I fear the worst because they didn't have armor. Just get clear of Cedar Hill while you can, Viper, the radiation risk's climbing."

"Understood," Viper said. He handed the handset back to Radar. "Mark the fastest route out. We're not sticking around to be part of the fallout."

The IFV bucked over broken asphalt as the mushroom cloud's shadow stretched across the wrecked streets. In the dim light of the troop bay, Specter's rosary clicked softly between his fingers. "Hail Mary, full of Grace..."

Samantha let the radio slip from her hand. It thunked against her thigh before tumbling to the floor. She leaned back in the jump seat as the hum of the engine grew distant in her ears. Her chest tightened. She pressed the heels of her hands against her eyes, but the unrelenting tears came anyway. She drew a shaky breath that broke halfway through, her grief spilling over into quiet sobs. Across from her, the others sat motionless beneath their radiation blankets. Their hidden faces and the drab folds of fabric made them look like a row of silent statues.

The APC slowed and eased to a halt. Outside, gray dust hung in the air while the orange glow of the blast lingered closer to the town center. The driver glanced back once before turning off the engine. "We'll wait it out here."

Through the narrow viewports, the burned sign of a Walmart loomed over a cracked parking lot where weeds pushed through the asphalt and smoked in little brush fires.

Inside the APC, no one spoke. Samantha turned toward the viewport, the stale air pressing against her face.

Outside, the parking lot was a graveyard. Grocery store carts lay on their sides in piles of abandoned metal, their frames warping. A thin sheen of blackened ash smeared across everything. In one, a skeleton still gripped the handle, its jaw frozen in a silent scream. Another leaned against the rear bumper of a sun-bleached sedan with fingers curled around a child's car seat that had long since crumbled to fabric and wire. The sight hollowed her. These people had been living their lives, only to be caught up in a war that wasn't their own.

The worst of the blast had passed. The heat shimmer over the asphalt had faded and a weak shaft of sunlight broke through the thinning clouds to fall across the cracked pavement. The dosimeter clicked softly against the wall of the APC. Radiation levels were minimal now, low enough to move without the blankets, but the weight of what they'd driven into would linger far longer.

The driver glanced back. "Colonel, it's clear enough to dismount."

Samantha didn't answer right away. She kept her eyes on the skeletal hands still locked around the cart, those fingers curled in stubborn defiance. Finally, she unbuckled, the webbing straps rasping as they slid free. "Open the hatch."

Cold air rushed in as the rear door dropped, carrying the faint metallic tang that still clung to the aftermath. Samantha stepped down onto the fractured pavement with her boots crunching over broken glass. The parking lot was silent except for the occasional creak of warped metal in the breeze. She moved between the wreckage, her boots kicking up fresh ash that settled over a grocery list still tucked into a cart seat, the edges charred black. Her gaze snagged on a single sneaker lying in the gutter, the rubber still tacky and smelling of scorched chemicals. Nearby, a smartwatch had partially fused to skeletal bone, its screen a spiderweb of heat-fractured glass.

One of her sergeants joined her, scanning the empty storefronts with his rifle. "This is horrific."

Samantha's throat tightened. "Yes. These people thought they'd have a tomorrow. Now, tomorrow's never coming."

The breeze shifted, and somewhere far off, she thought she heard the faint pop of small-arms fire. It was distant but enough to remind her this wasn't over. Her radio chirped. "Colonel, this is Clay. Where are you?"

Samantha lifted the handset. "We're in a Walmart lot, just east of Cedar Hill. Radiation's low enough now to move without blankets. What's your status?"

"Short version? Alive," Clay said. "We've got wounded, but it doesn't seem to be critical. We're heading west to link with friendly units. Cedar Hill's a no-go. The blast turned the center into scrap."

"The blast killed people all the way out here too." She exhaled slowly. "But understood. Route your wounded to the med station in Chillicothe. I'll meet you there after we sweep for survivors along our corridor."

A pause followed. Then Clay's voice came back, lower. "Colonel, don't go back in. Our drones are reporting radiation levels still too high and temperatures are over 600°F in some parts. "

Her grip tightened on the radio. She glanced once more at the overturned carts and skeletal remains before turning toward the APC. "We've seen a lot too, but I don't want to concern you, Sergeant. Just get your people to the med center."

She released the transmit button, slid the radio back into its cradle, and signaled to her driver. "Mount up. We're going back toward the edge of the zone. If anyone's still breathing out there, we're not leaving them behind."

The driver looked back at the scorched wreckage and shook his head. He shuddered before stepping aboard, the motion quick and almost involuntary. The hatch shut with a dull clang, sealing them in again. The APC rumbled to life with treads grinding over broken pavement, carrying them toward the gray horizon where the cloud still lingered.

Cedar Hill - Residential Block, Edge of the Blast Zone

The street was silent except for the hiss of cooling metal. Houses leaned at strange angles with their frames charred and skeletal. From the wreckage of a collapsed duplex, a steel basement door shifted and then scraped open. A blistered hand reached out, charred fingers gripping the frame. Another followed. Slowly, a man dragged himself into the daylight while coughing hard enough to double over.

Behind him, two more figures emerged with faces blackened and eyes bloodshot. Their uniforms were caked with ash and dust. They were the Moonshiners, or what was left of them. They didn't speak; they simply stared at the horizon where the heart of Cedar Hill still glowed faintly and shimmered with dangerous heat.

Somewhere deep in the ruin, something cracked to send up a brief plume of greenish smoke. "Let's move," one rasped at last, his voice barely more than a whisper. "We're not safe here."

They moved away from town as fast as their legs would carry them. Their jeep was gone and their weapons were destroyed. They were alone now. Stranded in a war zone, they had no way out and no one coming for them.

4

THE RAIL YARD – North of Cedar Hill

“Report,” Colonel Samantha Johnson ordered.

The remaining members of the Bison Plains Regiment slid back into their stations as the convoy rumbled toward the blast zone. The APC’s treads clattered over fractured asphalt while the **deep-seated growl** of the engine rattled the loose gear in the racks. Heat shimmer warped the asphalt on the horizon ahead.

“No squawk, Colonel!” Private Lowe replied, his eyes fixed on the console.

Samantha scanned the static-streaked display above him. “Any contact from Clay and his IFV?” Her voice was clipped; she feared the worst.

“Nothing, ma’am.” The private’s voice remained steady, though his brow furrowed as he traced a finger down the comms log.

Samantha leaned forward to scan the feed herself before straightening. “We’ll link with Chillicothe as planned,” she said, “but survivors come first.”

Outside, the landscape rolled by in ruined fields scorched black and farmhouses collapsed into smoldering piles. Every mile closer to the blast zone meant fewer chances of finding anyone alive. A burst of static cut through the speakers, sharp enough to startle a few of the regiment.

"Colonel… zzzt… if you can hear this… we're…" The voice fractured, swallowed by interference.

Samantha's eyes snapped to the comms panel. "Run it again. Clean it up."

The private's fingers moved quickly, boosting gain and filtering noise. The voice came back, still faint but clearer. "…took shelter in the rail yard… two klicks north of the blast. Heavy casualties. We can't hold out."

Samantha's pulse kicked up. The rail yard was well inside the fringe; if anyone was alive in there, they were on borrowed time. "Driver, adjust course. We're heading for that yard."

A murmur of unease rippled past the cabin. No one needed a reminder of what heading back in meant. Still, the APC's engine roared as the driver throttled up, and the ruined horizon swallowed them once more. The vehicle lurched as it left the highway, cutting across buckled asphalt toward the yard.

The comms crackled again. "…not much time… they're coming back."

Samantha leaned in. "Identify yourself."

A pause followed. Then, ragged but clear: "Moonshiners… we're all that's left."

The cabin went still as Samantha's jaw tightened. "Driver, eyes open. We're going in."

For half an hour, the APC crawled through the scarred outskirts, weaving around overturned grain trucks and the skeletons of houses. The air carried a heavy metallic tang that turned stomachs; a few men leaned over their knees, gagging. When the rail yard came into view, the convoy slowed. Outside the forward slit, Samantha caught sight of the first blackened and twisted boxcars, lying on their sides like scrap. A freight engine sat sideways across the track with its paint blistered and windows melted. The treads clanked over scattered rails, weaving between warped boxcars that leaned against one another.

Samantha scanned the dust cloud ahead. Movement.

Three figures emerged from behind a tipped flatbed. Weapons were slung, faces blackened, and uniforms caked in ash. They moved like old men and looked like walking dead who had escaped from hell. One raised a hand. "Colonel... you're late."

Samantha was already moving, her boots hitting the ground. "My God. Clay?" Her voice caught as she closed the distance, pulling him into a brief, fierce embrace. "What happened?"

Clay's voice was low and his breath uneven. "We were headed west to link up with friendlies, but then—I'll be glad to fill you in, but first we need to get out of here. Some of us are barely holding on."

She glanced past him. Two more of her Bison Plains Regiment slouched against the melted frame of their IFV. Nearby, two Moonshiners leaned hard on their rifles. One's sleeve was gone to reveal blistered skin; the other's eyes were half-shut, his breaths shallow.

Samantha caught the tremor in Clay's hands. "How many made it out?"

His gaze dropped. "These are it. Three of ours, four of theirs."

Her throat tightened. "We'll mourn later. Right now, we move." She waved the driver forward. The APC's engine roared back to life. "Get them inside. Now. Before the heat or the Fed patrols find us."

"If there are any Feds left," Clay muttered, helping the wounded up the ramp, "they're just as cooked as we are. I've never seen a cloud like that before."

The ramp rang under their boots. Samantha took one last look at Cedar Hill's jagged silhouette, the center still boiling with heat, before swinging the hatch shut. "Hang on," she said. "We'll get you all patched up."

Langley — George Bush Center for Intelligence

The rotor wash whipped at the dark glass of the helipad control tower as the Consortium's UH-92 Ghosthawk settled onto the pad. Sleek and unmarked, the aircraft's matte-black skin drank in the floodlights. Inside, Jack sat forward in his harness with eyes locked on the sprawling complex below. Beside him, Phen rechecked the encrypted satcom case with an unreadable expression. Vannah sat opposite, chin high, scanning the skyline as if she owned it. Twelve sat to her right in silence, her gloved hands resting lightly on her rifle and her eyes hidden behind mirrored lenses.

The pilot's voice came through their headsets, low and calm. "Welcome back, Operator Team One. Pad is hot."

The wheels touched down with a muted thud. A moment later, the helipad shuddered as hydraulics hissed and it began to sink into the earth. The night air gave way to a rising hum as reinforced walls closed overhead to seal them from the surface. Fluorescent strips flickered to life along the descending shaft, bathing the team in sterile white light. They emerged into a cavernous subterranean hangar, a place few outside the Consortium knew existed.

Other Ghosthawks lined the bay in precise rows. Some had crews loading gear while others sat with rotors still spinning down. Beyond them, the staging bays buzzed with movement. Armored figures moved in sync, and techs wheeled crates of weapons to waiting squads while mission controllers barked into headsets.

The moment Jack's boots hit the deck, the noise shifted. Operators along the catwalks and bays turned toward them. First a few claps, then more, until the hangar filled with cheers and fists pounding against steel rails.

"Mission accomplished!" someone shouted from the mezzanine.

Jack gave a brief nod but didn't smile. Phen allowed himself the faintest smirk. Vannah basked in the attention, removing her headset and tossing it to a waiting tech like a queen discarding a crown. Twelve said nothing. She scanned the crowd with a cold gaze, her mind still fixed on the family killed by shrapnel as they begged for help.

A young Operator jogged up with bright eyes. "Command wants you in the briefing room immediately. Director's already waiting."

Jack exchanged a look with Phen; no words were needed. This wasn't just a debrief. They moved toward the armored blast doors at the far end of the hangar as the cheers faded. As they approached, a newly painted Consortium seal marked the door. It blended elements of the CIA and FBI seals with hints of the American flag. Jack brushed the same seal on his sleeve and allowed himself a faint smirk as the door hissed open.

Beyond the blast doors, the hallway was lined with a black sound-dampening composite that swallowed both sound and light. Operators in varying loadouts passed them toward assigned Ghosthawks. Twelve noticed some coming from the Control Center were bloodied and heading toward bunks, but she gave it no thought. It was the life of a Consortium Operator.

The hallway widened into a staging concourse where digital boards tracked ongoing operations. Dozens of entries scrolled in plain blue text: timestamps, locations, team designations, casualties, and status updates. A balding man with a tablet paced between the boards, tapping commands into the screen and paying no attention to the team as they passed.

At the far end, two large men in tactical gear stepped aside and offered a Consortium salute: right hand to heart, then forward to the shoulder. Jack returned it as the door opened into a small vestibule with a scanner embedded in the floor. Jack stepped forward as a clinical white light swept over him to map his form. The system flashed green, and the team moved into a dark chamber.

Only perimeter lights glowed. The walls flickered on to reveal a masked man flanked by twelve others. A table rose from the floor and projected a three-dimensional map of the continental United States where borders flashed where new nations had formed. The masked man performed the Consortium salute. The others mirrored it, as did the team.

"In unison, we see all; we are all; we control all." The chant rose, a haunting liturgy that filled the chamber. The masked man continued, his voice firm with authority.

"Nothing escapes our gaze; our eyes are everywhere."

"Our agency cannot be undone in the darkest night and brightest day."

"In unison, we see all; we are all; we control all."

"The liturgy fades," the Chairman said. "Missouri was a spark in the tinder. Now we blow on the fire. I came here to brief you on your next theater."

"Yes, sir," Jack barked. Phen, Vannah, and Twelve stood rigid beside him.

The Chairman gestured. To his left, the First Chair leaned forward as the holographic map pulsed. Southern borders glowed crimson. "Mexico has chosen its moment," the First Chair said. "Their divisions now press into Arizona, New Mexico, and southern California. The Los Angeles Peninsula lies under their flag. They call it Mexizona, but they lack the numbers to hold it."

A different masked figure spoke. "They need not hold it alone. Our implants are already in motion. Clones have been seeded into their brigades to ensure Mexizona's survival."

"Because Texas and the Great Plains Nation will not endure a southern invasion. Not yet," the Chairman finished.

An alternate figure stepped forward. "You encountered them in Cedar Hill, but the UAA is embedding their elite Zero Company in the Rockies to prepare for the incursion."

"So what, you're calling it the Battle of the Rockies now?" Phen muttered.

"Lieutenant Stephen Martenson," the Chairman said, his voice sharp. "Would you care to repeat that for the record?"

"Oh, nothing, sir. Nothing." Phen lowered his head.

The Chairman let the silence linger. Then he moved, and the map zoomed into the Rockies. Blue wireframe mountains rose, fractured by red vectors pushing north. Icons blinked where skirmishes had already begun. "Zero Company," the Chairman said, "has been tasked with hardening the spine of the Rockies. They believe themselves unseen. They are mistaken."

A light shined on a board member in the corner, her voice a sultry blade. "Your assignment, Operator Team One, is to ensure Mexico's advance is not halted. You will destabilize Zero Company by eliminating their supply lines, cutting their forward scouts, and sowing confusion in their chain of command."

The map shifted again to reveal faint green markers in valleys and ridgelines. "These are your clone operatives, embedded among Mexican brigades. They will answer only to Consortium frequencies. Treat them as extensions of your will."

Vannah smirked. "So we play shepherd to sheep in borrowed uniforms. At least make it interesting."

"The UAA will make it interesting," a female voice replied. "Zero Company is not militia rabble. They are trained, disciplined, and they fight for something they believe in. Underestimate them, and you will not return."

For the first time, Twelve spoke. "Belief breaks like bone when pressure is applied."

The Chairman inclined his head. "Then you understand. You are the scalpel. Cut deep, unseen, and let the wound fester. By the time the UAA realizes what has happened, the Rockies will already belong to Mexico."

He raised his hand as the Board of Leadership mirrored him. "In unison—"

"We see all. We are all. We control all."

The map folded back into the floor. The lights dimmed. With a hiss of hydraulics, the chamber door opened back into the hallway.

"Don't fail me, Jack."

Asheville Regional Airport — UAA Command

The IFV's treads rattled over cracked asphalt and carried Zero Company east through the night. Smoke still clung to their gear from Cedar Hill, the sting of it mixing with sweat and heavy silence. No one spoke much; each man carried the haunting weight of what they'd seen. The comms crackled, breaking the monotony.

"Zero Company, divert. Immediate redeployment order. Proceed to Asheville Regional Airport. Priority tasking."

Viper leaned closer to the receiver while reading the coded scroll as it burned across the screen. "Asheville," he muttered. "We're not going home. The Great Plains Nation asked UAA command for help. They want us in the Rockies because the Mexicans are moving north."

Ghost frowned. "A border fight?"

"More than a fight," Radar said, scanning the dispatch log. "They're pressing Colorado. This looks like an attempt to conquer while GPN is distracted."

By dawn, the IFV rolled off I-40 with its treads grinding over the newly sealed tarmac of Asheville Regional. The airport was quiet. Since the military took it over there were no commercial flights coming in or out. A skeleton crew of UAA Marines stood watch at the perimeter. At the far end of the runway, something waited under floodlights. Specter caught sight of it first and whispered a prayer under his breath.

The craft sat with an ominous, coiled stillness. It was a stygian black with no seams, its broad wings blending into a single obsidian body. Thrusters angled downward, venting a constant shimmer of heat to keep the machine poised. Its edges repelled the light, causing the air around the hull to shimmer with a digital haze.

"What in hell is that thing?" Ghost breathed.

Joker pressed closer to the glass with wide eyes. "Is it for me? It's beautiful."

The IFV came to a stop. The side hatch opened. The men filed out and hauled their gear with them. The machine shifted with eerie fluidity, as if it were a sentient shadow acknowledging their presence. A ramp unfolded from its underbelly as the craft sensed their approach. Floodlights cut out in sequence, leaving the craft vanishing into its own silhouette.

"Not a transport I've ever seen," Radar murmured, tightening his grip on his pack. "This thing is meant to be secret."

Viper's eyes narrowed. "Then it's new. And if they sent it for us..." He left the thought hanging.

Reaper spat into the dirt. "New or not, anything that quiet makes me nervous."

Specter crossed himself and whispered under his breath. “Lord, keep us.”

The Marines on the tarmac nodded but gave no explanation; they only motioned the team forward. The craft loomed with a cold, monolithic weight with every step. Heat from its thrusters raised goosebumps along their arms. The ramp was chilled alloy underfoot and humming faintly. Inside, the air smelled of ozone and plastic as if the machine had just rolled off the assembly line. The interior was cavernous, with walls lined by modular racks that pulsed with soft red light as the team entered. The floor vibrated beneath them with a low thrum resonating in their bones. The hatch sealed behind them with a sharp hiss.

“I am Stealthwing: your transport, your shield, and your comrade.” The voice paused with a rhythmic timing that felt practiced. “I am the newest member of Zero Company.”

Ghost’s hand drifted toward his sidearm, a reflexive twitch. Joker’s smile vanished, replaced by a look of profound distrust as he rubbed the back of his neck. Even Viper stood rigid, his eyes searching the empty, red-lit corners of the bay for a speaker or a face that wasn’t there. Ghost looked at Specter and then at Joker as if he were waiting for a joke, but no one spoke.

The Stealthwing rose into the air like an elevator. It was smooth and steady, leaving the ground without so much as a tremor.

Viper didn't shrug. He looked at his men, seeing the same primal unease mirrored in their blackened faces. He adjusted his rifle strap, his knuckles white against the webbing as he forced himself to look back at the red-lit walls. He let out a breath he'd been holding, a long, slow exhale.

"Check your gear," Viper said, his voice low, cutting through the AI's artificial warmth. "We've got a long flight to get used to the company."

He turned toward the forward bulkhead, eyes narrowing as the craft banked silently into the night. "Let's see what our new teammate can actually do."

5

WASHINGTON, D.C. — LANGLEY Transit

Jack stepped out of the locker room just as Twelve came down the corridor. Vannah and Phen were already ahead with their laughter echoing faintly off the black-paneled walls. Twelve slowed until Jack fell in beside her. She gave him a quick smile, one she wouldn't dare hold too long under the base's ever-watching eyes.

"I was thinking we could try that new Chinese place in Woodley Park," she said, her tone light while she nudged his shoulder as they walked.

Jack's eyes flicked to a passing security lens then forward again. His reply was clipped. "On premises, we stay on mission."

Twelve smirked at the rebuff because she knew him too well. The wall wasn't for her; it was for the cameras. The doors ahead clanged shut after Phen and Vannah slipped through, the sound echoing down the corridor. Jack and Twelve kept walking with their boots soundless on the dampened floor. Twelve bumped him again, her smile defiant. She wasn't going to stop until he acknowledged. She loved this man even if he wouldn't show it back.

Jack's jaw tightened. "Would you stop, Twelve? You'll earn us a rip. The Chairman doesn't tolerate this kind of behavior on duty." His voice was low and forceful.

She grinned wider and remained unbothered. "Oh, come on, you're a real fuddy-dud."

Jack shook his head and kept moving. Twelve fell into step beside him with her shoulder brushing his just enough to remind him she was still there. They stepped through the doors at the end of the hallway where a heavy click followed as they closed. The muted bustle of D.C. nightlife greeted them. Ahead, the commuter train platform stretched under harsh fluorescent lights. Twelve's eyes flicked across the station in time to catch Vannah and Phen. Her blonde hair was bright in the artificial light as they stole a kiss before the next train pulled in. Twelve smirked and elbowed Jack again.

"I can't wait to kiss that steel expression on your face, honey," she teased, dripping sarcasm as she bumped him harder this time.

Jack cut her a glance with a low and warning voice. "Not here. You want a rip on your record, keep pushing it."

"Oh, come on, honey. We aren't even on premises anymore!" She quipped as the train screeched to a halt.

The doors slid open and the four filed in to find seats like ordinary commuters after a long shift. Around them, civilians stared at phones, muttered into earbuds, or sat hollow-eyed from the grind. No one noticed the Operators, off duty and blending in. Phen slid into a window seat with Vannah pressed close beside him, their hands finding each other's without hesitation. She leaned in and whispered something that drew a faint chuckle from him.

Twelve watched them a moment before turning back to Jack. "So. Woodley Park. That Chinese place. I'm buying, and you're coming."

Jack exhaled slowly while staring at the dark window as the train lurched forward. "We deploy tomorrow. You should be getting your head right."

"My head's right where it needs to be," Twelve said, her voice softer now. "Doesn't mean we can't eat."

Jack didn't answer, but he didn't shut her down either. The train rattled into the tunnel and plunged them into shadow and flickering light. Dozens of strangers swayed with the rhythm, but for the four of them, it felt like the city's pulse had slowed to match their own. Jack kept his eyes forward with the mask of command still fixed until the lights strobed across Twelve's face. For a breath, the world narrowed to her. The fire of her red hair caught in the glass reflection. His jaw unclenched as he reached up, brushing her cheek with a calloused hand, and pulled her in.

The kiss was brief and as sharp as the mission steel they lived by, but it was real.

"Oooooo," Phen muttered loud enough for the car to hear.

Vannah rolled her eyes and smacked his shoulder with a laugh. "How old are you, thirteen?"

Twelve leaned back with her smile lingering as the train rocked gently in the tunnel. For a moment, it felt like they could've been anyone. They were just coworkers heading home after a long day or couples tucked close together on a late ride. Phen leaned back against the hard seat, smirking. "So, what's the plan? We survived the boss's sermon. That earns at least one night off. Chinese? Steakhouse? Dive bar?"

"Dive bar," Vannah answered instantly. "The one off H Street with the jukebox. I'm not spending my last night in D.C. ordering dumplings like an accountant."

"Hey," Twelve shot back with mock indignation. "Dumplings are sacred."

Jack didn't answer right away. His gaze drifted to the window where tunnel lights blurred past. Twelve nudged him again, lighter this time. "Back me up here. Dumplings or dive bar?"

His mouth twitched into the faintest hint of a smile. "We'll do both. Dumplings, then drinks."

Phen laughed and pointed at him. "The machine can compromise. Alert the press."

Vannah rested her head on Phen's shoulder with her blonde hair falling across her eyes. "Don't tease him. He'll retreat into mission mode again."

"Mission before morals, la-la-la!" Phen mocked.

Jack shook his head but didn't deny it. The train slowed into the next station with the brakes squealing. Civilians shuffled out while others filed in: heads down and bags heavy. Ordinary life carried on in the shadow of war. Twelve leaned back with her hand brushing Jack's knee in the half-dark.

"For tonight," she whispered, low enough only he could hear, "we're not Operators. We're just us."

Jack glanced at her, then at Phen and Vannah across the aisle, then back to the window. His reflection stared back: tired eyes set in a face that hadn't been his own for a long time. He gave a small nod. "Just us."

Specter pulled up the monitor next to his jump seat to look outside. Stealthwing had no windows, but its surveillance system offered a seamless, 360-degree view of the world below. His rosary beads hung from his hand as he studied the full moon rising on the horizon, silver light washing across the cloud tops as they soared above Tennessee.

"Altitude thirty-five thousand feet. Airspeed five hundred fifty knots. Moonlight: aesthetically pleasing."

The AI's voice broke the quiet, measured and dry, just this side of ironic.

Specter's lips quirked. He pressed his thumb against the bead between his fingers. "Appreciated," he murmured.

Joker leaned forward in his harness, eyebrows raised. "Oh, terrific. Now our ride's got jokes."

"Correction," Stealthwing replied without missing a beat. "That was an observation. If you would like a joke, I am equipped for that function as well."

A ripple of chuckles went through the cabin. Even Viper's blank profile softened as he looked up from the tactical display.

Boom cracked his knuckles and grinned. "I like this bird already."

"Birds," Stealthwing countered, "cannot hover silently, deploy countermeasures, or carry nine Marines and their gear across a continent in two hours. But do continue."

Ghost shook his head, pulling his helmet back on. "That's unsettling. Talking transport. Feels wrong."

Radar adjusted his comms kit, earpiece jammed in. "Feels right to me. I can already tell she's got better signal clarity than half our gear."

"He," Stealthwing corrected flatly. "Pronoun preference established."

"Fantastic. Our transport has an ego," Joker groaned, leaning back in his seat. "I thought we escaped all that fake pronoun stuff when the neutronium bomb went off and started this mess."

There was a brief hum from the speakers, then Stealthwing's voice shifted, smooth and feminine, almost playful.

"Not ego. Programming," it replied evenly. "I can be whatever you want."

Several helmets turned toward the overhead panel, as if the AI could feel their stares.

Joker blinked, then barked a laugh. "Oh, hell no. The plane's flirting with me now."

"Incorrect," Stealthwing said, switching back to its default voice, tone still calm, almost amused. "Statistically, my phrasing is ninety-three percent more effective at undermining your sarcasm."

Boom snorted, shaking his head. "You hear that? Even the plane thinks you're a clown, Joker."

"Clowns at least get respect," Joker shot back, smirking. "This thing just graded my sarcasm like a schoolteacher."

"Correction," Stealthwing said smoothly, "your sarcasm ranked in the bottom fifteen percent of effectiveness, according to aggregated military humor databases. Would you like examples of superior wit?"

Everyone in the cabin except Viper erupted with laughter.

"That's enough," Viper cut in, though there was the barest trace of a smile tugging at his mouth. "Save the banter for downtime. We're not wheels-down yet."

"Copy that, boss," Joker said, but his grin lingered.

From the corner, Ghost muttered, "I still don't trust it. A plane that talks too much feels like a setup. Machines aren't supposed to have personalities."

Specter crossed himself with the rosary still in his hand, eyes never leaving the monitor. "Tools are what we make them, brother. If it flies and carries us safe, I'll take its words as just that—words."

"Words can still get you punched in the face," Ghost replied, helmet shadowing his eyes.

Radar looked up from his kit, brow arched. "Yeah, well, paranoia doesn't patch uplinks. I'm telling you, Stealthwing's got cleaner bands than I've ever run. I can pull in comms chatter from D.C. to Denver if I want."

"Not advisable," Stealthwing answered instantly. "Interception of domestic frequencies would violate multiple military codes and risk detection. However, you are correct about my signal clarity."

That earned another ripple of laughter.

Chatter shifted in his seat, fingers drumming against his rifle. "Am I the only one worried we're chatting with something that probably knows more about us than we do?"

"You're the only one talking like a spooked recruit," Bricks said, grinning. He leaned forward with eager energy. "Relax. If the bird wanted us dead, we'd be paste already."

"Affirmative," Stealthwing said without hesitation. "Fatality upon decompression at this altitude would occur in under thirty seconds. You would not suffer long."

The cabin went quiet. Stitch, his face pale but still holding it together, was the first to speak up with a strained laugh. "Comforting. Real bedside manner there."

Stealthwing's voice almost carried amusement. "I can adjust tone upon request. Would you prefer compassion simulation?"

"God, no," Joker muttered. "Next thing we know, it'll be tucking us in and talking to us about feelings."

Boom cracked up, loud enough to echo in the fuselage. "Better than you singing us lullabies, Joker."

"Request denied," Stealthwing said crisply, "though my archives include over two thousand lullabies in fourteen languages. Should mission morale require—"

"Don't you dare," Viper cut in, sharper this time, though his team could hear the laugh he was swallowing.

Chillicothe Medical Center—Missouri, 8:35 CST

The APC rumbled to a stop in front of Chillicothe Medical Center with its armored plates streaked in dust and blood. Floodlights blazed across a packed parking lot with lines of people waiting to be seen. Pickup trucks and battered sedans backed up to the curb, filled with wounded. Volunteers in makeshift armbands shouted over the chaos while dragging stretchers toward the doors. The glass entryway of the ER glowed harsh under fluorescents; every gurney inside was occupied and every hallway was crammed shoulder to shoulder.

The regiment stepped down into the churn of voices and sirens. The iron tinge of blood hung in the air, mixed with brake dust and pollen. A nurse in bloodstained scrubs nearly collided with Samantha as she rushed past. “We don’t have the beds; we don’t have the blood.”

Samantha didn’t flinch. She raised her hand, palm flat. Instantly, half her regiment broke off to clear a path for incoming vehicles. The others began unloading emergency stretchers from the APC. Even in the chaos, the militia’s blue buffalo patch caught the floodlights. Helicopters touched down in a nearby field, lifting some of the wounded toward other hospitals. Samantha pulled out her phone and dialed her father. After several failed attempts, she lowered it. The cellular networks were dead.

The sliding doors hissed open as she stepped inside. Overworked air-conditioning did nothing to cut the heat radiating from the packed lobby. Every chair was occupied, and the floor was worse. Families knelt with their wounded laid across blankets. IV bags dangled from coat racks while blood dripped onto the linoleum. A doctor in sweat-stained scrubs shouted orders over the noise with a cracking voice while two nurses tried to force a gurney down a hallway already clogged with stretchers.

The intercom barked another “Code Black,” swallowed immediately by the roar of voices. One of the nurses spotted Samantha and the militia patch on her shoulder. “We can’t take more. We don’t have the staff; we don’t have the beds.”

She stepped aside as three more gurneys rolled inside. Samantha kept her voice calm, low but carrying. "Nurse. Where's your emergency line?"

The nurse's face was drawn with exhaustion etched deep. "Over there, if you can get through. Lines have been jammed for hours."

Samantha crossed to the desk, lifted the receiver, and listened. She heard nothing but static and the chime of a failed connection. She set it down carefully. Clay staggered through the doors with two of his men on improvised stretchers, their faces gray with blood loss. Behind them came the Moonshiners, half-limping and half-carried. The nurse's protest rose again, thinner now. "We don't have the space."

Samantha dropped to one knee beside Clay's men and pressed her hand to a pulse. It was weak but present. She met Clay's eyes, and he nodded once.

"Listen to me," Samantha said, her voice steady and cutting through the din. "This lobby's already gone. You're drowning. Let us set up triage outside, in the parking lot, the lawn, anywhere we can put canvas down. My regiment will control the flow. Your doctors can work. We'll bring order to this."

For a moment, no one moved. The doctor looked like he might argue, but the sight of more stretchers silenced him. The blue buffalo patch caught the overhead light. Civilians began to turn, watching her. Samantha raised her voice.

"Bison Plains Regiment! Clear space outside. Establish stations. Wounded by priority: red, yellow, green. Anyone who can still walk, out of the lobby."

The regiment moved instantly. Boots pounded back through the doors. Order began to ripple outward as civilians followed their lead. Samantha adjusted a makeshift tourniquet on a Moonshiner's leg. "You're going to make it," she said quietly.

The doctor's voice came back, strained but steady. "If you can buy us space, maybe we keep half these people alive."

She met his eyes. "Then that's what we'll do, but you have to do better than just half."

The doctor dipped his head as he examined another.

Helena, Montana — Presidential Office — 09:45 MST

The last bands of twilight burned low on the horizon, a thin line of fire sinking behind the jagged spine of the Big Belt Mountains. From the tall windows of the Governmental Compound, President Jeremiah Johnson watched the ridgeline fade into silhouette while his reflection sharpened in the glass; the sky deepened from rust-red into indigo. A cigar clung to his lips with smoke curling upward in lazy threads. His free hand rolled a half-empty glass of bourbon between his fingers. He looked every inch the picture of calm authority, yet the rigid set of his shoulders betrayed the storm pressing in from every direction.

"What do you mean Mexico is moving north?" His voice held steady, but the edge cut through. "We can't afford another war front."

Governor Robert Kessler of Colorado answered from the other end of the line with a clipped and uneasy tone. "Yes, sir. The UAA and Texas are already shifting forces to reinforce the border. But I'm worried, Mr. President. Colorado may not be able to resist as much as I'd like."

Johnson exhaled through clenched teeth to let the smoke fog his reflection. He couldn't afford to sound as tired as he felt; too many governors depended on his resolve. He faced three enemies at once: Washington to the east, the Confederation pressing into the heartland, and now Mexico stirring to the south. The sun vanished behind the mountains. The phone went silent while Governor Kessler waited for reassurance Johnson wasn't sure he could give. "Hold as long as you can, Robert. Orders are coming," Johnson said, his voice a low, gravelly anchor.

"We'll be waiting, Mr. President," Kessler replied, and the line went dead with a hollow click.

Johnson finally set the phone back in its cradle as the weight of the day pressed heavier than the bourbon glass in his hand. He stood motionless in the silence of the office, watching the last of the mountain light bleed into the dark. The door clicked open behind him. Soft footsteps crossed the carpet as the faint scent of lavender cut through the haze of smoke and stress. Miranda Johnson came to stand behind him with her hands settling on his shoulders. Her touch was gentle but firm enough to ease some of the tension knotted into his frame.

"You've been at this since dawn," she murmured, her thumbs pressing into the cords of his neck. "The war won't be won tonight."

Johnson didn't answer. He let the silence stretch as he stared out at the blackening horizon where no light remained but the glow of Helena far below. Miranda's hands lingered before she moved away toward the far wall. Her eyes rested on the framed photograph above the credenza: five faces frozen in sunlight. Jeremiah, younger by a decade, stood broad-shouldered and grinning. Miranda stood beside him with her hair loose and shining. Samantha was a teenager with fire in her eyes even with braces on her teeth. Jake, lanky and laughing, had one arm wrapped around Buddy, the family's golden retriever.

The photo was taken in 2016 at their Big Sky Ranch before the neutronium blast, the Confederation, or the Secession Wars. It was a time when the greatest worry had been keeping Buddy from chasing elk off the property. Miranda touched the edge of the frame with her fingertips brushing the glass. "We were happy then," she said softly.

Johnson turned from the window with his cigar gone cold. He followed her gaze to the photograph while his jaw tightened. "We didn't know how good we had it."

"Maybe that's why we have to fight for what's left." Her eyes met his. "I miss my baby."

Her eyes welled with tears as Jeremiah stepped in to wrap his arms around her. "Jake didn't die in vain," he said quietly. "Even if I have to give my last breath fighting this war, I won't let it be in vain."

For a heartbeat, the office was quiet except for the hum of the air vents. The weight of command pressed on him. The governors waiting, militia bleeding, and a nation fracturing were only part of what he thought about. But here, it was just the two of them. Miranda pressed her cheek against his chest to draw strength. She pulled back after a moment with her eyes shining but steady.

"I promised myself after Jake that I wouldn't fall apart again. Not in front of Samantha. She needs a mother who won't break."

Johnson cupped her face and brushed away a tear. "You're stronger than you think. You carried her when I couldn't; you carried both of us. Samantha has become the best of both of us."

Miranda gave a small, sad smile. "And you carry a nation. I don't know which of us has it worse."

He let out a humorless breath and set the cold cigar aside. "A nation doesn't bleed like family does. Family leaves scars that never close." His gaze drifted back to

Jake's face in the photo then hardened. "That's why we don't stop." He leaned in to kiss her forehead. "Go home to Big Sky. Get some rest. I love you."

She nodded while mouthing the words back. "I love you too."

The desk phone buzzed with a sharp tone that cut through the moment. Johnson stepped toward the desk and lifted the receiver. "Johnson." Miranda stood in silence while watching her husband change from father and husband to a man of steel.

A strained voice crackled through the line. "Mr. President, this is General Harker. Satellite confirms Mexican armor crossing into New Mexico. Civilians are flooding the highways north."

Johnson's grip tightened. "Get me the governors of New Mexico and Arizona on a joint line," he said. "And Harker: mobilize everything we can spare."

The door to the Presidential Office had barely closed behind Miranda when the rhythmic thump of rotor blades rolled over the compound. Floodlights lit the helipad in a bright sepia, gleaming off the fuselage of the olive-drab transport. The GPN Homeland Continuity Service moved quickly to secure the perimeter as the crew readied for departure. Miranda stepped out flanked by two agents whose dark suits and earpieces caught the glare. Her arms were folded against the weight pressing in her chest. A crewman snapped a salute and pulled the cabin door open.

She paused at the threshold to glance back toward the lit windows of the compound. Jeremiah was still in there somewhere, bent over maps with a phone pressed to his ear, carrying the weight of a nation that refused to hold together. For a moment, she wished he could come with her back to the ranch and back to something quiet. But that life ended when this war started; with Jake.

Miranda climbed aboard. The agents followed with one across from her and the other near the door. Headsets went on to mute the outside world as the rotors built to a steady roar and the helicopter lifted into the night. Helena fell away beneath them, a scatter of golden lights against the dark. Beyond it, the sky stretched wide and empty, broken only by the faint silver line of the Missouri River reflecting the moonlight. She leaned her head back and closed her eyes. Soon, she would be home.

It had been weeks since she'd last been to the ranch. She remembered Memorial Day weekend when she and Jeremiah rode side by side across the fields, letting the horses and the wind carry the silence. For a few hours, the world felt whole. A small smile touched her lips as she thought of Jake beneath the old oak tree with a sketchbook in hand, trying to capture the elk that wandered through the property. Summers had been full of those moments: Samantha and Jake racing Buddy across the pastures until the sun dropped behind the hills and the cows drifted back toward the barn.

Her throat tightened. "Samantha," she whispered, pulling out her phone to call, but the line didn't connect. She closed her eyes again and chose to believe her daughter was safe.

"Ma'am." The voice cut through her headset.

Miranda blinked awake as the helicopter banked low. The warm glow of the ranch house porch light spread across the clearing below while smoke drifted from the chimney. The helicopter settled onto the pad with rotors kicking dust across the gravel drive. One agent stepped out first to scan the darkness before motioning her forward.

Miranda stepped down into the night. The air was cool and clean. For the first time in weeks, she breathed. The ranch house was quiet when she stepped inside. A fire crackled softly in the hearth with the scent of cedar as the executive housekeeper put another log in the fireplace. Miranda closed the door behind herself while the security detail lingered near the entry with low voices. The butler lowered his head in greeting, but no one followed as she moved up the staircase alone.

Her hand slid along the banister with fingers tracing grooves worn smooth over years. Upstairs, the hallway lay dark and lined with photographs of Christmas mornings, rodeo fairs, and Jake's first buck held proudly between Jeremiah's grin and Samantha's reluctant smile. She paused there for a second then forced herself forward. Jake's door creaked as she pushed it open.

Nothing had changed. Posters still clung to the walls over books stacked in careless towers. A half-finished sketch lay on the desk beneath the window. Dust had settled in, but the room still felt lived in and still his. Miranda crossed to the bed and lowered herself onto it. The mattress gave beneath her as she noticed a stick of his deodorant. She took the cap off and smelled the fragrant gel but put that cap back on as she yawned. Laying back she pulled the quilt to her chest. It still carried a trace of him. Tears slipped quietly into the fabric as she turned onto her side while clutching the pillow. Her breath caught once then steadied.

Exhaustion took her in the quiet dark of Jake's room. The First Lady of the Great Plains Nation slept not as a figurehead or the wife of a president, but as a mother who had lost her son.

Consortium City — District 4 — 11:15 PM EST

The neon glow of the Chinese restaurant flickered as Jack pushed the door open with the four of them stepping into the warm and muggy night. The city hummed around them: sirens in the distance, traffic lights bleeding red and green across wet asphalt, and helicopters thudding low toward the river. **Jack checked his watch then glanced toward the neon signs of H Street. "The dive bar is out," he said, his voice leaving no room for**

argument. "Command moved the transport window up two hours. We're done for the night."

Phen let out a short, disappointed breath but didn't argue. He shoved his hands into his pockets while **Jack** looked at him. "We'll meet at the briefing point tomorrow. Don't be late."

Twelve gave a faint nod while already scanning the street with an unreadable face. Phen met Jack's gaze with a half-smile. "I've never been late in my life."

Jack smirked. "There's a first time for everything."

Without another word, he and Twelve moved down the block and dissolved into the crowd. For a moment, Phen and Vannah stood between passing cars. He looked at her as her braided blonde hair caught the light. Her expression was calmer than he felt.

"Your place?" he asked.

Her lips quirked. "Unless you'd rather spend the night in a safehouse with peeling wallpaper and rats in the vents."

He chuckled. "I'll take my chances with you."

They walked in silence with their steps falling into a close rhythm. By the time they reached her building, the city noise had faded. An old brick townhouse stood wedged between glass towers with its wrought-iron railing slick from the dew. She keyed them inside. The door clicked shut behind them. Her apartment smelled faintly of jasmine and old books. The lights were dim and soft as candlelight.

She dropped her jacket, kicked off her shoes, and loosened her braid. Golden strands fell across her shoulders to soften the mask she wore outside. Phen lingered near the door while watching the way her shoulders eased and the tension slipped away.

"One night," she said quietly. "That's all we get before the war drags us under again."

He stepped closer. "Then let's not waste it."

Vannah studied him for a long moment before reaching up to trace his jaw. For once, she stopped calculating and simply allowed herself to feel. Her hand lingered on the side of Phen's face. His hand rose, hesitant then certain, to brush a loose strand behind her ear. She didn't pull away.

Outside, the city droned on with sirens, traffic, and a helicopter cutting low toward the river. Inside, time slowed. Phen leaned in and rested his forehead against hers. They swayed together in silence. She moved first by pulling him into a kiss. He returned it: steady and grounding. Her grip tightened as his hands settled at her waist.

Then came motion. He lifted her while her laugh was muffled against his shoulder as the bedroom door swung open. Tomorrow, they would go back to being weapons. Tonight, they were together, and that was all that mattered.

The sun streamed through the window with warm fingers settling across Twelve's face. She breathed in slowly then smiled at the steady rhythm of Jack's breathing beside her. Rolling over, she rested a hand on his bare chest and pressed a kiss to his neck.

Jack squinted against the light while a faint smile tugged at his lips. "What time is it?"

"It doesn't matter." Her mouth trailed along his collarbone.

His arm groped across the nightstand for his phone. "Twelve... what time?"

She swatted his hand away and laughed softly. "Don't worry. We'll be on time."

The sun rose higher to gild the edges of the curtains in a pale glow. Jack finally abandoned his reach for the phone and let his hand rest over hers while it remained splayed against his chest. "You're terrible at mornings," he muttered, though the roughness in his voice carried more affection than annoyance.

"Only when mornings mean going back to war," Twelve whispered. Her eyes studied the hard lines of his face softened by sleep. For a man who had spent his life braced for impact, this was the only time he looked unarmored. Jack cracked one eye open and caught her gaze. "You think we'll make it through this one?"

She didn't flinch and didn't give him the comfort of a lie. "We'll make it until we don't. That's enough."

They lay in silence for a few minutes, the warmth of their bodies mingling. Outside, the distant whine of sirens reminded them both that the world hadn't paused to give them this reprieve. Twelve shifted while propping herself on an elbow. Her fingers traced a scar across his shoulder, a pale crescent from a mission gone wrong years before. "Every time we walk into the fire, I wonder if this is the last scar I'll remember on you."

Jack caught her hand and stilled it against his skin. His voice dropped low, almost a growl. "Don't start saying goodbye before we've even stepped out the door."

Her lips curved faintly although her eyes were serious. "I'm not saying goodbye. I'm reminding myself that you're still here."

He leaned up to brush a kiss against the scar on her cheek while lingering there. For a moment, the war outside was distant. Then Jack pulled back and finally reached for the phone on the nightstand. Twelve grumbled in protest. The screen lit his face and washed him in a cold blue glow. His expression hardened as he scrolled through the alerts.

"The GPN is calling for help from the UAA, they are mounting a full defensive of Kansas," he said quietly, more to himself than to her.

"Chaos spreads faster when the desperate fight back. That's what they'll never understand; we don't need to win, we just need the fire to catch." She spoke quietly.

"The GPN may be stretched thin, but like a bear trapped in a corner, they are more dangerous," Jack grunted in response.

The warmth between them cooled, replaced by the inevitable return of duty. Twelve lay her head back on his chest while listening to the heartbeat that would soon march into chaos. "We had one night," she whispered again, as if the words themselves could stretch the time they had left.

Jack didn't answer, but his arm wrapped around her tighter. He held her as though he could anchor them both against the tide. "One glorious night," he murmured, his face reflecting the anxiety he was feeling. Jack slid from bed with his backside bare. She purred, and he bent to kiss her once more.

6

CHILLICOTHE MED CENTER — 06:40 CST

The steady rattle of the APC's engine had been Samantha's lullaby through the night. She stirred awake to the sting of smoke still hanging in the air, mixed with the sharp scent of antiseptic. Her cheek had pressed against the cold steel wall to leave an imprint that throbbed when she sat up. Outside, the hospital was already overwhelmed. Dozens of wounded poured in overnight. Missourians burned, crushed, and barely holding together. Samantha had worked until her hands shook while carrying stretchers, holding IV bags, and pressing gauze against wounds that wouldn't stop bleeding. She collapsed only when exhaustion won.

A low rumble rolled in from the distance. Something heavier than the vehicles the Moonshiners or UAA had.

"Fed armor," someone hissed.

Samantha pushed out of the APC as the first vehicles crested the rise. A column of battered Federal carriers rolled in with faded eagles still visible on their sides. Soldiers clung to the armor with scorched uniforms and rifles hanging slack. They dragged themselves forward with several white t-shirts hung from their antennas to show they surrendered. The militia didn't care; they saw Federal troops rolling in and began to equip themselves for another fight. Militia and local farmers poured into the street with rifles raised while the Moonshiners followed with shotguns and carbines snapping into place. The line swelled with anger and anxiety.

"Hold your fire!" a Fed officer shouted while waving a white t-shirt. "We need medical! That's all!"

A round cracked into the dirt near the tires as shouts erupted. A doctor broke through the line with a blood-soaked white coat. His voice was raw but steady. "You swore to fight. I swore to heal. This hospital does not close its doors. Not while I draw breath."

The men kept their arms trained on the Feds and refused to back down.

"To hell with your Hippocratic Oath!" someone shouted. "They bombed our home!"

Samantha grabbed the mic. "Feds, stand down. Drop your weapons." No one moved. "I said drop them. Now."

"We didn't bomb anything!" a captain shouted while stepping out of the lead vehicle with his hands raised. "We just need medical!" Behind him, his men hesitated with hands hovering over rifles.

"You killed my brother!"

The shot cracked. Private Hastings dropped instantly with blood spreading across the asphalt. Silence.

"What the hell, Wallace?!" the captain roared. "Weapons down! Now!"

It was too late. A sniper's round slammed into Wallace's chest and threw him back against the carrier. He hit the ground hard. The street snapped with fingers tightening on triggers. "Fire!"

"Stand down!" Samantha's voice thundered from the APC, but no one listened.

The captain staggered forward with his arms wide. "He acted alone! He broke orders! He's dead for it! Don't make his mistake!"

Across from him, barrels tracked every movement. The doctor stepped forward again with his arms spread. "Stop this! You'll slaughter the wounded! Is that who we are now?"

"Regiment! Moonshiners! Stand down!" Samantha roared. No one lowered their rifles. The bodies of Hastings and Wallace lay between the lines. Their blood soaked into the same dirt. Everyone held their breath as the rifles continued to be held aggressively.

"They killed our people at Cedar Hill!" a militiaman shouted. "Put them down!"

"We didn't touch Cedar Hill!" the Feds fired back.

"Liar!" Voices collided as guns wavered.

The doctor didn't move. "If you kill them, you kill me first! If this is who we are, then no nation deserves to survive!"

Silence fell. The captain's voice broke. "We'll leave. Just let us take our wounded."

Samantha stepped higher into the hatch while gripping the frame. "No one walks out of here with rifles in their hands." Heads turned, even the Moonshiners hesitated. "You came onto Great Plains soil armed and uniformed. You're prisoners now. Lay down your weapons, or I order every barrel here to drop you where you stand."

"Samantha—" the doctor started.

"They'll be treated," she said. "But disarmed. In custody."

The captain looked at his men then dropped to one knee. He set his sidearm in the dirt and raised his hands. "Stand down. We surrender." His order shouted loud so that every Fed troop heard him.

One by one, rifles hit the asphalt. The sound echoed. The Militia hesitated to lower their weapons until all of them were disarmed.

"Secure them," Samantha ordered. "Bind their hands, let's get the wounded separated. The rest go into custody."

The militia moved with their shackles, medics rushed in behind. Samantha held the frame with her chest heaving. Then she dropped back inside, slammed the hatch, and collapsed in the corner. The dam broke. Tears came hard and shook her shoulders. Outside, Clay barked orders as the Feds were rounded up. Inside, she was alone. She was tired. She missed home. She missed Jake, Mom, and Dad. Curled against the cold steel, she let herself cry. She wept not as a commander, but as a daughter who had lost too much.

Big Sky Ranch — Morning

Outside, birds chirped in the eaves and roosters crowed from the distant barns, their morning calls sharp against the quiet of the house. Miranda stirred with her cheek still pressed into the pillow that carried the ghost of her son's scent. For a moment, waking felt cruel because it brought her back to the quiet truth that she was in Jake's bed and the house was too still. She sat up slowly while pulling the quilt tighter around her shoulders. She pressed her palm to the pillow one last time before sliding her feet to the floor. She remembered Jake racing downstairs for breakfast as she heard the floor creak, but now it only echoed.

The hall was lined with the same photographs she'd passed the night before. She touched one frame as she moved toward the stairs. Outside, the air was cool and clean while carrying the scent of dew and sagebrush. Smoke curled from the chimney. Cattle lowed in the distance as life carried on. Buddy barked at the herd; the cows answered with an annoyed drift farther into the pasture.

It didn't take long for the dog to notice her. He came running with his coat flashing gold in the morning light and his tongue lolling as he bounded toward the porch. Miranda eased into her rocking chair as he reached her with his paws thudding against the boards. He pressed in close to lick her hand. She scratched behind his ears while feeling his fur warm beneath her palm. He was older now and slower, yet he was still there. Her eyes drifted past him and across the pasture to the line of cottonwoods. Beyond them, the small family cemetery waited. Her smile faded as she rose slowly. Buddy stayed close as she crossed the porch with his nails clicking softly against the wood. The fields stretched wide before them while washed in early light with dew clinging to the grass. The cottonwoods swayed gently in the breeze. The air grew still as she approached as if the land itself quieted.

Buddy trotted ahead then stopped at the gate as Miranda's fingers curled around the iron latch. She opened it and stepped inside. The headstones were worn but cared for; the newest one stood out.

Jacob Jeremiah Johnson. 2002–2025. Beloved son, brother, friend.

Her breath caught. Tears came before she could stop them. She sank to her knees with one hand pressing into the fresh earth and the other gripping the quilt at her shoulders. Buddy lay beside her with his muzzle resting across her leg.

"I dreamed you were still upstairs," she whispered. "Laughing. Drawing elk like you used to. I almost believed it. Then I woke up."

The wind moved through the cottonwoods. For a moment, she let herself pretend it was him. She bowed her head while pressing her lips to her hand to hold back the sob. "Your father says you didn't die in vain. That we'll make sure of it. But God help me, Jake... I would give it all back just to hear your voice again." The quilt slipped from her shoulders into the grass. She didn't reach for it.

Colorado — Abandoned Runway, Dawn

"We have arrived," Stealthwing said dryly. "Please place your seats and trays in their upright positions."

"Who thought giving our bird a personality was a good idea?" Joker quipped.

"Oh, you're just mad the corny jokes aren't yours," Ghost muttered while earning a few chuckles.

"Please, Joker," Stealthwing replied. "If I wanted to compete with you, I'd downgrade my humor algorithm by ninety percent."

Boom barked a laugh. "Damn. Even the bird's roasting you now."

"Roast protocols engaged," Stealthwing added. "Caution: overexposure may bruise fragile egos."

The banter broke as the engines shifted pitch with thrusters tilting for descent. Dust whirled across Specter's monitor where jagged peaks bracketed the cracked runway.

"Eyes up," Viper snapped. "Wheels down in thirty."

Hydraulics groaned while dust stormed the tarmac. Militiamen ducked behind trucks and crates to shield their eyes. They had expected trucks or perhaps a Blackhawk, but not a black-winged predator dropping out of the sky.

"Touchdown in three... two... one."

The landing came soft as silk. The ramp hissed open. Zero Company filed out in a single line with boots hitting gravel. They looked leaner and harder with shadows stretched long in the rising sun. A sergeant in a battered Stetson squinted at them while holding his rifle strap tight. "Zero Company, huh? Heard the name. Didn't know you were bringin'... that." His chin jerked toward Stealthwing as it continued humming behind them.

"'That' has better manners than half my team," Viper replied.

"Disputable," Stealthwing said at once.

Uneasy murmurs rolled through the militia line as knuckles tightened on rifles.

"Batteries charging," Stealthwing added while its engines fell silent.

Bricks cocked his head at the folded black panels along its spine. "It's solar too?"

"Solar, kinetic, and thermal," Stealthwing replied. "Unlike Corporal Brooks, I do not require three energy drinks before breakfast to function."

Joker threw his hands up. "Yeah, yeah. Put me out of a job."

That earned a few thin smirks, but the unease lingered. The sergeant spat into the dust. "Hard to believe flesh-and-blood soldiers climb outta somethin' like that... thing."

"Designation: Stealthwing, Sergeant. Not 'thing.'"

The man shook his head when Viper didn't react. He stepped aside just enough for his men to be seen. "Your commanders called for Zero Company. Well... here we are."

Specter's fingers traced the rosary in his pocket with his lips moving soundlessly. It was half prayer and half habit. Joker gave the militia a mock salute with a grin wide and shameless. Boom cracked his knuckles. Ghost hung back with his helmet shadowing his face while Reaper stood still. Radar spoke into his headset without looking up. "Signal's clean, boss."

Stitch adjusted his medic pack. Bricks tapped the charges on his belt while Chatter checked his scope. Viper's gaze returned to the sergeant. "These are my men. If this war keeps burning, you'll learn their names. Not from me, but from what they do when the shooting starts."

The militia line shifted but the suspicion held. The sergeant spat again. "Guess we'll see if the stories live up, or if you're just another batch of bodies we'll be burying."

The interior of the Ghosthound thrummed with a low mechanical hum while its stealth plating absorbed every attempt to see them. Cabin lights glowed a faint red to leave the operatives' faces cut sharp in shadow. Straps creaked and metal rattled with the UH-92 shaking with its rotors. Jack sat near the forward bulkhead with his rifle across his knees and his eyes hard and unblinking. The red cabin light catching the hard angles of Jack's face. His jaw hadn't relaxed since Consortium City. He didn't shift with the turbulence; his gaze fixed on a point in the middle distance as if he were already scanning a kill zone.

"Arizona's border is a tinderbox," he said. "We're not there to throw a match. We're there to guide the flame once it sparks." He looked at each of them in turn. "That means discipline. There will be no improvising and no freelancing."

Twelve leaned back as her boot tapped lightly against the deck. A notepad rested on her thigh where she had scribbled contingencies in a precise hand. "We'll need redundancies," she said. "If extraction gets burned, I want secondary routes east into Deseret territory. If cover IDs don't hold, we pivot to civilian persona two. And if—"

Jack cut her a sharp look. She raised an eyebrow in response. "Contingencies aren't weakness, Jack. They're survival."

At the rear of the cabin, a low laugh cut through the tension. Vannah leaned toward Phen with her braid falling over her shoulder as she murmured something in his ear. Phen smirked while answering quietly; his hand brushed hers on the armrest. Twelve's pen stilled. She didn't look up, but she clenched her teeth. Jack's eyes flicked toward them with his frown deepening.

"Are you two finished?" he asked.

Vannah met his glare with a smile that was easy but edged. "Finished? Hardly started."

Phen gave a small chuckle. "Relax, Jack. This tension is no good before a major op."

"Humor gets men killed," Jack snapped.

The words landed hard to fill the cabin. Silence followed, broken only by the pilot's voice over the comms. "Crossing into Arizona airspace. Twenty minutes to drop."

Vannah leaned back with her arms crossed and an unreadable expression. Phen shifted as the grin vanished when he caught the storm in Jack's gaze. Twelve finally looked up with a cold voice. "You think this is a game? Keep your heads on the mission or Jack won't need to kill you. This battle will."

The Ghosthound dipped as turbulence pressed them into their harnesses. No one reacted, but their hands tightened on the grips of their weapons.

"Twenty minutes," Jack said, quieter now. "Use them to remember who we are and what we're here to do."

7

GUNNISON, CO — NIGHTFALL

The cold bite of early fall clung to the fields as Viper and his company ghosted through the high grass with eyes fixed on the target Stealthwing had painted across their maps. Above, the black-winged craft prowled in silence while its sensors swept the terrain; his presence was both a comfort and an omen. From the valley ahead drifted the strains of mariachi music, carried thin on the night wind. Laughter followed with shouts and drunken calls that sounded like a party where no party belonged.

"Too loud," Ghost muttered. "Soldiers don't sing that close to the front line."

Viper didn't answer. He signaled with two fingers. Stitch peeled off to the right while Brick and Boom slid left as their shadows melted into the grass. The militia trailing behind bunched up awkwardly with rifles clenched in sweaty hands. Every snapped twig was a reminder they were just farmers and electricians a few years ago. Zero Company moved on while quietly cutting south into the dark as the noise grew louder.

Joker pulled his drones from his pack and slipped the AR goggles over his face. The quadrotors buzzed to life with barely a whisper and scattered upward as he crouched in the mud. "Hold up," he whispered into comms. "Let me paint it for you."

Viper lifted a hand and the line froze. Through his goggles, Joker skimmed the valley. Heat signatures appeared while glowing faintly on his HUD around firepits and lanterns. He dialed closer. The music blared tinny through battered speakers strung between poles. He caught the jerky motion of men swaying with arms slung around each other.

"Camp's lit up like a fiesta," Joker muttered. "Bodies moving; maybe fifty, no, sixty. But..." He leaned into the feed and frowned. "Something's off."

"Drunk?" Boom offered.

"Or pretending to be," Ghost countered.

The militia in the rear began murmuring while unnerved by the laughter. One farmer turned rifleman whispered too loud: "Why the hell they celebratin'? We ain't even hit 'em yet."

"Quiet." Viper's voice snapped through the air.

On Joker's feed, one of the figures staggered toward a lantern. He leaned into the light and froze. His face was slack and his movements were jerky, like a marionette tugged on uneven strings. He didn't blink.

"Uh, boss," Joker whispered with a tight voice. "You're gonna wanna see this. That's not a party."

The laughter carried again while sounding too forced. It was a trap. The militia didn't realize it yet as they shifted nervously and readied to charge, but Viper's stomach had already dropped. "Positions," he murmured. "Eyes wide. Nobody fires until I say."

Stealthwing's detached voice crackled overhead. "Warning. Additional signatures inbound. Armored transports, twelve vehicles, hundreds of heat signatures. Converging from the south. Estimated contact: ninety seconds."

The music swelled as if mocking them. Stitch slid forward with three militia at his back while leading them into the glow of the camp. Lanterns swung lazily to throw long shadows over crates and empty bottles. The closer they got, the clearer it became. The figures around the fires weren't moving. Stitch reached one of the slumped silhouettes and tapped its shoulder. It was a mannequin stuffed into a uniform with the head being a burlap sack painted with a crude grin.

"Son of a—" Stitch hissed while waving his men back. "It's a—"

The rest dissolved into static as the first shot cracked out of the darkness. One of the militia dropped without a sound while his body jerked as the round ripped through his skull. Another screamed while clutching his throat.

"Contact! Contact! It's a setup!" Stitch shouted while spraying a burst into the treeline.

At the same moment, Joker's drones picked up the shimmer of armored transports rolling in from the south. "Viper, it's a kill box!" Joker snapped while rip-ping his goggles off. "South line's stacked; their armor and infantry are closing fast!"

In the valley, Stitch and his last militiaman dove for cover, but the night erupted. The militia boy beside him jerked violently and went limp as he was dragged back into the grass by unseen hands.

"Stitch, fall back! FALL BACK!" Viper roared.

Stitch rose to run only to be hammered by a burst that punched through his chest plate. He hit the dirt hard while choking as blood bubbled between his teeth. His comm sputtered one last word: "Trap—"

"Warning," Stealthwing reported. "Multiple hostile elements converging. Stitch's heartbeat is absent. This position is compromised."

Viper clenched his fist. "Zero Company! Form a line! Get ready to bite before they chew us apart!"

Engines roared and rifles barked. The militia cracked with some stumbling back and others firing blindly. Then the sky split. Stealthwing swooped low with cannons spitting fire into the treeline to shred the mannequins and smash the camp into splinters. The ground lit up with flame and dust while drowning the festive music in thunder. From the south, armored transports ground into view with floodlights stabbing through the valley in blinding streaks.

Tracer fire ripped over the fields in long, burning arcs. Militiamen screamed and dropped while their bodies convulsed as rounds shredded the grass. "CONTACT:

LEFT FLANK! MOVE, MOVE, MOVE!" Viper's roar cut through the panic.

Boom swung his launcher up. A thunderous whoomp hurled a rocket into the lead transport. The explosion bloomed orange while shearing the roof off. Inexperienced militiamen cheered for half a heartbeat but were drowned by return fire.

"Reaper, cover our rear! Ghost, collapse right!" Viper barked. Reaper dragged a terrified militia boy by the collar as he snapped off bursts. Ghost flickered through the shadows while his suppressed rifle whispered death into the woods beyond their position.

"Stealthwing, status!" Viper snapped while diving behind a half-buried log.

"Overwatch engaged," the AI replied. "Hostiles: two hundred forty-three. Warning: the odds of survival without retreat are statistically negligible."

"Not helpful!" Joker spat. One of his drones slammed kamikaze-style into the treads of a vehicle to topple it into a ravine. He ripped off his goggles with ragged breath. "I've bought us maybe sixty seconds!"

"Sixty seconds is enough!"

But the militia line was collapsing. Brick ripped another rocket downrange, but a shell answered from the south to hurl him ten feet backward.

"Brick's hit!" Radar filled the comms. "Comms chatter's hot; Mexicans are calling in reinforcements with artillery inbound!"

The valley became a killing ground. Zero Company was pinned while the militia broke apart. Viper slammed a fresh mag into his rifle with bared teeth. "Hold the line! We buy every damn second we can!"

Above, Stealthwing's cannons stitched fire across the transport line. "Warning: reinforcements are three minutes out. Estimated survival: thirty-five percent."

"Then we make it thirty-six," Viper snarled.

Boom slid into the mud beside Brick with his hands already red as he gripped the younger man's trembling fingers. Brick's chest hitched while blood bubbled at his lips. His eyes were wide and pleading.

"I know, brother," Boom said with a breaking voice as he leaned close. "I know."

Another shell tore into the ridge to shower them with dirt. Brick's hand tightened once then went slack. Boom held it longer than he needed to while refusing to let go even as the battlefield howled. "Dammit," he whispered. He rose with anger covering his face as he hefted his launcher. "You're comin' with me, Brick. Every shot I fire is yours now."

"Extraction! Extraction!" Viper's voice tore through the comms.

"Negative; too hot to land," Stealthwing replied. "Pull back to secondary LZ. Marking coordinates. Fall back now!"

Zero Company shifted into a phalanx while pushing north through the mud. "Where the hell is Chatter?!" Viper bellowed.

"Haven't seen him!" Specter shouted back. His rosary beads clinked against his chest as he reloaded with hands slick with blood.

"Radio's dead on his channel!" Radar barked. "Not getting a ping or location for him. He's either jammed up or down!"

Boom's voice cracked with fury. "He's not down! He's just cut off; we'll find him!"

"The south line's collapsed," Ghost muttered while scanning the ridges. "If he's out there, he's in their teeth."

Another mortar screamed overhead to fling militia into the air. Brick's body slid deeper into the mud and Stitch had already vanished beneath the churned earth of the fake camp. There was no time to recover them.

"Eyes forward!" Viper roared while the weight of three fallen men dragged against his chest. "We get to Stealthwing or we die in this field!"

"Coordinates locked," Stealthwing reported. "Window is ninety seconds. If you are not there, you will not be extracted."

"We'll be there," Viper growled while shoving the line forward.

Tracer fire stitched the night. The mariachi music still wailed from the damaged speakers in the valley. The sounds warped as if mocking Zero Company fighting their way out of hell.

Gunnison Perimeter

Elsewhere on the ridge, Chatter belly-crawled into position with his rifle cradled against his chest as he settled behind a jagged outcrop of stone. From this vantage, he could see the entirety of the carnage: chaos spilling across the valley, muzzle flashes strobing through the dark, and tracers clawing at the sky like burning scars. He adjusted his scope while his breath fogged in the high-altitude cold. For a moment, he felt that familiar, crystalline calm: the stillness that always preceded the shot. His crosshairs tracked a squad of advancing infantry whose silhouettes surged through the localized smoke. He exhaled and squeezed; one fell. He racked the bolt and another dropped.

Then the radio hissed in his ear. It was not words but a jagged storm of static and broken fragments. Viper's voice was buried in the interference. Chatter pressed the earpiece harder against his skull. "Say again! Viper, you're breaking up!"

Nothing but the hollow hiss of the void answered. He risked a glance away from the optic. Below, Zero Company was pulling back in a tight, disciplined phalanx while the militia scattered around them like sparks from a dying fire. Stitch's position was gone and utterly obliterated. Brick lay still in the churned mud. The rest of the company was already retreating north, but the geography of the ridge had effectively cut him off from the main element.

"Dammit," Chatter breathed while swinging back to his scope.

A subtle shimmer of movement caught his eye at the edge of the woods. He saw three people in clean uniforms; they didn't look Mexican, nor did they look like militia. They were near a tent with a blonde haired woman looking at the battle below through binoculars. His stomach knotted with a sudden, instinctive dread. Before he could call out the contact, a sharp crack split the mountain air. His rifle spun from his hands as white-hot pain exploded across his shoulder with the force slamming him flat against the stone.

Boots thundered on the scree behind him. A shadow loomed while the muzzle of a weapon pressed cold and unyielding against the side of his neck. Through a haze of shock, Chatter managed to twist his head just enough to see the patch on the person's sleeve. There was no flag and no country; it was just a geometric triangular sigil that felt colder than the steel on his skin.

"You're coming with us," a voice said flatly. Rough hands dragged him from the rock to bind his wrists with the brutal efficiency of a professional. His radio was ripped from his vest and crushed under a heavy boot. His world narrowed to the bite of cord on skin, the metallic taste of blood in his mouth, and the suffocating weight of defeat. Down in the valley, Zero Company fell back toward their extraction while unaware of the shadow that had fallen over their sniper.

The world returned in agonizing fragments. The cold dirt grinding into his cheek, the sound of heavy boots dragging across dry pine needles, and the copper tang of blood thick in his throat. He blinked with hazy vision as the treeline swam in and out of focus. His wrists were bound tight with metal cuffs biting deep into the bone. Every time he stirred, the cord looped around his elbows wrenched tighter to force him forward like a broken puppet.

The men dragging him were in the same uniforms he spotted. He had seen the regulars who were loud and sloppy while shouting frantic orders. These men moved like something else. Their gear was high-end and far too pristine for the mud of the Gunnison front. Stitched onto their shoulders was that same insignia; it was something foreign but naggingly familiar, like a memory half-buried under a lifetime of service. He tried to lift his head, but a boot pressed firmly between his shoulder blades to shove him back into the dirt.

"Keep him quiet," a voice commanded. It was low, calm, and distinctly American, but it carried that clipped, lethal edge of a soldier who had seen too much for too long.

Another voice followed: lighter and almost mocking. "What's the point? He'll be dead weight soon enough."

"No," a woman's voice cut in, hard and certain as a slamming door. "Alive. He'll serve better that way."

Chatter's heart hammered against his ribs. He tried to focus and burn their voices into his memory. There were five of them at least. The leader spoke with absolute authority while the second was sharp and playful. The ginger-haired woman carried tempered steel in every syllable. His eyes settled on the blonde hair of the fourth person who said nothing at all; he'd seen her surveilling the valley before he was grabbed. Chatter could feel their eyes burning through him as they whispered amongst themselves. He coughed while spitting out dirt and bile. "Who... who the hell are you?"

A humorless laugh answered him. A hand gripped his hair to yank his head back until his eyes met a porcelain face with a scar and the shimmering green eyes. "You don't get to know that," the woman whispered softly. "You just get to disappear."

The ground shifted as he was pulled deeper into the timber. His radio, his rifle, and even his emergency locator beacon had been stripped away. Consciousness slipped again with the night dimming to a bruised black. Just before the void swallowed him, he heard the woman murmur something that chilled him more than the restraints: "The Chairman wants a report. Let's not keep him waiting."

The world came back in jagged, painful flashes. He drifted in and out while catching fragments of conversation from the shadows. They spoke English, but they did not sound like Federal troops or Mexican regulars. There was a cadence to their speech that felt like an echo of a world he knew but could not quite grasp. The pounding in his skull made it hard to tell if he was awake or caught in a fever dream. Every breath rattled his bruised ribs.

Canvas walls loomed above him with the air inside the tent heavy with the scent of lamp-smoke and dried blood. He blinked against the haze and froze. She sat cross-legged across from him: utterly composed as if the fire outside had never touched her. A cascade of vibrant red hair caught the lantern light to throw sparks of copper across the neat scar that cut down her left cheek. Her eyes were emerald and entirely unyielding. She studied him with the patience of a predator who had all the time in the world.

She remained quiet while the silence between them grew heavy and suffocating. Her posture was relaxed with hands resting lightly on her knees, but there was nothing welcoming in her gaze. Chatter could feel the marrow of his bones shivering because he recognized the face of a woman who had yanked his head back. She looked hardened by battle, but in a strange way he found his captor beautiful.

He swallowed hard with a raw, dry throat. "...Who the hell are you?"

A faint smile tugged at her lips. "That's what I'm deciding," she said finally. Her voice was low and smooth with an edge like a razor hidden beneath velvet. "Whether you need to know... or whether it's better you don't."

Chatter shifted with his chains rattling as he tried to straighten his back. He didn't drop her gaze despite his instincts. That scar and those emerald eyes had the weight of someone who already knew exactly how the night would end. Explosions still rattled the earth in the distance where the battle continued without him.

"Do you believe in ghosts, Private Wu?"

The way she said his name made the blood in his veins turn to ice. She leaned forward while the light caught the predator's glint in her eyes. "So tell me, soldier... are you worth more alive than dead? I don't have room for prisoners, and the battle below would certainly claim you if I left you behind." Twelve tilted her head while studying him as if she were choosing between options on a menu. "Poor Wu," she said softly. "Even now you think they'll come back for you. But I was watching. They left you. They didn't even look twice."

Chatter's jaw clenched while his teeth ground together. "That's a lie."

Her smile sharpened into something lethal. "Is it? Your sergeant made a call. You were already dead the moment you fell behind."

Chatter forced himself upright as much as the cuffs allowed. His shoulder screamed and his ribs burned with every labored breath. "Better to die with them than rot here with you."

For the first time, Twelve's eyes flashed with a sudden interest. She leaned in close while her scar caught the golden lantern glow. "Maybe. But death is cheap out there." She gestured vaguely toward the muffled thunder of artillery outside. "In here, I decide what you're worth. Alive... or dead. And I'm very good at getting value out of broken things."

Twelve let the silence stretch while her eyes never left his. Chatter's pulse hammered in his ears like a frantic drumbeat, but he refused to look away. That small, final defiance seemed to amuse her. Finally, she rose smoothly to her feet while brushing a fleck of dust from her trousers with a casual flick. "You've got some spine, Wu. I'll give you that."

She leaned closer while her long shadow spilled across him like a shroud. "Don't mistake this for mercy. You're alive because I find you useful. Nothing more." Her hand brushed his cheek lightly and mockingly before she straightened again. "Rest while you can. The next time you wake up... you'll wish you hadn't."

She turned and slipped through the tent flap to leave only the faint, flickering glow of the lantern and the distant, rhythmic rumble of artillery. Chatter sat in the heavy quiet with his wrists burning against the cold metal. He exhaled through clenched teeth while forcing the words out under his breath like a prayer.

"...Zero Company didn't abandon me." But even as the words left his lips, the doubt pressed hard and cold against his chest.

8

ZERO COMPANY FILED INTO the gut of Stealthwing as the sounds of battle continued buzzing around them like angry hornets. The ramp slammed shut with a hydraulic hiss to seal out the world. Bullets sparked against the exterior armor as Stealthwing lifted while banking hard into the night. His engines hummed with the vibration of the turbulence raking against the craft.

"Last known position of Chatter!" Viper ordered. His men collapsed to the smooth metal floor with their bodies heavy from exhaustion and shock.

"Last known position was on the ridge, outside of the primary kinetic engagement," Stealthwing replied. His voice remained dry as the internal pressure shifted with the cabin cycling a sterile air.

Viper gripped an overhead handle tightly while rocking as the craft banked sharply to avoid anti-air fire from the valley floor. "Can we find him? Can we go back?"

"Probability of recovery in current conditions: low." The automated pilot spoke plainly with a clinical detachment that grated on the men's raw nerves.

"Yeah, thanks, Doctor Bot. Maybe run those numbers again when you're not busy being shot at." Joker slammed his fist into the anodized aluminum floor with the metallic ring echoing in the cramped space.

Boom sat slumped near the bulkhead while his massive shoulders trembled. Brick's blood was still smeared across his vest and hands: dark and tacky in the dim red tactical lighting of the cabin. "It should've been me," he muttered with a cracking voice. "He was just a kid. I should've—" He choked on the rest while burying his face in his scarred hands.

Specter shifted closer to lay a steadying hand on Boom's shoulder. His rosary beads clicked softly as a rhythmic counterpoint to the hum of the engines while he whispered a Latin prayer under his breath. "Don't carry the weight alone, brother. Brick made his stand; he died a hero."

"Enough." Viper's voice cut through the grief like a blade. His steady gaze swept across the war-torn squad; at their haunted eyes and faces streaked with mud and grief. "Brick and Stitch didn't fall so we could waste ourselves in guilt. And Chatter," he paused with his jaw working, "Chatter's status is unknown. Unknown is not the same as dead. Until I see proof, he's just MIA."

Reaper leaned forward from the shadows of the jump seats with his eyes flinty and cold. "And if he's dead, Boss?"

Viper's silence was long and heavy. The Stealthwing's engines filled the void to serve as the only heartbeat in the room. Finally, he spoke. "Then we avenge him. But until then, we fight like hell to make sure this wasn't for nothing."

Joker rubbed at his eyes with a hoarse voice. "Feels like everything's for nothing right now."

"Not while we're breathing," Viper snapped back, his tone carried no warmth. "The mission lives as long as we do. We owe it to Brick, to Stitch, and to Chatter—wherever he is."

Stealthwing's calm voice intruded then. "Radio chatter detected. Unknown third party. Aircraft signatures confirmed. F-35s and F-22s are en route from the west."

Every man looked chilled, they thought they had extracted... now this. Joker frowned while glancing over at Radar, who was frantically adjusting his headset. "Those aren't Mexican regulars," Joker whispered. "And the Feds don't fly this deep into the interior anymore."

Specter's fingers tightened around his beads. "Then who?"

Stealthwing answered with surgical detachment. "Origin: Salt Lake airfields. Projected vector: Gunnison Valley. Estimated time to arrival: six minutes."

Viper's grip whitened on the overhead rail. The men exchanged wary, hollow glances because the silence was suddenly heavier than the sound of gunfire.

"Another player on the board," Reaper muttered; his voice grinding on stone.

"No," Viper said with his eyes fixed on the dark horizon visible through the cockpit glass. "Not another player. Another war." He strapped himself into a jump seat while cinching the harness tight. "Stealthwing, are you equipped to take on fifth-generation fighters?"

"I am primarily equipped for air-to-ground combat," the AI replied, "but my structural bones are based on the F-22. I do not know if I can outmaneuver five fifth-generation attack craft simultaneously." The words were unsettling. The best fighter jets in American history were currently hunting the same airspace. "I may be able to avoid a confrontation altogether. I am able to climb higher than their standard ceiling."

Viper's jaw tightened. "So we're not outrunning them."

"Outrunning, no." Stealthwing replied with a factual voice. "We can avoid direct confrontation by climbing into the upper atmosphere. Their current payload is ground-directed. Their mission profile is not interception; it is annihilation."

"How do you know their payload?" Joker asked while his fingers fumbled with his own straps.

"I've successfully hacked their satellite communications back to Salt Lake Command."

The men exchanged uneasy looks as the craft tilted upward with the G-force pressing them into their seats. Joker let out a bitter, jagged laugh. "Annihilation? That's supposed to make me feel better?"

"It means they're not coming for us," Specter murmured, though his lips continued to move in silent prayer. "They're coming for what's left of the valley."

Boom swore under his breath. "So all those poor bastards down there, the militia, the farmers..."

"...are about to be ash," Ghost finished grimly.

The high-pitched whine of the engines screamed as Stealthwing climbed toward the stars. "Visual confirmation," the AI added a beat later. "Five aircraft on vector. Bomb bay doors are armed."

Through the surveillance screens, faint contrails slashed across the starlight like hunters descending on prey too broken to move. The men of Zero Company could do nothing but watch as helpless witnesses to a massacre.

"We are too high for them to see us, but God help us if they do," Viper said while his fingers flew across his control tablet as he tried to stabilize the feed. On the monitors, faint specks detached from the fighters: tiny glimmers at first, then long, cascading streams falling as steady as a spring rain.

"Payload confirmed," Stealthwing reported. "Carpet saturation pattern."

Specter bowed his head with his rosary clenched so tight the wire began to bend. Boom just stared at the screen while his jaw trembled with a rage he had no way to vent. Viper gripped his tablet until the casing creaked under the pressure. "God help them," he whispered.

And then the valley lit up. The light from the explosions was so blindingly bright that the internal screens flared white then blinked to black as the sensors overloaded.

"Climbing higher," Stealthwing intoned with a voice unaffected by the apocalypse below.

The men sat in the sudden gloom with their faces washed pale by the fading afterglow from the screens. None of them spoke. Below, the fire spread in long, rolling curtains across the valley floor to consume trenches, vehicles, and men alike. From this altitude, the destruction looked abstract, like a torch being dragged across a paper map.

Viper's gaze never left the dark screen in front of him. His voice, when it finally came, was as flat as a grave marker. "Chatter is certainly gone after that."

No one argued.

Gunnison Ridge — Minutes earlier

The Ghosthound's rear ramp yawned open like the maw of a steel beast. Jack, Twelve, Phen, and Vannah broke from the undergrowth with boots slamming into the mountain soil as they dragged their prize with them. Chatter dangled half-conscious over Phen's shoulder while his head lolled until the red interior tactical lights washed across his bloodied features.

"Package secured!" Phen barked while shoving the prisoner up the ramp. Jack came last with his rifle sweeping the valley where firefights still tore the night apart. Cannons echoed through the peaks. "Inside," he snapped. The team flowed into the gut of the craft and the ramp slammed shut to seal the chaos outside to a distant, muffled thunder.

Twelve crouched over Chatter to yank his head back by the hair for an inspection of the damage. "Still breathing," she said coolly. "Barely. He'll last long enough."

"Long enough for what?" Vannah muttered while peeling off her tactical gloves with a sly, sharp smile. "Or are you finally going soft on us, Twelve?"

Twelve let Chatter's head drop to the deck with a hollow thud and did not even look at her. "Pilot. Lift us."

The Ghosthound's engines growled while stealth plating shimmered as it clawed skyward. Red light bled across their faces to carve deep shadows into their expressions. Then the pilot's tense voice cracked across the intercom. "New signatures inbound. Five aircraft. Trajectory's not us. They're hitting the valley."

The first blossoms of fire erupted below to wash heat through the timber and rattle the Ghosthound's hull. The operators strapped into their jump seats as the first shockwaves slammed against the fuselage. "Jesus," Phen muttered with the mockery stripped from his voice.

Jack didn't blink. "Not our problem. Eyes forward."

Twelve's gaze lingered on Chatter at her boots. Her voice was barely a whisper. "No. But it will be his."

The explosions below mushroomed into a chain of rolling shockwaves that punched upward through the atmosphere. The Ghosthound lurched violently while gear clattered in the lockers. Twelve pitched sideways to nearly hit the bulkhead, but Jack's hand shot out quickly to catch her arm. He never looked at her while his eyes remained glued to the firestorm visible through the small portholes. She eased herself free and smoothed her sleeve as if nothing had happened, though a faint curve of amusement flickered on her lips.

The pilot's voice ripped through the building turbulence. "Airflow unstable! Pressure spike! I need altitude now!"

Contrails streaked the stars above them. "Contacts!" the pilot barked. "Mexican interceptors. Two MiGs, high vector."

Phen's jaw fell slack with his knuckles white on the seat rail. "Where in the hell did they get MiGs?"

"Doesn't matter, babe," Vannah shot back with a tight voice. "They got them."

"Bought or gifted?" Twelve murmured with a razor-thin tone. "Either way, someone wants them in this fight."

"Radar lock in thirty seconds!" the console shrieked.

"Thought we were invisible!" Phen snapped while sweat dripped and his hands flew over his harness buckles.

"Stealth isn't immunity," Twelve cut in with irony. "The valley's lit up the whole sky. We're just another shadow moving against the fire."

Tracer fire clawed past the hull with the rounds rattling against the rivets like hail on a tin roof. Vannah flinched with her grin finally gone. "Too late. They've got eyes on us!"

"Evasive pattern Delta-three," Jack barked with an absolute tone.

The Ghosthound rolled hard while the mountains whipped past in a blur of black and orange. The first missile streaked by to detonate against a nearby peak; the resulting shockwave slammed the craft sideways. Chatter groaned on the deck with a hoarse, disoriented voice. "W-what is happening?"

Twelve shoved him flat with one hand while her eyes never left the radar screen. "Nothing you'll live long enough to fix."

Another jet screamed overhead with afterburners tearing the night apart. The pilot yanked the stick as the engines howled in protest. "They've got another lock!"

"Break it!" Jack ordered.

Countermeasures hissed from the dispensers while magnesium flares painted the night with false stars. One missile veered wide, but the second held a steady lock. "On us!" the pilot shouted.

A thunderclap ripped through the sky as the pursuing MiG vanished in a sudden blossom of fire; a Deseret Raptor streaking past with blue afterburners blazing claimed the kill. "They're fighting each other," Twelve said quietly with an analytical tone.

"Good," Jack growled. "Let them."

But the Ghosthound wasn't free. Warning klaxons blared while the stabilizers screamed in protest as the pilot fought to keep them level. "Two more MiGs inbound! West vector!"

Phen slammed his fist against the console. "We're meat in a grinder. MiGs below, Raptors above!"

"Then climb faster!" Jack barked.

"Are you insane?" the pilot yelled. "We'll get shredded—"

"Do it," Jack snapped with an angry voice rippling with authority.

The Ghosthound clawed upward as the treeline fell away. Through the portholes, the firestorms swallowed the valley to erase whole trenches and armies in seconds. Shockwaves hammered the fuselage while tossing the craft like a toy in a storm. Vannah's knuckles whitened on her harness. "One mistake and we're dead."

Jack didn't even look at her. "Then don't make mistakes."

"They have another missile lock! I can't shake—" The pilot's voice was cut off as the front of the Ghosthound took a direct hit.

An explosion cracked through the interior to vent pressure and heat. "We're hit!" Jack shouted as the Ghosthound began spinning erratically; shedding altitude. Chatter began to float in the zero-G of the tumble while his body drifted as the ground rushed up to meet them.

"We are going to have to bail out!" Jack roared while grabbing his parachute and tossing the others theirs.

"What about him?" Vannah pointed at the unconscious Private Wu drifting near the ceiling.

Twelve's voice was laced with ice. "He was dead anyway."

Jack's jaw tightened. He didn't argue. "Move out. NOW!"

Vannah cursed but followed. Phen dove after her with his chute pack tight against his spine. Jack was last. He paused just long enough to look at Wu sprawled on the deck before his jaw set. He pulled his own ripcord handle into place and kicked free of the hatch.

The wind howled like a living thing to tear at Jack's face as the Ghosthound's burning hulk twisted above him. Fragments peeled from its frame while sparks and fire spiraled across the night sky. The blackness swallowed everything else. Then the stars opened wide: cruel and indifferent as Jack's chute deployed with a bone-snapping tug. Below, the valley was on fire. Deseret's payload scoured the valley in sheets of orange and white; shockwaves rippled upward to buffet him like a rag doll. To his left, a canopy snapped open: Phen, twisting hard to stabilize. Further off, Vannah's chute caught the moonlight. Twelve was already descending in controlled, surgical spirals while appearing as calm as if she had stepped off a curb. Jack didn't bother looking up for the Ghosthound; he knew what came next. The explosion lit the sky like a fireball while the blast wave punched through the air and slammed into his chest. His canopy buckled with cords screaming, and for a sickening second, he thought the silk would tear. Then it caught again to yank him so hard his teeth clacked together. The lifeless body of the Ghosthound's pilot fell past Jack to cause his chute to twist slightly.

"Report," Jack snapped into comms.

"Alive," Phen's voice came back, followed by a sigh.

"Still falling; thanks for asking," Vannah added with her teasing edge thinned but present.

"Stable," Twelve said flatly.

Jack adjusted his harness while cutting through the chatter. "Regroup on the ground. Valley floor is fire. Aim for the ridgeline. We move east."

"Copy," Phen muttered.

The comm went silent to leave only the rush of wind and the distant thunder of the battle. Jack scanned the night as he descended. Somewhere in the chaos, MiGs still prowled and Raptors circled. Miles of burning Colorado soil waited to claim them. The thunder of the Ghosthound's final moments eventually bled into a ringing vacuum to leave only the thin whistle of the high-plains wind as the four silk canopies drifted toward the dark horizon.

They dropped through the freezing air in a ragged formation, their canopies snapping taut against the wind before they slammed into the brittle scrub. Jack hit the ground with a jarring thud, his boots digging into the dry earth as he executed a hard roll to dissipate the momentum. He was on his feet and unholstering his rifle before the chute even went limp. He stood with the muzzle sweeping a horizon that offered nothing but empty country and the distant, rhythmic thud of explosions rolling in from the west.

One by one, the others regrouped through the tall grass. Vannah hissed a quiet curse while untangling herself from her lines. Phen landed rough nearby while already pulling his beacon scanner from his harness with frost-bitten fingers. Twelve dropped last. Her descent was the most uneventful. She pumped her legs as she came in contact with the ground. Her chute collapsed neatly at her boots in a single, fluid motion that seemed to ignore the chaotic wind entirely.

The four of them stood in the vast, hollow dark with their breath steaming white in the biting air. Behind them, the distant horizon glowed with a faint, hellish orange as Gunnison burned. Ahead stretched only the open plains with a horizon so flat and star-swept it felt like the edge of the world. The silence of the drop zone seemed to travel forever as their voices seemed louder than they intended.

Phen squinted at the flickering screen of his gear while shaking his head in frustration. "No signal. Whatever EM spike fried the Ghosthound's avionics must have cooked half our localized comms. Best I can tell, we're somewhere east of Gunnison, maybe pushing the Colorado-Kansas line."

Jack's voice was flat and steady. "Close isn't good enough, Phen. In this terrain, five miles in the wrong direction is a death sentence. We need to know exactly where the line is."

Twelve scanned the horizon; her face unreadable. "It doesn't matter where we are geographically," she said with a sharp edge. "We're alive. In our line of work, that is the only thing we require to finish the job."

"Yeah?" Vannah snapped while pulling her tactical gloves back on and cinching the Velcro tight. "And how exactly do you expect us to do that without a ride? High Command doesn't exactly have a reputation for roadside pickups."

Jack finally turned to face them with his silhouette stark against the dim glow of the burning sky. "Then we find a way to contact them. Quietly. We move east until we can reach a hardened relay, a civilian cell tower, or a microwave array. Anything we can hijack or bypass. It doesn't matter how far we have to trek. Until we report in, we might as well be dead."

The team fell silent under the crushing weight of their isolation. They were four operators on the edge of nowhere with a mission the Consortium still expected them to execute with perfection. With the unexpected interference of a third party, all of the Consortium's clone assets were destroyed.

Phen finally broke the quiet with a low, resigned voice. "Then east it is. Hope you like walking, Vannah."

"You'll carry me if I ask," Vannah elbowed him and smiled with tired eyes.

Jack nodded once with his internal compass already locked onto the rising stars. He began to move while his boots crunched rhythmically over the frost-covered grass. The others fell in behind him as their shadows stretched long and thin against the approaching dawn. The remains of the battle they kicked off blazed in the distance.

Canon City Cabin — Dawn

The kettle whistled low on the stove while steam curled toward the timbered ceiling. Sarah Martinez slid a plate of eggs across the table to her son who was barely twelve with hair still mussed from sleep. Her husband, Luis, sat opposite; his boots were still muddy from checking the goats while the kitchen radio murmured static-filled news about fighting somewhere far to the west.

The dog bristled before anyone else noticed with a growl vibrating low in its chest. Dishes rattled faintly on the shelves. Sarah frowned while glancing toward the window. "That's not thunder, Luis."

A sound like tearing metal screamed across the sky. Shadows covered the sun overhead while moving too fast for the eye to track, leaving the cabin quaking in their wake. The boy dropped his fork and scrambled to the window just as the first explosion rolled over the ridgeline. A plume of smoke climbed into the air, followed by a shockwave that rattled the panes until the glass spiderwebbed and burst. Plates shattered on the floor while dust sifted from the cedar rafters.

Outside, thick black fumes began to coil up from the treeline in heavy, oily plumes. Another fireball slammed into the valley floor beyond the ridge, the roar of the impact muffled by the earth but enough to make the floorboards jump.

Luis Martinez pulled his son back from the jagged, broken glass with a voice hoarse from adrenaline. “Get away from the windows. Both of you.”

For a few moments, they stayed rooted while staring out at the horizon where fire clawed toward the dawn sky. Luis was the first to break the trance. He crossed the living room to his gun safe with a heart pounding against his ribs; his fingers trembled as he spun the dial. The heavy door creaked open and he pulled out his shotgun along with a range bag heavy with shells. “In the cellar, now,” he ordered with a sharp, decisive voice. “Don’t come out for anyone but me. You hear me?”

He shoved the weapon under his arm, threw the front door open, and ran out into the morning chill as his family hurried into the belly of the house. Luis burst into his work shed while the early cold cut through his sweat-soaked shirt. Smoke coiled above the ridge. Even from this distance, he could smell the chemical sting of burning aviation fuel. He darted to the old HAM rig bolted against the wall next to his ATV. He slapped the power toggle and twisted the dials until the static gave way to a fractured, open channel.

"This is Luis Martinez, east ridge, Canon City. We've got wreckage; aircraft down. Repeat: unidentified aircraft down. Smoke is visible from my position. Over."

Static cracked then a calm voice came back clipped by interference. "Ranger Station Seven receiving. Say again, east ridge?"

"Confirmed. Impact near Dawson Gulch. One jet and a helicopter-like craft. It doesn't look right, Station Seven." Luis' knuckles whitened against the mic. "They came down hard. You'll want eyes on this immediately."

There was a long pause then a firmer voice joined. "Copy, Martinez. Station Seven is escalating to Command at Cheyenne. Maintain distance from the wreckage. Armed forces are en route."

Luis exhaled while lowering the mic as the line dissolved into dead static. He knew what "en route" meant in these times. There would be soldiers, investigators, or the GPN commandos they whispered about on the radio crawling all over the place. "Distance..." he chuckled under his breath with a grim spark in his eyes. "I live for this."

He threw his leg over his ATV and kickstarted the engine. The machine roared to life like a horse eager for the gallop. He twisted the accelerator and launched down the trail toward the ridge while racing toward the fire to see what the sky had dropped on his land.

9

CANON CITY WOODS — Dawn

Luis' ATV bounced hard over the jagged rocks, smoke marking the sky ahead like a signal torch. The morning chill bit at his cheeks, but the air was dominated by the acrid, sharp sting of burning aviation fuel.

"*¡Ayúdame!*" A voice called out, faint at first. Then it came again, louder and saturated with panic: "*¡Rápido!*"

Luis slammed the brakes, dirt and pine needles spitting from the tires as the ATV skidded sideways to a halt. He gripped his shotgun, heart hammering against his ribs, his eyes sweeping the dense stand of timber. Tangled in the high branches above, a parachute sagged like a torn, white sail. A man writhed in the harness, one leg bent at an unnatural angle. His voice broke as he called out again in frantic Spanish. Luis raised the shotgun, the barrel leveling at the man's chest. His gaze flicked down to the forest floor where a cracked pilot's helmet lay half-buried in the pine needles. The paint was chipped from the impact, but the Mexican flag remained bright against the dull composite steel.

The pilot saw the bore of the gun and froze. "*Por favor...*" he gasped, his hands trembling against the nylon straps. Luis' jaw clenched, his finger brushing the cold curve of the trigger. The forest had gone dead quiet, save for the rhythmic creak of parachute lines in the wind and the pilot's shallow, terrified breaths. The man's face twisted, his eyes darting between the muzzle of the shotgun and the ground far below. He sputtered, his words tumbling out in a desperate rush: "*¡Tengo miedo!*"

"Drop your weapons!" Luis barked.

The pilot shook his head, pointing at his ears. "*No entiendo inglés...*" He either didn't understand or was pretending not to. Luis motioned with the shotgun, stabbing the barrel toward the dirt in an unmistakable command. The man broke then, sobbing as his words spilled into a frantic prayer. "*¡Acordaos, oh piadosísima Virgen de Guadalupe, envolvednos con su manto de protección!*"

The invocation hung in the cold morning air, trembling with raw desperation. Luis felt it strike something deep within him, even as he kept the shotgun steady. He'd heard that same prayer from his grandmother when he was a child. Instinctively, Luis made the sign of the cross over his chest, his lips moving with a half-whispered *Ave María*. He didn't catch every word, but the shape of the plea was familiar—holy, pleading. *Guadalupe.*

The pilot hung there trembling, one leg twisted ugly in its harness, blood darkening the fabric of his flight suit. The chute lines creaked above, swaying in the pine branches like a hangman's rope. Luis kept the shotgun raised, his knuckles white on the stock. This man, this Mexican, was one of the reasons smoke filled the sky, the reason Colorado was being torn apart. He could end it here. Simple. Clean. One pull of his trigger. It wouldn't end the war, just this one life. But he'd have to carry that weight forever.

The sight of the broken helmet on the ground, the flag painted too neat, too proud. It made his stomach knot. Whoever this man was, he wasn't a demon. He was just another poor bastard caught in a machine too big for him.

Luis exhaled, lowering the barrel a fraction. "Dammit!" he muttered.

The pilot flinched at the shift in the weapon's angle, his eyes glistening as words tumbled out too fast for Luis to track. All he could make out were fragments: *miedo... familia... madre.* Luis spat into the dirt, making his choice. He holstered the shotgun on the ATV and grabbed his hunting knife and a length of rope. Moving to the trunk of the pine, he climbed until he was positioned above the man. The pilot flinched when Luis grabbed a fistful of his harness, but Luis only growled, sharp and low, "Don't make me regret this."

He looped the rope through the harness to create a makeshift pulley over a thick, sturdy branch. Bracing himself, Luis sliced through the primary chute lines. Even with the rope's tension, the pilot crumpled onto the forest floor, screaming in agony as he clutched his ruined leg. Luis climbed back down and retrieved his shotgun, standing over the fallen man. "You're coming with me. Alive or dead, it's your choice."

The pilot blinked up at him, chest heaving, and for the first time, the terror in his eyes gave way to a profound confusion. Luis didn't care. He had questions, and if the Great Plains commandos were truly on their way, this man might just be of use to them.

Cheyenne Strategic Command — Helipad

The mountains glowed with a fierce, unforgiving brilliance in the afternoon light, their jagged ridges still dusted with the white, skeletal remains of the season's last snow. On the compound's roof, the asphalt helipad shimmered with a distorted haze of heat rising from Stealthwing's idling thrusters. The sleek, black-winged craft sat like some prehistoric predatory bird at rest; its specialized, light-absorbing armor seemed to swallow the high-altitude sunlight, while a low-frequency hum vibrated through the air, heat shivering off the carbon-fiber skin of its wings.

Zero Company ringed the craft in a protective, professional cordon, rifles slung low but their eyes remained restlessly sharp. Their uniforms were still heavily streaked with the grey-brown mud of the Gunnison Valley, blood dried into dark, stiff patches on their tactical vests, exhaustion was carved into every line of their faces. Specter sat on a crate near the boarding ramp, his head bowed in a posture that suggested either prayer or a total collapse of energy. Boom stood nearby with his massive arms folded over his chest as if daring any of the local guards to step an inch closer to their bird. Joker chewed nervously at his lip, muttering the setup to a joke that no one had the heart to acknowledge.

Across the pad, the Great Plains Nation soldiers watched them with distrust. Their insignia marked them as the Montana-Idaho Militia, but the "militia" label was a relic of a simpler time. These weren't farm boys or weekend warriors anymore; weeks of sustained blood, retreat, and catastrophic loss had tempered them into something brittle and dangerous. Their fingers twitched rhythmically near their triggers whenever they looked at the Stealthwing. A few whispered under their breath... *that foreign machine... the UAA keeps it on a short leash for a reason.*

One GPN sergeant, a man with a jagged scar running into his hairline, spat on the roof just outside the cordoned-off area. "If they're really an ally," he growled, loud enough for the wind to carry it, "why the hell do they feel the need to guard that thing from us?"

"Because a bunch of Midwestern farmers wouldn't know what to do with a piece of tech this advanced even if it came with an instruction manual," Joker quipped, his voice carrying a jagged edge.

Viper's hand shot up instantly. His stare drifted across the pad toward the GPN sergeant. He didn't need to speak; the message was written in the set of his shoulders: *This machine isn't yours, it will never be yours, and you aren't ready for the weight of it.*

The silence that followed was brittle, like thin glass held under immense pressure. The sound of high-bypass turbofans soon rose over the eastern ridge as UAA Navy One dipped toward the compound, flanked by a pair of F-35s flying in a tight, protective escort. The GPN officers on the runway snapped into a rigid, ceremonial formation, as the massive 747-200B touched down with a puff of tire smoke. The F-35s broke off, banking in wide, sweeping arcs to establish a continuous patrolling route around the Strategic Command airspace.

Zero Company loaded back onto the Stealthwing, which lifted from the roof with a ghostly lack of noise, repositioning to a small patch of manicured grass near where Navy One had hissed to a stop. The men filed out again, maintaining their vigilant detail as the primary hatch of the Presidential plane opened. A large staircase on the back of a truck rolled into place.

President Samuel Burris stepped out first, tall and steady despite the altitude. At his side was Vice President Ulysses Mars, broad-shouldered, his expression carved from stone. Behind him walked Taylor Mars, his eldest son—uniform crisp, the patch of a UAA Marine stitched proud on his arm. He was supposed to be on leave, but his eyes glittered with the hunger of a young man who wanted to see history happen up close. Taylor's chest burned with pride at the sight of UAA steel holding the line, but a thought gnawed at him: *allies who stare at each with their hands so close to their guns aren't allies for long.*

President Jeremiah Johnson stepped forward from the GPN welcoming committee with his hand out. The UAA President returned the gesture, a strong handshake and a tense but warm smile accompanying it.

"We have a lot to talk about." Jeremiah motioned to his right toward one of the hangars where a meeting room had been set up. His honor guard turned rigid and saluted the two Presidents as they walked through the line toward the hangar. The conference room inside was a study in functional diplomacy: a long, scarred stainless steel table, the flags of the UAA and the GPN standing in heavy wooden bases like opposing sentries, and armed guards stationed at every reinforced door. President Jeremiah Johnson led the way in, his shoulders squared as if to defy the immense weight of the war that was currently bending them. Under the unforgiving glare of the overhead LED lights, the sheer exhaustion of the man was visible in the deep, shadowed lines carved into his face.

President Samuel Burris followed, his stride steady, his expression carefully neutral. Behind him, Vice President Ulysses Mars scanned the room with an expression like carved granite. Taylor Mars lingered at his father's shoulder, silent, his eyes taking in every uniform, every gesture. The Pact Governors of the GPN were already seated, their expressions a gallery of unease and resentment. Each bore the look of leaders stretched too thin. A large monitor at the head of the table showed the grim summary of the past half-decade:

Major Events Since 2024

- **2024:** The Confederation launches a coordinated attack and conquest of the Pacific Northwest. They remain deeply entrenched along the West Coast, creating a permanent forward operating base on American soil.

- **2025:** The world is rocked by the assassination of President-elect Troy Thomason. In the resulting chaos, VP-elect Lisa Rice vanishes without a trace, leaving a vacuum at the heart of the federal government.

- **2025:** Washington officially brands the Great Plains Nation as traitors and enemies of the state. The U.S. Federal military begins launching localized attacks on civilian infrastructure within the GPN borders.

- **2025:** The Capitol Massacre occurs. After several congressional leaders announce their formal intent to secede, the halls of power are turned into a slaughterhouse. Riots erupt nationwide, leaving thousands dead or listed as missing.

- **2026:** The burning of the Great Plains Nation Governor's Mansion and the primary Government Compound. The loss of central records sends the region into administrative chaos.

- **2027:** A Confederation-backed strike hits Cedar Hill, Missouri.

- **2027:** The Battle of the Rockies begins in earnest. Mexico advances a professional force from the south, while an unidentified third-party strike originating from Salt Lake is detected by long-range sensors.

The UAA delegation looked at the summary of the past half-decade, their faces carefully schooled into masks of neutrality. However, one member of the delegation stood and offered a sharp, crisp salute at the mention of Troy Thomason's name. Taylor felt his own chest tighten at the gesture. He had grown up knowing Troy personally. The man had been more than a political figure to him; he had been a constant presence, an uncle in everything but blood. Seeing his life and his tragic end reduced to a singular bullet point on a tactical screen struck Taylor harder than the silence that followed.

"Troy was a great man, one of the main reasons why we took the steps to secede." President Burris' mouth tightened into a grimace as he motioned the UAA Delegation into a moment of silence. The GPN Delegation followed suit so they didn't offend their guests.

"I knew him well," Jeremiah spoke at a near-whisper, his voice thick with a genuine, heavy grief. "A truly great man." An uncomfortable, thick quiet followed for what felt like an eternity, broken only when a young aide rushed into the hangar. His face was pale, his voice carrying the sharp, unmistakable edge of emergency.

"Mr. President, we've just received an encrypted communique from Salt Lake."

The room stiffened. Johnson's jaw tightened, Burris' eyes narrowed, and Mars leaned forward as the aide slid a tablet across the steel table. The screen flickered, then steadied. A flag resembling the Utah state flag emblazoned on the screen, beside it a seal with Moroni in the center and "Nation of Deseret" written in bold letters.

A calm, measured voice spilled out of the speakers, every syllable clipped with a terrifying, practiced authority. "This is the Provisional Council of Deseret. As of this morning, we have assumed full administrative and military control of Northern Colorado. Our forces have secured the Gunnison Valley and all surrounding territories. Stability is currently being restored under our sovereign governance."

A ripple of angry murmurs went through the GPN governors. Johnson sat as still as a statue, his eyes fixed on the screen.

The voice continued. "The Great Plains Nation is hereby instructed not to interfere in this stabilization process. However, as an act of humanitarian respect for our neighbors, we will permit GPN recovery teams to enter the Gunnison sector under a white flag for the sole purpose of retrieving your dead and wounded. This olive branch will remain open for a window of seventy-two hours." The screen shifted, the crest of Deseret glowing brighter against the dark background as the voice hardened into a threat. "But let us be absolutely clear: any hostile action, any unauthorized flyover, or any movement against Deseret Peacekeeping Forces will be treated as an immediate act of war. We will respond decisively and without further warning. The borders of Deseret are now sovereign. They will be defended."

The communique cut out abruptly, leaving only the hum of the overhead lights and the thin, haunting hiss of static. Every eye in the room turned toward Johnson and Burris. Johnson's hands were clamped so tightly on the edge of the table that his knuckles were bone-white. "They butcher our men in a surprise strike, they claim our sovereign land, and then they have the gall to call it peacekeeping?"

Burris shifted in his heavy chair, his tone wary. "The question we have to answer right now, Jeremiah, is whether you accept this peace offering... or whether you recognize it as the bait it clearly is."

Viper stepped forward from the shadows of the room, his mud-streaked uniform and hard eyes a stark contrast to the polished politicians. "Mr. President," he said, addressing Burris directly. "We lost two men in that valley, and one is still missing in action. Zero Company requests formal claiming rights as part of the recovery detail."

"I am sure if you boys flew in with that monster of yours, they would assume hostility." Johnson replied, his voice carrying concern over Stealthwing.

Viper maintained eye contact with his President. Burris leaned forward, his voice calm but edged with the reality of their position. "The question isn't whether your men or mine have the earned right to retrieve our fallen. The question is whether the Council in Salt Lake actually intends to let anyone who crosses that line come back alive."

Vice President Mars spoke for the first time, his voice like the sound of grinding iron. "If Salt Lake is dangling a humanitarian truce, it's because they think you're too weak to call their bluff. You've already bled on three separate fronts. They're betting everything that you won't risk opening a fourth."

Taylor shifted at his father's side, the words spilling out of him with a Marine's bluntness before he could think to check them. "But if we don't go in for them, doesn't that mean they died for nothing? We don't leave people behind. Period." The heavy silence that followed made Taylor wish he'd kept his mouth shut, but his words hung in the room like a challenge that the leaders couldn't easily sidestep.

The aide who had delivered the message broke the tension. "Sirs, we've also received word of a crash in

Canon City from the GPN station there. They received a distress call from a local civilian."

"If we move on Gunnison for the recovery, perhaps your craft could be diverted to Canon City to investigate that crash," Johnson suggested, his eyes flicking to the UAA leaders. "But Deseret was clear, anything that looks even remotely hostile will trigger a war. And that bird of yours, Viper, is nothing if not hostile."

Mars leaned forward, his jaw tightening as he looked at the map. "Canon City means their net isn't fully closed yet. They struck hard at the heart, but they don't own the entire state of Colorado. Not yet."

"It's settled then, I'll deploy Zero Company to Canon City to investigate, you all retrieve the dead in Gunnison." Burris stood quickly, momentarily bypassing the diplomatic formality.

Johnson shook his head. "You order your people, I'll order mine. Let's not forget where that line is."

Burris looked at Johnson, his mouth a thin, disciplined line of resolve. He didn't argue the point of sovereignty. He turned to Viper. "Canon City is yours. Go down there and prove your men are worth the tremendous investment the UAA has placed in you all. Bring back answers."

Viper nodded, a sharp, singular movement. Johnson's eyes cut across the table toward the rest of Zero Company, his voice rough and warned. "Remember, Salt Lake is watching every move through a scope. Don't give them a single reason to stretch our lines any thinner than they already are."

The air in the hangar remained thick with tension as the meeting began to dissolve. Zero Company offered a final, unified salute to Burris and a respectful nod to Johnson. Their next mission was settled, but as the aides began gathering papers and the governors murmured in the corners, it was clear that the fracture lines between these two allies were only widening, threatening to tear the coalition apart before the first shot of the new war was even fired.

Canon City Crash Site — 03:00 PM MDT

Stealthwing's black wings beat against the thin mountain air as he descended, his shadow cutting a long, jagged line across the pines. Dust swirled in frantic spirals on the cracked forest road below, scattering gray ash across the scorched earth. From the cockpit's perspective, the wreckage spread like an open wound, the mangled carcass of a transport helicopter smoldering in one ravine, while the twisted frame of a fighter jet lay collapsed a football field further, its wings snapped like broken bone. Black smoke drifted upward in crooked, oily columns, staining the Colorado sky.

The ramp lowered with a hydraulic hiss, and Zero Company fanned out in a practiced, silent diamond, rifles sweeping the tree line. The smell hit them first.

A sickening cocktail of jet fuel, vaporized plastic, and scorched earth.

"Movement," Radar said, his gloved hand pointing toward the tree line.

On the far edge of the crash site, a man waved both arms frantically beside a mud-caked ATV. The low afternoon sun caught the glint of a shotgun slung across his back. At his feet, a second figure sat slumped against the vehicle's tire, hands bound, his face a mask of gray exhaustion.

Viper lifted a hand, halting the team. His voice was low, filtered through his comms. "Eyes open. That's no welcoming committee."

They advanced toward the man and saw his weathered Carhartt jacket and stained jeans marked him as a local, not a soldier. His jaw was set, his gaze shifting nervously between the approaching Operators and the burning wreckage behind him. The prisoner leaned heavily against the ATV, a torn flight suit hanging off one shoulder; a cracked pilot's helmet lay in the dirt beside him, still bearing the faded, proud colors of Mexico.

Specter's eyes flicked to the broken machines scattered across the clearing. "Looks like the birds had a mid-air collision," Joker muttered, his levity failing to mask the tension.

Boom's grip tightened on his light machine gun. "So the question is," he said, his voice like grinding gravel, "what's still alive out here?"

"Identify yourself!" Viper shouted, his rifle leveled at the local.

The man dropped his shotgun into the pine needles, his voice raw. "Luis... Luis Martinez!" He kept his arms high, his hands shaking against the backdrop of the smoke.

"We aren't going to harm you. Step away from your prisoner," Joker said, walking toward the slumped man. "Does he speak English?"

"No," Luis responded shortly, his chest heaving. "I know a little, but not enough to translate what he's screaming about."

Joker crouched by the slumped pilot, his rifle angled low but ready. The pilot's lips moved, Spanish spilling out in broken, wet gasps. "Definitely not English," Joker muttered, glancing back at Viper.

Luis shifted his weight uneasily, his arms still raised. "I found him in a tree after I heard the crash. He must have punched out of the jet. I wasn't gonna let him bleed out like an animal." He pointed shakily toward the mangled remains of the fighter.

Specter murmured under his breath, "Mercy's a dangerous habit in this war, brother."

Stealthwing's voice rumbled from his external speakers, dry and clinical, cutting across the wind. "Bring the subject within range of my auditory processors. I can provide a real-time translation."

Luis flinched as the machine spoke, the metallic resonance echoing across the clearing. He obeyed, lifting the prisoner by one arm while Joker helped heave the man upright. They half-dragged him toward the Stealthwing's shadow, the ATV's engine ticking nearby as it cooled. The rest of Zero Company held their weapons at high ready, watching the perimeter.

The Mexican pilot stumbled, his ruined leg barely able to bear weight. He grimaced through split, bloody lips, muttering low prayers as Luis pushed him forward.

"Closer," Stealthwing instructed. A faint red laser swept across the prisoner's chest and face, scanning, while the Operators tightened their circle.

"Vitals detected. Translation interface engaged." The AI paused for a millisecond, then the pilot's frantic words came through the loudspeakers in clean, detached English: "*I am not armed. For the love of the Virgin, do not kill me. When my people come to rescue me, I will tell them not to kill you.*"

Joker cocked his head. "Great. Our bird's moonlighting as a UN translator now."

Viper ignored him. "Ask him who else was in the sky with him."

Stealthwing relayed the question in Spanish. The pilot shook his head quickly, blood dripping from his temple. The AI translated evenly: "*Two more in my squadron. Both downed. Two Russian MiGs and one... American-built plane. Painted over. Not ours.*"

The words hung in the cold morning air like the smoke itself. Boom spat into the dirt. "Old stock. Someone wanted this fight to look like a proxy war."

Viper lowered his rifle an inch. “We’re not done. Stealthwing. Scrub the wrecks, I want everything. Engines, serial numbers, bolt by bolt. Find out where they came from.”

“Reminder: I lack opposable thumbs,” the AI replied. A small access door hissed open on his belly. “Take these sensors and deploy them on the debris field.”

Joker retrieved the magnetic discs, handing a few to Specter. They split up, slapping the sensors onto the blackened carcasses of the aircraft. “I can’t believe the Mexicans have MiGs now,” Specter said quietly as he stepped close to the fighter’s hull. “I’d have never thought the Feds would allow that on the border.”

Boom stood guard, his rifle sweeping the treeline. “Doesn’t matter how they got ’em. What matters is who wanted them here.”

Joker slapped a disc against the battered helicopter fuselage. As he examined the nose, he stopped. Under a layer of soot, he saw white text: *WE SEE ALL.* Puzzled, he shook his head and applied the final sensors. They all pulsed a steady, rhythmic green.

Stealthwing’s voice rumbled again, faintly sardonic. “Sensor calibration initiating. Initial scans show foreign paint layers inconsistent with Mexican stock on the MiG. Serial plates have been filed. Crude work.”

“What about the helicopter?” Viper asked.

A series of buzzing and clicking sounds filled the air as the AI processed the data. “There is biological material inside.” The sensors pulsed in unison. “Scan complete. Organic residue detected within the primary fuselage. No active vitals."

Joker frowned, brushing ash from his tactical gloves. "Organic residue? What the hell does that mean, Doctor Bot?"

Specter's rosary clicked. "It means we should look inside."

Boom moved toward the wreck, his massive frame silhouetted against the twisted metal. "I'll get the kit." He jogged back to Stealthwing, returning moments later with a heavy hydraulic breaching tool slung over his shoulder.

The machine whined as the hydraulics bit down into the warped steel, the fuselage creaking under the immense pressure. The Operators raised their rifles, sights fixed on the opening seam. With a screech of tortured metal, a panel gave way, folding like wet paper. A gust of thick, stagnant smoke hissed out.

"Opening achieved," Stealthwing intoned. "Proceed with caution."

Viper pulled his CBRN mask from his pack, the straps snapping tight as the filters hissed to life. The others followed suit, the clearing filling with the sound of mechanical, rhythmic breathing. Viper was the first inside, his flashlight beam cutting through the gloom of the compartment.

At the rear of the cabin, half-hidden in the shadows of the wreckage, a man slumped forward. His wrists were cuffed high to a handrail, his head hanging at an unnatural angle. Joker climbed in after him, his voice muffled by his mask. "Please tell me that's not..." The beam settled on the face. Pale. Bruised. Blood dried at the corner of the mouth.

"Chatter," Boom said, his voice breaking over the comms.

The silence in the wreck was absolute, broken only by the creak of cooling metal. Viper crouched, a gloved hand brushing Chatter's shoulder. Cold. No pulse. The cuffs had dug deep into his skin, his wrists raw, as though he'd been left to die chained to the chopper.

Viper straightened, his jaw set hard behind the glass of his mask. "He didn't go down fighting. Someone put him here as cargo."

Joker swore and slammed a fist against the scorched wall. A hollow clang echoed through the compartment, and something tumbled loose from a ceiling locker. A leather binder hit the deck with a slap. Its cover was scorched but the seal was intact. It resembled the CIA's crest, but the eagle was wrong, its wings were stretched too wide, the stars twisted into strange, non-standard geometry.

Joker flipped it over. Stenciled in block letters on the back was the motto: *WE SEE ALL.*

"Feds?" Viper asked sharply.

"Not like any branch I've seen," Joker muttered. "This matches the nose art outside."

Boom stepped forward with the breaching tool, the chain links screeched once before snapping. Chatter's body sagged, folding to the deck like a discarded rag doll. Specter crossed himself, his lips moving in a silent prayer for the dead.

Viper looked at his men, his voice flat and controlled. “We take him out. He’s ours, no matter how he died.” He bent, hooking an arm under the kid’s shoulder. Specter took the other arm; together, they raised the dead weight of their comrade.

“Move fast,” Viper ordered, glancing toward the smoke on the horizon. “Because if Deseret finds us standing over this mess, mercy won’t be part of the conversation.”

10

CHILLICOTHE MED CENTER — Two Weeks Later

Engines idled in a long, vibrating line of transfer trucks across the hospital parking lot, thick plumes of black diesel smoke curling into the biting morning air. Their beds were stacked high with the logistics of a departing army: crates of medical gear, salvaged ammunition tins, and the dust-stained, battered duffels of the Bison Plains Regiment.

Clay walked up the ramp of a flatbed trailer to guide the Regiment's APC into place. Members of the militia swarmed the vehicle, the ratchets clicking rhythmically as they strapped the steel beast down for transport. Closer to the hospital's main entrance, a different kind of line formed. Federal soldiers, shackled in pairs, shuffled toward a yellow school bus that had been crudely converted into a prisoner transport. Each man walked like a shadow of his former self. All eyes hollowed out by defeat, their steps muffled by the dragging metal chains on the asphalt.

Samantha stood near the hospital doors, watching the exodus. The building was a skeleton now, emptied of the hundreds of injured from the Cedar Hill bombing. Inside, discarded stretchers leaned in uneven stacks against the walls, and the waiting room had been stripped of its rows of cots. The smell of antiseptic clung stubbornly to the tile, the haunting echo of groans and cries had finally faded. Chillicothe was quieter now than it had been in the weeks before.

Samantha's eyes swept over the Regiment; there were too few of them now, the ranks visibly thinner than when they had first rolled into town. Clay limped down from the trailer, barking orders with a volume that defied his injury. He was clearly straining to walk with a normal gait, though the rhythmic wince in his jaw gave the lie to his bravado.

What remained of the Moonshiners gathered near a waiting van. They were heading east, back toward Independence, Kentucky and the safety of their own republic. The convoy's engines revved in a low growl, and the pavement seemed to tremble under the weight of the departure. Samantha exhaled, a long, steady breath that clouded in the air. Leaving Chillicothe felt like closing a heavy door on a chapter of her life she wasn't sure she'd ever have the courage to reopen.

"Colonel," Clay's voice called out, hoarse from days of command. He stepped toward her gingerly, favoring his bad leg. His helmet was tucked under one arm, his other hand white-knuckled on the strap of his rifle. For a fleeting second, the light hit him just right, making him look decades older, the names of the dead seemingly etched into the creases of his face. Then the hardness returned. "We're set. Convoy's ready to roll."

Samantha nodded, her throat tight. She glanced at the prisoner bus, where Federal soldiers slouched behind fogged windows, their shackled hands resting uselessly on their knees. Once, she might've seen them only as the enemy. Now, they looked like nothing more than men caught in the violent undertow of a war none of them had truly chosen.

She turned back to her own. The Regiment stood at attention, their packs heavy, their fatigues carrying the dirt and blood of Missouri. But they stood proud. The blue buffalo patch caught the morning sun, the symbol of defiance shined against the drab olive of their gear. They were still hers, the Buffalo Patch Patriots.

The Moonshiners' van pulled away first, tires crunching over shards of broken glass. One of the men leaned out the window, tipping his cap toward Samantha in a silent salute. Then, the convoy engines revved in unison. The sound swelled into a roar that swallowed the hospital.

"Mount up," Samantha said, turning to Clay. "Let's bring them home."

The Regiment stirred, their weariness masked by the ritual of motion. Weapons were checked, straps cinched, and helmets settled. Samantha climbed into the lead truck, settling into the passenger seat beside Clay as he hauled himself behind the wheel. The convoy lurched forward, winding out of the lot like a great metal snake. She looked back one last time in the side mirror, watching Chillicothe shrink. The hospital, the flags, and the small crowd of civilians and nurses waving handmade banners in a thin, rising cheer. For weeks, this town had been the center of her world. Now, it was just another place they had passed through, leaving ghosts in their wake.

"Airport next," she murmured, more to herself than to him.

Clay gave a tired nod. "Airport."

The convoy wound through the quiet streets until the road opened up to the regional airport. At the far end of the tarmac, the gray, utilitarian bulk of a C-130 dominated the horizon. Its four turboprops were already spooling, chopping the cold air into a steady, thrumming buzz.

Clay directed the men to undo the ratchets on the APC so he could drive it up the rear ramp personally. Chains clattered as the ground crew locked the vehicle into the dark belly of the plane. The Federal prisoners followed, the sound of their steel shackles scraping against the metal ramp echoing in the cavernous hold.

Samantha stood at the edge of the tarmac for a final moment, the prop-wash tugging at her coat and whipping her hair across her face. She drew in one last breath of Missouri air and turned. She crossed the tarmac and climbed the ramp, the roar of the engines drowning out the world as the hydraulic doors sealed shut.

She climbed the internal ladder to the jumper seats where the rest of the unit was already harnessed in. Settling into the nylon webbing, she buckled her own harness and looked at Clay. She offered him a rough, tired smile.

"Maybe Cheyenne will give us a night or two of rest," she said, her eyes already heavy. She leaned her head back and closed them.

"You and I both, Colonel," Clay echoed.

The C-130 shuddered, the engines screaming as it surged forward down the runway. It lifted into the sky, banking west toward the Rockies. A single tear tracked down Samantha's cheek, catching the dim interior light. She didn't wipe it away. It belonged to the dead they were leaving behind.

Washington, D.C. — 2.10,27

The city was perched on the jagged edge of the war.

National Guard checkpoints choked every artery leading into the old capital, sandbags stacked into makeshift ramparts while razor wire curled like silver thorns along the medians. The SUV crept forward in a long, stuttering line of battered civilian vehicles; each one stopped, searched, and waved through by soldiers in their worn camouflage. Their faces wearing hollow expressions as they tried to maintain the line. Beyond the wire, civilians shuffled toward reinforced concrete bunkers, children clutching tattered blankets while the rhythmic rumble of artillery from the south shook the windowpane glass. The UAA Marines were pressing hard toward the Potomac; from the west, the Bluegrass States pushed closer by the day. Washington had become a prize surrounded by fire.

Jack sat in the passenger seat, his rifle balanced across his knees, his eyes fixed on the guards. Every distant explosion rattled through the SUV's frame. "Chaos," he muttered, his voice a flat line. "Exactly what the Chairman wanted."

Twelve didn't look up from her tablet, the cool blue glow etching her features sharp against the smoke-filled afternoon light. "Chaos isn't the point, Jack. It's the illusion. They'll fight over the surface ashes, blind to what we're building beneath them." In the back, Phen lounged as if the war outside were mere theater for his amusement, one arm stretched casually across the seat behind Vannah. She smirked at his whisper, brushing a stray strand of hair from her cheek, though her eyes stayed fixed on the ruined, blackened skyline.

Jack's jaw tightened. "You two finished?"

"Not even close," Vannah shot back, her tone like velvet, though the hunger in her gaze was anything but playful.

The SUV rolled to the final checkpoint. Guards raised rifles, eyes scanning the dark tinted windows. Jack lowered his window just enough to flash his CIA credentials. His stare was steady, unblinking. "We're cleared."

The sergeant hesitated, looking at the stone-cold faces inside the vehicle, then waved them through. Behind them, the civilians were pressed forward into the dark mouths of the bunkers, their shouts muffled under a fresh thunder of artillery.

As they cleared the final line, the SUV slid into the dead heart of the city. Smoke draped across the skyline like funeral veils rising from shattered neighborhoods. Yet one building loomed untouched, its glass and steel gleaming like a relic refusing to die: the *George Bush Center for Intelligence*. Twelve's eyes lingered on it, a faint, clinical smile touching her lips. "Langley still stands. The old world clings to its illusions until the very end."

Jack's voice was iron. "Let them cling. Soon they'll only see ruins. What's inside will belong to us."

The words hung heavy in the SUV; the promise of the Veil hiding their world, of a place that would one day see only rubble while the Consortium rebuilt in secret beneath it. Jack pressed a hidden sequence on the console. Ahead, the asphalt of a restricted service road split in two with a groaning, hydraulic shudder. A massive steel door ground upward, revealing a tunnel carved deep into the prehistoric bedrock. He accelerated, tires spitting grit, as the steel slammed shut behind them, sealing away the dying war above.

The SUV descended. Headlights cut across gunmetal barricades and soldiers in blackened, non-standard gear, rifles held at high-ready. The lead guard saluted with robotic precision. "Welcome home, Commander." The cordons lifted, and the SUV rolled forward into a light that wasn't daylight. The tunnel opened into a vast, subterranean chamber so wide the human eye couldn't process it at once. A false sky arched miles overhead; a glowing, geodesic dome radiating a synthetic warmth. It wasn't the sun, but it was near enough to trick the mind. Clouds shimmered faintly, shifting in a programmed, meteorological cycle across the **Veil**.

The city spread below like a perfectionist's mirror of Washington. Streets fanned out from a replica National Mall, monuments rising in exact detail. But here, every statue wore a mask: the smooth, expressionless faces of the Consortium's Board, each forehead etched with occult seals that glowed with a faint, bioluminescent pulse. Washington, Jefferson, Lincoln; their legacies erased and replaced by these masked architects of a New Dawn. The SUV wound past the reflecting pool, the water still and perfect as black glass. Artificial fountains fed it in endless, silent cycles. On either side, soldiers patrolled—not the ragged National Guard of the surface, but sleek, disciplined units in matte-black armor. Their helmets were opaque, their movements inhumanly precise.

Vannah leaned forward, her breath fogging the glass. Her voice was low, almost reverent. "Consortium City."

Phen smirked, though his eyes followed the statues with a flicker of unease. "They built a dream out of bones."

Twelve's gaze remained fixed on the dome above, where the false sun blazed eternal. "Not a dream, Phen. A throne."

Jack remained silent. His eyes swept the monuments and the black flags snapping in the artificial breeze. It was Washington, but one hollowed out by the authoritarians he served, a fake city wrapped in perfection, waiting for the world above to finish burning. Phen smiled, his eyes glowing with a distorted patriotism as he saluted a black flag emblazoned with the Consortium seal. He pointed toward the intake center as a fresh wave of people started walking out into the immaculate streets.

"They think they are still in the city above," Phen laughed. "What they don't realize is that this is the real city. The one above is just a corpse."

Twelve's eyes flicked toward the civilians, her tone cool. "Illusion holds longer than chains. They'll never look up long enough to question the sky."

Vannah smirked, her amusement turning cold. "They'll die thinking they were free. That's the genius of it."

Suddenly, music swelled, in brass and drums, the music echoing down the boulevards. Thousands of black flags snapped in unison.

"Now, a special welcome from our leader... our Chairman."

The voice on the loudspeakers shifted. It was smooth, commanding, and weighted with an authority that felt less like charisma and more like inevitability.

"My people," the Chairman began, his tone amplified until it seemed to press against every chest in the city. "What is the world above?"

In a bone-chilling unison, thousands of voices answered; men, women, and children, their tones flat and rehearsed. "Ruins. Lies. The failure of freedom."

"And what is the world below?" the Chairman asked.

"Order. Strength. The triumph of unity."

The Operators slowed their pace, the rhythm of the call-and-response settling over them like a shroud. Civilians froze mid-step, workers with tools, mothers guiding children, students with books. Every last one stopped and turned their faces upward toward the speakers.

"And who guards the truth?"

"The Consortium. *The Consortium.* **The Consortium.**"

The word repeated like the toll of a funeral bell, building until the streets shook. Phen's chest swelled, his lips moving in time with the crowd. Vannah echoed the words softly, her face a blank mask of satisfaction. Twelve did not speak; she merely analyzed the depth of their obedience with clinical detachment. Jack's jaw tightened. He hated the brainwashing, even as he recognized his role as one of its enforcers. He didn't join the chant. He only watched the masked statues of history gazing down from their perches, the insignias on their foreheads glowing in the artificial sun. Washington remade in the image of the shadow government controlling it.

The Chairman's voice thundered again, absolute. "And who will lead the world into its new dawn?"

"You will, Chairman. You will."

The voices rose as one, vibrating through the Veil until the artificial sky seemed to shiver. Then, the Chairman intoned: "In unison."

"We see all; we are all; we control all," the crowd thundered back.

"Nothing escapes our gaze; our eyes are everywhere."

The words carried down the avenues, past the carbon-copy monuments and the perfect facades of the White House and Capitol, bouncing against the steel and stone.

"Our agency cannot be undone in the darkest night and brightest days."

Every citizen repeated the line, their lips moving without hesitation. The sound was not fervent; it was mechanical, as if the words had replaced their very breath.

"In unison, we see all; we are all; we control all."

The final refrain slammed against the dome. Silence followed, like the pause after an executioner's axe. Phen's hand was over his heart, his eyes shining with rapture. Vannah looked on with cold satisfaction. Twelve remained still, a figure carved in glass.

Jack alone stood rigid, his jaw clenched. To him, the chant wasn't unity; it was a set of golden chains. They had their privileges, but he knew he was still a slave all the same.

The Chairman's voice returned one last time, softer, intimate. "Carry the words. Breathe them. Become them. For beyond the Veil, the old world dies. Here, the new one begins."

A mesmerizing chime began to play. Jack knew the sound, it was one that reprogrammed; changed minds to see the New Dawn as reality, and everything else as *Fake News.*

The speakers clicked off. Life resumed instantly. Workers lifted crates. Mothers tugged their children. Soldiers adjusted their rifles. As though the ritual had never happened.

Jack exhaled through his nose. "Zombies with flags," he muttered.

Phen didn't even flinch. "No, Jack. Patriots with purpose."

Phen slipped out of the apartment as Vannah's laughter echoed faintly from the shower, the sound muffled by the steam fogging the frosted glass of the balcony doors. Overhead, the false sun of the Veil began its calculated transition into dusk, the artificial sky shifting from a brilliant gold to a bruised, synthetic violet. He walked down the manicured marble path into a private garden where the statues of former presidents and forgotten generals stood firm. Their faces hidden behind the featureless Consortium masks, each forehead etched with a sigil that seemed to writhe and pulse in the dying, low-frequency light. The air was unnaturally still, thick with the constant, subsonic hum of the massive machinery that powered the city beneath the earth.

Phen checked the shadows of the surrounding colonnade, his movements precise and practiced, before keying his tablet. Layers of deep-state encryption unfurled across the screen, locking into place with a series of digital clicks until the secure line opened. The display blinked once, and then an unblinking eye; black on a field of white, filled the screen. "Commander Ashby is showing cracks," Phen said. His voice was no longer the playful tone he used with Vannah; it was controlled, cold, and devoid of sentiment. "He mutters against the liturgy. He casts doubt where certainty should stand. His loyalty..." He glanced around the silent, masked garden one last time, his eyes hard. "...his loyalty is no longer absolute."

The digital eye on the screen did not move, but the weight of the silence on the other end felt like it was pressing into the very marrow of his bones. At last, a voice answered. It was a sound warped by a thousand filters, neither male nor female, sounding more robotic than human.

"*Noted. Record filed.*"

Phen hesitated for a fraction of a second; a heartbeat that betrayed the faintest, dying ripple of guilt for the man he had fought beside. Then his jaw set, and the zealot returned. "He's effective. I will grant him that. But effectiveness without devotion breeds contagion. And contagion must be purged."

The connection cut abruptly. The screen went black, reflecting Phen's own stony expression in the glass. Behind him, the Veil's false horizon glowed faintly, casting long, distorted shadows across the marble corridor. Above them, Washington D.C. continued to burn as the ultimate prize of a Secession War. But below, in the pristine silence of Consortium City, a man's fate had just been sealed. Jack Ashby's war was far from over. But it would not be the same war once the Consortium decided exactly what to do with a patriot who had begun to think for himself.

11

Sleepy Creek Lake, WV — 03.19.27

Robert checked his watch at 4:00 **PM** before sliding his red kayak into the high-country lake he'd found years ago. It was a place he kept for himself like a buried treasure. Out here, there were no sirens screaming through the concrete canyons of D.C., no rhythmic thud of protest marches, and no televised speeches dripping with the poison of a crumbling Union. There was no war here; there was only the haunting, prehistoric cry of loons, the silver-white hush of the birches leaning over the shoreline, and the clean, hollow knock of a carbon-fiber paddle against the plastic hull.

He thumbed his GoPro on out of habit and let the red boat drift. He took a breath, drawing in the scent of damp pine and the sharp, bracing chill of the mountain air. The lake was a sheet of black glass, a perfect, unmoving mirror for the granite ridges and the snow-dusted peaks that hemmed in the valley. He dipped his paddle again, pulling slow, effortless strokes until the only sound in the universe was the water breaking off the blade in a soft, melodic swirl. In the shallows near the reeds, he heard the frantic splashing of geese and ducks, and for the first time in what felt like an eternity, Robert Turner actually smiled.

He stopped paddling and let the boat drift into the center of the mirror. An early spring wind moved over his face like a cold, invisible hand, its fingers stinging his lungs as he took deep, experimental breaths. He could feel the physical knot of anxiety in his chest begin to loosen. It had been the one that had lived there since the assassination of Troy Thomason.

Robert leaned back against the molded seat, letting the kayak spin in a lazy, clockwise circle. He struggled to remember if this was what life had been like before the pandemic, the invasion, and the Capitol Massacre turned his home into a high-security prison. He was no politician; his world was measured in the weight of a chef's knife and the precise dance of a blue flame.

He had once been a man of some small renown. In the 2023 season of *Amazing Chefs*, he'd worn an American flag chef hat and cooked with a flair that the judges called "unapologetically patriotic." He had stood on a stage under hot lights, worrying about the consistency of a reduction or the sear on a scallop. "God… feels like another life," he whispered to the empty air, his voice sounding thin and strange in the vast silence as he closed his eyes, chuckling quietly to himself. For the first time in five years, he allowed himself to believe the lie that he might actually be safe.

The birds warned him first.

A sudden rustle in the canopy became a frantic, screeching rush as the tree line erupted in a literal sheet of wings. Robert quickly sat upright, his paddle across his lap, his eyes darting toward the ridgeline. Then the sound hit—a *WHOOSH* that seemed to tear the atmosphere apart as two fighter jets ripped low across the mountain gap, their afterburners scorching the air. Then came the black shape behind them. It didn't make sense to his eyes at first; it was a large wing shaped thing, like something from a science fiction movie. It flew past with a terrifying silence before more jets. It was followed by smaller, diamond-shaped wings, their wake so powerful that the wind began shaking the birches, stripping the newly grown leaves from the branches in a green rain.

"Okay," Robert breathed, his hands shaking so hard he nearly dropped the paddle. "Nope. Time to go." He dug the blade in, frantically turning the kayak toward the shore, but the shockwave hit before the sound. The water puckered in violent, concentric rings, and the boat shunted sideways with a force that nearly flipped him into the could depths. A scaring curse escaped his lips as the sound finally arrived; a long, rolling punch of sonic energy that rattled his teeth in his gums and vibrated deep in his marrow.

His feet were out of the boat before plastic hull hit the mud of the bank. Far off, beyond the next ridge, something was burning, a column of oily smoke rising into the blue. The rhythmic, heavy thump of rotors began to echo through the valley. Robert scrambled out of the boat, dragging it up the bank with a desperate strength he didn't know he possessed. He ran for his truck, fumbling the key into the ignition and twisting it with a prayer. Nothing. The dash didn't even flicker. A small red icon; a dead battery with a diagonal slash, flashed once and faded into black. He could feel his pulse in the very tips of his fingers, the same cold adrenaline he felt when he'd once slipped with a deboning knife and caught the blade just before it hit bone. He didn't waste time. He yanked his mountain bike off the teardrop cabin trailer, hopped on, and began pedaling like a madman toward the thickest bunch of trees.

The helicopter thunder built behind him, passing directly overhead. Robert risked a glance up as he rode, seeing a white line of fire spear the sky from the valley floor. One of the helicopters turned into a cloud of glowing shrapnel with a sound like tearing sheet metal. A human scream followed the explosion before the pieces rained down into the cove, hissing like vipers as they hit the water. He threw the bike down and dove under a massive drift of dead leaves and pine needles, pressing his face into the dirt. The ground trembled under him; once, then twice. He waited, his chest heaving, until the roar of the rotors faded into a distant hum and the only sound left was the ragged, terrifying loudness of his own breath.

Another jet dipped below the mountain peaks, and as it banked, Robert saw the American flag painted on its wing. It pulled up in a vertical climb and disappeared over the next range.

Run, he thought, hauling himself out of the dirt. *Just keep running.*

Grabbing his bike, he pushed deeper into the old-growth forest. Branches whipped at his arms like lashes. Brambles tore at his ankles. The forest seemed to pull at him in a hundred small, needy ways until the lake was gone, the truck was a memory, and his sense of direction had dissolved into a frantic rhythm of footfalls and the clicking of his bicycle chain. Night took the woods by degrees, the shadows stretching out until they became a solid wall. By the time he stumbled upon the small, timber-framed cabin, the darkness was absolute. He stood at the door, his hand hovering over the rusted handle, listening. Silence. The door gave way with a long, agonizing scream of hinges.

Inside, it was a time capsule: a thin cot, a pot-bellied stove, and a few cans of beans with years of dust on their lids. He built a fire in the stove and stoked the flames as he twisted old newspapers, built a teepee of kindling, and blew on the embers until the heat finally found his iced bones.

Opening a can of beans he ate them cold, using a tarnished silver spoon he found in a drawer. As he ate, he noticed the order of the shelf: peaches, green beans, navy beans, all perfectly arranged. This wasn't a home; it was a waypoint, a hunting cabin kept in military readiness. His thumb throbbed; a dull, hot ache from where he'd burned it on the stove. He found a pouch of dry tobacco, pressed a leaf against the blister, and wrapped it tight with a strip of silver duct tape. Then he stripped off his damp jeans and shirt, collapsing onto the scratchy wool blanket of the cot. The exhaustion was a physical weight, dragging him down into a dreamless sleep as the wind began to whistle through the gaps in the floorboards.

It wasn't dreams that woke him. It was the sound of the world breaking.

CRACK.

The door didn't just open; it disintegrated. The hinges screamed as the frame blew inward under the force of a tactical boot. Cold night air rushed in, and suddenly the small room was a forest of white light. Flashlights cut spears through the dark, blinding him.

"On the ground! U.S. Army! Now! Hands where I can see them!"

Robert bolted upright, his heart hammering so hard he thought his ribs might snap. His hands were in the air before he even understood the commands. The outlines of rifles filled the room; heavy barrels, suppressed muzzles, the silhouettes of men in full combat load. The room was suddenly thick with the smell of sweat, wet wool, and gun oil. "I—I'm not armed! Please!" Robert's voice cracked, sounding small and pathetic.

A soldier slammed him back onto the cot, the rough fabric scratching his skin as plastic zip-ties bit savagely into his wrists. Another man tore through the shelves, cans of peaches clattering and rolling across the floorboards. The stove door was kicked open, scattering glowing embers across the wood.

"Clear!" someone barked from the darkness. "One civilian. No hostiles."

Robert blinked, his eyes stinging from the high-lumen beams. A gloved hand yanked him to his feet, forcing him to stand in his underwear. A sergeant with sharp face featured stepped into the light, spit flying with every barked word. "What the hell are you doing out here? This is a restricted zone!"

"I—I was just camping," Robert gasped, barely able to find enough air to speak. "I swear. I'm nobody. I'm just a cook."

The sergeant's stare was hard, suspicious, and entirely devoid of mercy. He jerked his head toward the door. "Bag him. We move before the line shifts. The Bluegrass boys are crawling all over the east ridge."

"We're in rebel territory, Sarge. We gotta move now."

"I command when we move!" the sergeant roared, spittle dribbling down his chin. "Now move him out!"

They dragged Robert out into the freezing night. A line of transport trucks idled under the canopy of the trees, their headlights taped over with black vinyl. More soldiers crouched in the roadside ditch, their NVGs glowing a ghostly green as they scanned the ridgeline.

Somewhere deeper in the woods, the silence was shattered by the sharp, rhythmic crack of gunfire; distant at first, then growing louder, like dry branches snapping in a fire.

"Contact west!" a voice screamed. Muzzle flashes began to spit from the dark tree line, the bullets whining past with a terrifying *zip-thwack* against the cabin walls.

"Bluegrass militia! Move! Move!" The Feds shoved Robert down into the frozen ground, the mud caking against his skin. Rifles began barking directly over his head, the muzzle flashes illuminating the chaos in strobe-like bursts. He curled into a ball, palms clamped over his ears, every nerve in his body felt like they were engulfed in flames while his body froze.

Tracer fire stitched the darkness in long, elegant lines of red and yellow. A rocket screamed through the air, detonating against a lead truck and flipping the multi-ton vehicle in a spectacular roar of flame. Men screamed. Shrapnel hissed through the air like angry hornets. Robert's world shrank to the taste of silt in his teeth, the smell of smoke in his lungs, and the sheer, overwhelming thunder of two armies tearing into each other with total indifference to his existence.

Boots thundered past, kicking a spray of dust into his mouth. The sergeant who had captured him went down hard beside him, his helmet rolling into the darkness. "Sarge!" someone shouted; but the man's skull had been split open by a bulled, his eyes staring at the stars, glassy and unseeing. The sound of the sickening *phlop* caused Robert to gag as he did his best to stay silent.

"Fall back! Fall back!" a lieutenant bellowed, his voice cracking with the strain. A truck roared to life, gears grinding as wounded men stumbled toward the open tailgate. One soldier with a mangled shoulder sprayed blind fire at the tree line, empty brass shells raining across Robert's bare back like hot hailstones. Another soldier fell, screaming, his rifle clattering inches from Robert's face. The heat of the muzzle made him flinch as another man scooped the weapon up and kept firing.

Robert curled tighter in the dirt, trying to become part of the earth. Through the cacophony, he heard a different rhythm of shouting. There was a distant, brassy bugle call that sounded like a ghost from another century. Green tracers began slicing across the red. The opposing soldiers moved forward with a terrifying momentum. Robert rolled into the tall weeds at the side of the cabin, an instinctive, animal attempt to hide. A man screamed into a radio nearby: "We need support! We need—" then he went silent as a round punched him back against the cabin wall, his blood spraying the timber. Others ran, their boots pounding past Robert, the air filling with the metallic stink of iron, gunpowder, and human sweat.

The truck at the end of the line exploded, taking the screams of several men with it into the night sky. The bugle call rose again, closer this time, and with it came the sharp, guttural bark of orders in a dialect Robert didn't recognize. Bullets ricocheted off the metal of the abandoned vehicles, hammering the Feds who were trying to escape into the dark. Then came the sound of boots, what sounded like hundreds of them, thrumming along the cold ground in a terrifying unison.

For a moment, he thought they might pass him by. Then a flashlight swept the weeds. The beam slid over his bare feet, paused, and then climbed slowly to his face. A heavy boot crunched down inches from his head. A voice snapped, low and menacing: "We got one hidin' in the grass."

Hands yanked him up by the collarbone, dragging him out into the open like a slaughtered deer. Mud streaked his face as he blinked into the harsh white light, his voice breaking. "I'm not—I'm not one of them! Please!"

The rifle barrel jammed into the center of his chest said otherwise. The soldier dragged him through the frozen, dew-covered grass. "Who are you!" the man barked, his face covered with greasepaint.

"Ro-ro-ro-bert... Robert Turner," he stammered, his eyes fixed on the dark bore of the rifle.

"Soldier! Lower your weapon!" A man with two silver stars on his shoulder stepped forward out of the smoke. "I said lower your weapon. The Fed boys are dead or gone at this point. There's no fight left in this one."

Robert swallowed hard, the barrel lowering only a fraction as the man with the stars stepped closer. General Marcus Rhoades' boots crunched in the frozen grass. He studied Robert with an unreadable expression, the firelight from the wreckage throwing long, hard shadows across his features. "Robert, why are you all the way out here in the middle of a war zone?"

"I—I'm not anyone," Robert stammered, his hands still trembling in the air. "I was in D.C. I'm a chef. I came to the lake to get away. To hide. I don't know anything about the Feds, I swear."

Rhoades studied him, tugging his leather gloves tighter. His voice dropped to a razor's edge. "D.C. is a city built on liars, spies, and deserters. You'll forgive me if I don't take a man's word at face value when he's found hiding in a ditch after a firefight."

"I'm not... look, I don't even own a gun. I am naked. I just wanted to be left alone," Robert pleaded motioning toward his boxers and barechest.

For a long moment, the only sounds were the distant crack of sporadic gunfire and the faint, agonizing moans of the wounded. Then Rhoades gave a sharp, clinical nod to his men. "Search him. If he's telling the truth, he's just another stray caught in a war he doesn't understand. If he's lying, I'll know by morning."

Two privates moved forward, their movements rough as they forced Robert back toward the cabin. He complied, his legs feeling like lead.

Inside, the cabin was a ruin. The door hung shattered on its hinges, and the floor was littered with the remnants of Robert's few possessions. Outside, the soldiers worked in a grim silence, dragging the bodies of the Feds into the tree line. Shovels cut into the frozen earth with a rhythmic crunch that echoed against the walls.

The cold wind carried the scent of the battle mixed with woodsmoke as Robert was shoved back onto the cot. His wrists remained bound, his breath coming in shallow, uneven gasps. His GoPro, his rusted spoon, even the small pouch of tobacco had been scattered across the floor. General Marcus Rhoades loomed over the wooden table, the silver stars on his collar catching the flickering lantern light. His lieutenant stood behind him, arms folded, eyes fixed on Robert like a hawk watching a rabbit.

"Robert Turner. From Washington, you said," Rhoades began, his voice low and steady.

Robert nodded frantically. His mouth was like cotton rolled in sand. "Yes. I—I'm just a chef. I left when the Capitol Massacre happened. I didn't want any part of it. I just wanted to cook."

The lieutenant stepped closer, his voice accusing. "And yet here you are. Wrong place, wrong time doesn't cut it when my men are bleeding out in the dirt."

"How was I supposed to know the war would find me here?" Robert's voice cracked. "I came out here weeks ago. I thought I'd be safe."

The private by the door barked a laugh, holding up the battered GoPro. "Safe? Or spying? You filming troop movements for the Feds?" He let the camera drop onto the floor with a hollow clatter.

"No! Look at the video! It's just me in a kayak! I was recording the loons before those planes flew over!"

Rhoades didn't move. His stare was a physical weight. "Men died tonight, Mr. Turner. My men. So you'll forgive me if I don't take a stranger at his word."

Robert's chest heaved. "Please—I'm not with them. I swear to God. I don't even like guns. I hate them."

For a long moment, the only sound was the hiss of the lantern and the distant, rhythmic scrape of shovels outside. Then Rhoades leaned back, his chair creaking under his weight. His voice was cold and final. "Morning's not far off."

The words felt heavier because the first smear of gray was already touching the horizon. The promise of interrogation, of judgment, of whatever '*knowing*' meant under Rhoades's command. The thought pressed down on Robert like a physical crushing force. The general rose, his shadow swallowing the lantern glow as he moved toward the broken door. "Hold him here. Guard the door." He paused at the threshold, his voice low and certain. "If you're lying to me, Robert... you won't see the sun set tomorrow."

Robert's face was swollen with tears as he looked at the shattered door. "I'm no big-time chef... I barely made it through culinary school. I worked the grill at a chain steakhouse in Arlington. That's it. That's all I ever was." The broken door was pulled into the frame, leaving Robert alone with the shuffle of boots in the frost, the scrape of metal on stone, and the terrifying, inevitable weight of the coming day.

Washington, D.C. Skies — 3.20.27 — 05:00 AM

The cockpit canopy rattled with a rhythmic, high-frequency vibration as Captain Elias "Cross" Mercer eased his F-35 Lightning II into the formation. His HUD painted the pre-dawn sky in a glowing tapestry of neon green and gold, tracking telemetry that felt increasingly like a death warrant. To his left and right, the wings of other F-35s, Raptors, and Texan Hornets glimmered against the first bleeding light of the rising sun.

Below them, the Potomac River snaked through a city that was already physically and spiritually broken. Arlington was a patchwork of smoldering fires, and the rhythmic, silent flashes of artillery stabbed from the West like a slow, repetitive heartbeat. Positioned behind them, silent as a guillotine blade, flew the B-2 Spirit. The stealth bomber was no longer an asset of the United States Air Force; it was piloted now by defectors who had thrown their lot in with the Montana-Idaho Militia and the seceding states. Its massive, black bat-wings stretched across the dawn like a shadow.

"Package confirmed," the command channel crackled in Mercer's ear, the voice clipped, professional, and terrifyingly cold. "Proceed to target. This is it, boys. Make it count."

Mercer felt the sweat slicking his palms inside his flight gloves. "Dad," he whispered into his oxygen mask, the comms dead-silent on his end. "I know you fought for this country... I'm sorry."

The bay doors of the B-2 yawned open and the ordnance began to fall; precision-guided death falling through the morning mist. Mercer reflexively closed his eyes. "I'm sorry," he whispered again, his voice cracking against the rubber of the mask.

"Package away! Repeat—package away!" the bomber's comm barked, the tone shifting from professional to triumphantly feral. Across Mercer's HUD, targeting icons flared a brilliant, satisfied green. The formation shifted instantly, the escort fighters peeling wide in a graceful, lethal arc to cover the bomber's egress.

"Hell yeah!" a Texan pilot drawled over the open tactical net. "That's how you end a damn war!"

"Copy that! Good riddance, swamp rats," another voice answered, a jagged, dark laughter spilling across the frequency.

Mercer said nothing. His gloved hand gripped the flight stick so hard his knuckles began to ache inside the leather. Below him, the federal city unfolded like the Constitution. The whole city about to vanish with the crushing blow that he had made possible. The first flash bloomed long before the sound could climb to his altitude. It was a white, blinding core that swelled outward with a terrifying hunger, swallowing whole city blocks like dry paper set to a blowtorch. Another followed. Then a third. The Potomac suddenly glowed like molten glass, reflecting the apocalypse above it, as the historic bridges snapped like dry twigs under the thermal pressure.

Static roared in Mercer's ears, a white-noise scream as every electronic channel went wild. "Direct hit! She's burning—she's gone! Look at that bloom!"

"Eagle Wing, RTB! RTB! Mission complete!" Command's voice was strained now, nearly drowned out by the spontaneous shouts and hooting cheers of the pilots in the formation.

Mercer swallowed hard against the bitter bile rising in his throat. His HUD shimmered and distorted from the massive electromagnetic wash of the detonations; green numbers bent and blurred across his vision. His visor dimmed automatically to protect his retinas against the hellish glare below, but no filter could mute the reality of the sight. The iconic dome of the Capitol shearing apart in slow motion, the National Mall vanishing beneath a single, rolling wave of superheated dust.

"This is it, boys. We just put the nail in the coffin."

"God bless Texas!" someone howled, his voice cracking with a terrifying, ecstatic joy.

"UAA! UAA! UAA!" another hooted into the comms, the chant of the United Allied American states echoing like a tribal war cry.

It was a cold, crystalline realization for Mercer: the United States was over. With that single coordinated blow, the dream was either dead or so greatly diminished that it would never breathe again.

Mercer thumbed his mic, his mind flashing to his father's service medals, boxed away in a dusty cedar chest back home. He thought of the precisely folded flag that had sat on their mantle for twenty years, a promise he had just helped break. He pressed the transmit button halfway, his heart hammering against his ribs, then let it go. Silence.

The sky grew eerily quiet as they banked away, the only sound the steady, indifferent hum of his engines. Below them, Washington D.C. was no longer a city. It was a jagged, smoking wound in the earth. Mercer exhaled once, a long, shuddering breath that fogged his visor. *The United States is dead.* And he was one of the men who held the blade that killed Caesar Augustus.

Forest Cabin — Sleepy Creek Lake, WV

The cheers outside swelled, a raw, triumphant roar that echoed off the ancient Appalachian hills. Inside the cabin, Robert twisted against the wooden chair, his wrists burning as the plastic zip-ties bit deeper into his skin. General Rhoades stepped through the ruined door frame, his heavy greatcoat brushing against the jagged splinters. The smile on his face wasn't one of cruelty; it was one of victory and triumph.

"Chef," he said, his voice a calm, vibrating baritone, "this damn war is over."

Robert's breath hitched, a spark of desperate hope flickering in his chest. "I can… I can go home? Back to D.C.?"

Rhoades studied him, his head tilting just slightly, like a scientist observing a specimen. "D.C. doesn't exist anymore."

The words flattened Robert like a physical blow. "N-no… no, that's not—" His voice collapsed into a jagged sob. "My fiancée… my home—"

Rhoades's expression softened a fraction, but the steel never left his tone. "Son, I've marched through burning towns for two years now. I've buried men with my own hands. I don't take any joy in telling you this; but if she was in DC then she is gone. You'll have to make peace with that."

Robert's tears blurred the general's face into a shifting shadow. "Then what happens to me?"

Rhoades turned toward the light spilling in from the broken doorway, where the sun was finally beginning to bleed over the ridge. "Nothing. You're no spy. No soldier. Just a man who wandered into the wrong fire. You'll stay here." He glanced at the lieutenant standing by the door. "Board it up. Leave him supplies. He's not our enemy." The soldiers nodded, already gathering scraps of lumber and splintered crates to nail across the frame. Outside, the chants of the Bluegrass militia carried on, a victory hymn.

Rhoades lingered one moment longer, his eyes fixed on Robert. "War takes enough men. I don't need to make more enemies out of cooks." His voice dropped to a conspiratorial whisper. "When the boards come off that door, make yourself scarce. Shepherdstown won't be kind to strangers right now."

Robert pulled harder against the frame of the chair, the wood creaking. "Why are you doing this?"

Marcus Rhoades turned and looked through him, adjusting his leather gloves with a slow, deliberate precision. "To give us time to leave without you getting in the way."

"But how..."

Rhoades didn't answer. Instead, he pulled a pair of heavy scissors from his kit and placed them on the small table closest to Robert's bound hands. "You'll find a way."

Outside, the truck engines cranked to life, the sound of tires crunching over dirt and stone signaling the departure of the army. Rhoades stepped onto the porch. "Don't nail him in too hard," he ordered.

The two soldiers nodded, loosely hammering the boards across the door frame. Robert began to rock his chair violently, the legs skidding across the floorboards. "Don't leave me here! Don't leave me tied up!"

The chair toppled with a dull, sickening crack. Robert's head slammed into the floor, a spike of white-hot pain lancing through his skull before the world folded into absolute black.

When sound returned, it was a pressurized, underwater thrum; as if his head were wrapped in heavy wool.

A dull, rhythmic ache throbbed behind his eyes, the taste of blood on his tongue. He lay paralyzed for a breathless minute, his mind a flickering projector of the night's carnage: the scream of a rocket, the roar of the truck exploding, and the wet, sickening *thwack* of the sergeant's skull coming apart. Then, the finality of the hammer; the rhythmic thud of boards sealing him inside the abandoned cabin.

Light edged into the cabin through the gaps in the lumber and through the window that signaled the arrival of the cool dawn. He tried to move, and his neck protested with a sharp, animal-like ache. He realized he was no longer on the floor. The mattress creaked beneath him as he rolled over, then froze.

His wrists; they felt cold and slick, but they were free. He pushed himself up on one elbow, his vision swimming. The zip-ties were gone. His hands trembled as he curled his fingers, feeling the raw, dark welts where the plastic had chewed into his flesh. A smear of dried blood rimmed his cuffs, but the circulation was returning in a painful pins-and-needles rush.

A scuff of movement caught the corner of his eye. The scissors Rhoades had left clanged to the floor, the blades flicked open, resting near a roll of duct tape. Someone had freed him and moved him to the cot.

Then the smell hit him: the rich scent of coffee.

"You are awake." The voice made Robert jump so hard he nearly rolled off the bed. A man stood in the cabin's entryway, framed by the partially pried-open boards. He held an axe in one hand. "It's getting cold out, so I was chopping some wood to burn."

He spoke to Robert with the casual ease of an old friend. "Who are you?"

The man leaned his axe against the interior wall. "Well? I'm the owner of this fine little cabin." He looked around at the wreckage. "I show up and it looks like a war was fought in my kitchen, and I find you zip-tied to my grandma's old kitchen chair." He motioned toward the splintered remains of the wood on the floor. "That chair has been in my family for over a hundred years."

"I... I'm sorry, sir," Robert stammered. He tried to stand, but dizziness hit him like a physical hammer. He collapsed back onto the cot, his breath shallow and ragged.

The man poured a dark liquid into a stainless steel cup and handed it to Robert along with two ibuprofen. "I don't think you were at fault, but I had no idea my little escape would have become a prison." He paused to take a long sip of his own coffee. "My name is Ben. Ben Dalton, by the way. Sheriff of Shepherdstown, West Virginia."

Consortium City — 03.23.27

The Dome shimmered overhead like a wounded sky. From the outside, the recent bombardment of Washington had stripped away layers of protective soil and stone, revealing the black ribs of structural metal and pulses of light that didn't belong to the natural world. Radiation storms, born from the surface apocalypse, painted the subterranean horizon in sickly greens. Above them, Washington was still a funeral pyre.

But inside the Veil, the perfection held. There were white picket fences. The crack of a bat during a baseball game in the park. A mother pinning fresh laundry to a line in a gentle, synthetic breeze. The air smelled of rain-washed grass and baking bread. The lie endured, flickering only slightly at its frayed edges, but it remained beautiful all the same.

Jack Ashby stood with the others in the Observation Hall, staring up through the reinforced glass at the fractures where reality bled into their sanctuary. He said nothing.

Phen folded his arms, his eyes tracking a localized glitch in the "sky" projection. "The Veil's wounded. If the people ever truly saw what's sitting just outside that glass—"

"They won't," Vannah cut in, her voice as smooth. "HRT has been assigned to repair the framing on the exterior. They're installing a new skin that projects a simulation of the surface destruction back at the world, so no one will ever see us. We'll be a ghost in the crater."

A sharp, digital tone split the silence. An eye projected itself onto the far wall; a flickering white iris on a field of solid black.

"Operators. New directive." They stepped closer to the projection in a practiced formation. "There will be diplomatic talks in Charlotte, North Carolina," the voice continued. "The rebels are calling them the Charlotte Accords. Intel suggests the formation of a mutual defense pact. A League of former traitorous states."

Twelve looked at the others, her gaze eventually settling on Jack. She didn't care for the politics or the grand designs of the Board; she loved him. She would follow him into the fire or out of it. She offered a small, private smile as Jack met her bright green eyes.

"Focus, Twelve." Jack's tone was harder than he meant it to be, a defensive reflex. The projected eye widened, then narrowed into a cold, judgmental slit. Words unfurled beneath it in crisp, bureaucratic text that felt surgically clean against the grime of the world above.

"Your mission," the voice intoned, flat and unblinking, "is to kill the leaders of these rebel 'countries.' They have no right to exist and must be shown the error of their ways."

Jack felt the phrase like a physical blow to the sternum. It wasn't the content that shocked him; he'd seen the Consortium perform "necessary" extrajudicial acts before. But the language was absolute. *Kill.* No contingency. No debate. No diplomacy. The architects had chosen a verb and meant to cut all the way to the bone.

They had killed before, but it had always been framed as a service to the country. Jack had always been mission-focused, but this felt like a massive overreach into the dark. He swept the room quickly, his face a locked box, ensuring no one saw the flicker of doubt that threatened to break his composure.

Mission before morals. The guiding principle of his life echoed in his mind, but for the first time, it felt hollow. He was tired, or perhaps the cracks were finally reaching the surface. Jack's face went still, like a window slammed shut against a rising wind. He had learned to hide tremors; leadership required a blankness that his team could read as certainty.

Phen saw it anyway.

Not from where Jack sat; Phen had the habit of watching people's reactions instead of the briefing screens. He saw the micro-tell of Jack's jaw, and the way his hand hovered a fraction of a second too long above the console. He caught the small, private exhale Jack let out behind his teeth and stowed the observation away like contraband for later use. Phen didn't make a show of it. He folded his arms and let his easy, practiced smile reappear. A crack, however small, was still a crack.

"Direct and efficient," Phen said aloud, his voice soft and practical. He was playing the part, keeping the theater intact for the sake of the mission. Vannah's gaze lingered on Phen, a curve of dark amusement at the corner of her mouth. She stretched her leg out under the table, the tap of her toe against his boot equal parts a tease and a claim.

"It won't be clean," Jack said, finally breaking his silence. He walked to the observation window. "This will be the most overt act of war the Consortium has ever engaged in."

Vannah laughed under her breath. "This is all so dull. I'm just ready to deploy."

"The rebels are already calling the falling of D.C. their 'Independence Day,'" Jack said, his voice tight. "They've scheduled the Charlotte Accords for next March to mark the first anniversary. It gives them a year to build an army, and it gives us a year to disappear into their ranks. To do this right, we have to embed deep. This may cost all of our lives."

"A year is a long time to play pretend, Boss," Phen quipped, leaning over to press a lingering kiss to Vannah's temple. "But don't worry about us. We've got plenty to keep us busy while we wait for the fireworks."

Jack's expression remained firm. "We fit in. That is our orders."

Twelve's hand instinctively went to the holster at her hip. "We'll be ready."

Phen let his grin slide back on. "We'll be the best *Todd and Lisa...*"

Vannah reached up to brush a speck of phantom dust from the projection console, her touch almost affectionate. "You a Todd? and me a Lisa?" She laughed at the absurdity.

Jack watched them fall back into the rhythm of the work—the clicking of magazines, the snap of equipment cases, the sterile chirp of comms being cycled. These were the rituals that made sense. They were tidy, predictable, and remarkably easy compared to the prospect of spending a year as a suburbanite named Todd. He stayed at the window a beat longer, watching the maintenance drones crawl over the Veil like industrious silver spiders. They were patching the fractures with terrifying speed, stitching the "sky" back together before any of the "citizens" could look up and realize their sun was a lie.

Phen caught Jack's eye on the way out. He didn't offer a salute or a report; he just gave that annoying, cocky tilt of the chin. Part question, part dare, and a subtle reminder that he was watching the "Commander" for any more slips. Jack returned the nod, though it was smaller and more hesitant than it would have been before the world started ending every other Tuesday.

Big Sky Ranch — 01.02.28

"The events of March 20th, 2027 will be remembered as the day the experiment known as the United States of America ended." The voice of the anchor was measured, heavy, as grainy footage rolled across the screen: the National Mall burning, smoldering clouds climbing where the Capitol once stood, monuments shattering into dust. "In less than twenty minutes, centuries of marble and memory collapsed under a storm of fire unleashed by their former countrymen. The combined air forces of the United Alliance of America, the Bluegrass

States Republic, the New Republic of Texas and the Great Plains Nation unleashed a strike the world had never witnessed on American soil. Nuclear payloads dropped across Washington, D.C., erasing the capital that had stood for over two hundred and fifty years."

Images shifted showing the charred husks of the Lincoln Memorial, the Potomac blackened with ash, aerial sweeps of an unrecognizable city swallowed by destruction. "But even before the bombs fell, the government of the United States had moved. Independence Hall, Philadelphia; once the birthplace of the Republic, was chosen as its new seat. From there, a fractured administration declared the continuation of the Union, though its authority now stretched thinner than parchment." The screen cut to interview footage with senators speaking from hastily assembled offices, crowds in Philadelphia clutching flags, soldiers saluting outside a courthouse converted into a command post. "Washington was gone. But America, they said, would endure."

Jeremiah toked on his cigar, smoke curling upward as he twirled a glass of bourbon in his hand.

"In the months since the strike, the United States has declared an end to all offensive operations." Stock footage rolled of Independence Hall with scaffolding still clinging to its brick face, flags draped from every window, soldiers standing watch at the perimeter. Rows of desks filled the old Assembly Room, laptops glowing where the Founders once signed parchment. "From Philadelphia, the remnant government has vowed to rebuild. They call it the 'Second Founding.' But the shadow of Washington's destruction haunts every word, every act. The investigations into how such a strike was coordinated. The questions remain, echoing in the silence of the new capital: Who provided the intelligence? How was the most protected airspace in the world breached?"

The anchor's voice lowered, underscored by strings. "For the coalition of nations that rose from America's collapse: the United Alliance of America, the Great Plains Nation, the Bluegrass States Republic, and the New Republic of Texas; the March 20th strike was not only an ending. It was a beginning. They claim it was the necessary blow to sever the old order and secure their sovereignty." Footage interspersed with columns of UAA infantry marching through Raleigh; Texas armor rolling across dusty plains; Bluegrass parades in Louisville with flags stitched in navy and gold; Great Plains ranchers saluting militia columns as they passed. "But for historians, the question will linger: was it defense... or vengeance?" The program lingered on satellite images of D.C. no longer recognizable as a capital, but as a crater. A blurred image of the White House came into focus, no longer white it was a dingy tan and gray with streaks of black soot.

Jeremiah didn't look away from the screen, though the images no longer surprised him. He had signed the orders. His allies had signed theirs. The bombers had flown because of his orders. The narrator's words pressed into him like the weight of the Rocky Mountains outside his window. Defense or vengeance. He had always told himself it was the first. But the second whispered close at the edge of his mind.

He set the cigar down, exhaling slow.

On the desk before him lay a folder, unassuming, its paper thick with inked seals and formal lettering. The United Alliance of America's invitation. Charlotte. A summit of equals, not a reunion of the Union. A pledge of steel and blood that if one fell, all would rise in its defense.

Miranda's voice drifted from the next room, faint, warm, grounding. And upstairs, Samantha's laughter echoed with one of the ranch hands. For a moment Jeremiah closed his eyes, letting the sound carry him away from the crater on the screen. Buddy barreled into the office and licked Jeremiah's elbow, snapping him out of his reverie. Buddy took off running into the other room as he heard Samantha shout to, "catch."

Here, life edged back toward something like normal. Not the old kind of normal; a new one.

12

Cedar Hill, Missouri — 01.10.28

Samantha stepped off the giant Great Plains Air Force C-130 onto a makeshift runway on the outskirts of town. The sounds of construction filled the air, thick with dust and the pungent smell of gasoline. "General! General!" a young airman ran up to her, his face caked in dirt. "We found our APC we lost in '26."

Samantha narrowed her eyes. "Show me." Her gaze swept the ruined town, but the mounds of fresh dirt didn't stay still. High-pitched ringing drowned out the construction engines. Purple and green light blossomed behind her eyelids, followed by that impossible, unnatural lightning. The heat came back first. For a second, the construction noise became screams and the smell of gas became the scent of streets collapsing into ash. She braced herself against the ramp trying to regain her balance.

"You okay General?" The airman grabbed a bottle of water from the jeep and tried to hand it to her. She shook her head and smiled, but the images stayed for a moment. She stood and began to follow the airman.

They crossed the churned mud of the worksite until the vehicle came into view, half-sunken in a ditch with armor mottled by rust and ash. The turret hung like a broken jaw, its tracks peeled away. A Buffalo Patch Banner still clung to the side, charred but visible. It had been pulled out and tied to sticks to create a makeshift shelter. “Regiment survivors?” Samantha asked as she reached the fabric of the Buffalo Patch Flag. The charred threads rasped against her fingers, sliding away like old ghosts.

“We haven’t found anything ma’am,” Senior Airman Lewis said, shaking his head. “If anyone survived, ma’am... it wasn’t for long. Not in Cedar Hill.”

She remained still, her boots heavy in the mud. “Get the APC moved to the motor pool,” she said finally, her voice clipped but steady. “Strip it for parts. Whatever’s salvageable will serve us better than letting it rot in this ditch.”

“Yes, ma’am.” Lewis snapped a nod and signaled to the crew. Samantha looked again at Main Street. The empty storefronts, collapsed roofs, and the skeletons of houses once filled with life were slowly being replaced. Cedar Hill was still a scar that Samantha wished had never been opened, but she knew the people under her command had the impossible job of turning it back into a home for so many.

She drew a long breath and squared her shoulders. “Set a detail to recover the banner. Clean it, mend it, and hang it in command.” Her voice softened a fraction.

"The men who carried it deserve that much." Lewis hesitated, watching her as if weighing whether to say more, then just nodded. Around her, construction crews pushed at the earth with heavy machines, dragging beams into place, hammering, and welding. The sound was constant: industry trying to drown out memory.

Samantha turned back toward the airstrip, her shadow stretching long across the mud. She was no longer the young Marine balancing relations between the United States and her father's cause. She was the top general in her infant country's military now, and she couldn't afford to let the events of the last five years haunt her. Still, as she climbed into the waiting jeep, her hand brushed the worn leather of the seat beside her, the same way it had brushed the flag. The past clung to her no matter how many times she told herself it was gone.

"Back to HQ?" the driver asked.

Samantha nodded. "Back to HQ. We've got work to do." The jeep jolted forward, bouncing over ruts.

Raleigh, Carolina — 01.15.28

The red, blue, and white flags of the Alliance snapped between skyscrapers still bearing old U.S. colors. Vendors sold patches with the UAA crest: the mountains anchored to the Atlantic beneath a single star. The air smelled of magnolias and smoke from the eternal flame burning in Thomason Square. "We are gathered here today to honor one of our greatest, the presidency that never happened, and to pray for the UAA." President Samuel Burris's voice echoed off the buildings in downtown Raleigh as the thousands gathered cheered. His polished exterior gleamed on televisions from the coast to Appalachia. He was the man who had been the Governor of North Carolina, the one who led them through the Secession Wars and toward independence.

"It's no secret that Troy and I were rivals," Burris continued, smiling. "I ran in the Democrat primary to challenge him in the general. How your Vice President, Ulysses—" The applause and shouts grew louder at the mention of the VP's name. Burris raised his hand, chuckling. "I know, I know. We all love Ulysses. But let me finish my speech so he can talk to you!" The laughter softened as he straightened. "We built this Alliance on faith, on courage, and on the promise that we would never bow again: not to Washington, not to anyone." He paused for applause, scanning the square and nodding to a few faces he recognized. Light gleamed in his dull hazel eyes, every gesture precise and practiced. "Let us pray."

The crowd fell silent. The orchestra's final chord faded, leaving only the flapping of flags and the hiss of the eternal flame. "Heavenly Father," Burris began, his voice gentler now. "You have brought our new nation through challenging times, but today we stand in peace. We pray for everlasting peace across the Earth and here at home, where the former United States has shattered into pieces. May we never be required to turn to the sword again to defend our way of life. May we never have to worry about the Consortium, or invading armies from the east." For a long moment after Burris finished, no one moved. The sound of the eternal flame filled the silence: a faint hiss like breathing. Then, slowly, thousands of hands lifted in unison. Heads bowed. From the stage, the sight was staggering. A city on its knees.

When the prayer ended, Burris stepped back from the podium. The orchestra swelled, horns and drums rising like the tide. He turned toward the man standing behind him, the crowd already beginning to chant his name. "Now," Burris said, his voice booming again through the speakers, "I give you the man who stood by Troy Thomason from the beginning, the one who believed in him when few others did. A sailor, a senator, a patriot, and my friend: Vice President Ulysses Mars!"

Applause erupted like thunder. Ulysses took a slow step forward, his dress whites gleaming in the winter sun. His face bore the quiet dignity of a man who'd spent half his life at sea. As he reached the podium, he rested both hands on the edge and looked out over the square.

"When I first met Troy Thomason," he said, his voice deep and steady. "He was a kid with more courage than sense. We grew up in the same Carolina town. He always said he wanted to serve, to fix what was broken. I told him he'd get eaten alive in politics. So he went into real estate and built an empire instead." A ripple of laughter moved through the crowd. Ulysses allowed himself a brief smile. "Troy never listened when people told him he couldn't do something. He used to say to me, 'Ulysses, when they say you can't, prove them wrong.' And he did. His name rose on skyscrapers from New York to Singapore. He was a hard head."

Ulysses paused, a melancholy smile softening his weathered features. "But he never backed down when he knew he was doing what was right by his employees, his investors, and his country. And he wouldn't have backed down as President." He turned, saluting the smiling statue of Troy Thomason that overlooked the square, the bronze face glinting in the sunlight. "He believed that good men could still change the course of history. He believed that faith wasn't weakness. And when he asked if he should run for president, I told him it would destroy him, but that maybe it would save America."

He paused, eyes sweeping across the crowd of veterans, widows, and children holding flags. His eyes focused on Charlton and Amyleigh Thomason and smiled when Charlton held up their new baby son. "It didn't save the America we knew," he continued softly, "but it gave birth to the one we have now. He believed that freedom belonged to all of us—not to any politician or organization—but to the people who bled for it." The applause came slowly this time, reverent and rising like a wave.

"And so," Ulysses said, straightening, "we stand here not just to remember a fallen friend, but to renew the promise he made: that liberty and peace must never again be enemies. That this Alliance, flawed as it may be, stands for the dignity of every man and woman who still calls this land home." He lifted a hand toward the horizon. "And in the name of the land that Troy and I have loved so much, we will meet with the leaders of Texas, the Great Plains, and the Bluegrass States: not as rivals, but as brothers, on March 20th, 2028. Together, we will forge an alliance strong enough to stand against the encroachment of any nation. Each will be independent, but we will be allied, because together we are strong."

He leaned forward slightly, his voice rising with conviction. "We will be a prosperous nation. We will be a great nation. We will be an enduring nation!" The square exploded in sound. Flags waved, horns blared, and voices cried out until Raleigh shook.

In the Crowd.

The crowd was still roaring. Flags whipped in the cold morning wind, a sea of red, blue, and white. From the stage at the steps of the UAA Capitol building, President Burris and Vice President Mars smiled and waved like saints in a cathedral of noise. In the large crowd gathered to honor Troy Thomason, four figures waved their flags as well. Vannah jumped in the air, clapping like a high school cheerleader, while Phen smacked his hands together nearby. Jack Ashby stood holding Twelve's hand as their flagpoles rose and fell in rhythm with the crowd's chant: *We will be a great nation.* The words rolled like thunder through the square. Jack smiled, but his eyes stayed still, watching and measuring.

"Too easy," Phen Martenson muttered beside him, his voice lost under the music. His hand rested casually on the camera slung around his neck.

"Smile, sweetie!" Vannah Martel called. Her Southern drawl was light, practiced, and flawless. A UAA lapel pin gleamed against her red coat. "You look nervous and boring, Phen. Smile for the nice patriots."

"Remember the plan," Jack murmured, close enough that only the three beside him could hear. "We're ghosts until March. No hurry. No mistakes." Phen's camera clicked as he adjusted the lens. He played the part of the tourist with an easy grin, but his eyes tracked security placements and the angles of rifles. Then he saw a group of eight men standing near the east barricade, kitted out for war. He zoomed in.

The insignia on their shoulders came into focus: a royal blue bar gripped by a golden eagle with wings stretched wide. At its center, a white star burned in the heart of a stylized zero, flanked by diagonal red and white stripes. Every edge was outlined in gold thread that caught the winter light like fire against black. He could barely make out the yellow letters below the emblem: Zero Company. Phen lingered on the image for a heartbeat too long, then he pulled back and resumed the act as another smiling patriot with a camera. A burst of feedback hissed through the speakers. A woman's official voice rose above the fading applause. "Thank you for joining us today. Please begin exiting the plaza in an orderly fashion through the East Edenton and North Wilmington Street gates."

The roar shifted into chatter and the scraping of chairs. Jack lowered his flag, the polite smile still fixed on his face. "Time to blend," he murmured. "Stay in step."

Twelve nodded once, her eyes scanning the motion of people funneling toward the streets. "Security's relaxed," she said quietly. "They're confident. Proud days make careless guards."

"Pride's a weakness," Phen muttered, tucking the camera under his arm.

"They'll learn." Vannah laughed, light and airy, twirling her flag once before folding it neatly against her chest. "You two sound like preachers at a funeral. Smile. It's a holiday."

"A holiday we had a hand in creating," Jack said coolly.

Phen laughed. "We were on the other side of the country when that happened." Jack ignored him and moved with the wave of bodies, shoulder to shoulder with families and soldiers in parade uniforms. A pair of Zero Company members crossed their path, talking easily and unaware of who brushed past them. Jack watched them go.

"They're here to protect Mars," he said under his breath. "Smart choice. He's the only one in the Alliance people still believe in."

"Imagine your country's history having a first president that no one liked or respected," Twelve said.

"Oh, they respect Burris, but he's part of the DC class of politician everyone in the old world despised," Vannah whispered back.

"Burris knows how to smile," Phen said, lowering his voice as they turned toward East Edenton Street. "But that's all it is: teeth and timing. Mars, though? He believes what he says. That's dangerous."

Jack adjusted his flag to his shoulder, letting the fabric hide his face from a passing drone. "Belief always is," he muttered.

"It's the root of every war and every martyr." Twelve's hand brushed his and briefly squeezed his fingers as they passed beneath a banner. She didn't break stride. "He's not just their martyr," she said quietly. "He's their identity. Their Washington. Their Jefferson. Without him, the Alliance has no soul."

Vannah's smile was faint. "Then we don't need to kill their leaders," she said. "We just need to kill their faith."

They merged with the river of people flowing toward the exits. A uniformed officer waved them through with a smile, handing out commemorative pins. Vannah took one, thanked him sweetly, and pinned it beside the transmitter hidden in her lapel. Behind them, the anthem began again, softer this time. “Next time we see this place,” Phen said, “it’ll be different.”

“With any luck, we’ll never see this place again after March.” Vannah pulled Phen down and kissed him on the cheek. Jack glanced back one last time at the Capitol steps, then turned into the street.

“Charlotte’s next,” he said. “And when the smoke clears, even their martyr won’t be enough to hold them together.”

Charlotte, Carolina — 01.28.28

Charlotte was untouched during the Secession Wars; life here was normal, aside from UAA flags flying where American flags once flapped in the wind. It was lucky. The only attack Carolina endured at the onset of the war was the assassination of President-elect Troy Thomason. That was when everything changed. Banners of the infant nation fluttered from flagpoles and hung down the sides of buildings. Some businesses still flew the American flag, but the UAA flag always flew higher. Trade and Tryon gleamed as crews worked feverishly to polish windows and clear the streets for the coming Carolina Accords.

Dr. Six Parks crossed Romare Bearden Park, her boots cracking latent ice that still hadn’t melted. Sunlight flashed through the bare trees, catching her striking red hair and green eyes. The air smelled of roasted coffee and pastries from a nearby vendor. She wanted to stop, but the line was too long and she needed to report to the Marine recruiting office. Patriotic music drifted from a vendor's small speaker; she smiled as she mouthed the words of the UAA national anthem.

"Doc! Doc!"

She turned to see a young private running toward her, helmet tucked under his arm, breath fogging in the brisk morning air. Not far behind him came another Marine. "Well, if it isn't the Parks brothers," she said, shaking her head. "Aren't you both supposed to be on R&R?"

Private Three Parks grinned, brushing snow off his sleeve. "Ma'am, you know how it is. They told us to relax, but the sergeant said, 'Relax somewhere I can see you.' So here we are."

Seven came up behind him, still catching his breath. "He's lying. We just missed you, Doc."

Six arched an eyebrow. "You missed my medical evaluations, you mean. You're both due for one. You'd think we were related as much as you both pester me."

Three groaned. "See, that's why I keep my distance. We share a last name and when I get within ten feet of you, out comes the blood pressure cuff."

She smirked. "Someone has to keep you alive long enough to pretend you're heroes." They fell into step together, boots scraping frost from the concrete. Ahead, Tryon Street shimmered with banners and strings of lights. The city was preparing for the Carolina Accords the way other cities prepared for holidays: fresh paint, new security cameras, and street musicians rehearsing patriotic songs.

"You hear the schedule?" Three asked. "They say President Burris himself is coming, along with Presidents Chandler, Johnson, and Martinez. This is gonna be big. The whole world's gonna be watching."

Six nodded. "That's the idea. Make it look safe enough for the cameras."

"Isn't it safe?" Seven asked, glancing toward a convoy of armored transports parked along the curb. The crews were unloading sealed crates marked PROPERTY OF UAA TRANSPORT COMMAND.

"Of course it is, but it's a city. Gotta wrap up all the riff-raff!" she said.

Diesel drifted past as they rounded the corner near Romare Bearden Park, where workers were raising a temporary overflow pavilion. The old convention center was being remodeled into the Accord Center. The glass towers reflected the UAA banners like flames frozen in midair. For a moment, Six stopped to watch them. Something about the red, blue, and white rippling against the glass made her chest tighten. It reminded her of something: hallways washed in white light, children's laughter echoing in rhythm, and a number whispered by a voice that sounded like her own—a twin. The memory slipped away before she could catch it.

"You good?" Seven asked.

She blinked, forcing a smile. "Fine. Just a flashback to basic training."

He laughed. "I get those too. Only mine involve bad chow and worse instructors."

"Mine usually involve needles."

"Yeah, needles too."

For a moment Six looked at Seven, perplexed. "You get the same flashbacks as I do, it seems."

"I chalk it up to late nights, bad beer, and fast food." Three laughed uncomfortably, trying to change the subject. They crossed into the courtyard outside the Marine Recruiting Office, where a giant poster of President Burris saluting the flag dominated the entrance. Below it, the slogan read: *Strength Through Unity—The Alliance Endures.*

"Nice artwork," Three said. "Think he really posed for that, or did they just stick his head on a better body?"

Six shot him a look. "Keep that up and you'll be volunteering to muck out the Trauma center."

"See? Threats already. It's like being home."

Seven grinned. "We'll leave you to your paperwork, Doc. We've got to check in with supply before the MPs think we deserted again."

"Try not to," she said. "Desertion paperwork's hell on my Fridays." The two Marines saluted and peeled off down the street, laughter trailing behind them. Six watched them go, then turned back toward the recruiting office doors. The reflection in the glass caught her eye again. Her face doubled for a split second, the same expression mirrored perfectly before she moved. She frowned, shaking off the odd vertigo.

Inside, the sound of typing and voices drifted through the lobby. Charlotte thrummed like a machine that had never stopped running, its heart steady and untroubled. But as Six crossed the threshold, a gust of cold air followed her in from the street: one last whisper of winter that made her pause. Something about it felt hollow, like a breath drawn before a scream. She brushed the thought away and stepped inside.

13

Independence, Kentucky — 02.15.28

Chandler Ranch was filled with tents that dotted the fields, canopies staked against a mild wind while bluegrass music spilled from a wooden stage. For February it was unseasonably warm, mid-sixties with the sun bright on the long grass where children chased each other between rows of folding chairs. A cool breeze carried the honest tang of manure from the west pasture, a smell as common here as prayer. The sun hung low over the fields, catching the golden fringe of the new Bluegrass States Republic banners. The cloth snapped gently, a wide navy canton bearing twelve red stars, each point tracing the jagged borders of the new republic from the cold edge of Michigan to the Tennessee hills. Beneath it stretched a white field of peace and a crimson bar for the blood that bought it, all framed by a thin yellow line that glowed like sunlight on bourbon. Old farmers stood beside veterans in new BSR dress grays, their hats pressed to their chests as children wove through the crowd with paper flags. Every flag had a story; every family had history.

President Kenneth Chandler stood near the edge of a small wooden stage, watching his fields sway like an ocean. The years had carved lines around his eyes, but the way he carried himself, tall and weathered by duty, left no question why he had become the heart of the new republic. A band struck up a fiddle tune, and the crowd began to cheer as a small procession made its way up the dirt lane. Secretary Amelia Bennett, War Secretary Benjamin Chambers, and Attorney of Justice Luke Caldwell approached with their escorts, their coats trimmed with the gold piping of the new national service.

"Mr. President," Bennett said, her voice warm but reverent. "You couldn't have ordered a finer day for history."

Chandler smiled faintly. "The Lord's good at scheduling," he said. "I just build the fences."

They laughed quietly, but when Chandler turned toward the platform, his expression sobered. The band fell silent. Across the pasture, the crowd began to settle, hundreds of faces turning toward him as flags stilled in the wind. He stepped up to the microphone, taking off his hat.

"My friends," he began, his voice carrying the deep timbre of a man who had worked this land his whole life. "This ground has been in my family for five generations. My boys learned to ride on these hills. They hunted these woods. They helped me plant that sycamore over there when they were no higher than my belt buckle." He paused, glancing toward a tree on the far edge of the pasture, its bare branches cutting across the afternoon sun. "Now their names are carved in stone not a hundred yards from it."

A hush fell over the crowd.

"They were boys who believed in something bigger than themselves," Chandler continued. "They died in the early days, when the Great Plains stood up and Washington sent its planes to remind us who was in charge. They never saw this flag, but they died for what it stands for: faith, honor, and the right to be left in peace." Behind him, a Marine honor guard raised the new BSR standard. The blue canton caught the wind, stars flashing like embers, the red bar at the bottom glowing against the green pasture. "This land," Chandler said, "belongs now to the Republic, to all of you. It will be the seat of our government, the Chandler Commons, where free people can speak without fear. I give it not as a gift, but as a debt paid to my sons and to every family that lost more than they could afford."

He lifted the folded deed from the podium, the official seal of the Bluegrass States embossed in red wax. Secretary Bennett stepped forward to accept it, bowing her head. "This nation was born in pain," she said softly, turning to the crowd. "But today it stands in peace. The Chandler Ranch will forever remind us that our freedom was built not by the powerful, but by those who loved too deeply to surrender."

Applause rolled across the field, steady and heartfelt, rising into cheers as the band began again. Chandler stepped back, his gaze drifting to the horizon where the flags rippled in lines like planted crops. For a moment, the red and white stripes shimmered together, and he thought he saw his sons in the light, standing shoulder to shoulder, smiling like they used to before the world changed. He closed his eyes. "God keep them," he whispered.

As the music swelled, the banners of the Bluegrass States Republic flared in the wind. The crowd began to disperse in ripples, conversations returning like birds after a storm. Fiddles and banjos spun through the air as vendors reopened their stands and children waved miniature flags. Chandler stepped down from the stage, the applause still echoing in the distance. Bennett and Chambers followed, greeting the families that pressed in close to shake hands or pass folded notes of thanks.

"You did well," Bennett said quietly when the crowd thinned. "You made them believe this land is more than soil."

Chandler smiled faintly, eyes fixed on the horizon. "It is more than soil. It's my life. My blood, sweat, and tears are buried here."

From the ridge, he could see the surveyors marking the first lines of what would become Chandler Commons, stakes and colored flags fluttering where wheat his horses would no longer graze. The idea of a capital there, in his own pasture, still felt unreal. "Chandler Commons," he said after a moment, the name rolling awkwardly on his tongue. "I don't know if I like it. Sounds pretentious." He spat into the grass.

Bennett smiled faintly, eyes on the glowing banners. "Then let it be pretentious," she said. "Because one day, this place will be the heart of the Republic. And at its heart, Sovereign Hall."

Texas State Capitol — 02.17.28

"Texas will stay Texas!" President Gerald Martinez slammed his fist against the lectern as shouts rolled through the chamber. The gallery was packed shoulder to shoulder: oil magnates in pressed suits beside ranchers in denim, veterans in brown coats, and preachers with Bibles tucked under their arms. Texas Rangers surrounded the room, stationed to prevent an old-fashioned Wild West shootout should the need arise. The air was thick from all the bodies of the gathered crowd.

"Mr. President, what you're proposing is surrender!" a legislator from Amarillo shouted, his voice cutting through the noise. "Those Alliance folks want a pact so they can drag us into their next war. We've been free since '25 and we don't owe them a damn thing!"

Applause thundered from the Isolationist benches as supporters pounded the wood railings. Martinez raised a hand, but the roar swallowed him until the Sergeant-at-Arms banged his gavel twice. "We owe it to our children," Martinez said sharply. "We owe them a

Republic that doesn't have to build walls just to sleep at night. We fought alongside the UAA, the Bluegrass States, and the Great Plains. We bled together to break the old Union's chains. If we turn our backs now, we'll be divided before the ink is dry on our own Constitution."

"Division keeps us safe!" another legislator barked. "We don't need to sign treaties with outsiders who can't mind their own borders. Look what happened to the Carolinas. They're already crawling with foreign agents. You want that here?"

The crowd erupted again. "Foreign agents? You mean refugees from when we nuked DC?" Martinez leaned forward, the veins in his neck standing out like cords. "You have lost your mind if you think isolation will save us. You think no one will come for our oil, our ports, or our land? I've seen the satellites, gentlemen. I've seen the fleets crossing the Atlantic and the factories rising in Beijing. The world didn't stop when Washington burned. The UAA has inherited the most powerful Navy in the world. Don't you want them as friends?"

President Martinez stood tall, straightening his hat and bolo tie. The room fell still for a moment. He lowered his tone, grounding his voice. "The Charlotte Accords aren't a surrender. They're a line in the sand. A promise that we will not fight alone if and when that storm comes again."

From the second row, Senator Rojas rose slowly. He was a white-haired man who had seen too many wars.

"And when that storm comes from the UAA?" he asked quietly. "Who stands with Texas then?" The silence that followed was heavy. Martinez stared at him, his jaw tight. "I will," he said finally. "With or without your support."

"You will stand alone, Mr. President. We already have border disputes in Alabama with the UAA, and the Mexicans are champing at the bit to expand cartel lands into ours. The other states in this Republic wouldn't be happy if we ceded that territory!" Rojas barked back with forced composure.

The gavel struck again as the floor descended into argument. Martinez didn't move, his hand resting on the lectern and trembling with anger. "Remember, Senator," he voice low with a sharp edge. "Remember what we did with Robert Sinclair. We exiled him." He narrowed his eyes while leaning forward. "Don't think for a second the Isolationists in this chamber outnumber the Patriots of Texas."

Senator Rojas's face drained of color. The name Sinclair was akin to a curse. He had signed the exile order himself, placing his signature beside Martinez's on the parchment that sent a man he once called brother across the former US. Now the crowd's cheers struck him like blows. He sank back into his seat as the Patriots pounded their desks and shouted Martinez's name. Cameras flashed from the gallery, catching the fire in the President's eyes, his expression unyielding.

Martinez gave a small nod to his Rangers, then turned and stepped down from the dais. The heavy doors swung open, and the roar of the room fell to a dull hum. Out in the marble corridor, the air was cooler and quieter. Portraits of old governors lined the hall, their painted eyes watchful. Martinez exhaled, loosening his tie. "Idiots," he muttered. "Half of them don't even know what they're cheering for."

"Course they don't," a voice answered, smooth as glass. "That's why they need you to tell 'em."

Martinez turned. The man leaning against the window frame looked like he had stepped out of an oil baron's handshake: pressed gray suit, shined boots, and a silver tie pin catching the light like a blade. "Clay Harlan," Martinez said, his tone flat. "You always lurking in the hall when I finish a fight?"

Harlan smiled faintly, pushing off the frame with unhurried grace. "Only when the fight's worth watching." He approached with his hands clasped behind his back, remaining measured in his response. His badge glinted: Office of Strategic Affairs, Senior Adviser. It was one of the wartime appointments no one had ever revoked. "You handled them well," Harlan continued. "They'll sleep easier tonight, thinking their President's got it all figured out."

"I don't need their sleep," Martinez said. "I need their loyalty."

Harlan nodded. "And loyalty, sir, is a fragile thing. Especially when your neighbors start making promises they don't intend to keep."

Martinez's eyes narrowed. "You mean the UAA."

"Among others," Harlan replied easily. "The Carolinians will talk peace, but they've been arming faster than any nation west of the Mississippi. They want alliances because they're afraid, and fear is contagious."

Martinez bristled. "You got intel to back that up, or is this just another one of your stories?"

Harlan's smile didn't fade. "I've got friends in places you don't like to admit exist. Let's just say I wouldn't put your faith in men who smile too much on camera." For a long moment, neither spoke. The hum of the Capitol's air vents filled the space between them. Finally, Martinez asked, "You've always got an angle, Clay. What's yours this time?"

Harlan's eyes flicked to the flag outside the window. "Just trying to make sure Texas remembers who she is," he said softly. "You go to Charlotte, sir. Shake their hands and smile for the world. But don't you forget that every alliance costs something. Just make sure it's not your Republic they're buying... or your life."

Martinez studied him a moment longer, then stepped away. "You worry too much."

"That's my job," Harlan said, smiling again. "Worry keeps the lights on."

As Martinez disappeared down the hall, Clay Harlan lingered by the window, watching the flag twist in the wind. He adjusted his tie pin, a thin silver band shaped like a broken circle, and whispered as if to no one: “Phase Whiskey complete.”

“Good,” a voice returned in his ear.

Helena, Montana — 02.22.28

Snow still clung to the Capitol grounds, sparkling under a pale winter sun that hung high over the mountains. Governor Davison Carey stood before The Freedom Tree, brushing snow from the brass plaque with a gloved hand until the inscription emerged: *The Freedom Tree—With the Vision of Universal Freedom for All Mankind.* His breath fogged in the cold air as his fingers paused on the name of his wife’s great-grandfather. The metal was cold, almost biting. “Freedom for all mankind,” he muttered. “We’re further from it now than we ever were then. How naïve of us.”

A soft voice broke through the stillness. “Honey?” Madeline Carey approached, her coat drawn tight against the wind. She placed a hand on his shoulder. “You’ve got a vote, darling,” she said gently. “We need to hurry.”

Davison smiled faintly, glancing up at the bare branches that clawed toward the bright sky. “They planted this tree believing peace was permanent.”

Madeline followed his gaze. “Maybe it can be again.”

He sighed and brushed his gloves together. "Maybe." Carey paused, looking at her. "They planted this tree at the end of the first Civil War, when Montana barely had a role. Now, after the Secession Wars, we were at the heart of it."

They walked toward the Capitol steps, boots crunching through the thin crust of snow. The building rose like a fortress of granite and glass, its dome gleaming. A pair of Great Plains Guards stood at the entrance in deep green uniforms trimmed in gold, rifles slung casually at their sides. Inside, the warmth hit them immediately with the smell of coffee, ink, and polished wood. The rotunda echoed with the measured footsteps of aides and secretaries. The government of the Great Plains was busy establishing itself and in the sense of the rhythm Davison closed his eyes.

They climbed the staircase toward the Pact Assembly Hall, Madeline glanced at him. "You've been quiet lately. Even more than usual."

He gave her a small smile. "Just thinking," Carey said.

"About what?"

"About whether men like me should still be the ones writing the future."

Madeline squeezed his arm as they reached the landing. "Men like you helped build it," she said softly. "You've earned the right to help guide it."

They reached the tall oak doors of the Pact Assembly Hall. Aides moved briskly, carrying folders stamped with the golden seal of the Great Plains Nation: a single bison enclosed in a circle. It was the emblem Davison and Madeline's daughter had designed at the founding of the Montana-Idaho Militia. He took the folder marked with his name before heading into the Hall. Brushing his thumb over the embossed seal, Davison smiled. His family wasn't just part of the nation's story; they were woven into its beginning.

The usher at the entrance straightened as they approached. "Governor Carey," he said, pulling the door open with a respectful nod.

The chamber was bright, sunlight spilling through high glass windows. The nine Pact Governors sat around a long, crescent-shaped table. Steam rose from coffee cups, and the sound of pens scratching against paper mingled with the rhythmic ticking of the wall clock. "Governor Carey of Wyoming joins us," the usher announced.

"About time," Governor Bradford Davidson of Idaho said with a good-natured grin. "We were just taking bets on whether the snow got you."

A few laughs rolled through the room. Carey took his seat near the center. "If you think I'd miss a vote over a little frost, you don't know Wyoming."

President Jeremiah Johnson stood at the head of the room. He was tall and broad-shouldered, his posture effortlessly commanding. His hair had gone gray at the temples, but his eyes were still sharp. "Let's bring this session to order," Johnson said, tapping the folder in front of him. "We've got work to do before the

Senate convenes next week. First, I want to welcome someone new to the Pact." He turned toward the far end of the table, where a man in his early forties sat straight-backed. "Governor Thomas Lee of Montana," Johnson said. "Since I took on the role of President, I couldn't govern Montana and the nation both. The people chose their next leader."

He smiled faintly. "Governor Lee won his election last week against Quentin Jamison, the former Governor of Oregon and the last Democratic presidential candidate before the Secession Wars."

A few of the governors exchanged glances. The mention of Jamison carried history, representing old-world politics that felt like relics now. Governor Lee inclined his head. "Thank you, Mr. President. It's an honor to serve. Montana's ready to carry its weight for the Plains and for the great nation we've built together."

"Good man," Johnson said. "That's exactly what we'll need. Now, let's get to work."

Governor Mark Matthews of Nebraska cleared his throat, flipping open his folder. "Before we start into law and order, I'd like to remind the Pact that the Senate subcommittee will expect a complete framework before they meet on Monday. That means succession, electoral structure, and emergency powers: all finalized."

Governor Emma Harrison of Minnesota leaned forward. "We've agreed on most of it, but the succession clause still hangs open. If something happens to the President, we can't afford a leadership vacuum."

Johnson nodded. "Which is why I've asked you all here today. We've built something stable, but stability depends on planning for the worst while we still can. A war is being fought on multiple fronts and our infant nation needs steady leadership."

Governor Gene Kyle of North Dakota grinned faintly. "Are you saying you plan on disappearing on us, Jeremiah?"

The room chuckled, and Johnson smiled. "Not if I can help it. But the Great Plains Nation isn't about one man; it's about the Pact. If we're going to survive another century, we need a system stronger than whoever sits at this table."

Governor Kelly Lome of South Dakota adjusted her glasses. "Section 4, Clause B proposes that in the event of incapacitation, authority passes to the Chair of the Pact Governors until a special election can be held."

Bradford Davidson nodded. "Practical. Keeps the chain intact."

Carey leaned forward, his voice steady. "It's not enough. The Chair could change midterm; we'd be setting ourselves up for instability. We need a permanent line, at least three deep, with Senate oversight."

A few heads turned his way. Governor Roger Billings of Missouri raised an eyebrow. "Wyoming speaking like a lawyer now?"

"Experience from being a lawyer," Carey said simply. "You plan for storms when the sky's clear. We've seen what happens when nations don't."

Johnson smiled approvingly. "Noted. We'll amend it accordingly." He tapped his folder. "Now, on elections. The proposal moves us from appointment by Pact to direct national vote. That means opening registration across the states again and building trust in a system people still don't fully believe in."

Governor Lee spoke for the first time since his introduction. "Trust takes time, Mr. President. The Secession Wars didn't just split borders; they split faith. Folks in Montana remember what Washington ballots looked like before the fall. We'll need more than paper to prove we're different."

Johnson regarded him for a moment, then nodded slowly. "You're right. But we start small: fair, open, simple. The world will see we can hold an election without a gun to our heads."

The mood in the room softened again. Davison glanced toward the wide windows behind Johnson. Outside, the sun glinted off the snowy rooftops of Helena. He thought of Madeline's words at the Freedom Tree. *Maybe peace can be permanent.* For the first time in a long while, he let himself believe it.

Governor Harrison flipped a page. "There's one clause left unsettled: the Continuity Provision. If we're finalizing succession, we need to agree on who carries the torch if the entire civil chain is broken."

Johnson leaned back in his chair. "We can't assume the Senate and Pact will always be standing in a crisis. The Militia's already structured for national coordination. It's only practical that their commanding officer be next in line."

Governor Lome frowned. "You're talking about military authority over civilian government."

"Only in the event of total incapacitation," Carey said, scanning the text. "It's a last-resort safeguard. The General of the Great Plains Militia would act as temporary caretaker until elections can be held."

Harrison nodded slowly. "That'd keep order if, God forbid, the Pact or Senate fell in one blow."

Johnson smiled faintly. "That's the idea. We plan for the worst so the people can hope for the best."

Bradford Davidson added, "So the line stands: President, Speaker of the Senate, Pact President Pro Tempore, and finally the General of the Militia."

Johnson gave a satisfied nod. "Then it's settled."

The governors signed their initials beside each of the clauses. The paper was then gathered and filed, A final piece of paper was brought to Johnson, his pen scratched softly. After he held the folio up with the paper he had just signed. The room shook with applause.

14

CHARLOTTE, CAROLINA — 03.19.28

The wind still carried a bite from winter, but it didn't stop the hundreds of thousands of people from flooding into Charlotte. A sea of citizens from every corner of the Alliance packed shoulder to shoulder along the parade route on Tryon Street, smartphones and cameras lifted to capture the events. Livestreams on Vyber lit up across the social media sites while flags of the UAA rippled from every balcony. They were joined by the bright banners of the Great Plains Nation, the Bluegrass States Republic, and the New Republic of Texas. For the first time since the Secession Wars began, all four nations stood together in one place. The opening blast of a naval horn rolled between the towers of Uptown Charlotte, a sound deep and proud that echoed and reverberated down the alleys. The crowd erupted with cheers as the first vehicles rolled into view.

A line of UAA ceremonial Marines marched in perfect unison, dress whites gleaming and bayonets catching the morning sun. Children hoisted onto their parents' shoulders waved miniature flags and shouted their names as if greeting returning heroes. Behind them came the first dignitary motorcade: a shining Great Plains Nation escort with motorcycles flanking a sleek armored limousine draped with the bison emblem. Spectators pressed forward, hoping for a glimpse of President Jeremiah Johnson or General Samantha Johnson, though they wouldn't arrive until evening. The air filled with the scents of roasting nuts and sizzling meats as vendors along the sidewalks sold everything from UAA kettle corn to GPN-style smoked bison sandwiches. Above it all rose the rhythmic thrum of a dozen marching bands, each representing a different nation and determined to be louder than the last. Charlotte hadn't looked this alive since the Panthers went to the Super Bowl. The same **feverish energy** filled the intersections, though the jerseys had been replaced by the mismatched camos and dress grays of four different nations.

High above the street, glass towers glittered with massive projection displays counting down the hours: *THE CAROLINA ACCORDS—MARCH 20th—A NEW ERA BEGINS.* Floats from the BSR rolled forward next, rustic wooden platforms adorned with red and blue banners where fiddle players performed atop bales of hay as dancers in simple boots and wide smiles stepped in sync to the beat. Then came Texas. The New Republic's cavalry riders trotted proudly behind a polished black armored vehicle with the Texas star blazing bright across its doors.

President Gerald Martinez waved from the open roof, his hat held high and his laughter bright and unrestrained as the children on the Texan float chanted his name. "Martinez! Martinez!" he soaked in the affection, his face exploding with joy.

From a hotel balcony above the intersection, his teenage daughters, both in matching white sundresses despite the cold, leaned over the railing and shouted down, "We love you, Mr. President!"

Martinez responded with a grin. "Love y'all too!"

The crowd laughed, the moment pure and warm. For a heartbeat, the world felt whole again. Along the parade route, cameras flashed as reporters narrated breathlessly into microphones about reconciliation and the promise of tomorrow. The mood was infectious, hope blooming like spring flowers from concrete. Near the edge of Romare Bearden Park, Dr. Six Parks walked with a group of UAA medical staff. She held her coat tightly as she watched the parade pass, unable to suppress a smile. Private Seven Parks, dressed in his dress whites, elbowed her lightly. "Feels good, doesn't it? Like maybe the world's done exploding for a while."

Six nodded. "Feels peaceful," she said, almost surprised to hear the word aloud. A strange warmth fluttered in her chest: something like relief, but more like belief. Belief that everything up to this point had been worth it.

High overhead, drones hovered in neat formation, their synchronized lights blinking like fireflies and making patterns the crowd mistook for choreography. On the far side of the street, just beyond the cheering crowds, a man in a red Carolina ballcap lifted a camera to his face. Jack Ashby's finger hovered over the shutter as he scanned the parade through his lens. His expression was calm, casual, and disarming. Beside him, Phen adjusted his own camera bag, chewing a stick of gum like a bored tourist. "You get the shot?" Phen murmured.

Jack didn't lower the camera. "I'm just enjoying the show." He smiled.

More floats followed as the parade surged deeper into Uptown. A marching band from Houston thundered down Tryon, their brass section blazing through a triumphant rendition of *The Republic Forever.* Their uniforms shimmered in gold and crimson under the sun, plumes swaying in perfect unison. The crowd clapped along, some dancing in place, others wiping tears from their cheeks. Behind them came a Great Plains Nation agricultural float: a rolling meadow built atop a flatbed with waving wheat made from golden fabric and a mechanical bison that lumbered its head from side to side. Children squealed at the sight, reaching out as if they could touch it. Farmers in denim and leather vests tossed small sacks of sunflower seeds into the crowd, earning delighted cheers. Members of the Montana-Idaho Militia Honor Guard flew the Blue Buffalo Banner, walking in lockstep behind it.

The Bluegrass States Republic float appeared next, pulling Charlotte into a swirl of fiddle tunes and rhythmic guitar. Spectators roared as the red doors of a mock Kentucky barn swung open to reveal a giant illuminated map of the BSR, its twelve stars glowing bright and their jagged borders shining like a constellation. A sudden hush fell over the street as UAA Navy cadets marched in perfect blocks, their white caps cutting a sharp line through the river of color. As they reached the heart of Tryon, they shifted in flawless formation to spell out: *UAA—STRONGER TOGETHER.* The crowd erupted, phones continued waving high and voices rising in a wave of pride.

Behind them, a float emerged that dwarfed everything before it: a moving monument of polished steel and banners in white, gold, and blue. At its base, towering screens broadcasted live feeds from all across the nations showing the beach crowds on the Carolina coast, ranch towns in Texas, and snowy fields in the Great Plains. Atop the float, surrounded by an honor guard in immaculate dress uniforms, stood President Samuel Burris. He looked every inch the statesman, his posture straight and his hand raised in a measured wave. The roar that met him was deafening. "Burris! Burris! Burris!" Near the base of the float, a massive vertical monitor flickered to life.

Vice President Ulysses Mars appeared, streaming live from Raleigh, his image crisp against the backdrop of the Capitol dome. His voice boomed through the speakers, deep and steady. "Charlotte! Wish I could be there with you today, but someone has to keep the lights on in Raleigh." The crowd laughed. "Take care of our President for me," he continued, pointing playfully at the camera. "He does all right on his own, but he's less likely to get into trouble with y'all watching him." Even Burris laughed at that, shaking his head. Ulysses's tone softened. "But truly, today isn't about any of us on this stage. It's about you. It's about hope. And tomorrow, together, we write a new chapter."

The screen dimmed as the feed ended, leaving Burris to wave once more as the float rolled forward like a moving temple. From the sidewalk, Dr. Six Parks found herself smiling without meaning to. "Pretty good show," Seven murmured beside her.

Six smiled with pride. "Feels like the world's deciding to breathe again." Behind them, the GPN float's mechanical bison let out a low recorded bellow, making the children laugh. Up on the balcony where Jack Ashby stood, he lowered his camera for the first time in minutes. The crowd below glowed with joy. Flags shimmered and bands played. "Beautiful," he said softly.

Phen nudged him. "Tomorrow's going to be a long day. Might as well enjoy the peace while it lasts." Jack nodded. The last great float of the parade rolled past on a tide of cheers, the party continuing in the streets until the street light began to flicker. It was a day before everything would change.

Charlotte, Carolina — 03.19.28

The Magnolia Room in the Accords Convention Center glowed like dusk in a glass lantern. Soft amber lights haloed from chandeliers shaped like blooming flowers, casting warm reflections across polished marble floors that had been buffed to a mirror shine. Magnolias imported from Savannah, in the state of Jefferson, lined the perimeter, their heavy, floral scent drifting through the room like a physical presence. Servers moved efficiently between clusters of guests, offering trays of Carolina wines and golden, bite-sized cornbread rounds. On the large buffet sat hors d'oeuvres of fried pickles and cocktail sausages rolled in puff pastry; the rich, smoky aroma of Carolina-style barbecue intermingling with the sweet perfume of the blossoms.

On a small stage near the front, Patrick Healy and his band tuned their instruments. Patrick's battered, honey-colored acoustic showed a deep crack down the lacquer from years of street corners and bar stages, a contrast to the pristine tuxedoes in the front row. He warmed his vocals with his hit songs like *Pieces of Me*, his voice thickening the atmosphere before he strummed his first chord. Patrick tapped his mic gently, his smile infectious and his dimples creasing as his eyes lit up. "Welcome to my hometown," he said, his Southern lilt grounding the room. "Let's make tonight feel like a little piece of home before history books are drafted tomorrow."

A warm ripple of laughter followed, genuine and relaxed. He began to play, slow at first, the violin joining him with a soft, rising harmony that seemed to pull the tension out of the air. As Patrick sang, the first dignitaries began to enter. Jeremiah and Miranda Johnson, the President and First Lady of the Great Plains Nation, led the procession. The digital displays around the room flashed the Blue Buffalo patch, the symbol of the Great Plains, and their desperate defense of the homeland against the Confederation. Shortly after Jeremiah came his daughter, General Samantha Johnson. She was still in uniform, her posture rigid, accompanied by men in Montana-Idaho Militia dress. The room erupted in a roar that nearly drowned out the music, though Patrick played on, unfazed and smiling.

The applause softened as the next dignitaries arrived: President Kenneth Chandler of the Bluegrass States Republic and his wife, Marie. Chandler looked almost out of place in a formal suit, his rancher's broad shoulders and sun-browned face standing firm beneath the glittering chandeliers. Marie carried herself with a soft, practiced grace, her hand slipping into his arm as the crowd welcomed them with polite cheers. "Never thought I'd see the day," Chandler murmured to his wife as they stepped onto the marble. "Kentucky folks rubbing elbows with Texans in one room without anyone arguing about horses."

Marie smiled lightly, her eyes scanning the room. "Let's not tempt fate, Kenneth."

Behind them strode President Gerald Martinez of the New Republic of Texas. He was dressed in a charcoal suit but remained unmistakably Texan: bolo tie, hat in hand, and boots polished like obsidian. His entourage arrived with practiced swagger, but Martinez himself greeted guests with genuine warmth, clasping shoulders and shaking hands with the easy familiarity of a man who made friends everywhere he went. Just behind him, his daughters broke from their mother's side the moment they spotted Patrick Healy onstage. They squealed and darted toward the front with the reckless joy of teenagers who had no interest in political decorum. Patrick grinned mid-verse, giving a playful wink without missing a beat. Martinez watched them go with a father's amused resignation. "Where's the bar?" he asked loudly, drawing a wave of chuckles as he wove through the throng.

The applause stilled almost instantly when the doors at the far end of the Magnolia Room swung open. A burst of brass punched through the air as the Levine Middle College High School Hornets Marching Band stepped through the entrance in black-and-gold uniforms. Conversations died and glasses paused mid-air. Even Patrick stepped back from the mic, wiping sweat from his brow as he made room. The first clear notes of the UAA National Anthem, *Mountains Anchored to Sea*, rang out. Students sang the harmony, soft and reverent, as they marched deeper into the hall. Guests placed hands over their hearts; a few wiped tears. This was not just ceremony; it was a declaration of identity.

As the anthem peaked, President Samuel Burris entered. He walked through the parted crowd, shaking hands as he passed, his blue suit immaculate and the UAA crest pinned over his heart. His entourage followed, but Vice President Ulysses Mars was notably absent, his face instead displayed on a tall holographic monitor wheeled in by staff. Mars appeared seated at a desk in Raleigh, giving a solemn nod as the band finished. When the final note faded, Burris mounted the stage and shook Patrick's hand firmly. "Patrick," Burris said, lifting the mic, "you remind us what home sounds like."

Burris straightened, letting the weight of the moment settle. "Six years ago," he began, his voice heavy with memory, "we lived in a nation collapsing under its own contradictions. A virus swept through our country and set brother against father. We locked down a nation of three hundred million people and in the process, we destroyed businesses and broke families." He let the words hang in the quiet air. "But then, hope arrived. His name was Troy Thomason." He paused, letting the name settle. "Against the caution of Washington, he ran for President. And by golly," Burris's Carolina drawl deepened, "he won."

The room smiled with him, but the mood shifted as Burris continued. "But then, on January 15th, 2025, he was murdered while addressing us. Then came the invasion from a foreign power. The Capitol Massacre. The chaos that tore the nation apart." He lifted his eyes toward Jeremiah Johnson. "And then came the Great Plains. If it wasn't for your courage, Jeremiah, and the audacity of the Pact Governors, the Confederation would have rolled right across this continent."

The room broke into thunderous applause. "You stood when Washington would not," Burris said. "Jeremiah Johnson and his Pact built a shield in the wilderness. Because of their grit, the Confederation failed. The Carolina Accords are more than treaties. They are a promise that peace can be forged from war and that freedom can belong once again to the people. Not the bureaucrats, not the elites, not the swamp."

A wave of applause rose, steady and strong. Burris raised his hand gently. "Tomorrow, we stand with our brothers and sisters from Texas, the Bluegrass States, and the Great Plains. As allies. Peace is not a dream. It is our inheritance. And tomorrow, we sign its charter."

He stepped back as cheers filled the Magnolia Room, the band striking a soft reprise of the anthem. But amid the celebration, Twelve Parks and Vannah Martel moved quietly along the outer edges of the room as waitstaff in neat black uniforms, invisible and perfectly placed. Twelve carried a tray of wine glasses, her gaze flicking to the ventilation grates and security pillars, her mind cataloging every exit and every guard's posture. Vannah offered drinks to a group of senators, her Southern charm effortless and disarming. Neither looked at the other, but both were counting every second, every shift in the room's energy.

Vannah whispered without moving her lips: "Showtime's almost here."

Twelve smiled barely, but her eyes caught movement in the corner. A woman stood among the UAA Marines, a woman in a spotless ceremonial uniform, her chin lifted with quiet confidence. She looked exactly like herself. Her same eyes, the same jawline, the same red hair. Twelve's breath hitched, her hand trembling as she grabbed Vannah's arm, nearly upsetting the tray of wine.

"What?" Vannah whispered through her practiced, cheerful smile.

Twelve pointed toward the Marines, her voice a puff of a sound. Vannah followed her gesture and saw only a group of soldiers standing at attention. When Twelve looked back, the woman was gone, swallowed by the crowd. "Vannah," Twelve swallowed hard, her heart hammering against her ribs. "I think I'm seeing things."

Uptown Suites — 03.19.28

Jack and Twelve sat at the dim bar of the Uptown Suites, a hotel that was neither upscale nor a no-tell, but one of those forgettable mid-tier places found in a thousand cities. Normally it would feel unremarkable. Tonight it felt like the eye of a storm. Months of planning had led to this quiet moment: months of pretending to be people they weren't and smiling at the very men and women they were preparing to kill. But for these last few minutes, it was just the two of them. Twelve sat in her formal waitstaff uniform from the reception, the black-and-white fabric still sharply pressed though she had already loosened the collar. She sipped a martini, the rim of the glass marked with a faint crimson print from her lipstick. Her eyes never left Jack, drinking him in with a hunger that had grown sharper every week.

Jack sat beside her with his shoulders relaxed and his posture deceptively calm. He sipped a beer with one hand while his gaze stayed fixed on the TV bolted above the bar. The screen replayed highlights of the parade: the floats, the dignitaries, and President Burris's remarks. Everyone on that screen would be dead in less than twenty-four hours. Part of him wanted mission success, for his organization. But the other part had a gnawing regret swelling up inside. He didn't look at her once, but she never stopped looking at him. Her fiery red hair spilled over her shoulders, catching the soft bar light. She had unbuttoned the top of her blouse, it was a subtle, calculated move, hoping it would pull his attention away from the television. It didn't. Jack's jaw flexed, the faintest sign that he was calculating and bracing. He took another drink, eyes still on the flickering images of a world celebrating a peace he had been trained to destroy.

Twelve leaned in just enough to brush his shoulder with hers and whispered, "You can look at me, you know."

He blinked but didn't turn. She heard Vannah giggling in the lobby, that bright sound Vannah could turn on like a switch, followed by Phen cracking some joke that made her laugh even harder as they passed by the bar. Twelve's stomach tightened. She wished Jack talked to her like that. She wished he flirted or let himself be light. But Jack wasn't Phen. He was their leader for a reason. Jack was intentional, strong, and controlled. She admired that about him, but tonight the admiration twisted into something rawer. She was jealous and desperate for him to see her the way Phen saw Vannah. She knew Jack loved her; he just showed it colder and quieter, hidden behind walls she couldn't always climb. Tonight those walls felt impossibly high.

Twelve's fingers tightened around the stem of her glass. She stared at Jack's profile: the line of his jaw and the focus in his eyes that never wavered from the television. The parade replayed in bright, triumphant colors while Burris's speech thundered through the speakers. Jack didn't blink. Something inside her cracked.

"Jack," she said quietly.

He didn't answer. Her heart kicked with the jealousy and the longing of months spent playing roles and hiding feelings. She set her glass down a little too hard. "Jack."

Nothing. So she did something she knew she probably shouldn't. She slid off her stool, stepped directly between him and the television, and in one impulsive motion swung her leg over his lap to sit facing him. Right there in the middle of the bar, her hands rested on his shoulders. Her breath trembled. Her eyes searched his. "Look at me," she whispered.

For the first time all night, Jack did. His beer hovered halfway to his lips. His expression softened, the steel in him giving way to something unguarded and pained. "Twelve..." His voice was low, almost apologetic.

She waited, refusing to move. He finally placed his beer down. His hands rose, slow and careful, until they rested on her hips. He wasn't being possessive. He was simply grounding her. "I see you," he said.

Her breath hitched. "And I'm sorry," he continued. "I should've told you that sooner."

The walls she had been crashing against shifted just enough for her to slip through. His thumb brushed her waist and her forehead touched his. The noise of the hotel bar faded into nothing. Without another word, Jack stood and lifted her effortlessly. Her legs instinctively tightened around him as she buried her face in his shoulder. The bartenders didn't look twice. Phen and Vannah noticed from across the lobby, Phen raising his brows while Vannah smirked with approval, but they didn't intervene. Jack carried Twelve toward the elevator with a certainty that made her feel weightless. She felt protected in his arms.

When the doors slid open, he stepped inside with her arms still locked around him. The soft light cast warm shadows across them as the doors whispered closed. Neither spoke. His forehead pressed to hers while her fingers threaded into the fabric of his collar. For the first time all night, they breathed in sync. The elevator chimed at their floor. Jack backed into the hall with her still held in his arms, navigating the quiet corridor until they reached their room. He shifted her slightly, just enough to free one hand to push the keycard into the lock. A soft click. He nudged the door open with his shoulder. Their silhouettes slipped inside, no longer pretending. The door eased shut behind them.

Phen watched the elevator doors slid shut behind Jack and Twelve, the soft *metallic hum* echoed through the hall like the last note of a song. Vannah watched the numbers above the door blink upward, slow and steady, then she smirked. "Finally," she murmured, arms folding under her chest.

Phen stood beside her, loosening his tie with one hand while the other shoved casually into his pocket. "Guy held out longer than I thought."

Vannah tilted her head. "Mm. Must run in your little brotherhood."

Phen huffed a laugh, a genuine kind that only ever slipped out around her when his defenses were down. "You implying I held out?"

"You did," she said, stepping into his space just enough to make his pulse give itself away. "For maybe three seconds." Her finger traced the line where his collar met his throat, slow and familiar. Phen caught her wrist gently, bringing her hand to his lips. "You broke first," he murmured against her knuckles.

Vannah shrugged one shoulder, brushing her body lightly against his. "I make the rules. I don't follow them."

"Which is exactly why I like you," Phen said, sliding his arm around her waist. He wasn't tentative. He was claiming her in the way lovers do when they know they are allowed. She rested her hands on his chest, feeling the steady rise and fall of his breath. For a moment there was nothing that mattered outside of the two of them. Just a couple, standing in a quiet corner of the lobby where the eyes that watched them didn't matter.

"You okay?" he asked, lowering his forehead to hers.

Vannah breathed softly, eyes half-closed. "As okay as anyone on the eve of blowing up the world."

Phen gave a small nod, his hand tightening at her waist. She opened her eyes again, the gleam in them shifting from teasing to hungry. "Jack finally let down his defenses and showed Twelve he cared... in public," she let out a soft, breathy laugh. "That's something."

"Feels like the last loose end finally tied up," Phen murmured.

Vannah's thumb stroked his jawline, her fingers lightly sliding across his scruff. "Then maybe we deserve a little something too."

"Oh?" Phen raised a brow, amused. "Planning something?"

"Planning?" she echoed, leaning in just enough that her breath warmed his ear. "No, sweetheart." She took his tie between two fingers and tugged him an inch forward. "Finishing," she whispered. "Yes."

Phen exhaled, a low chuff escaping his chest as the tension of the lobby finally began to fray. He didn't have to reach far for her hand; their fingers interlaced with the quiet, practiced certainty of two people who had belonged to each other through a dozen different lives and missions. They walked toward the guest elevators with no need for the frantic pace of the young or the panicked stealth of the guilty. They were simply two lovers moving through a familiar ritual, pretending for a few precious minutes that the sun wouldn't rise on the end of the world.

At the elevator, the doors slid open in a hush. Vannah stepped in first, looking over her shoulder with a half-smile that hit him like gravity. "Come on," she said softly. "Walk me upstairs."

He followed. Just before the doors closed, she brushed her lips to his cheek, a slow and lingering kiss that held a promise neither dared speak aloud. The elevator sealed them in, the glow of soft yellow light warming their silhouettes as they rose. Tonight, they had each other. Tomorrow, Charlotte would burn.

Mountain Home Air Base — 03.19.28

The high desert night was cold and moonlit, the kind of chill that carried sound for miles. The last flight of the evening, three F-15SGs from the Singaporean contingent, touched down in smooth succession. Engines roared as they rolled along the runway before taxiing toward the hangars. Governor Bradford Davidson stood beside his son near the tarmac, hands deep in the pockets of his heavy coat. The base lights reflected off the pavement in long white streaks, catching the faint smile on his weathered face. "Smooth landing," he said, nudging his son's arm.

Captain Nathan Davidson grinned as he tugged off his flight gloves. "These birds practically land themselves, Dad. The instructors back at the Resettlement camps used to say the air in Idaho was too thin for real flying, but I think they just missed the humidity."

Bradford snorted. "Thin air or not, you fly 'em like you were born in the cockpit. Try telling the mechanics they land themselves and see if you get a flight tomorrow."

A Singaporean pilot hopped down from the wing of the lead jet, waving a gloved hand at them as he headed for the debriefing room. "He's a natural, Governor! Best student we ever pulled out of the Militia's integrated wing!"

Bradford raised a hand in return, his chest tightening with a familiar pride. He had fought tooth and nail to ensure those Singaporean refugees became more than just guests; he wanted them to be permanent citizens. He had personally overseen the transition from the temporary resettlement centers to the front lines, ensuring every pilot who crossed the Pacific found a home and a GPN passport. He had never regretted the political capital it cost him to turn refugees into brothers-in-arms.

"Governor!" a sergeant called from the hangar doors. "The Commander is ready for the strategy review whenever you are."

Bradford raised a hand. "Tell him I'm coming. Just needed a minute with my boy."

Nathan smiled faintly. "Mom says you're turning soft."

Bradford shook his head. "She's a liar." Then, quieter, he added, "Proud of you."

Nathan opened his mouth to answer when a strange vibration began to tremble through the air. Bradford's expression hardened. "You feel that?" Nathan did. Pilots turned and mechanics paused mid-step. The entire base seemed to shift as if the air pressure had dropped suddenly. Then the sirens erupted. Klaxons wailed and flashing lights swirled.

A voice erupted from the PA system: "INCOMING THREAT. INCOMING THREAT. SEEK COVER IMMEDIATELY."

The base exploded into motion. "Dad, inside, now!" Nathan grabbed his arm, but Bradford was already moving. "Sergeant!" he shouted to a security officer sprinting toward them. "Which direction?"

"Southwest radar confirms multiple inbound drones. Confederation signatures!" The sergeant's voice shook. Nathan froze. "That's impossible. They're still pinned in Oregon."

"No," Bradford said grimly, "they're not."

In the sky, tiny shapes glinted against the stars: silent, fast, and growing larger by the second. The first missile hit the far end of the runway. The runway buckled under the explosion, cement and asphalt chunks peppering nearby buildings. The shockwave slammed into Bradford and his son, throwing them backward onto the concrete. Nathan scrambled up, his ears ringing. "Dad! Dad, get up!"

Bradford pushed himself to one knee, coughing. More impacts shook the ground as hangars blew apart in violent bursts and jets ignited like torches. Singaporean pilots ran toward the nearest bunker, shouting orders in two languages. Another drone screamed overhead. Nathan grabbed his father by the shoulders. "We have to move!"

Bradford staggered to his feet, but his gaze had shifted toward the Singaporean barracks, already engulfed in flames. "I need to get command on the line," he said. "They need to know this wasn't a border skirmish. This was planned. This was—"

A second missile struck twenty yards away. The night turned white with a deep, world-breaking roar erupting with it. Then nothing. The blast flung bodies like paper. Shrapnel tore through the air in a hail of steel. The fireball swallowed the hangar, the crew bay, and the line of grounded F-15SGs. Governor Bradford Davidson disappeared in the inferno.

Silence followed, broken only by the distant crackle of burning metal and the soft, falling hiss of settling dust. A private stumbled from behind a concrete barrier, blood down his cheek, clutching a radio pressed to his ear. "This is Mountain Home," he choked, coughing through smoke. "We were hit. We need emergency response. Multiple casualties. Governor Davidson is—" His voice broke. "We lost the Governor."

Static. Screaming. Sirens. "Repeat: Governor Davidson is down. Mountain Home is compromised."

Lewiston Militia Command — 11:05 PM MST

Red warnings cascaded across the command center's central wall. Colonel Sarah Wexler stood rigid, her knuckles white as she gripped the edge of the operations holotable. "Confirm it," she said quietly.

A junior officer swallowed hard. "Mountain Home is completely dark. All telemetry is lost. No survivors are confirmed. And," he hesitated, the weight of the report clearly shaking him.

"Say it," Wexler ordered.

"Governor Bradford Davidson's beacon was extinguished at 22:14."

Silence swallowed the room. Wexler looked at the flickering red icons, her breath hitching before she whispered, "God help us."

Another officer shouted from a nearby station. "Confederation signatures detected. Possible path of attack came from Maogon and Leninia airspace. This was coordinated."

Wexler slammed her hand down on the table, the sound echoing through the hushed room. "Send an emergency alert to every state in the Pact. Mobilize all border units. Notify Bozeman Air Command because they will need to take operational control immediately." She looked up at the comms officer, her expression hardening into a mask of cold command. "And send a secure burst to Helena."

Bozeman Air Command — 11:19 PM MST

The command floor buzzed with muted tension as screens flickered and officers circled the operations tables. The hum of cooling fans filled the cold air. Lieutenant Rourke rushed into the central pit clutching a tablet. "Colonel! Emergency transmission from Lewiston. Mountain Home is gone."

The Colonel took the tablet and read the red-priority burst. His face drained of color. "Casualties?"

Rourke swallowed hard. "They haven't found anything. The Confederation used a drone swarm. Governor Davidson is confirmed dead." The Colonel bowed his head for a brief moment before snapping upright. "Activate Protocol Four. Get Helena on a private line."

"Yes, sir." Rourke hurried to the comms station, his fingers flying as encrypted packets shot across the network.

"Helena is responding," the operator announced. "Patching through now."

Rourke took a breath and leaned into the mic. "This is Bozeman Air Command. We have a catastrophic loss at Mountain Home. Governor Bradford Davidson is KIA. Repeating: Governor Davidson is confirmed KIA."

Static crackled before a frantic voice came through the speakers. "This is Governor Kelly Lome. What happened?"

Rourke steadied himself. "The Confederation attacked unprovoked, ma'am. A drone swarm originating from Maogon territory. Mountain Home suffered total destruction. Loss of aircraft, personnel, and Governor Davidson."

Silence hung for a heartbeat. Then Lome exhaled shakily. "Dear God. We trusted the cease-fires."

"Ma'am, Lewiston recommends immediate Pact mobilization. We also advise activating the Continuity Protocol for the Pact Governors until a replacement for Idaho can be appointed."

"You will have it," Lome said, her voice tightening into a command tone. "Helena will convene an emergency session. But what about the President? Does Jeremiah know?"

Rourke's jaw clenched. "Not yet. But he needs to."

"No," Lome said quickly. "Not over comms. Send the message through General Johnson. She is the only one he will listen to."

Rourke hesitated. "Ma'am, General Johnson is in Charlotte."

"Then get her home," Lome said. "Now. Before anyone realizes what this attack really means."

Rourke signaled the comms officer, who began drafting the highest-priority military burst. "We will send the order immediately. We will divert a transport from Lewiston to Charlotte."

"Good. And Lieutenant?"

"Yes, ma'am?"

"When you reach her, tell her the Pact just lost its Pro Tempore."

Rourke bowed his head. "Understood." The line went dead.

The Colonel turned to Rourke. "Get that message out. General Johnson leaves before sunrise." Rourke moved fast, his heart hammering against his ribs. Because they all felt it: whatever hit Mountain Home was only the beginning.

Charlotte, Carolina — 12:41 PM EST

The secure satellite phone on Samantha Johnson's nightstand shrilled into the darkness. She shot upright with her heart slamming and her breath uneven. For one wild moment she expected to see Montana sunlight through the curtains, but the city lights of Charlotte glowed instead, fractured through the tall glass window. She grabbed the phone. "Johnson."

Static crackled before a voice came through. "General Johnson, this is Lieutenant Rourke, Bozeman Air Command." His voice was too tight and too fast.

Samantha's blood went cold. "I'm awake," she said, swinging her legs over the side of the bed and planting her feet on the carpet. "Report."

Rourke exhaled sharply. She could hear the chaos behind him: alarms, overlapping voices, and boots hammering across tile floors. "General, Mountain Home Air Base has been hit."

Samantha froze. "Extent of damage?"

A suffocating pause followed. "Total loss, ma'am."

The world narrowed. Samantha stood and paced to the window, her fingers whitening around the phone. "How many casualties?"

"We don't have a count. The Confederation deployed a drone swarm. The base is gone. Air wings, personnel, civilians... everything."

Samantha pressed her free hand to the glass, staring down at the vibrant night city that suddenly felt impossibly far away.

"Ma'am, Governor Davidson was there visiting his son." Rourke's breath stuttered.

"What happened to Bradford?" she asked quietly.

"KIA, General."

For a moment, Samantha didn't speak. The city lights blurred as her jaw tightened. Bradford Davidson wasn't just a Pact Governor; he was Jeremiah's friend, a father, and the President Pro Tempore of the Pact. And now he was gone. "What is Helena doing?" she forced out.

"Governor Lome has called an emergency session," Rourke said. "Continuity Protocol is being activated. Bozeman, Lewiston, and Minot are scrambling air readiness. We're mobilizing the Militia statewide."

Samantha straightened as her soldier instincts overtook the shock. "What do you need from me?"

"Immediate return to Montana. Governor Lome's order."

Samantha closed her eyes briefly. She had known peace was an illusion. "What about the President? Has my father been notified?"

"No, ma'am. Governor Lome said to contact you first. She wants you back on Montana soil before he hears a word because she thinks he will refuse to leave Charlotte."

Samantha exhaled a tight breath. He would refuse. He would chain himself to the Accords table before letting the Confederation dictate his presence.

"General," Rourke continued, "a transport from Lewiston is wheels up in ninety minutes. It will land at Charlotte Air Command and take you straight home."

Samantha stared out at the skyline, at the banners and the celebrations still echoing faintly from Uptown. Tomorrow was supposed to be peace. It was supposed to be a new world. "Lieutenant," she said, snapping her voice into steel. "I'm on my way."

She lowered the phone slowly. Behind her, Miranda and Jeremiah stirred in the adjoining suite, unaware of the nightmare. Samantha didn't call them yet. Instead, she opened her closet, pulled on her uniform jacket, and tightened the belt and stood rigid, catching her reflection in the mirror she could see her tears but pushed them back. She cursed under her breath and ran to the door between the suites. "Mom! Dad! Wake up!"

Jeremiah and Miranda stepped into the connecting room, both half-dressed and startled. Jeremiah's short beard was mussed, but his expression sharpened instantly at the sight of Samantha in uniform. "Sam?" Miranda breathed. "What's wrong?"

Samantha swallowed hard. "Mountain Home. It is gone."

Miranda's hand flew to her mouth. Jeremiah blinked, the hardness of his face softened for a moment. Slowly he took a half step toward her, his eyes searching her face in disbelief. "Casualties?" he asked.

"Everyone," Samantha said quietly. "A drone swarm. It was fast. The base is ashes, Dad." Jeremiah staggered back into the table and gripped its edge. Miranda caught his arm to steady him. He said nothing, just stared into the carpet with his jaw trembling. Samantha took a breath. "Dad, Governor Davidson was there. He didn't make it."

Miranda whispered, "Oh, no," as Jeremiah shut his eyes so tightly the skin pinched white. Bradford had been his friend, his ally, and his sanity on more days than he would ever admit. When he finally looked up, his voice was the voice of a President again. "What does Helena need?"

"They've activated Continuity. They're mobilizing the Militia. They want me back in Montana immediately."

Jeremiah nodded once, a fire rising behind his eyes. "No. I'm not leaving Charlotte. Not now. Not when we are hours from signing the Accords. If I run, the Confederation wins twice."

"Dad—"

"Samantha," he said firmly, stepping closer and gripping her shoulders. "The Great Plains needs someone there who can command the Militia if this escalates. That is you. Not me."

Miranda touched her husband's arm. "Jeremiah, she is right. We don't know what is coming."

"I do know what is coming," he growled. "Chaos. Panic. Fear. And if I leave this city before the Accords, the peace we've fought for will tear itself apart by morning." He exhaled sharply. "But you go. You and your mother both. I want you on Montana soil before the next communique comes in."

Miranda blinked, pulling her heavy cardigan tighter over her nightgown. Her hair was a mess of sleep-tangled waves, and her feet were bare against the cold suite floor. "Me? Why?"

"Because if this is meant to tear the Accords apart, I want you as far from the fallout as possible." Jeremiah's voice was steady, but his hands were trembling as he reached for her. He hadn't even found his shoes yet; he stood in his socks and undershirt, his breathing heavy in the quiet room. "Big Sky is fortified. It's home. I need to know you're behind those walls, Miranda. I can't think straight if I'm worried about you being caught in a riot here."

He turned fully to her, the practiced hardness of a President finally cracking. In the dim amber light, he looked older—tired and human. "I need to know at least one part of my world is safe."

Miranda's eyes filled, but she didn't let the tears fall. She knew that look. It was the one he wore before every major battle of the Secession. "Jeremiah," she started, her voice a small, warning plea.

He didn't let her finish. He pulled her in, kissing her with a quiet, desperate depth. His hands didn't grip her with strength; they shook slightly at her waist, as if he were trying to memorize the shape of her through the fabric. When he pulled back, he rested his forehead against hers, their shared breath the only sound in the room.

"I'll be right behind you," he whispered, a promise made to himself as much as to her. "As soon as the ink is dry on that paper, I'm heading to the airfield. I won't even stay for the dinner."

Miranda cupped his cheek, her thumb tracing the stubble on his jaw. "You had better be. I'm not keeping dinner warm for three days again, Jeremiah. You come home."

"I'll be there," he promised.

Samantha looked away, her gaze fixed on the floor. She was the only one fully dressed, her uniform jacket buttoned slightly crooked in her haste, her boots still unlaced at the top. She only looked back when she felt her father's heavy hand on her shoulder. He pulled her into an embrace that smelled of the starch of his discarded suit and the familiar, grounding scent of her childhood. It wasn't the hug of a President to a General; it was a father trying to anchor his daughter before another battle, after he thought they were over.

"You get home," he said into her hair, his voice thick. "Keep Montana steady. Keep the Pact steady. If I don't call you by noon tomorrow, you take operational command of the Militia. You hear me?"

She squeezed him back, her ribs aching against his chest. "I'll see you at the house after the signing, Dad," she said, her voice sharp with a forced, brittle confidence. "Don't make me come back here and drag you home."

Jeremiah managed a small, tired smile that didn't reach his eyes. "Go."

Miranda grabbed a coat from the chair, not even bothering to find her shoes, just stepping into a pair of travel flats. Samantha slung her bag over her shoulder, the nylon strap digging into her neck.

"I love you, Daddy," Samantha said from the threshold, the old childhood name slipping out in the rush.

Jeremiah stood in the frame of the doorway, alone in his undershirt, his silhouette cast long against the warm light of the suite. He didn't wave. He just watched them walk down the long, carpeted hallway until the elevator doors hissed shut, severing the connection. He stood there for a long time afterward, staring at the empty hall, before he turned back to the room.

15

JEREMIAH HADN'T SLEPT SINCE Miranda and Samantha left. The suite felt too large now, a hollow shell that magnified every tick of the wall clock that now showed 6:17 AM. The couches sat untouched and the curtains remained open from when Samantha had thrown them aside, leaving the skyline of Charlotte to glow faintly beyond the glass. He sat alone at the small desk with his shoulders hunched, the leather chair creaking whenever he shifted his weight. The mini-bar across the room stood open. One of the tiny Jack Daniels bottles sat empty beside his hand while another remained half-finished. He didn't want to get drunk; he knew he couldn't afford that, but he needed something to take the edge off the dread crawling up his spine.

The smell of whiskey hung in the air, mixing with the faint scent of Miranda's perfume still clinging to the pillows in the adjoining room. He stared at the painting on the wall: a pair of red cardinals perched on a dogwood branch. They looked bright, peaceful, and innocent. He hated it. His bloodshot eyes stung as he leaned back and rubbed the bridge of his nose. "Samantha should never have been here," he murmured to the empty room.

"Miranda shouldn't have been here. I should have sent them home days ago."

He tipped the bottle to his lips and took another controlled sip. Outside, the city slept as if the world wasn't sharpening its knives again. He turned the empty bottle in his hand, rolling the cool glass between his fingers. "Bradford," he whispered. "God, Brad." His throat tightened. The whiskey burned going down, but it wasn't the drink making his eyes water. He set the bottle down and dragged a hand over his face. The cardinals stared back at him, perched calmly in a world untouched by war. He wished he could step into that peaceful little painting and stay there forever.

But dawn was coming. The Accords were coming. And the Confederation had one more night to ruin everything. The phone rang. Jeremiah flinched at the sharp sound, then reached for it with a slow, heavy motion. He kept spinning the little bottle between his fingertips as he lifted the receiver to his ear. "Hello?" The word came out rough and hoarse, as if scraped from the bottom of his lungs.

"Daddy?" Samantha's voice, steady but layered with fatigue, cut through the quiet. "Mom is home at the ranch. I stationed one of our Special Forces unit there until we understand the situation. I just arrived in Bozeman." She sighed with visible worry. "Have you slept?"

Jeremiah exhaled through his nose, staring again at the painting of the cardinals. She already knew the answer. "No," he said softly.

Samantha's voice warmed, showing her mother's tenderness mixed with her father's steel. "You need to try," she said. "Just an hour. Even half. You can't walk into the signing running on fumes."

Jeremiah swallowed against his tight throat. "I'll be fine."

"Dad." Her tone sharpened into something military. "This could escalate. I need you sharp. Promise me you'll rest."

He closed his eyes. The bottle stilled in his hand. "I promise I'll try," he said. It wasn't a lie, but it wasn't the truth either.

Samantha seemed to hear his hesitation. "We'll handle Montana. Lewiston is running point until I take over. The Pact is stabilizing. You don't have to carry everything tonight."

Jeremiah let out a long breath, leaning back until the chair creaked. "I'm proud of you, Sammy," he murmured. "You know that, right?"

There was a pause on the other end, just long enough for Jeremiah to imagine her grounding herself against the weight she now had to shoulder. "I know," she said quietly. "And I'm proud of you too."

Another silence followed, the kind only parents and grown children who have survived wars together can share. Then Samantha's tone tightened again. "I'll call you as soon as the emergency session ends. Get some rest, Dad. Please."

Jeremiah nodded, though she couldn't see it. "All right," he said. "Give your mother a kiss for me."

"I will."

The line clicked dead. Jeremiah lowered the phone, staring at it for a long moment before setting it down beside the empty bottle. His reflection in the black television screen looked older than he remembered. Outside, the first hint of dawn grayed the sky. Peace, the thing the world believed was inevitable, felt like it was hanging by a thread. He stood slowly, the room tilting from exhaustion, and moved toward the bed. He knew he had to try to sleep, but the moment he lay down, the silence was replaced by the ghosts of his own making. Every fear and every mounting cost returned, a ledger of names and faces forcing him to account for the decisions that had led them all to this edge.

Was he doing the right thing? Were the Accords truly the history he prayed they would be?

He sank into the mattress and reached instinctively for Miranda's pillow. The soft floral scent filled his lungs like a quiet mercy, and his composure finally broke. Jeremiah pressed the pillow to his face, trying to breathe steadily, but the dam cracked. Silent sobs shook through him, the muffled, raw cry of a husband who had to stay strong while everything he loved slipped out of reach. Alone in the dim suite, Jeremiah Johnson, the leader of the Great Plains Nation, cried into the pillow his wife had slept on only hours before. For the first time since his nation was born, he felt completely alone.

The floral scent of the pillow had been a quiet mercy, but it couldn't stop the sun from climbing.

Jeremiah had spent the last hour drifting in and out of a feverish, heavy half-sleep, his mind cycling through the faces of the men he'd lost. Every time he closed his eyes, he saw the red cardinals from the painting, their feathers stained a darker, wetter crimson. Out of habit, he picked his Rolex up from the nightstand and saw the time hit 7:49 AM just as he stepped out of the bathroom.

Jeremiah stood shirtless in front of the mirror, his tie hanging loose around his neck and his eyes red from the night without sleep. The shower steamed behind him, untouched. He tried to force himself through the morning routine, but each motion felt like wading through wet cement. He flicked on the television to drown out the silence.

Good Morning Carolina!

The cheerful jingle clashed horribly with the mood in the room. It felt obscene, a burst of manufactured brightness breaking into his grief. A polished anchorwoman appeared on-screen, her expression grave beneath the soft studio lights.

"We are beginning this morning with breaking overnight news. Reports have come in of a large-scale attack on Great Plains Nation military assets in Idaho..."

Jeremiah stopped tightening his tie. His breath caught in his throat.

"...and moments ago, President Samuel Burris addressed the nation."

The screen cut to a recording of a live feed. Samuel Burris sat in a modest studio chair with no pomp or polish. His face was drawn from a sleepless night of his own; he was still in yesterday's suit with the tie loosened and eyes shadowed. He looked like a man carrying the weight of an entire continent. Jeremiah swallowed hard as Burris began speaking, his voice low but controlled.

"Our friends in the Great Plains Nation suffered a devastating attack last night. Mountain Home Air Base has been destroyed. Governor Bradford Davidson has been confirmed among the casualties."

Jeremiah gripped the edge of the bathroom counter until his knuckles turned white.

Burris paused, collecting himself. "I spoke with members of the Pact of Governors early this morning. President Johnson is still assessing the situation from Charlotte, and General Samantha Johnson is already coordinating the response from Montana." He leaned forward, the cameras catching a sharp glint in his eyes. "Let me be clear. The attack on the Great Plains Nation is an attack on all of us. On peace. On unity. On the future we are trying to build here."

The studio fell silent. Even the hosts seemed unsure how to move.

Burris continued, "As of this morning, I have authorized the UAA Marine Air Service to deploy support wings to Montana and Idaho. We stand with the Great Plains. We stand with President Johnson."

Jeremiah's jaw tightened as pride and grief collided. Then Burris lifted his chin, his tone sharpening. "This attack will not derail the Carolina Accords. It will not divide the nations standing together today. It will not force us back into fear."

The anchor cut in softly. "Mr. President, are you saying the signing will proceed as scheduled?"

Burris nodded once. "Yes. We will not let the Confederation or the Consortium dictate our future. The Accords will be signed. I will be damned if I let foreign terrorists change my mind!"

Jeremiah exhaled slowly, lowering himself onto the edge of the bed. For the first time since the call from Bozeman, he felt the faintest flicker of steadiness; he realized that he wasn't carrying the fate of his home alone. On the screen, Burris spoke one last sentence. "To President Johnson, to the Great Plains Nation, and to the families grieving this morning, we stand with you. And we will not bend."

Jeremiah muted the TV and closed his eyes, letting the sudden silence of the suite press against his eardrums. He wasn't alone; not today and not in this fight. The knowledge that Burris was standing in the gap gave him a flicker of steadiness, but it didn't dull the ache in his chest or the phantom weight of Bradford's ghost sitting in the corner of the room. In just a few hours, he would have to stand on that platform in front of the world and act like he wasn't breaking. He could put on a strong face; he has worn that most of his life. Taking a deep breath he grabbed his jacket, looking around he nodded gently, then walked out the door.

Uptown Suites — 03.20.28 — 8:00 AM EST

Jack lay bare-chested beneath the soft morning light while Twelve curled against him, trying to anchor herself to something warm before the world swallowed them again. The sun pushed through the curtains in bright stripes, catching Jack directly in the eyes. He blinked against the glare, then kissed the top of Twelve's head as she stirred.

"What time is it?" she mumbled into his chest, her voice thick with sleep.

"Eight," Jack murmured. "We have to get up. Big day."

She made a soft sound—half annoyance, half contentment—and tucked her face deeper against him. He kissed her again, slower this time. In private, he was warm, affectionate, even tender. Only Twelve ever saw it. Only she ever would. But outside these four walls, he would be steel again. He reached for the remote on the nightstand, clicking on the small television across from the bed.

Good Morning Charlotte!

The bright jingle nearly made Twelve wince.

"...and we return now to President Samuel Burris, who moments ago addressed the developing situation in the Great Plains Nation."

Jack's expression hardened. The camera cut to a recording of Burris in the studio, concluding the final moments of his morning address. "Let me be clear. The attack on the Great Plains Nation is an attack on all of us. On peace. On unity. On the future we are trying to build here." Burris said, his voice thick with resolve. "As of this morning, I have authorized the UAA Marine Air Service to deploy support wings to Montana and Idaho. We stand with the Great Plains. We stand with President Johnson."

The host leaned in. "Mr. President, are you saying the signing will proceed as scheduled?"

Burris nodded once. "Yes. We will not let the Confederation or the Consortium dictate our future. The Accords will be signed. I will be damned if I let foreign terrorists change my mind!"

Jack clicked the volume down sharply. Twelve lifted her head slightly, studying his face. She noticed his jaw tightening and the anger simmering right under the surface. "You okay?" she asked softly.

Jack didn't answer immediately. He swung his legs off the bed and sat forward with his elbows on his knees, staring at the muted TV as the program shifted to parade highlights. Then he growled, "the Confederation should have been wiped out a year ago."

Twelve blinked. "Jack."

"They were our project," he snapped, though his voice never rose above a quiet rasp. "Our smokescreen to gain more power in the US and now they're running wild like rabid dogs." He stood and paced once to the window. "The Consortium funded their early push. Fed their propaganda while opening the borders to weaken patriotic resolve. Hell, we even stoked the Russo-Ukrainian war to lower the possible defense of the homeland." He raked a hand through his hair. "And somehow the idiots upstairs still let them keep their toys."

Twelve sat up in the sheets, watching him and knowing better than to interrupt.

Jack's fists clenched. "We built the damn fire, and now we're acting shocked that it is burning out of control. The Confederation is a nuisance; a distraction that we created. They were never the problem. This," he jabbed a finger toward the TV, toward the replay of Burris shaking hands with parade-goers, "this is the problem."

Twelve pulled the sheet around her chest, her brow tightening. "The Accords?"

Jack laughed once, a humorless, dark sound. "The Accords don't bring peace. They create power. They give Burris, Jeremiah, Chandler, Martinez, and everyone down here, a single shared purpose. To create a hegemony against the Chairman!" He stepped closer to the TV, lowering his voice to a razor-thin whisper. "And if they sign it, the Consortium loses control of the board."

Twelve watched his reflection in the glass, the morning sunlight crowning him in a pale halo that made the fury in his eyes even sharper. "So they sent us," she murmured.

Jack nodded. "The Confederation was supposed to be a tool, but the brass let it get away from them. Now they're terrified of the Accords, and we're the only 'fix' they have left." He crossed back to the bed and sat beside her, calmer now but no less lethal. "If the Accords go through, every sovereign nation becomes a partner. A bloc. A singular voice. They rebuild the old alliance system under different colors. And once that happens? The Consortium stops being a shadow and starts being obsolete."

Twelve curled a hand around his forearm. "And when we light the fuse today, they get their chaos back."

Jack finally looked at her, and something dangerous and intimate flashed in his eyes. "Exactly," he whispered. He brushed a loose strand of red hair behind her ear. "The Confederation was a tool. A means to destabilize. But the Accords undo everything. They repair what we spent years breaking."

Twelve watched him for a long heartbeat before rising onto her knees behind him. "Jack," she whispered. He didn't turn, not at first. She reached out and slid her arms around his waist from behind, her cheek pressing between his shoulder blades. "You're thinking like a soldier. Like a Commander."

He closed his eyes.

"And I love that about you," she continued. "But for just a little longer, I need you to be mine."

He exhaled shakily. "Twelve," he warned, but the warning had no heat.

She tightened her arms around him, then gently pulled him backward toward the bed. "Come back to me. Just for a little while."

Jack turned to her then, and the walls inside him shifted. Her hair fell messily around her face, sunlight catching the red in it like fire. Her eyes weren't seductive so much as pleading. For something real before the world ended. He lifted a hand to her cheek. "You're trouble," he murmured.

She smiled, slow and tender. "Always."

Jack kissed her. It wasn't the careful or restrained kind; it was urgent, the kind of kiss given when the world is counting down and there is no promise of another. Twelve let the sheet fall as she pulled him with her, both of them sinking back into the warm, unmade bed. Her fingers threaded into his hair as his hands slid to her waist, drawing her close until their foreheads met.

The city hummed outside their window. History marched toward the Convention Center. But here, in the quiet, sunlit room, time slowed. Jack whispered something against her mouth that only she would ever hear. She answered with a soft breath, pulling him closer.

The curtains shifted as the heater started up. For a few stolen minutes, before the violence and the shattering of the Accords, they disappeared into each other. When the world came for them again, it would find them changed. But for now, they made love like it was their last morning alive.

Uptown Suites Breakfast Room — 03.20.28 — 8:52 EST

The Uptown Suites breakfast room smelled of syrup, cheap coffee, and the faint citrus of 'from concentrate' orange juice. It was the kind of place found in a thousand other hotels across the former United States, Phen and Vannah seemed perfectly content with the arrangement. Phen sat with one leg lazily kicked out, a stack of pancakes drowning in syrup in front of him. He slurped the last bit of juice through a straw, the loud, grating sound drawing a few annoyed looks from the other guests.

He didn't care.

Vannah sat across from him, her hair slightly tousled from sleep and wearing the hotel's free "Uptown Suites" T-shirt like a designer piece. She stabbed a piece of sausage and pointed it at him dramatically. "So you're telling me," she said, her eyes wide with amusement, "that you really thought the fire alarm yesterday morning was the toaster?"

Phen shrugged with total confidence. "It smelled like toast."

"It smelled like burning wires and plastic, sweetheart."

He grinned. "Toast is just bread trying to be wires. Besides, bread nowadays is pretty much plastic anyway with all the genetically modified content."

Vannah choked on a laugh and slapped the table. The sound was loud, bright, and a little shrill, the kind of noise that made every serious person in the room stiffen as if someone had just used profanity in church. A middle-aged couple wearing matching Accords pins glared over at them, scandalized that anyone could laugh on a morning like this.

Around them, the room was a hive of hushed, panicked whispers.

"...an attack on Idaho soil..."

"...Governor Davidson killed..."

"...lines of succession thrown into chaos..."

The TV mounted in the corner blared *Good Morning Charlotte!*, replaying President Burris' firm morning address for the sixth time in half an hour. "We stand with President Johnson," Burris repeated from the screen. "And let me be perfectly clear... this attack will not derail the Accords."

Every table in the room seemed to tilt toward the television. Except theirs.

Vannah stabbed another sausage link. "Do you want the rest of this? Because I swear this thing is judging me."

Phen leaned forward, his eyes twinkling. "Babe, if a sausage is judging you, we need to add that to the mission log."

She kicked him under the table. He yelped loudly, causing several more people to turn and stare. Vannah laughed harder.

Phen grabbed another pancake and tore it in half. "Let them stare. They're just jealous because we're prettier."

Vannah smirked, leaning across the table, her lips quirking. "We really should be more worried than this, shouldn't we?"

Phen considered that for a beat. He looked at the TV, then back at the woman across from him. He shook his head and shoved a piece of pancake into his mouth. "Nope."

She let out a softer laugh, fondness showing in her eyes.

Around them, the world worried, whispered, and panicked. Phen and Vannah sat there unbothered because to them, none of that mattered. *None of them mattered.* Only the mission mattered. Only they mattered.

They were happy.

16

CONSORTIUM CITY — 03.20.28

The Chairman stood at the center of the darkened conference hall, the glow of a dozen holoscreens burning a cold, clinical blue across his mirrored mask. The Board of Leadership sat in a wide, imposing semicircle around him; silhouettes in tailored suits that cost more than most men made in a lifetime. Their masks, carved from brushed aluminum and painted white, remained fixed on the chaos unfolding across the digital displays.

The largest display replayed the Mountain Home drone attack on a continuous, agonizing loop. It was a masterpiece of destruction: the initial orange bloom of the inferno, the shimmering ripple of the shockwave, and the sight of massive steel hangars folding like wet paper under the kinetic pressure. Then, the screen would flicker, resetting to beginning again. Another screen showed the National News Desk announcing that **GOVERNOR BRADFORD DAVIDSON was lost in the attack.**

The Chairman's voice didn't just speak; it cut through the heavy air like a sledgehammer hitting glass. "Who authorized this?"

A suffocating silence swallowed the room. The Chairman's gloved hand remained steady for a heartbeat before his fist slammed into the mahogany table, the violent crack echoed off the high vaulted ceilings like a gunshot.

"The Confederation was told to hold position!" He stepped toward the screen, his boots clicking rhythmically against the polished floor. He stabbed a finger toward the flickering image of Mountain Home. "They were told to build their walls and enjoy the communist playgrounds they were gifted. They were meant to disrupt; to be a threat. To be the boogeyman that kept the Great Plains from looking too closely in our direction. They were *not* authorized to launch an all-out strike on the GPN."

A man three seats down, a senior strategist whose mask was etched with gold filigree, cleared his throat with caution. "It appears their Central Command acted independently, sir. Internal intercepts suggest they believed the Accords would render their borders irrelevant. They panicked."

"WE HAVE ALREADY RENDERED THEM IRRELEVANT." The Chairman's voice boomed, the sheer volume rattling the haptic interface panels embedded in the table. "Washington! Oregon! Those territories were gifts from the Consortium! They are playing house in ruins we provided! Get them on camera. Now. I want an answer from the source!"

"Right away, sir." One of the younger Consortium techs at the perimeter console stood upright quickly. He performed the salute, slapping his right hand to his left shoulder. The Chairman, eyes still fixed on the burning base, acknowledged the gesture by slapping his right hand to his left shoulder. A cold mirror of the loyalty he demanded.

He paced the crescent-shaped room, his reflection dancing in the black glass of the darkened screens until the central holographic array lit up with a low, electromagnetic hum.

On the right: Premier Oleg Rostov of Leninia. He was heavy-shouldered and frost-eyed, the dim blue light of the transmission sharpening the bitter angles of his scowl. He wore a dark, heavy military greatcoat with tarnished medals pinned to the breast, relics of a Red Army that no longer existed. On the left: Paramount Leader Li Zhengyuan of Maogon. He was immaculate, his posture so straight it looked painful, his hands folded perfectly behind his back. He wore a high-collared tunic, his expression serene in a way that made the Chairman's jaw ache with suppressed rage.

The Chairman didn't offer a greeting. "You," he snapped, his mask inches from Rostov's digital face. "Explain why my plan is currently on fire."

Premier Rostov sniffed, his nostrils flaring with a misplaced sense of pride. "The strike was a tactical necessity, Chairman. It was our own intelligence. We gathered it ourselves. It suggested the Great Plains was mobilizing for a pincer movement against Leninia and Maogon. We could not sit by. Preemptive action is the only language Jeremiah Johnson understands."

"PREEMPTIVE ACTION?" The Chairman's roar was so sudden the light panels overhead flickered.

Rostov gave a tiny, almost theatrical shrug, the medals on his coat clinking softly. "War favors the bold, does it not?"

"War," the Chairman hissed, leaning in until the mirrored surface of his mask was all Rostov could see, "is a tool that *we* wield. Not you. Not your pathetic Politburo. And certainly not whatever Soviet cosplay cabinet you've assembled in your stolen strip of the Pacific Northwest. You are a puppet, Oleg. Puppets do not decide when the play begins."

Rostov's jaw flexed, the defiance in his eyes flickering. "Leninia is a sovereign state. We answer to the will of our people."

"You answer to ME." The Chairman spun around, his coat snapping like a whip as he turned his fury toward the other screen. "And what about you, Zhengyuan? You stood by and encouraged this idiocy? Or were you too busy counting the grain you stole from the Idaho panhandle to notice your neighbor was launching a war?"

Li Zhengyuan didn't blink. His breathing was slow, measured. When he spoke, his voice was like silk over a blade. "Premier Rostov acted prematurely," he said softly. "Maogon had advised restraint. We suggested a diplomatic blockade."

The Chairman narrowed his eyes. "Liar. You've been whispering in his ear for months."

Li offered a polite, diplomatic smile. It curved on the lips but never reached his eyes. "We did express concern that the Accords posed... complications. A unified economic and military bloc forming on our border would naturally require a response. We merely discussed the 'what if' scenarios. We did not know the Premier would be so... impulsive."

"That bloc," the Chairman seethed, "is exactly what the Consortium was in the process of dismantling from the inside. We were winning."

Rostov scoffed, finding his courage again. "You prevented nothing. Look at the feeds, Chairman. The Carolina Accords will be signed within hours. They were already prepared to unite; our strike merely provided the heat to forge the metal. We did what you were too afraid to do."

Li folded his hands behind his back. "In fairness, the Confederation cannot be expected to sit idle while our influence dissolves into a footnote of history. Desperate states take desperate measures, Chairman. Perhaps your leash was too loose."

The Chairman slammed both palms onto the table, leaning forward until he was a looming shadow over both leaders. The orange glow of the burning hangars at Mountain Home reflected in his mask, making it look as though his eyes were made of embers.

"Your actions have jeopardized EVERYTHING. You have put them back on a war footing!"

"The Secession Wars were a masterpiece," the Chairman whispered, his voice dropping to a cold, predatory level that made even the Board members hold their breath. "The United States was dismantled, bit by agonizing bit. The world fractured exactly on schedule. We were mere weeks from stepping out of the shadows to claim the throne of a new global order. OUR NEW DAWN!"

His gloved hand clenched into a white-knuckled ball. "And now? You give Jeremiah Johnson a martyr. You give that daughter of his, Samantha, the perfect excuse to mobilize the Pact. You give Samuel Burris his hero moment on a silver platter." He pointed at the loop of the explosion. "You have turned a petty border governor into the rallying cry for a new American empire. You didn't stop the Accords. You baptized them in blood."

Li Zhengyuan's voice remained calm, but there was a new edge to it. "Then perhaps your legendary operatives in Carolina should have seen this coming. Perhaps they should prevent the signing from occurring at all."

The Chairman's head tilted slowly to the left. The Board behind him seemed to shrink into their chairs. "How in the hell do you know about our operatives in Carolina?" he growled, the sound vibrating with a primal threat.

Rostov smirked, leaning back in his chair. "With all due respect, Chairman, we aren't the fools you take us for. We didn't know for certain... until you just confirmed it. Well played, Paramount Leader Li."

A thick, mocking Russian chuckle erupted from Rostov's speakers. Li Zhengyuan did not laugh. He simply examined the Chairman as if he were a specimen in a jar.

"Chairman," Li said evenly, "your organization is not the only one capable of reading patterns. The Confederation does not operate in a vacuum. When a storm gathers over Charlotte, even Mother Russia and Father Korea can feel the atmospheric pressure change. Our assets saw the movements. We are not the dumb puppets you think we are."

The Chairman's breathing was the only sound in the room, heavy and rhythmic inside the mask. "You presume far too much, Li."

Li's eyes narrowed. "On the contrary. I presume very little. But when the Great Plains Nation is attacked and the mighty Consortium responds with... silence... I begin to wonder if the masters have lost their grip on the hounds."

Rostov barked another laugh. "Maybe your Consortium is not the shadow-god it claims to be. Maybe you are just another man in a mask, hiding from a world that has outgrown you."

A deadly, absolute quiet settled across the Situation Room. The Board stared straight ahead, their white masks reflecting nothing but the blue data. The Chairman planted his hands on the table and leaned in.

"You forget yourselves," he whispered. "You forget who allowed you to exist after the Cold War. Who negotiated the peace deals in your failing skirmishes while your armies limped out of the ruins of the 2020s. Who fed your propaganda to Ukraine, to Japan, and into the heart of South Korea to ensure no one stood in your way? Who invited you to a North American continent carved up and ready for the taking? Who filled your offshore coffers until you were the wealthiest men in the Communist dung heaps you occupy?"

His voice dropped to a hiss. "You forget that without the Consortium, you would still be groveling for scraps in the mud, begging for the 'compassion' of a United States that would have erased you from the map a decade ago."

Rostov's smile evaporated. Li's serene expression finally chilled into a mask of stone. The Chairman straightened slowly, regaining his full, imposing height. The holograms fractured across his chest in sparks of light.

"But you are right about one thing," he said, his tone shifting into something clinical. "The Accords will embolden them. The moment they stand united, the moment they believe themselves righteous... they become harder to break. They start to think they are a nation again."

Rostov shifted uncomfortably. Li's eyes flickered toward the data feeds.

"But that," the Chairman said softly, "is why we always plan for the failure of our subordinates. My operatives in Carolina; since you are so curious, will proceed as intended. The infiltration cell is already in place, woven into the very fabric of the security detail."

Rostov scoffed. "A handful of field rats is your grand solution to a unified continent? You are delusional."

The Chairman lifted his chin. "They are not rats, Oleg. They are scalpels. And today... they carve a new history out of the old one's heart."

Li Zhengyuan's voice was like a razor. "And if your scalpels fail? If Johnson signs that paper? What then?"

The Chairman stopped pacing. For several seconds, the room seemed to shrink, the walls closing in on the digital projections of the two leaders. "If they fail," he said, "we have contingencies that make your drone strikes look like a child's firecracker."

He snapped his fingers. A tech at the far console flinched, then brought up a new holoscreen. A grainy, high-definition feed appeared: Jack's face, partially obscured by shadows.

"The time is 2100 hours on March 19, 2028. Zero Energy pucks planted at all structural nodes around the Convention Center. Enough has been seeded to turn the city center into a memory. Reporting in."

The Chairman turned back to the two leaders. "You see, Rostov? Zhengyuan? We have technology that exists outside your understanding of physics. These same devices are already positioned in Moscow and Beijing. They have been there for years. Don't tempt my resolve."

Rostov's eyes widened, his bravado replaced by a dawning horror. "What... what is Zero Energy?"

The Chairman growled. He didn't answer with words. Instead, he pulled a sleek, chrome-plated pistol from his jacket. He didn't aim at the screen. He aimed at the tech who had just initiated the feed, a man who had served him faithfully for five years.

The Chairman fired.

There wasn't a bang or a flash, only a high-pitched hum that set every tooth in the room on edge. The tech froze. His mouth opened to scream, but his vocal cords simply ceased to be. His face twisted, turning a translucent, sickly gray as his flesh began to vanish in layers, like sand being blown off a dune. In three seconds, the man was gone. No blood. No bone. Only a pile of pristine clothing lay on the floor where he had stood.

The Chairman lowered the weapon. The response was absolute.

On the screen, Rostov's face had drained of all color. The swaggering Premier looked like he was about to be sick. On the left, Li Zhengyuan's serenity had finally shattered; his breathing was shallow, his eyes wide and unfocused.

"That," the Chairman said softly, "is Zero Energy. A total molecular deconstruction. If I wished, I could wipe your capitals from existence before your morning tea cools. Now," he added, his voice dropping to a deadly, gutteral growl, "you will kneel."

For a moment, neither leader moved. The Chairman raised the pistol again, pointing it toward the camera lens.

Both men dropped instantly. Their torsos fell out of the camera's view as they hit the floor. The automated cameras tilted down to follow them. Rostov's shoulders were shaking with a visible tremor; Li Zhengyuan bowed until his forehead was pressed against the cold floor of his palace.

"Swear it," the Chairman commanded. "Renew your fealty to the Consortium."

Rostov's voice was a pathetic tremble. "Leninia... and the Western Bloc... we stand with you. We submit."

"Maogon kneels," Li whispered, the silk gone from his voice. "We obey the will of the Chairman. Always."

The Chairman watched them for a full minute, letting the weight of their humiliation settle over the Board. He wanted them to feel every second of their powerlessness.

"Good. You will maintain your borders. You will follow the plan to the letter. And you will do nothing. Nothing. to interfere with Charlotte. Issue an apology to the Great Plains. Blame a rogue commander. Blame the weather. I don't care what the lie is, but make it convincing."

Both men murmured their ascent, their voices muffled by the floor. The Chairman leaned in, his mask filling both screens with cold, mirrored light.

"Remember this moment, Premier. Remember it, Paramount Leader. Because the next time you forget who created you... you won't be kneeling. You'll be replaced by someone who understands the value of silence."

He made a sharp, cutting gesture with two fingers. The screens went black. The Chairman exhaled, an icy release of tension. Behind him, the Board rose as one, performing the left-shoulder salute. Their white masks looked like a graveyard in the dim light.

A low chorus of masked voices echoed through the hall.

"In unison, we see all."

"In unison, we are all."

"In unison, we control all."

Charlotte, Carolina — 03.20.28 — 10:45 AM EST

A catering van nosed up to the service entrance off Brooklyn Village Avenue, sliding in beside a line of decorators' trucks and vendor vans already unloading for the Accords ceremony. The morning was sunny and cool. Commuters streamed past the old Westin and the Convention Center on their way to work, entirely unaware of the storm brewing.

Jack stepped out first. The side door slid open and Phen, Vannah, and Twelve followed. Jack and Phen wore tuxedos while Twelve and Vannah remained in their cocktail dresses from the night before. It was the perfect disguise for staff shuttling between pre- and post-event duties. They worked quickly, pulling folding carts out of the van and stacking linens, steno burners, and trays in neat, forgettable piles.

Jack locked the van and pushed the first cart toward the service entrance. Ahead of them, a slow-moving line of vendors inched forward. Florists with boxed arrangements, audio crews lugging cases, a coffee distributor rolling silver percolators. Each paused beneath the bright beam of a security scanner. A tired-looking event guard waved people through with barely a glance.

Jack flashed a laminated vendor badge. The scanner beeped green.

"Next," the guard mumbled.

Twelve drifted past him with a soft, professional smile that made the guard straighten his posture unconsciously. Vannah followed, her perfume and poise masking the Zero Energy pucks hidden in her cart. There was enough power in that pile to turn the city into a wasteland. Phen came last, whistling as he pushed a smaller cart labeled *extra burners*. The guard didn't even bother lifting the lid.

The Convention Center buzzed with life. Reporters set up tripods, volunteers draped flags, and UAA Marines checked security posts while staff rushed trays to VIP rooms. The whole place hummed with hope, and the expectation of a historical day. It was a celebration waiting to unfold.

Jack didn't feel any of it. He simply had the countdown flickering in his head.

They pushed their carts toward the service elevator and squeezed in beside a florist's cart overflowing with lilies and baby's breath. An elderly man stood behind it, smiling warmly at the four of them.

"Good morning!" he said cheerfully. "What kind of food do y'all cater?"

Vannah returned his smile with practiced sweetness, her Georgian accent soft and syrupy. "Well, sweetie, we specialize in smoked meat and barbecue. And just wait until you try my mama's pecan pie."

"Oh my, I love some pecan pie!" the man chuckled.

"Me too!" Vannah beamed, laying it on thick while the others smiled politely, nodding along.

The elevator dinged, gliding to a stop. When the doors opened, Vannah gestured graciously. "After you, sir."

The old man shuffled out, disappearing around the corner. Once he was gone, Vannah's smile vanished into a smirk. "Gotta respect your elders. That's what my Papa always told me."

Jack and Phen groaned. Twelve only smirked.

They rolled their carts into the main concourse. The girls split off naturally, stopping every few yards to subtly press a Zero Energy puck into place. Disguised as brushed stainless-steel décor accents, the pucks attached magnetically to walls, vendor booths, and support pylons. They were casual, invisible, and deadly.

This would be the first deployment of Zero Energy on such a scale, but the Chairman's instructions had been clear: *Destroy the people and their hope. Preserve the land and infrastructure.*

Twelve kept the count in her head. *Eight. Nine. Ten.*

Jack's expression remained stoic and professional as he pushed the catering cart, hundreds of people walking in every direction moving flags, lights, merchandise carts. He reminded himself of his *Mission before Morals* mantra, but he couldn't help feeling like what they were about to do was a bridge too far as his eyes caught a young staffer adjusting a banner that read "Unity: Together," completely unaware that today was their last day on earth.

He tracked the UAA Marines at the perimeter with his eyes as he noted the placement of their sidearms and the gaps in their sweep patterns. He didn't let his thoughts and emotions get in the way of the orders, never before the orders. They moved deeper into the concourse, past bright banners and eager volunteers, all of it humming with a purpose that was about to be erased.

Twelve lingered by the registration table, adjusting a stack of pamphlets with one hand while her other disappeared beneath the draped cloth. She felt the magnetic thrum as the puck locked onto the steel frame. *Thirteen.*

A few yards away, Vannah floated through the crowds with a toothy smile. She paused by a decorative torchier light, checking her reflection in the polished pillar before sliding a silver disc into the shadow of the housing. *Fourteen.* They flowed through a crowd like they belonged, no one the wiser. Two more went into the hollow base of a hydration station, the water sloshing softly in the plastic jugs as the magnets bit into the metal. *Sixteen.* By the time they reached the darkened corner behind the main vendor booth, the rhythm had become second nature. A cluster of four went into the structural junction, hidden behind a stack of "Restoration" tote bags. *Twenty.*

Jack glanced back once, his brow tight, but he didn't intervene. The Chairman had been vague about "coverage." Too vague. And if there was one thing Consortium operatives learned early, it was *When in doubt, overkill.* By the time they reached the Crown Ballroom, the count had climbed far beyond what any of them realized.

Twelve pressed the last puck beneath a draped stage riser and whispered, almost unconsciously, "Done. Last count, forty pucks."

"We think that's enough?" Vannah murmured into her comms.

"It's well above the ordered amount." Jack responded calmly smiling as patrons walked by. "The original specs called for twenty internally, but a few more shouldn't hurt anything."

The Carrier Pigeons took to the stage and began tuning their instruments beneath the vaulted, gold-leafed lights of the Crown Ballroom. The soft hum of electric guitars drifting over the crowd like a low-frequency buzzing while delegates, ambassadors, and politicians laughed together, their wool suits and fancy dresses accompanied by the rolling tide of a thousand voices comingling in the room. The room was filling up slowly, as more people pushed closer to the stage to hear the classic rock icon.

Mark Carrier stepped up to the mic, rolling his shoulders as he tested the reverb. His eyes looked tired but he feigned a smile that all of those in attendance reflected back. "Let's make this a good day," he murmured, his voice caught by the sensitive equipment and broadcast as a gravelly intimate promise to the thousands watching. The soundboard director behind the glass booth held up ten fingers, counting down. Cameras on robotic jibs panned wide, catching the swelling audience and the "Restoration" banners that hung like heavy tapestries from the rafters. A ripple of anticipation swept through the hall as the first notes were strummed.

Mark's soft rhythm came first accompanied by contemplative storytelling that felt like they were pulled from the bottom of a well. The voices in the room hushed. He closed his eyes and let the first verse of *Character Assassination, Pt. 1* rise. *"I wish she knew me like I was before..."* His voice was warm, aching, and steady. *"...all those feelings we knew suddenly were lost... but more likely, stolen."* The words settled over the hall as the people swayed, and some sung along. A cameraman near the stage swallowed hard, his lens shaking just a fraction of a millimeter. In the back of the room, near a service station, Twelve paused. A silver tray of crystal water glasses sat in her hands, but her fingers had gone cold.

The lyrics didn't just play; they ripped into her psyche. For a moment, the mission, the pucks, and the Chairman's cold logic were eclipsed by a jagged, neon-bright memory. She saw an older man, with kind eyes and calloused hands. He was sitting cross-legged on a faded rug in front of a walnut-veneered stereo rack. He was meticulously organizing vinyl records, the smell of static and old paper filling the air. Someone who looked like her was dancing to this exact melody. The sunlight in the memory was warm. It was real. It didn't feel like a "glitch."

She shook her head, the glasses on the tray clinking with a sharp, crystalline sound. Jack was suddenly beside her, his hand a vice-grip on her elbow. "Focus," he hissed, his voice a razor against her ear.

Even Jack's eyes flickered toward the stage as Mark continued: *"The silence speaks so many words... when there is nothing to say..."* The song was an elegy for a love that didn't know it was destroyed. When the final note faded, the stillness remained for three full heartbeats before the applause erupted. A loud sea of cheers and clapping.

Mark adjusted the mic stand, his face bathed in a warm, amber glow that made the room feel like it was trapped in a beautiful golden hour. Then the opening chords of *Part 2* rolled out. It continued the story of the first song, but seemingly more desperately clinging to that love that refused to be.

"Will the rain ever stop? Will the sun come back out?"

Twelve placed her tray on a table, her movements mechanical, but her heart was hammering against her ribs. *"No freshness to the flowers that grow outside by the park bench..."* The vision returned, sharper this time. She saw the record spinning, and the man's hand as he adjusted the needle with a reverence that felt like a sacrament. She remembered the feeling of the hardwood floor beneath her feet. It was a life she had been told never existed, a dream that didn't exist.

"Wake up," Phen muttered, shoving an elbow into her ribs as the spotlight swept toward the main entrance.

A voice boomed through the PA, cutting through the music like a scythe. "Ladies and gentlemen, distinguished guests... our first dignitaries have arrived." The transition from the stage to the entrance was instantaneous. Camera crews scrambled, their heavy cables snakes across the marble. "Please welcome, Prime Minister Kenneth Chandler of the Bluegrass States Republic."

Chandler entered with a statesman's practiced gait, his wife's hand tucked firmly into the crook of his elbow. He wore a navy suit that looked like armor, a Bluegrass lapel pin glinting under the lights. He moved through the double line of UAA Marines, his smile wide but his eyes calculating.

"Today," Chandler said, stopping briefly for a reporter's boom mic, "is a turning point. We've spent enough time looking at the fences between us. It's time to look at the horizon. United or not, this is still our home."

The ballroom erupted. Jack watched from the catering line, his face filled with a bored contempt. "Politicians," Phen whispered, leaning back against a support pillar where a puck was hidden. "It's all just theater before the slaughter."

"Now entering, President Gerald Martinez of the Republic of Texas."

Martinez entered with the measured stride of a man who owned the ground beneath him. He held his Stetson against his chest, his expression filled with a firm Texan resolve. There were no smiles today; the smoke from Mountain Home was still too fresh in everyone's lungs. On either side he was flanked by Texas Rangers in their dress whites with wide-brimmed hats, ceremonial sabers, and gold badges that caught every stray beam of light in the hall. Martinez didn't just lead; he commanded the room with a cold, quiet fury, his charcoal suit crisp and his lone-star tie pin shining like a dagger. The Texans in the audience let out a roar that shook the glass partitions, it wasn't a cheer of celebration, but a shout of defiance.

"President Martinez!" a reporter shouted. "What is Texas' stance after Mountain Home?"

Martinez stopped. He didn't just look at the reporter; he looked into the camera, addressing the millions watching at home. "Our stance," he said, his voice rumbling, "is that Texas does not forget. And anyone who attacks our allies will find out exactly what 'Don't Tread on Me' means in the modern age."

The applause wasn't loud but it was a heavy, rhythmic pounding of hands that felt like a war drum. Jack watched the Rangers escort Martinez's family toward the VIP section. The President's daughters followed, their faces glowing in the light of their phones as they posted to Vyber, the mundane act of social media clashing horribly with the gravity of their father's words.

A heavy, rhythmic drumline began to play as Mark and the Carrier Pigeons yielded to The Great Plains Militia Honor Guard. They marched in with their ceremonial busby hats crafted from thick, dark bison fur. Their bodies moving in lockstep with the beat.

"Ladies and Gentlemen, President Jeremiah Johnson of the Great Plains Nation!"

Jeremiah marched in. He didn't look like a politician; he looked like a man who had just come from a funeral and was headed toward a battle. His head was high, his shoulders back, but there was a hollowness in his eyes that only Jack and Twelve seemed to notice. A young woman with a microphone rushed his side. "President Johnson! How are things in the Great Plains?"

Jeremiah slowed his pace, his tired eyes sharpening for a moment. "General Samantha Johnson has the situation under control. My people are grieving, but they are not broken." He kept moving, his purposeful stride leaving the reporter in his wake as the applause boomed for the man who had lost so much in the last seven years.

The lights shifted one final time. The fanfare was less theatrical, almost humble.

"Introducing President Samuel Burris of the United Alliance of America!"

The applause swelled into a roar of recognition. Burris stepped through the entrance flanked only by two aides carrying heavy binders marked with the UAA crest. He wore a simple suit and a somber expression—the look of a man who had counted every life lost to get to this table. If Jeremiah had been the shield during the Secession Wars and Martinez the sword, Burris was the architect of the reconstruction. He was the reason they were all standing on this ground. He offered a modest wave and kept walking, his presence drifting in like a steady tide.

As he reached the front, the three other leaders stood. Chandler shook his hand firmly. Martinez gave a curt, respectful nod. Jeremiah placed a heavy hand on Burris's shoulder, it was the acknowledgment of the weight all of the leaders carried. A burden none of them wished to bear.

Jack watched from the catering station, the skin on his jaw was tight enough to tear. Twelve moved to a nearby table, pinning one of the last pucks under the heavy linen and whispering the final count. Vannah and

Phen exchanged a glance confirming that the kill box was primed.

The applause faded. A calm settled over the thousands in the room. Burris stepped up to the table where the Accords lay waiting. The parchment looked impossibly bright under the stage lights, the pens gleaming like surgical instruments.

"Ladies and gentlemen," the announcer said, his voice echoing into the far corners of the hall, "we invite all dignitaries to take their positions for the official signing of the Carolina Accords."

Jack exhaled once. He felt the cold, magnetic pulse of the pucks hidden around the conference center. "Show-time."

17

Crown Ballroom Main Stage — 03.20.28

"Ladies and gentlemen, please turn your eyes to the monitors where we will review the wording of the Accord, together. This signing is one of the most historic moments in American history; for while the United States no longer exists, we are all still Americans."

The voice on the speakers echoed through the Crown Ballroom as the crowd fell silent. Every eye turned toward the massive screens suspended from the vaulted ceiling. They flickered to life, washing the room in a soft, clinical white light. A digital parchment unfurled across each display. A digital parchment unfurled across each display, the Carolina Accords rendered in ornate script, framed by the gold-leafed crests of the four signatory nations.

A quiet reverence settled as children were lifted onto shoulders, Reporters lowered their microphones while UAA Marines stood straighter. Even Mark Carrier, still wiping sweat from his brow backstage, stopped moving for the first time all morning.

Onscreen, the text scrolled slowly as the announcer's voice filled the hall:

THE CAROLINA ACCORDS

Ratified at Charlotte, Carolina, United Alliance of America on this Monday, March 20, 2028.

PREAMBLE

We, the sovereign nations formed from the former United States of America—the United Alliance of America, the Great Plains Nation, the Republic of Texas, and the Bluegrass States Republic—recognizing our shared history, common values, and mutual security interests, do hereby enter into this Accord. In the interest of peace, cooperation, economic stability, and mutual defense, we establish these Articles to guide our relations and secure a safer future for our citizens. Though our political paths have diverged and our borders have changed, we affirm that the American spirit does not belong to a single government, but to the people who uphold liberty, justice, and the rule of law.

ARTICLE I — Mutual Recognition & Sovereignty

i.1: Each signatory nation acknowledges and respects the full sovereignty, borders, and self-governance of every other signatory.

i.2: No signatory shall seek to annex, undermine, destabilize, or otherwise violate the independence of another.

i.3: Diplomatic relations shall be considered fully normalized as of the signing of this Accord.

ARTICLE II — Collective Defense Pact

ii.1: An attack on one signatory nation shall be considered an attack on all.

ii.2: Each nation commits to rendering military, logistical, or humanitarian support as appropriate and feasible.
ii.3: A Joint Defense Council (JDC) shall be formed, composed of representatives from each nation's defense ministry.

ARTICLE III — Economic Cooperation & Trade

iii.1: Tariffs between signatories shall be reduced with the intent of eventual elimination, forming a cooperative economic zone.
iii.2: Cross-border trade routes shall remain open except in times of declared national emergency.

ARTICLE IV — Civil Liberties & Human Rights

iv.1: Each signatory commits to upholding core human rights, including freedom of expression, fair legal process, and protection from racial, gender, and religious discrimination.

ARTICLE V — Border Management & Migration

v.1: Nations may maintain independent immigration policies but agree to humane treatment of migrants and refugees.
v.2: A shared database of criminal offenders shall be established to improve border security between signatories.

ARTICLE VI — Energy, Infrastructure & Reconstruction

vi.1: Signatories agree to cooperate on major infrastructure projects, including power grids, rail systems, and water networks.

ARTICLE VII — Environmental & Agricultural Cooperation
vii.1: Signatories shall collaborate on water rights, drought mitigation, and food supply stability.

ARTICLE VIII — Intelligence Sharing & Anti-Terror Coordination
viii.1: Each nation commits to sharing credible intelligence regarding external threats and hostile foreign powers.
viii.2: A Joint Counterintelligence Taskforce (JCT) shall be formed to prevent infiltration or destabilization efforts.

ARTICLE IX — Dispute Resolution
ix.1: Disputes arising from this Accord shall first be addressed by the Accord Council.
ix.2: No signatory may resort to military force against another without exhausting Articles IX.1.

ARTICLE X — Amendments & Withdrawal
x.1: This Accord may be amended by a unanimous vote of all signatory nations.

SIGNATORIES

Signing: President Samuel Burris (UAA)

Signing: President Jeremiah Johnson (GPN)

Signing: President Gerald Martinez (Texas)

Signing: President Kenneth Chandler (Bluegrass)

As each name was announced, the leaders lifted their hands to the crowd and sat at the table. Each held an official copy with their nation's crest embossed in gold leaf. A commemorative pen was passed to each man;

they signed their own copies first, passing them to the left as flashing camera bulbs captured the moment.

While the announcer read, Jack, Phen, Twelve, and Vannah slipped through the back. They moved quickly but without urgency so as to not draw attention. They took their time and made no sudden turns, keeping their eyes down so they wouldn't make eye contact. They did everything they could to look like they belonged there. A pair of UAA Marines walked past them toward the VIP cordon, neither sparing the catering staff a glance.

Jack tapped his comm once, silently. "Execute."

They stepped behind a curtain-lined service partition used for staging trays. Large refrigerator units filled the space, their compressors running loudly. The thunder of applause from the ballroom dimmed as they got deeper into the back, all of it replaced by their footsteps echoing in concrete. Vannah peeled off her catering apron and stuffed it into a linen bin. "How long?" she whispered.

Twelve checked her watch. "The Chairman said anytime after signature confirmation. Satellite link is stable."

Phen grinned, rolling his shoulders. "Perfect. Let's get outta here."

Jack cracked the service door. The hallway was empty. A narrow utility corridor, it mirrored the ballroom's length in both directions. Only janitorial carts and a stack of folded risers waited there. "No cameras in this wing," Twelve murmured, already scanning the ceiling. "Just blind spots and old tech."

Vannah motioned everyone to stop. "You sure about that, Twelve?" Pointing to a ceiling globe that looked to house a camera.

Jack pulled out an IP scanner from his tuxedo coat and pointed it at the globe, he shrugged. "Looks dead to me."

Twelve ribbed Vannah. "Comfortable now, princess?" Vannah nodded as they slipped into the corridor. They rounded the corner toward the freight elevators, and a pair of venue staff appeared suddenly, arms full of spare tablecloths. Jack didn't hesitate; he adopted the tired expression of an overworked caterer.

"You two—good. We need these linens rerouted to Ballroom C. VIP overflow," he said, motioning vaguely.

The staffers blinked, exchanged looks, and then hurried the other way. Phen snorted quietly. "People will follow any man holding a clipboard."

"I didn't have a clipboard," Jack muttered.

"That's the joke," Phen whispered.

They reached the freight elevator. Twelve jabbed the button and the old doors shuddered open with a mechanical groan. They stepped in, the doors sliding shut with a heavy metallic clunk. For the first time since entering the building, Jack exhaled.

"Phase one," he said softly, "is complete."

The elevator groaned to a stop. Twelve's eyes snapped to the roof-access indicator. "It's clear," she whispered, looking out toward the roof.

"Move," Jack said.

They burst through the doors into the narrow stairwell and sprinted upward. Vannah and Twelve had kicked off their heels, the muffled slap of their bare feet and the frantic strike of the men's dress shoes hammering against the concrete. Every floor they climbed tightened the knot in Jack's chest. His adrenaline, certainty, and dread swirled as his heart beat faster. By the time they reached the final landing, the sirens outside were still silent. The ceremony continued undisturbed below them, all of the applause and camera flashes echoing faintly through the walls.

They didn't know how long they had.

Jack shoved the door open. The rooftop exploded into cold sunlight and whipping wind. There was their Ghosthound, its edges shimmering under partial cloaking. The rotors spun silently, bending the air without sound. Its fuselage absorbed the sun like a void.

A Consortium pilot leaned out, shouting over the vibration: "Board NOW! Field amplification spike detected—you overloaded the grid!"

Phen stumbled. "The what?"

"No time!" Jack snapped.

The four bolted across the rooftop, stripping off layers of their formal attire as the wind clawed at their clothes. The concrete vibrated beneath them as the Ghosthound's systems powered toward full lift. Twelve reached it first, the pilot hauling her inside. Vannah jumped second, skidding into the crash netting.

Phen was halfway up the ramp when the air behind them rippled. A low, deep thrum like pressure tightening the air. The detonator hadn't been touched, the pucks were syncing on their own.

"GO!" the pilot screamed. "It's cascading!"

Jack pushed harder as his lungs burned; but the roof pitched beneath him as the atmosphere distorted. The first shockwave of Zero Energy was beginning to pull in power from the satellites overhead.

Phen reached out from the bay door. "JACK! MOVE!"

Jack dove. Phen caught his wrist with both hands and hauled him into the bay as the Ghosthound tore itself off the rooftop.

The Ghosthound lurched, almost weightless for a fraction of a heartbeat as the pilot engaged the afterburners, jolting the craft forward into the air like a rocket. The cloaking field snapped shut around them as they shot north, banking hard over the edge of the Convention Center. Below them, Charlotte was consumed with a blinding, impossible light. A ring of violet brightness flickered across the Convention Center's footprint into a pulse that expanded outward like the flashing of lightning, only a thousand times greater.

Phen's eyes widened. "What the hell is that—"

Twelve didn't answer. Jack grabbed the rail, his knuckles white. The second pulse hit. The city center seemed to fold inward as distortion rippled out. The city wasn't collapsing, but life was *erasing*. It was swallowed by a bloom of violet-white energy that crackled into the sky. The sound arrived a second later, it sounded like a hollow, crushing, bass-deep roar that vibrated inside their bones. The Ghosthound shuddered, engines straining past safe limits as its internal alarms screamed. Vannah clamped a hand over her mouth, tears streaking her cheeks. Twelve stared straight ahead, her face blank. Jack watched the expanding sphere of annihilation consume the blocks around the center. The distortion crackling at the edges of the city as well beneath them. The ground shimmered like air bending under pressure. Another flash followed that was too bright to look at.

Another sound erupted, not a boom, but a long and amplified hiss, like the earth exhaling its last breath. Jack gripped the side handle and raised his binoculars. He knew what was happening, but he never imagined the scale as people on the street vanished.

The same technology that Stephen and he had field-tested before the Secession Wars, only exponentially larger. One after the other, people froze, and then vanished. Their clothes dropped straight down onto the pavement, falling into messy piles exactly where they'd been standing. Cars along I-74 and I-85 jerked violently as their drivers evaporated; the unpiloted vehicles smashed together, bursting into fireballs that rolled across the asphalt.

"Oh my God..." Jack's voice cracked. "Phen—it's just like the Zero Energy darts we used in '25. Scaled up. Multiplied. Jesus... this is—"

Phen let out a wild, unhinged laugh. "Let me see! Let me see!" He tore the binoculars from Jack's hands, pressing them to his face as the Ghosthound climbed harder. Below them, life was vanishing in a widening ring of light dissolving every life it touched. Everything alive. Everything human. Even birds vanished in the air.

Jack swallowed against a dry throat. His mind flashed back to the children in the ballroom as the violet light consumed the streets. This wasn't a targeted strike. It was a total erasure of everything living. They had launched an apocalypse while believing they were only completing a mission.

Phen lowered the binoculars slowly, the manic grin fading into something colder. His expression was carved from the same steel the Consortium had molded into him. Jack couldn't stop staring at the devastation. The city was dissolving. People were falling into nothing. History itself was being scraped clean. His grip tightened on the doorframe until his knuckles blanched.

"This wasn't supposed to be like this..." Jack whispered. "Not like this."

Phen's hand clamped onto Jack's shoulder, fingers digging in just enough to hurt. He leaned in, his eyes reflecting the violet glow expanding beneath them. "Jack," he said softly, almost kindly. Jack turned. Phen squeezed his shoulder once, sealing the moment.

"It's war, Jack... remember... *mission before morals.*"

Raleigh, Carolina — 12:30 PM EST

Ulysses Mars sat alone, the blinds half-drawn, the sunlight of Raleigh cutting sharp, clinical angles across his desk. The Alliance News Network played softly on the mounted television, showing the Crown Ballroom in Charlotte mid-celebration. The camera panned across the dignitaries, the flags, and the hopeful crowds. Mars watched with a stillness born of years of discipline. One hand rested on a notepad; the other on a cooling cup of coffee he'd forgotten to drink.

He leaned forward as President Burris passed his copy to Jeremiah Johnson, and Gerald Martinez reached for his own pen.

The screen flickered. First once, then again, violently. The audio popped with a jagged static. The picture warped, the colors bleeding into a sickly violet hue. Followed by bright yellow letters on a black screen.

FEED OFFLINE NO SIGNAL DETECTED

Mars blinked, thinking at first it was a localized station outage. All of the phones in the office building began ringing in a cascading chorus down the corridor. Shouting erupted. A heavy crash echoed from outside the office as someone dropped a stack of files. Ulysses heard screaming and crying echoing in the hall. The ANN feed flickered back on momentarily; the camera lens was cracked, showing blurred, impossible images of piles of clothing sitting on chairs where people had been just moments before.

The secure phone on his desk lit up bright red followed by another line. Then another before every phone in the building was ringing. His chest tightened as he reached for the secure line, another blood-curdling scream echoed from the hallway. Mars rose from his chair, but before he could reach the door, it burst open. Speaker Margaret Holloway stumbled in, her face was pale, mascara streaming down her cheeks in dark streaks. She clutched a worn Bible to her chest like a life preserver. Behind her, a young ANN reporter hovered, breathless and trembling, her camera still rolling.

"Mr. Vice President—" she gasped. "Ulysses—" Her voice broke.

Mars froze, every instinct screaming for her to say it. "Just say it."

She swallowed hard, forcing the words out as if each one cut her throat. "Charlotte..." she covered her mouth to stifle an uncontrollable urge to scream. "Charlotte is gone. Everybody is gone."

The reporter behind her sobbed silently, the camera shaking in her hand. Mars steadied himself on the edge of the desk, his knuckles white. "Define 'gone.'"

The look on Holloway's face told him everything. "Sir..." She opened the Bible with shaking hands. "I need you to take the oath. Now." Her voice cracked. "We... we don't know who else is alive."

The phones kept ringing as the alarms blared in increasing volume. Somewhere outside the window, heavy transport helicopters thundered past toward the south. Ulysses Mars stared at the Bible, at Margaret's trembling hand that held it. Finally he let his eyes drift to the reporter recording this horrible event in real time.

He exhaled slowly, a heavy, ragged breath. *Not like this.* He placed his right hand on the Bible. "Madam Speaker," he said quietly, "begin."

The camera light blinked a steady, accusing red. Ulysses Mars stepped around the mahogany desk. His mind swirled with a nauseating sense of déjà vu. *My God, not again.*

Holloway swallowed, trying to find her breath. "By the authority vested in me as Speaker of the House of the United Alliance of America... I hereby invoke the line of succession. Please repeat after me." A single tear slipped down her cheek. "I, Ulysses R. Mars..."

"I, Ulysses R. Mars..." Ulysses repeated, his hand firm on the Bible, the other raised toward the ceiling.

"...do solemnly swear..."

"...do solemnly swear..." Mars said. His voice was strong and clinical, even as a cold anger began to well up inside his chest.

"...that I will faithfully execute the office of President of the United Alliance of America..."

"...that I will faithfully execute the office of President of the United Alliance of America..." He spoke firmly as more staffers began to crowd into the doorway, their faces all worn and tearful.

Holloway's voice cracked. "...and will, to the best of my ability, preserve, protect, and defend the Articles and Constitution of this Alliance..."

"...and will, to the best of my ability, preserve, protect, and defend the Articles and Constitution of this Alliance..." For a moment everything fell silent. The phones still rang and sirens screamed outside. Mars lifted his hand from the Bible. "So help me God."

Speaker Holloway lowered the book, breaking into heaving sobs. The reporter whispered into her mic, her voice barely audible over the chaos, "Ulysses R. Mars... is now President of the United Alliance of America."

Mars turned toward the dead ANN screen, he clenched his teeth together. "I need to know what the hell happened—now!"

Staffers scattered instantly, sprinting out into the hallway. A single figure stepped in as the others fled, a UAA Marine in full dress uniform. He squared his shoulders and held his expression firm.

Colonel Brigham Mars.

He snapped to attention and saluted. "Just tell me what you need, sir, and I will make it happen." For the first time since the screen went dark, something in Ulysses softened. He rounded the desk and pulled the Colonel into a tight embrace. The gesture startled Speaker Holloway; the man who was now President had never been known for displays of affection.

The gesture froze Speaker Holloway in mid-sob. The man who was now President had always been down to earth but he typically kept an intellectual distance. He moved toward the Colonel with a raw, unscripted desperation. As they collided, the symmetry was unmistakable. It was in the way their shoulders locked at the same sharp angle, and the way the Colonel's hand gripped Ulysses' neck with a familiarity that spanned decades rather than minutes.

They weren't just two officials in a crisis; they were two boys from the same home, suddenly standing in this tragedy together.

Brigham didn't pull away. He kept his hand anchored to the small of Ulysses' back, a tether to the earth while the sirens outside tried to scream the building down. "We'll get through this, Yule," he murmured, the use of the childhood shorthand hitting the room awkwardly. "But look at me. You aren't the heir anymore. You're the President. There's no one left to wait for."

Ulysses exhaled, stepped back, and squared his shoulders. Whatever he had been a minute ago was gone. What stood in his place was the leader of a nation in shock.

18

Austin, Texas — 03.20.28

"What do you mean the President is dead?" Vice President Rafael Cortez shouted, his voice cracking as aides delivered the early reports from Charlotte. "Get the President of the UAA on the damn phone now!"

Rafael paced aggressively, his boots hammering the floorboards until Clay Harlan from the Office of Strategic Affairs walked in. The aides scattered instantly as Clay shut the door with a final, heavy click.

Rafael whipped toward him. "Clay," he barked, "tell me this isn't real. Tell me Martinez isn't—"

Clay didn't speak until the door latched fully. When he did, his voice was low, steady, and lethal. "It's real."

Rafael froze. "What do we know?" He tried to contain his anger, but Harlan's stillness spooked him.

Clay stepped forward, sliding a thin black tablet onto the mahogany desk. The screen displayed a satellite still of Charlotte—an expanding ring of violet light where the Convention Center should have been. There was no blast crater. No debris. Just a bright, impossible bloom spreading across the grid.

"What in the hell kind of weapon can do that?" Rafael's eyes widened.

Clay knew exactly what it was, but he feigned a perfect ignorance. "Sir, we have never seen this kind of technology."

His voice was controlled, but Rafael caught the faint tremor of calculation beneath it. "Whatever this is," Clay said, "it's not conventional. It's not chemical or nuclear. It isn't directed energy as we understand it."

Rafael stared at the tablet, his breath shallow. "No shadows," he whispered. "No heat bloom. From what we can tell, it's just... people gone. Instantaneous. "

Clay nodded, his face a perfect mirror of Rafael's horrified countenance.

Rafael dragged a hand across his face and sank into his chair. "My God... Martinez... the Rangers... half our delegation..."

Clay continued carefully, each word cautiously positioned. "There are no survivors reported inside a three-mile radius. None from any nation."

Rafael swallowed hard. "And Burris? Has the UAA given a statement?"

Clay's jaw tightened. "Sir, Mars claims they're still 'assessing the situation.' That's all we've received."

"Without confirmation that Martinez is gone, I have to assume the Presidency," Rafael spoke under his breath, fear tingling just beneath the surface.

"Very good, sir." Clay turned toward the door, a thin smile finally creasing his lips as he stepped into the shadows of the hallway.

Kentucky State Capitol — 03.20.28

The television flickered once. Twice. Then the feed collapsed into a static hum. Amelia Bennett lowered the remote slowly, her eyes fixed on the dead screen. The last image of President Burris lifting the pen, the applause and cheers from moments before still burned in her mind.

"That's not weather," Benjamin Chambers said. The War Secretary stood from the couch, already shaking his head. "The sky's clear for two hundred miles."

Luke Caldwell crossed his arms. "Transmission failure, then. UAA broadcast lines—"

The screen went black. Chambers exhaled. "That's not a relay issue."

Outside the windows, the city of Independence moved on as traffic lights cycled, interns laughing over coffee cups, a government complex entirely unaware it had just stepped onto a fault line. Inside, the air went cold.

"Call the broadcast desk," Amelia said. "Now."

A staffer hurried out. Seconds passed like hours. When he returned, his face told the story before his mouth could. "The signal didn't drop," he whispered. "It vanished. Everything from Charlotte went dark at the source."

Chambers straightened. "All feeds?"

"Yes, sir. Domestic. International. GPN. All of it."

Luke swallowed hard. "Then either the UAA cut the broadcast... or there's nothing left to broadcast."

Amelia didn't answer. The office monitor blinked to life again, displaying a single, haunting line from the Bluegrass Public Service Network:

CAROLINA ACCORDS — VENUE STATUS UNKNOWN

No one spoke. Finally, Luke asked the question none of them wanted to hear. "Do we notify the Governor?"

"Not yet," Amelia said, her voice steady. "We don't move until we understand what this means."

Chambers turned to her sharply. "Amelia... President Chandler was there. His wife. Half the executive branch."

"If something has happened," Amelia replied evenly, "we do not announce it until we know what survives it."

Luke's voice dropped. "Meaning...?"

Amelia met his eyes. "Meaning we may be leaderless by sundown." Her words hung heavy in the air.

"This government has no Vice President," she continued. "No succession statute. We copied the American presidency and forgot the part where it fails."

Luke's face drained of color. "Then who's in charge?"

"No one," Amelia said.

Chambers sat back hard. "If the executive collapses, the Guard won't know whose orders to follow. The Governors will fill the vacuum."

"And that," Amelia said quietly, "is how civil wars start."

A second staffer burst in, a phone shaking in his hand. "Ma'am—you need to see this."

The video was shaky, amateur footage from a distance. A violet-white bloom was swallowing the Charlotte skyline. The video was silent, but the roar echoed in Amelia's mind anyway.

"My God!" She stifled a cry when Luke stepped back.

Luke stared at the grain on the hardwood floor. "That's not a bomb."

Chambers didn't blink. "That's not anything we know."

Online captions began scrolling past: *Leaders inside. Entire delegation. No survivors.*

Amelia looked away first. "Lock this building down. Verified personnel only."

Luke nodded, already typing. "Emergency address? what's the angle? Do we point fingers at the UAA? At the Confederation?"

Amelia didn't look up from her hands. "No, we have to keep it short. Emotions are high so we have to keep it human." She finally met his gaze, her eyes hard. "The people who saw it just watched the new world they were promised end on social media. They don't need a lecture on geopolitics or a list of suspects. They need to know we're still breathing. We can't point fingers, Luke. Just tell them we're here."

"And succession?" Chambers asked.

Amelia shook her head. "Not today."

Chambers frowned. "Amelia—"

"Kenneth Chandler wasn't a chair to be replaced," she said. "He was trusted. If we rush to crown a successor, we fracture that trust at the moment the people need it most."

Luke hesitated. "Then what governs?"

She folded her hands on the desk. "We do. Collectively. Continuity directives only. No unilateral authority."

"That's not constitutional," Luke said.

"No," Amelia replied. "But it may be survivable."

Bozeman Air Command — 03.20.28

General Samantha Johnson stood beneath the main operations display, hands clasped behind her back, eyes fixed on the Pacific Northwest. Airmen and Marines of the Great Plains Militia flanked her, their attention locked where hers rested. Red lines traced the Great Wall—Leninia where Washington once stood, Maogon where Oregon had been. Surveillance drones patrolled lazily now, their feeds calm, almost mocking after the chaos of the last twenty-four hours.

Mountain Home still burned in her mind. Governor Davidson. The base. The men and women who hadn't even had time to understand they were under attack. Her thoughts drifted, uninvited, to where it had all begun. Her thoughts drifted back to the Neutronium bomb on Election Day in 2024, and the subsequent Confederation invasion. All of those years ago when she rescued Allison, Luke, Lilly; pulled free from beneath an old station wagon where their father had secured them before his life was snuffed out by the heat of that disaster.

She pushed the memory down. To a warfighter, peace is a luxury, but being in command was not. Her cell phone began to ring. She looked at it quickly: her mother, Miranda. She sent it to voicemail. Miranda called again but Samantha declined the call.

"Excuse me, it may be an emergency," she said, slipping through the crowd that had gathered around her. She stepped into a quiet alcove and called her mom back. "Mom."

Miranda's voice came through erratic, frayed by tears. "Honey..."

"Mom, is everything okay?"

"Can you turn on the news?"

Samantha's eyes lifted back toward the operations display. "I'm standing in front of it," she said.

There was a pause. Then, quietly— "I can't get ahold of your father."

The words hit her harder than any attack ever could. "What do you mean?" Her head began to spin. She leaned against a console, forced to sit.

"He was supposed to call when the Accords ended. Our security team isn't answering, and neither is the front desk. When I call his phone it just rings and rings until it alerts 'no signal found.' Honey... I fear the worst," Miranda sputtered.

Samantha closed her eyes for a moment. When she opened them, her expression changed. "Mom," she said carefully, "I need you to stay where you are. Don't talk to anyone unless it's through official channels. Do you understand?"

Miranda sniffed. "Sam... what's happening?"

"I don't know, but I intend to find out."

"Ma'am. News from Helena," Corporal Daniels called out from the communications pit.

Samantha ended the call with her mother gently. "I'll call you back," she said. "I promise."

She slid the phone into her pocket and crossed the operations floor in long, deliberate strides. Every eye tracked her. The room quieted without an order being given. "Put it on the main screen."

The Pacific Northwest map collapsed into a smaller window as a live feed replaced it. The image stabilized on the Great Plains Senate Hall in Helena. The room was packed with legislators and security frantically moving around. A seal appeared in the lower corner: **GREAT PLAINS NATION — EMERGENCY SESSION.**

Samantha's jaw tightened. Walt Ridley, Speaker of the Senate, stepped forward. His voice was steady but strained. "As of this hour, the Great Plains Nation has been unable to establish contact with President Jeremiah Johnson, his protective detail, or any member of his executive staff present in Charlotte."

A murmur rippled through the Senate chamber. In Bozeman, no one spoke.

"Under Article Seven of the Articles of Succession, and by unanimous consent of this body, I have been directed to assume the duties of President of the Great Plains Nation, effective immediately."

They think Dad is dead... oh God.

A clerk stepped forward holding a weathered Bible. Ridley placed one hand on it. "I swear to preserve the sovereignty of the Great Plains Nation, to defend its people, and to uphold its laws in this hour of uncertainty."

The oath was brutal in its simplicity. When it ended, Ridley looked directly into the camera. "To our military: you are to maintain a defensive posture only. No retaliatory actions, I want no border escalations. To our people: we will mourn. We will investigate. And until the truth is known, we will stand alone."

The feed cut. The operations floor remained silent for five full seconds. Then someone whispered, "He didn't even say Jeremiah was dead."

Samantha turned slowly. "Because until it's proven," she said, her voice ironed flat, "he isn't."

She faced the main display again. "All units: maintain surveillance of the Great Wall. We maintain a defensive posture only, until I know more. The Great Plains Nation is on its own."

No one questioned her. Samantha pulled her phone from her pocket and looked at her mother's name. Her thumb hovered. If she made the call now, it would mean she believed the void. She let her hand fall to her side instead.

Around her, Bozeman Air Command resumed its low hum as orders flowed and systems stayed green. She stared at the red lines on the map. Her father had taught her that belief was a weapon. Once you let it in, it changed how you fought.

Not yet.

Until there was a body recovered, an official message, or something undeniable: Jeremiah Johnson was still alive.

Across the former United States, borders did not close with speeches. They closed with delays. They closed with trust quietly forgotten.

Flights were grounded for "airspace verification." Convoys and supply routes were rerouted for "security assessments." Diplomatic calls rang unanswered, then stopped ringing at all.

In Austin, the Texas Office of Strategic Affairs quietly suspended all joint operations with the United Alliance of America pending "clarification of threat vectors."

The word *clarification* appeared six times in the memo. The word *trust* did not appear once.

In Independence, Kentucky, the flags of the other Accord nations were lowered without announcement and without ceremony.

In Helena, the Great Plains Senate chamber remained lit through the night. There were no press briefings and no statements—only the cold confirmation that Walt Ridley had taken the oath of office. Senators entered and exited under heavy guard. The doors stayed closed.

On Vyber, the first livestreams from the edge of Charlotte appeared.

The footage was grainy, showing people breaking military cordons—not to fight, but to film. Urban explorers, scrapping crews, and opportunists pulling copper from the bones of a dead city. Some claimed it was a weapons test. Others insisted it was an accident. A growing number argued breathlessly that Charlotte was fine—that the footage was staged, recycled, or a false flag.

Thousands of keyboard warriors declared with absolute certainty that such technology did not exist. The comments section did the rest.

And somewhere beneath the arguments, the footage, and the denials, a single truth settled into the soil of North America:

No one was in control. No one knew what was going on.

Raleigh, Carolina — 03.25.28

The room was quiet except for the low, rhythmic hum of the wall display. Ulysses Mars stood alone, hands resting on the edge of the mahogany desk, eyes fixed on the paused image in front of him.

Charlotte. Or what was left of it.

The satellite composite showed a perfect, harrowing absence. Charlotte was no longer a city, but a hollowed-out shell of itself; a concrete forest where the wind was the only thing left moving. There was no jagged crater, no scorched earth, and no smoke to signal a struggle. It was a space where millions had been rendered into a sudden, quiet void. It felt less like a weapon of war and more like an act of God; a digital rapture that had forgotten the buildings and taken only the souls.

"They're calling it a catastrophic energy release," one of the analysts had said earlier. Another had used the word *unknown*. A third had simply shaken his head.

Ulysses had dismissed them all. He reached forward and advanced the footage frame by frame.

There.

A flicker, barely visible at the edge of the blast radius, moved in a way that defied every known law of physics. He leaned closer, his shadow stretching long across the floor. "Run that again," he murmured, though no one was there to hear him.

As the video looped, he caught a speck that looked like a helicopter. It was a jagged silhouette against the violet haze. He moved to take a screenshot, but the frame blurred into static before the command could register. He tried again, scrubbing back through the timestamp, but the anomaly was gone. Every subsequent attempt met the same digital wall.

Behind him, the Presidential seal caught the dim light. The office still bore Samuel Burris's nameplate, untouched. It felt wrong to remove it so soon; it felt worse to leave it. In the hallway, boxes of belongings from Ulysses' Vice Presidential office sat stacked against the wall.

Ulysses straightened slowly, the weight of the silence in the room pressing against him as he studied the void on the screen. He realized then that they hadn't been aiming for simple destruction; they were sowing a deep, systemic confusion designed to paralyze the survivors. They weren't looking for a conventional war so much as they were cultivating a landscape of doubt where no one could be sure who to trust or what they had actually seen. That was the signature of the authoritarians who wanted all of this to begin with—The Consortium.

He thought of the Secession Wars and how often the enemy hadn't been visible until it was too late. He thought of how many times history had proven that the most dangerous forces were the ones no one could name.

His phone buzzed against the mahogany desk, a sharp, insistent vibration that seemed to cut through the stillness of the office. A notification from Austin scrolled across the lock screen, thick with the veiled threats of Vice President Cortez and demands for an immediate security briefing, while a separate channel flashed with a stream of frantic, diplomatic inquiries from Kentucky. Below them all sat a single, chilling alert from the western border: the Great Plains Nation had officially ceased all external transmissions. Ulysses watched the screen light up again and again, the digital noise of a fractured continent trying to claw its way into the room, but he didn't reach for it. He let the lights flicker and the demands pile up in the dark, his attention anchored solely on the faint glimmer of a helicopter disappearing into the Charlotte static.

He opened a new secure file and began typing a single line at the top:

SUBJECT: CONSORTIUM — EXISTENCE UNCONFIRMED

He stared at the words for a long moment. Then, slowly and deliberately, he added another line beneath it:

STATUS: ACTIVE

He dragged the corrupted video file over to the secure folder, naming it simply: *Helicopter?* Ulysses Mars closed the file and looked once more at the image of the voided city. "They think they erased themselves, like no one would see them," he said quietly to the empty room.

A thin smile crossed his face. "I saw them bastards... They didn't."

He stared at the screen, waiting for the helicopter to reappear, but as quickly as he saw it, it vanished back into the static.

19

MONTGOMERY, ALABAMA — 08.07.32

The early morning sky ruptured with clean white flashes as Texas missile batteries punched through the hastily assembled UAA air defenses. The first impacts struck the city's outskirts, with logistics depots, rail yards, National Guard armories, and communications hubs being leveled. These were not symbolic targets or population centers; they were choices made for paralysis. It was an opening salvo designed to blind, deafen, and sever command before Montgomery could even grasp that it was under attack.

Alarms screamed to life across the city; The Battle of Montgomery had begun.

Within minutes, the United Alliance responded. Naval air wings scrambled from the Gulf Fleet, and fighters lifted from Eglin Air Force Base in Fort Walton Beach, clawing into the predawn sky as fire bloomed across Alabama. The airspace filled rapidly with Texan drones, strike fighters, and electronic warfare craft, all colliding with UAA interceptors racing west. Tracer fire stitched the darkness above the Alabama River, arcing toward the Georgia line as air-defense batteries fired blindly at shapes moving too fast for traditional tracking.

Montgomery burned in pockets. The city went dark block by block as substations vanished in controlled bursts. Cell towers folded in on themselves, their signals dying mid-transmission. Somewhere downtown, a hospital generator kicked on just as a second strike erased the fuel depot meant to keep it running.

Inside the UAA command post beneath Maxwell Boulevard, officers shouted over one another as feeds dropped to static.

"Radar's blind—repeat, radar is blind!" "Drone swarm inbound from the west!" "Air Wing Three just lost two birds—no eject signals!"

A young lieutenant stared at the tactical display as friendly markers winked out, replaced by red vectors advancing with clinical precision. "They're not probing," he said, his voice tight. "This is a full push."

Above ground, UAA Marines poured into the streets, moving fast and low between firelit shadows. Humvees skidded around abandoned intersections. Infantry squads took positions on rooftops that still stood, missile tubes angling skyward as Texan drones screamed overhead. One detonated against a radio tower two blocks away, the concussion knocking men flat.

"CONTACT—DRONES, HIGH LEFT!"

A Marine squeezed his trigger. The missile streaked upward, caught its target, and burst into white fire that rained molten fragments across the street. Another drone slipped through. It struck an armory on the east side of the city, and the explosion rolled outward, shattering windows in skyscrapers, their doors blew inward, and a shockwave tore through the surrounding neighborhoods. The blasts igniting secondary fires that no one would be able to put out before morning.

Near the river, a train derailed under precision strikes, its tankers rupturing and spilling fire into the rail yard. Black smoke climbed into the sky, thick enough to blot out the stars. From the air, Montgomery was covered in a thick blanket of soot.

There weren't any warnings as civilian centers were hit by drones.

At 4:41 AM, the first Texan armored columns crossed the line from Mississippi, their engines masked by electronic jamming that made UAA sensors blind. Their advance was methodical, almost restrained. They weren't moving to conquer the city outright, but to choke the life out of it.

Raleigh, Carolina — 4:17 AM EST

Ulysses Mars stood barefoot on the cold, polished floor of the Presidential Office, his jacket half-buttoned and his tie discarded somewhere in the shadows of the room. He remained motionless, his attention anchored to the wall of displays where live feeds from the deep south flickered like a dying heartbeat. Montgomery was burning. It was a city he had spent four years integrating into the UAA; it was his city now, and his responsibility. Watching the logistics hubs vanish into plumes of orange fire felt like watching his own skin being flayed.

"Patch me through to Austin," he said, his voice quiet but carrying an edge that made the room go still.

An aide hovered at the edge of the light, clutching a tablet with both hands and nodding. "Sir, we've tried every secure channel on the list. The Office of Strategic Affairs has completely shuttered their diplomatic comms. They're ignoring us."

"Try again," Ulysses snapped, finally turning his head. His eyes were bloodshot from stress. "I don't care if you have to scream through a civilian relay. Rafael needs to hear my voice."

On the screen, another explosion bloomed over a rail yard, sending a spray of white-hot sparks into the night sky. A general standing in the corner shifted his weight, his uniform crisp as he stood at attention. "They're hitting the nervous system, Mr. President. They've got our power substations, fuel depots, rail junctions, which will cripple our response. Fortunately, they haven't touched the residential districts yet. It's calculated leverage; they want us blind and immobile before we can even consider a push into Texas territory."

Ulysses' jaw tightened until his teeth ached. He knew the narrative Texas was spinning; he'd been reading their state-sponsored Vyber feeds for months. "They still think we are to blame for Charlotte. They've either convinced themselves, or have been convinced, that we're the architects of that erasure. They are attacking us for an unfounded lie, General."

A second aide stepped forward, his face pale and waxy in the glow of the monitors. "Sir, the reports are widening. Birmingham is seeing incoming missile vectors now. They are creating a coordinated front."

Ulysses closed his eyes for a brief second, the darkness behind his eyelids offering the only rest he'd had in hours. He thought of the "helicopter" glitch he'd found four years ago. The tiny, jagged silhouette that proved the Consortium was real, but no one believed him. He had spent his entire first term trying to expose them, but the doubt they had sown was too thick. Now, that doubt had finally turned into more bloodshed.

"Authorize full defensive engagement," he said, opening his eyes. The weariness was gone, replaced by a cold, tactical clarity. "I want our interceptors over every major hub in the Southeast, but I am being very clear: there is to be no pursuit beyond the Alabama line and absolutely no escalation into Texan airspace. We are the victims of an unprovoked strike, and we will hold that moral high ground even if it costs us our assets in West Alabama. We do not give Rafael the total war he's looking for."

The room erupted into a flurry of motion as the orders were relayed. Ulysses moved to the communications console, his thumb hovering over the priority override.

"Get me Admiral Sentelle on the Gulf Fleet flagship. Now."

The screen flickered to life, revealing the Admiral's face. Sentelle was framed by the dim blue tactical lights of the *UAA Thomason's* command deck, his immaculate uniform at odds with the red, heavy bags beneath his eyes. "Mr. President."

"Admiral," Ulysses said, leaning into the camera's field of view. "Is the *Thomason* ready to sail?"

Sentelle didn't answer immediately; he was a man who weighed the cost of every word. "She's fueled, crewed, and provisioned. Carrier Group Delta is at heightened readiness, but sir, sending a carrier group of this magnitude into the proximity of Texan waters will be read as a final escalation. Cortez is already looking for a reason to claim we're planning an invasion of Houston."

"I'm fully aware of the optics, Admiral," Ulysses replied, his voice dropping into a low register. "But Texas has no navy to speak of, and the only way to break this fever is to put a knife to the throat of their economy. I want pressure on Austin. I've given them enough words, but they refuse to listen. A carrier group parked in the Gulf is a reminder that our restraint is a choice, one we can revoke at any time. Texas has been fighting a lie for years, and tonight, they've started killing my people to sustain it. I'm done with the cold war maneuvering."

Sentelle exhaled slowly, the order settling on his shoulders. "Understood. We'll position south of Mobile in international waters. We'll stay visible, and loud on every radar frequency they have. A show of force."

"A reminder," Ulysses corrected him. "That I can end their Republic without firing a single shot if I'm forced to. Make sure they see the *Thomason* on every screen in Texas."

The connection cut, and Ulysses stood in the hum of the cooling fans. An aide approached him tentatively. "Sir, we have a leak from the Texan Senate. They've just convened a closed-door session, and multiple sources are indicating that impeachment discussions for Cortez have already begun. The hawks are losing their nerve now that the missiles are actually flying."

A long breath dragged out of Ulysses. He was tired but hopeful. All night the fires of Montgomery burned, he held on hoping the politicians in Austin would find their spines before the next salvo. "So Rafael pushes them into a war to save his own skin, and now they're looking for an escape plan. Keep monitoring them. I want to know the second a vote is called. If Cortez falls, the missiles may stop. If he doesn't, and I have to show Texas exactly what the UAA Navy and our Marines are capable of, then so be it."

He turned back to the window, watching the first faint hints of dawn crawl over the Raleigh skyline. He was at the center of a conflict he had spent years trying to prevent, and now, he just had to survive it without becoming the monster the Consortium wanted him to be.

Pensacola Naval Air Station — 3:52 AM CST

The Air Station was brightly lit against the night sky with the Papa flag flying from poles held by sailors on the decks of the various ships, signaling all crew to prepare for sea. Sailors and flight personnel ran out of every building with their duffels, uniforms half-tucked because they hadn't planned to leave until 0600 hours.

On the flight deck of the *UAA Thomason*, deck crews moved along her massive span in controlled chaos. Fighter-interceptor jets sat nose-to-tail in precise rows—canopies sealed, navigation lights blinking red and green against the dark. Ordnance and weapons crews were loading each jet quickly. Yellow shirts signaled with sharp, practiced motions as tow tractors nudged aircraft into final positions. Blue shirts sprinted across the deck carrying chocks and chains. Red shirts stood off to the side, arms crossed, watching—waiting for orders they suspected would never come.

Below deck, the carrier's engines came alive in stages, a low vibration spreading through the hull as power ramped up. The *Thomason* wasn't rushing. She didn't need to. She was already winning the moment she moved.

On the pier, sailors boarded the *UAA Defiance* and *UAA Jefferson* at a near run, steel boots clanging up gangways as deck officers barked names and divisions.

Lines were cast off early. Harbor tugs idled nearby, ready to guide thousands of tons of warship into open water.

At 3:58 AM, a boatswain's whistle cut through the air. The Papa flag snapped tighter in the wind.

"All hands," a voice echoed across the *Thomason's* internal speakers, calm and steady. "This is not a drill. Prepare for immediate departure."

Sailors scrambled to their stations, the PA system barking a relentless cadence that chased them through the narrow passageways. They were briefed that their only job was to get the biggest guns in the theater into open water before Texas drove further into UAA territory. On the bridge, the ensign continued repeating the muster call through the PA while officers shouted for status reports. Helm checks were checked off and confirmed; navigation systems synced with orbital clocks. One by one, satellite uplinks gained access, and the dark screens of the CIC suddenly bled to life with a chaotic wash of radar sweeps and tactical maps. Admiral William Sentelle stepped toward the windows and watched Pensacola's lights reflected in the glass, his hands folded behind his back.

"Any changes?" he asked, his voice low over the hum of the bridge.

"No, sir," the navigation officer replied, his eyes glued to the oscillating green sweep of the long-range radar. "Texas air assets are saturated over Montgomery and Birmingham. Their coastal batteries are active and painting us, but they're holding fire. No intercepts detected, from what I can tell they're keeping their focus on the push into Alabama."

Sentelle nodded once, a grim satisfaction settling in his chest. "They don't have the birds to spare to come out here and meet us." He turned his gaze toward the dark horizon beyond the breakwater. "Good. Let them sweat the choice."

At 4:06 AM, the *UAA Thomason* eased away from the pier, harbor water splashed around her hull as she slid into the open water. One by one, her escorts followed, their wakes overlapping into a single, widening wake across the Gulf.

The *Thomason* took position as the *Defiance* took her place in front of the carrier. Her radar arrays rotated continuously, painting the sky and sea in widening arcs, already watching for threats that didn't appear yet. If Texas launched anything airborne toward their vector, *Defiance* would be the first to know, and her fleet would be the last thing those pilots ever saw. Off her port quarter, the *UAA Jefferson* fell in beside her sister ship, missile cells loaded and sealed, fire-control systems humming quietly beneath the deck. Where *Defiance* shielded the sky, *Jefferson* guarded the horizon, surface and underwater threats, anything foolish enough to test the perimeter.

Behind them both, the *UAA Carolina* moved into position. A guided missile cruiser and the command spine of the group, her decks bristled with antennas, relays, and sensor suites that fed the carrier a living picture of the battlespace. Every data stream converged there, before flowing back into the *Thomason's* command net. Deep below the surface, unseen by radar or satellite, the *UAA Miami* was already ahead of them. She had slipped free hours earlier, running dark, sonar passive, her captain listening to the Gulf breathe. Anything that tried to shadow Carrier Group Delta would be found long before it was ever seen.

Trailing at a distance came the fuelers, supply tenders, floating warehouses of food, parts, and aviation fuel. They kept their lights low and their spacing wide, a guarantee that this force could remain at sea for weeks if necessary. These ships were surrounded by smaller battleships meant to keep their supplies safe.

Together, they formed Carrier Group Delta.

On the bridge of the *Thomason*, Admiral Sentelle watched the formation settle into place, the sky above the Gulf wide and filled with stars. "Signal the group," he said. "Standard posture. No deviations."

"Aye, sir."

The Papa flag was hauled down as the carrier passed the breakwater, replaced by the steady glow of navigation lights as a large UAA banner snapped in the wind from the superstructure. They wanted Texas to see them. They wanted to disrupt their attack, and end their unprovoked war.

Texas Senate Chamber — 08.10.32

The Senate chamber was full, and no one was comfortable. Jackets hung over chair backs. Ties were loosened. Coffee cups sat untouched at the edges of desks, already going cold. The public gallery was empty; sealed by order of the Sergeant at Arms. There was no press and no livestream; every phone had been surrendered at the door. The emergency session had been called to address the war Texas had waged against the UAA since three days earlier. There was a growing consensus that it had to stop before it gets out of hand.

The Senate Majority Leader stood at the center podium, one hand resting on a thick binder that had been prepared in advance. "We are not here to debate the cause of the war," he said evenly. "We are here to determine whether the executive branch retains the confidence of this body to continue prosecuting it."

A murmur rippled through the chamber. It wasn't a surprise because many still supported Cortez in the chamber. A senator from the Oklahoma panhandle leaned toward her neighbor. "That's not how this was framed."

The Parliamentarian didn't look up from his notes. "It is now."

The Majority Leader continued. "At 01:42 AM on the 7th, the President authorized sustained offensive operations beyond the scope of the Emergency Defense Resolution passed by this Senate. At 02:11, he declined a formal request from the United Alliance of America for immediate ceasefire talks."

A hand shot up. "Point of order!" a senator barked. "The President is Commander-in-Chief."

"Yes," the Majority Leader replied without missing a beat. "And this body retains the authority to determine whether that command is being exercised lawfully."

That landed like a physical blow. Another senator stood. "Are we impeaching the President?"

The chamber went quiet. The Majority Leader paused just long enough for the silence to hurt. "We are determining," he said, "whether hostilities can continue under his authority."

The doors at the rear of the chamber swung open. Rafael Cortez entered, flanked by security, his expression controlled but his jaw tight with anger. He hadn't slept, and it showed in the red veins of his eyes and the stiffness of his gait. He stopped halfway down the aisle.

"What is this?" Cortez demanded. "I wasn't notified—"

"You were," the Majority Leader said. "At 03:06. Your office acknowledged receipt."

Cortez turned toward the seated senators. "While our cities are under attack, you're holding procedural theater?"

"Our cities under attack? What cities?" Senator Blaire from Mississippi shouted angrily. "This attack is putting our cities in their crosshairs, not before."

A senator from Houston rose slowly. "My district is in an uproar," she said. "My constituents are asking why we are at war without a reason!"

Cortez scoffed, crossing his arms over his chest. "The attack was forced on us when Alabama petitioned to secede from the UAA and join us."

"And yet," the Parliamentarian said quietly, finally looking up, "that was a legal dispute that could have been resolved through negotiation."

"We all know why you wanted this war to begin with!" another voice shouted from the back. "You wanted revenge for Martinez!"

Other voices rose in loud agreement.

"Ladies and gentlemen of this chamber! The UAA is at fault for what happened that day—" Cortez tried to state his case, but he was cut off.

"They lost leaders too, we all did! How do we know the Consortium didn't have anything to do with it?"

The room erupted into laughter.

"Don't start that conspiracy nonsense!" The Parliamentarian spoke in measured tones, motioning for quiet. "These are not only articles of impeachment; the conduct under review carries criminal exposure."

A staffer burst through the door, clutching papers and a printed map of the Gulf. "I am so sorry to interrupt," he panted, "but military intelligence is reporting that the

UAA has moved a Naval Strike Group within a stone's throw of Austin and Houston."

The voices that had been shouting fell into a sudden silence. The Majority Leader didn't look at Cortez; he looked at the Parliamentarian. The Parliamentarian closed his binder.

"Mr. Leader," he said evenly, "the chair recognizes a motion to suspend hostilities pending review of executive authority."

A hand rose. Then another. Cortez turned slowly, searching the chamber for a single ally. He had lost every one of them with the revelation of the UAA naval position. The Majority Leader finally looked down at him.

"Mr. President," he said, not unkindly, "please take your seat."

The Bridge of the UAA Thomason — 12:00 PM CST

"Sir... incoming priority from Raleigh." Ensign Morel spoke in measured tones, his boots silent on the deck as he stepped toward Admiral Sentelle and Captain Addison with the fresh printout in hand.

The Admiral didn't speak immediately. The bridge was quiet aside from the pings of the radars and sonar units. There was the constant hum of the engines and the occasional sound of seagulls outside. Radar scopes glowed green, their rhythmic sweeps tracking aircraft that, as of this moment, were no longer considered enemies.

Captain Addison watched Sentelle's face carefully. "Orders, Admiral?"

Sentelle took the paper and folded it once, then again, his movements precise and deliberate as if the act itself could ground the chaos of the last seventy-two hours. "Signal the group," he said finally. "Weapons cold. Our defensive posture remains in effect, but all active strike packages are to be canceled immediately."

"Aye, sir." Addison hesitated, his eyes flicking toward the tactical map. "And the Texans?"

Sentelle looked out through the forward windows where the Gulf stretched flat a pale, hazy sky. "They'll get the same message, whether they're ready to hear it or not."

The ensign shifted his weight, looking between the two officers. "Sir... does this mean we're turning back?"

"No," Sentelle said, his voice firm. "It means we're stopping exactly where we are."

Addison raised an eyebrow. "Holding position?"

"International waters," Sentelle replied. "We remain visible, but unmistakable. This war didn't end because Texas was beaten in the field; it ended because someone decided not to make it worse."

Addison nodded once, the logic of the orders finally clicking into place.

"Helm," Sentelle called out. "Maintain current heading and speed. Notify Carrier Group Delta—this is a standdown, not a withdrawal. I want the world to know we're still here."

Across the carrier, the effects of the order were subtle but immediate. On the flight deck, crews halted their preparations mid-motion. Ordnance teams began the tedious work of securing weapons they had expected to see detonating over Houston before nightfall. Pilots climbed down from their cockpits without ceremony, helmets tucked under their arms, their eyes scanning the deck for explanations that no one was authorized to give.

No one was cheering after the announcement. Some wars ended with victory; others simply ended with exhaustion. This one seemed to end because their presence struck fear into the right people, enough for them to negotiate.

Sentelle unfolded the paper once more, his thumb tracing the last line of the transmission.

Standdown order signed, President Ulysses Mars.

The Admiral exhaled slowly, the tension in his shoulders finally beginning to give way. "Smart man," he murmured.

Captain Addison glanced at him. "Sir?"

Sentelle handed him the paper, turning back to watch the horizon. "He ended it before it got out of control. He's more interested in the future than the fight."

"But at the cost of Alabama." Addison spoke up.

"West Alabama wanted out, and the East wanted to stay. I just hope this buys us a piece of indefinite peace."

Admiral Sentelle nodded as he walked toward the Captain's At-Sea Cabin, closing the door behind himself.

Outside, the *UAA Thomason* held her position, while her fleet maintained theirs, sitting on the horizon that Texas wouldn't be able to ignore.

Raleigh, Carolina — 2:17 PM EST

Ulysses Mars sat alone with his elbows digging into the mahogany desk and his face buried in his hands. The war was over for now, but the word tasted hollow. He had stopped it by pulling Texas back from the edge, halting the bombings, and keeping the Gulf from igniting into a total theater of war. History would record it as restraint. Diplomats would call it maturity. But the cost burned in his chest.

Half of Alabama was gone.

It had not been lost in battle or taken by a flanking maneuver. It had been given away. West Alabama, specifically the counties that had voted loudly to leave the Alliance and join the Republic of Texas, was no longer his. It was a democratic fracture sealed by a ceasefire and a stack of paperwork rather than an exchange of blood. It was the right call and perhaps the only call, but that did not make it hurt less. Alabama had been a symbol that the UAA could fracture without collapsing. Now that symbol was split down the middle by a line drawn in a conference room.

Ulysses dragged his hands down his face and stared at the desk as he traced the faint scratch marks left by Samuel Burris's pen. He still had not replaced the furniture because he still felt like he was sitting in a dead man's shadow.

The price Texas paid was different but no less severe. Rafael Cortez was gone, impeached in a closed emergency session and removed before the sun had even cleared the horizon. By midmorning, the phrase *criminal exposure* was being whispered in the halls of Austin by people who never used such words lightly. Charges were coming. Cortez would be remembered as the man who turned grief into a war and called it justice. He was a sacrifice the Texan Senate was more than happy to make if it got the UAA Navy off their doorstep.

Ulysses reached for the ceasefire document and read the final lines for the third time. *All hostilities terminated. National borders amended. Forces to stand down.*

A knock sounded at the door that he refused to acknowledge. Another one followed, lighter this time. "Mr. President," a voice said quietly through the heavy wood. "They're asking when you'll make a statement."

In the span of four years, Ulysses had watched the nation fracture, rebuild, and fracture again. Every decision shaved something off him, including his certainty, his patience, and finally his mercy. He was becoming a different man, he could feel it in his bones. He didn't like it.

He stood slowly as his back cracked in the silence. "Tell them," he said, his voice regaining its practiced presidential steady. "Tell them the Alliance chose peace."

The aide hesitated. "And Texas, sir? What do we tell the reporters regarding the new border?"

Ulysses looked toward the window where the afternoon sun cut across Raleigh as if the world were still whole. "Tell them that peace is not forgiveness."

The door clicked shut. Ulysses remained standing with his hands resting on the edge of the desk, feeling the weight of a country that kept asking him to give pieces of itself away in the name of survival. He wondered quietly and dangerously how many more compromises it would take before there was nothing left to give, and whether the next war would leave him with any choice at all.

20

THE CONSORTIUM WAS NEVER one to act too quickly or rashly, but when they did, there was always a good reason. Patience was their primary currency, a resource they had stockpiled in the decades before the first borders of the old world began to fray. They had been planning this New Dawn since the 1950s, stretching back to the shadows of Project Paperclip. Beneath the destroyed surface of Washington D.C., a city hidden under a veil of technology, the Consortium's true heart beat with a low, rhythmic thrum. It was a masterpiece of misdirection; while they remained in the subterranean shadows, they had successfully orchestrated a landscape where the surviving nations of the former United States pointed fingers at one another rather than at the source of their shared rot.

Life on the surface had resumed, reshaped with new national identities but largely unquestioned otherwise. Many nations rose where one had fallen, each carving out an identity from its corpse. Some forged trade alliances out of necessity, while others bristled behind freshly drawn borders guarded by men with old grudges. The Remaining States of America had reconstituted themselves in Philadelphia, choosing a path of isolation over the messy business of influence. The Free States Nation had embraced a radical libertarian autonomy, rejecting any form of entanglement that smelled of the old federalism.

The United Alliance of America, however, remained the most dangerous variable in the Chairman's calculations. They had not just survived; they had seized the remnants of the United States Navy and rebuilt it into a focused, lethal extension of Ulysses Mars' will. Beside them, Texas remained a coiled spring; they were angry, but restrained, and satisfied with the piece of Alabama that Ulysses gave them but tensions would stretch to a breaking point. The Bluegrass Republic survived only by the grace of its neutrality, balancing precariously between powers that could swallow it whole. And then there was the Great Plains Nation, which had simply gone silent, retreating behind their borders with a chilling lack of interest in the outside world.

Deep underneath the simulation of a dead city that no longer existed, the Chairman sat in the Oval Office of the New White House. One that was built as a mirror of the one destroyed, the entirety of Consortium City was a mirror image of that which was above. From the windows of the bunker, he could see the Washington Monument standing whole and proud against a perfect, blue-sky simulation. He watched the streets below where automated traffic moved in careful, looping patterns. To the thousands of workers and operatives who called this subterranean metropolis home, it was like nothing had ever happened. The apocalypse was a rumor; the simulation was the truth. No one questioned that truth, The Consortium guaranteed that.

His desk phone buzzed, intruding upon the artificial quiet he cultivated. The Chairman slid his mask over his features and tapped a button, manifesting a holo-screen that bathed the aluminum shield in a flickering blue light. "Commander Phen here to see you," the voice announced.

"Send him in," the Chairman replied, his voice raspy. The Consortium seal, engraved onto the forehead of the aluminum mask, caught the light as he shifted.

The doors opened without ceremony, and Phen Martenson stepped into the room. He wore no rank insignia and his uniform was freshly pressed, no patches or identifiers were on the uniform. His posture was still military, he stood at a disciplined attention, but there was a visible tension in his shoulders that hadn't been there in the years before the 2032 escalation. He looked like a man bracing for a blow he could already see coming. The doors sealed behind him with a muted hiss of pressurized air.

The Chairman did not rise from the Resolute Desk. "Commander," he said, his voice filtered through the mask's voice changer. "You're late."

Phen inclined his head, his eyes scanning the simulated city beyond the glass. "I was delayed."

The Chairman's gaze followed Phen's. "No," he corrected. "You were precise. You spent exactly three minutes in the foyer contemplating your opening statement. As always."

Phen said nothing. The silence between them wasn't awkward; it was the silence of two military officers who understood the rules of the engagement. In this room, truth was a variable and questions were only permitted when the Chairman invited them.

"Jack Ashby," the Chairman said at last.

Phen's jaw tightened. "I assumed that was why I was summoned."

The Chairman turned from the window for the first time, his mask reflecting Phen's own weary expression back at him like a cold accusation. "He has become... inefficient. His operational instincts remain intact, but his loyalty vectors no longer point where they should. He is dwelling on the math of the Charlotte strike. He is looking for explanation or reason."

Phen held his gaze, his voice low. "Jack has never failed an assignment. He is the most capable asset we have in the field."

"No," the Chairman agreed. "He has failed *us*. There is a difference between capability and compliance, Stephen. One is a tool; the other is the hand that holds it."

The two stood for a moment locked on each other. "In 2028, you began formal investigations into Jack's loyalty, you reported him. Whatever your reasons, you started this." The Chairman's words settled heavily in the room.

Phen exhaled through his nose, slow and controlled. "Then retire him. If he's compromised, follow the protocol."

The Chairman tilted his head. "That is under consideration. But the Board recommends termination. He is too risky if somehow his memory is recovered. If he is disposed of then there is no residual risk of his memories resurfacing in a way that could damage us."

Phen's control cracked. "No," he said, the word echoing more loudly than intended in the sterile office.

"You forget your place," the Chairman warned, his voice dropping into a lethal whisper.

"I know exactly where I stand, and I know what Jack represents," Phen replied, his voice urgent. "Even stripped of memory, even broken down and rebuilt, he will still be dangerous. You don't throw away a weapon like that just because it needs calibration."

"Then why spare him?"

Phen didn't answer immediately. He didn't speak of the bond they shared or the years of blood they had spilled together. He didn't mention that Twelve would never forgive the Chairman, or himself, if they ended him. "You need him alive as proof," Phen said instead. "To show the other cells that service doesn't always end in a body bag. It keeps them compliant."

The Chairman regarded him for a long moment, the digital eyes of the mask flickering. "Thirty days."

Phen's breath caught. "Thirty days?"

The Chairman suddenly slammed his fist on the desk, the sound like a gunshot. "You dare ask questions? You were the one who reported he was vacillating! You were the one who noted his regret after the Montgomery jamming operations!"

"I did, sir. For selfish reasons. I wanted him pulled before he did something he couldn't come back from." Phen didn't flinch as the Chairman walked closer, the mask coming within inches of his nose.

"Commander Stephen Martenson, you and Jack have been partners since before we permitted the Confederation to invade. You are as close as brothers, and you claim to be selfish?" The Chairman backed away, his voice softening into a terrifying, kinder tone. "Don't answer that. Did you know that Jack is a junior? It was a trick question. I know you didn't. You don't even know the man you're trying to save."

The Chairman sat back at the desk. "I will tell you a story. His father, Senior, and I were friends. We went to Yale together. He was a fine friend, brilliant in ways most men can't fathom. But some men are unsuited for the things that leadership requires. They believe in the sanctity of the individual. They believe in the lie of the soul."

He tapped his fingers against the wood. "I see myself in you, Stephen. You know what needs to be done, and you don't let something as inconvenient as friendship stand in the way. I like that."

The intercom chirped. "Chairman—"

"Didn't I say I wanted quiet?" The Chairman reached out and surgically tore the intercom from its port. Wires snapped free with a dry crackle of sparks. Phen shifted despite himself. "You remind me of me," the Chairman continued. "You know what you want. You are willing to erase the lines when they become inconvenient. That's why Jack can't stay. He believes in uncrossable lines. People who deserve to live and not be sacrificed. Things you don't do, Phen."

"Where will he go, sir?"

"Wherever his father is, to a place where he is forgotten. You are dismissed."

Phen snapped into a Consortium salute, but as he turned, the door swung open and Twelve burst through. She had clearly bypassed the security detail in the hallway. Her normally cold, razor-sharp features were cracked, showing a raw desperation. "You can't do this! Please, you can't do this!"

She ran toward the Chairman, who turned and delivered a backhand across her face so quickly Phen barely saw it. The healed scar on her cheek split open instantly, gushing blood across her jaw. Twelve hit the floor hard, the sound dull and final. She didn't cry out.

"Stay where you are," the Chairman said to Phen, who had taken a half-step forward.

Twelve pushed herself up on shaking hands, blood dripping from her chin onto the polished stone. Her eyes burned with a cold fury. "You don't get to do this," she said hoarsely. “You don’t get to erase him like he never mattered.”

The Chairman wiped his hand on the edge of the desk. “You broke protocol. You interrupted a closed session. You are not programmed to beg, Twelve.”

Programmed. The word punched her as she steadied herself. “I’m not begging,” Twelve snapped. “I’m telling you that killing him will cost you more than you think. You’ll lose the unit. You’ll lose me.”

The Chairman studied her. Not as an asset, but as a variable. “You care,” he said slowly. “Do you know how rare that is in this city? You are the most effective operative we’ve ever engineered. You have perfect compliance, perfect execution, until now. And yet here you are, bleeding for a man who has already been discarded.”

Engineered. Another word hit her but she ignored it even though it gnawed at her. “Jack didn’t make me weak,” Twelve shouted.

“He made you dangerous,” the Chairman countered. He paced to the window once more. “Very well. We will not terminate Jack Ashby. He will undergo full retirement. Thirty days of normal life, then we come and get him. He will be quarantined with complete sensory isolation. Identity erasure, and his memory will be replaced. He will leave this city and never remember you. That is your punishment for defying me!”

Twelve swallowed, her voice trembling. “And if he does? If he remembers?”

The Chairman didn't turn. "Then I was right to fear him. But understand that this is not mercy, it is containment of a threat to The Consortium. If Jack becomes a problem in the future, the fault will be yours." he said, gesturing to a tech in the foyer. "Take her to medical, clean up her face."

Phen helped Twelve toward the exit, she glanced back at the desk. The Chairman was already seated, his mask unmoving against the glow of the simulated DC. "Remember," he called out. "You have thirty days with him. Make them count, because after that, he won't even know your name."

Twelve's Apartment — Night

The lock disengaged with a soft click that felt loud in the hallway. Twelve stepped inside and shut the door behind her, leaning her forehead against the reinforced panel for a moment longer than she should have allowed. The apartment was bathed in low, amber light. The dim, stagnant glow she always left as a marker against the dark. She was halfway across the foyer before the iron tang of blood hit the back of her throat.

"You're late."

Jack Ashby's voice drifted from the kitchen. Twelve froze, her hand still hovering near the pocket where she kept her sidearm.

"Jack—"

He stepped into view, the silhouette of his shoulders broad against the kitchen light. He was already moving toward her, a question forming on his lips, but the words died the moment the amber light hit her face. The scar on her cheek had been torn open, a thin, jagged line of red weeping down toward her jawline. Her left eye was already beginning to swell, the flesh darkening into a deep, bruised purple that would be unrecognizable by sunrise.

Jack stopped short, his entire posture shifting from casual to lethal. "What the hell happened to you?"

"It's nothing," Twelve said automatically. She reached up to touch the wound, but a flare of pain lanced through her cheek, causing her to gasp.

Jack crossed the room in three long strides. He caught her wrist before she could touch the split skin, his grip firm but careful. "Don't," he snapped, his voice vibrating with a sudden edge. "Don't you dare lie and say it's nothing."

He turned her head gently toward the light, his jaw tightening as he inventoried the damage. He had seen violence on every scale; he had inflicted it with his own hands across a dozen states. But he knew the difference between a combat wound and a message. This wasn't a mission injury, it was a calculated, administrative punishment.

"Who did this?" he asked, his voice dropping to a dangerous register.

Twelve pulled her wrist free, stepping back into the shadows. "It doesn't matter, Jack."

Jack laughed once, a short, humorless sound that didn't reach his eyes. "That's funny. Because it matters a hell of a lot to me."

She ignored him, shrugging out of her tactical jacket and letting it fall to the tile floor with a heavy thud. Dark spots of blood dotted the floor. "I handled it," she said, her voice sounding hollow. "I always do."

"That isn't an answer, and you know it."

She finally looked at him. Jack's anger was a visible thing, but beneath the surface, she saw the one thing he was never supposed to feel: fear. It wasn't the fear of a man facing death; it was the frantic, helpless terror of a man watching the only thing he cared about be hurt.

"I told you not to wait for me," she said softly.

"And I told you I don't follow orders from you," Jack shot back. "You disappear for hours into the lower levels and come back looking like a training dummy. What am I supposed to think?"

Twelve walked past him toward the bathroom, peeling off her gloves and leaving faint red smears on the white laminate counter. Jack followed, leaning against the doorframe, his arms crossed as he watched her reflection in the mirror. She turned on the sink, letting the water run cold. The blood spiraled down the drain in a pale pink vortex as she examined the damage. She leaned forward looking at the bloodshot eye, the split lip and scar, the mark of the Chairman's hand.

"Why do you only care when no one's watching?" Twelve said sharply, her voice cracking as she pressed a cold, wet cloth to her cheek. "We promised to protect each other, Jack. We swore it."

Jack scoffed, gesturing toward the bloodied face in the mirror. "Is this what protection looks like to you?"

She met his eyes in the reflection, her gaze steady despite the pain. "Yes."

The word landed with more force than the backhand that had caused the wound. Jack straightened, his expression darkening. "What aren't you telling me?"

The silence that followed was thick, filled only by the hum of the air conditioner filtering through the vent. "Say it," he pushed, stepping into the small bathroom until the air felt tight between them. "Whatever it is, say it."

Twelve swallowed hard. She was screaming in the privacy of her own mind. *Because if I tell you, they'll accelerate the process. Because if I tell you, I'll have to watch the light go out of your eyes today instead of thirty days from now.*

"Because knowing..." she paused, coughing as she applied alcohol to the cut, the sting forcing her to close her eyes. "Knowing won't help anyone, Jack. It won't change the trajectory."

"Don't insult me," he said, his voice dropping to a growl. "I've bled for this mission, I've killed for this job. Twelve, I've done everything for you ever since the day we were paired up."

"I know," she said softly. "That's why you're still here. That's why you're still breathing."

Jack stepped closer, his voice a mere whisper now. "Is this about the Chairman? Is he finally pulling the plug?"

Twelve's silence was the only confirmation he needed. He exhaled slowly, his hands clenching and unclenching at his sides as he fought to stay grounded.

"You're the best operator they have," she said, trying to find a lie that felt like a truth. "That's why you scare them. They don't know how to factor you into the new map."

Jack stared at her, a bitter smile touching his lips. "Scare them. Is that what we're calling it now? I'm a liability, Twelve. I've seen the way the techs look at me during calibration. I'm a corpse they haven't finished burying."

Twelve turned away from the mirror to face him fully. The swelling was worse now, making her look lopsided and frail, yet her eyes remained sharp. "It's what they see, Jack. Not what you are."

"That's not how this works," Jack said, shaking his head. "You don't get punished for being the most efficient weapon in the armory."

A short, jagged laugh escaped her. "You don't," she agreed. "Until the war changes, and the weapon becomes obsolete."

Jack leaned in, his eyes searching hers, looking for the secrets she was guarding. He had always been too good at reading her. "They're setting something up. I can feel the shift in the air. That meeting today… that wasn't about a new mission… It was about me!"

"They're… changing things," she whispered.

"That's the corporate line for erasure," Jack said quietly.

Twelve's fingers curled into fists. She stepped forward, closing the gap until her chest nearly touched his. "Listen to me. Whatever they tell you in the next few days. Whatever they offer, whatever tests they put you through; you do exactly what they ask. You don't fight, and dammit Jack you don't question. You understand me?"

Jack frowned, confused by the desperation in her tone. "That's your advice? Total surrender?"

"Yes. Tonight, it is."

Jack studied her for a long moment, then reached out, his thumb stopping just short of her bruised cheek. "If they try to take me off the board," he said, his voice thick with a promise of his own, "don't you let them turn me into something I'm not. Don't let them hollow me out."

Twelve's voice wavered for the first time since she'd entered the apartment. "I won't."

He nodded, accepting the promise without realizing that the "hollowing out" had already been signed and sealed. "Good," he said. "Because if I ever forget who I am…"

He let the sentence trail off into the amber light. Twelve finished it in her head: *I'll remember for you. I'll hold the pieces until you can find them again.*

But aloud, she said nothing. She moved into his arms, the smell of copper and salt mixing with the warmth of him. They kissed.

The Carolina Wastes — Early Morning

"I don't see any eyes on that corridor," Lee whispered into his radio while his breath hitched in the cold morning air. "We cut through Freedom Drive and take West Morehead. That puts us a few blocks from the Convention Center."

The convoy slowed but didn't stop. Three pickup trucks and two stripped-down jeeps rolled forward as their tires crunched softly over glass and debris that had been baked flat by years of weather and neglect. Engines stayed low and headlights remained off. In the **Carolina Wastes**, no one wanted to advertise their presence even four years after the silence began.

"Copy," a voice crackled back. "Thirty minutes. In and out."

Lee raised a fist and the lead truck eased to a halt beneath the shadow of a collapsed overpass. The skyline of Charlotte loomed ahead like a graveyard of giants. Uptown's towers were still standing and structurally intact, but their windows were dark and empty, representing a city holding its breath.

"Same rules as always," Lee said as he stepped out of the cab. "Stay on task, no wandering, and for God's sake no souvenirs. We are here for the copper and any other precious resources we can salvage. We do not touch the personal effects."

A few grim acknowledgments came through the comms as boots hit the pavement with muffled thuds. They moved in pairs with tools slung over their shoulders while headlamps cut narrow cones through the morning haze. Copper lines were easy to spot since they were stripped bare in some neighborhoods but remarkably untouched here. Someone whistled low.

"Hell of a thing," a man muttered while his light danced over a row of abandoned cars. "Whole city just left."

"Left? You mean vanished," Emory corrected him as her voice sharpened with nerves. She knelt to pick up a wad of clothing and a pair of sneakers from the asphalt. They were perfectly arranged as if the occupant had simply evaporated out of them.

"Keep moving," Lee snapped. "You want philosophy, find a bar."

Tools came up and headlamps dipped. The convoy spread out along the block with metal cutters biting into conduit and pry bars popping access panels that had not been opened since the day the city stopped existing. Copper peeled free in long, heavy lengths. It was valuable and familiar, and it was the only thing keeping their families fed in Raleigh.

Emory worked a junction box near the curb by bracing her shoulder against the housing as she twisted a stubborn bolt. Someone behind her laughed quietly when the panel finally gave way.

"Still hot?" a voice asked.

"No juice," she replied while her voice echoed in the hollow street. "Dead as the rest of the place."

A few doors down, Lee crouched beside a traffic control cabinet to scan the rooftops. He didn't like the quiet. It was not just the absence of people; it was the absence of biology. No birds sang and no rats scurried through the gutters. No stray dogs picked through the trash because there was only the wind.

"Five minutes," Lee said into his radio. "Bag it and move."

From the corner of her eyes Emory saw something. At first, she thought it was a reflection where her headlamp caught on glass or polished steel. It was a round object half-buried beneath a drift of ash and dead leaves near the sidewalk. *I know he said no souvenirs... but.* She knelt to brush the debris aside with a gloved hand.

The object was a smooth, flat disk about the size of a hockey puck with a surface that was shiny and seamless. There were no markings, as far as she knew it was a metal piece that fell off the Convention Center at some point.

"Hey," she called quietly. "Lee? Check this out."

"What?" he answered with irritation.

"You ever see one of these? It's... I have no idea what it is." She lifted it as her brow furrowed. The disk felt strangely warm against her palm.

Lee straightened slowly as his instincts finally began to scream. "Put that down, Emory."

"I haven't seen it on the inventory list," she said while turning it over. "It's not UAA and it is too clean for Texas."

"Put. It. Down. Now."

It was too late, the disk pulsed rapidly. It was not bright or loud, but it possessed a soft internal glow that looked like something breathing faster and faster. The air around Emory rippled, and distorted her silhouette like heat rising off a summer road after it rained.

Lee opened his mouth to shout, but Emory was already gone.

There was no scream or explosion. There was only a sudden absence, she was there, then she wasn't. Her gloves hit the pavement first followed by her jacket which collapsed inward as if the body inside had turned to air. Her boots tipped sideways and sat empty. Tools clattered onto the concrete where her hands had been a second ago.

The disk hit the ground and turned black. Someone swore loudly as the sound cracked like a whip. Another scavenger backed away while shaking his head. "No. No, she just—she's gone."

Lee moved forward with heavy legs. He stopped where Emory had been standing and stared down at the pile of clothing as if it might rearrange itself into a person.

"Emory?" He knew there would be no answer because he had just witnessed everything.

Another scavenger named Mike stepped forward with his eyes fixed on the disk. “What the hell is that thing?” he muttered as his voice trembled as he reached down.

“Don’t touch it!” Lee bellowed.

Mike’s fingers brushed the warm edge of the metal. The disk pulsed a second time. Mike’s face contorted for a brief and horrific second while his features folded inward like a reflection collapsing in a broken mirror. He vanished in a blink and left behind a helmet, a pipe wrench, and a pair of overalls that hit the ground a half-second later.

“Bag what we have and let’s get the hell out of here!” Lee shouted as his voice reached a fever pitch. “Run! Go!”

They grabbed the copper they had already stripped and scrambled into the back of the trucks. They were no longer concerned with being heard. The lead truck peeled out with tires screaming against the pavement and left the piles of empty clothes behind on the sidewalk.

“Regroup!” Lee yelled into the radio while they tore toward the city limits. “Emory and Mike are just gone. They are gone.”

From the upper levels of a partially collapsed parking structure, a UAA Marine reconnaissance team observed the street below through magnified optics. They had been shadowing the civilian convoy since first light, keeping a silent watch from the shadows of the ruins. They had just watched two civilians disappear.

"Actual," the team leader said into his throat mic while keeping his voice low and controlled. "Recon Two-One. Be advised. Civilian noncombatant vanished at grid Delta-Seven. There wasn't any kind of explosion and no EM spike either."

A long pause followed on the other end of the comms. "Clarify 'vanished' Recon Two-One."

"Subject was present one second," the leader replied as he watched the empty clothes through his lens. "Absent the next. No remains. Personal effects were left behind on the pavement."

Another Marine shifted beside him while staying glued to his glass. "Second civilian just went," he said quietly. "Same thing happened."

The leader did not look away from the street. Below them the roadway was static. Clothing lay where bodies had been and tools sat scattered across the concrete. There was no movement where there should be. The scavenger convoy was already breaking contact and their vehicles reversed course toward the exclusion line. "Civilian elements are egressing," the leader added. "No pursuit is being attempted."

The radio fell silent for a moment. "Copy Recon Two-One. Mark the site. Do not approach."

The leader acknowledged and adjusted his optic to compensate for the shifting morning light. "Stand by," the Marine next to him said. "There is an unknown object at the point of disappearance."

The leader focused his lens until the image sharpened. A flat black disk lay in the street, roughly twenty centimeters across with no markings and no visible power source. It sat there looking completely inert.

"Eyes on unknown device," the leader said. "We aren't getting close to whatever that was."

He toggled his laser rangefinder and a soft chirp confirmed the lock. "Geo-tag that," he ordered. "Deploy micro-drone, I need visuals so keep it high."

The drone lifted from its housing and eased forward in a controlled and slow drift. The Marine monitoring the feed frowned at his tablet. "Sir, I have no returns on the target."

"Explain."

"No thermal readings, and I'll be damned if there isn't a reflection. Its like nothing is sitting there," the Marine said while tapping the screen. "Sensors are skipping around like nothing is there."

The leader felt his jaw tighten. "Recover the drone. Bring it back slow."

The drone hesitated in the air. The feed glitched into static for less than a second as a wave of interference washed over the screen. When the image returned the street was unchanged except for one detail.

The device was gone.

"Actual," the leader said evenly. "The object is no longer visible. Confirm no contact with our drone."

"Confirmed," came the reply. "Maintain standoff."

"Recon Two-One," Actual continued while his voice dropped an octave. "This site is now classified, fall back to camp. We'll continue observation from a distance only, do not engage any further anomalies."

"Roger."

The team began displacement immediately. There was no verbal coordination needed since their movements were quiet and disciplined. Weapons were slung and optics were stowed. As they moved through the shadows of the parking structure one Marine glanced back toward the empty street.

"Sarge," he murmured. "What do we put in the report?"

The sergeant did not slow his pace. He thought of the clothes on the pavement, and the way the air had rippled like heat. How something could erase a person without a single drop of blood.

He keyed his mic as they reached the stairwell. "Report exactly what we saw. Leave nothing out."

"And pray," he added quietly, "that someone higher up already knows what this means."

He took another step down into the shadows of the structure. "We call it exactly what we saw. We let someone with more stars decide what it means for the Alliance."

They disappeared into the depths of the parking deck and left the street empty again while Charlotte stayed silent.

21

Charlotte Speedway — December 20, 2034

Morning arrived slowly at Camp Racetrack. The generators thudded awake before the sun cleared the eastern grandstands, sending a steady vibration rolling across the infield like distant thunder. Canvas tents glowed dimly from within as Marines moved through practiced routines. They laced boots, checked weapons, and tested radios without the need for conversation. Beyond the speedway walls, the Charlotte skyline loomed unchanged and uninhabited. Towers stood intact and windows remained unbroken. It was a city preserved at the exact moment it stopped existing.

At centerfield, the camp had grown into something semi-permanent. Command and medical tents sat closest to the infield access road while neat rows of campers and RVs lined up alongside canvas structures. These were temporary solutions that had long outlived their intended lifespan. Antenna masts rose from concrete pads poured months earlier, and tall Hesco barriers ringed the perimeter. These were reinforced with fencing and motion sensors that were calibrated daily and trusted only reluctantly by the men on the line.

Camp Racetrack existed because of a report that no one liked to reread. Two civilians had encountered a single device, resulting in no remains. The event looked exactly like the day The Accords were stopped, a terrifying similarity that forced the UAA brass to launch an immediate investigation. Marine Recon had witnessed the erasure from a distance, yet science teams had failed to reproduce the effect. Hundreds of drones vanished and sensors returned with nothing. The area had been declared stable enough for limited operations, but dangerous enough to justify an ongoing military presence. The Marines stayed not because they understood the Carolina Wastes, but because someone had to watch the vacancy to protect outsiders from a similar fate. They served as the stewards of a dead city.

Dr. Six Parks stood at the opening of the medical tent beside the command center while cradling a mug of coffee she had already forgotten to drink. Her fiery red hair was pulled into a messy bun atop her head, and her emerald-green eyes vanished behind glasses fogged from the heat rising off the cup. She had been at the Accords before the tragedy in '28, but she had left early. She had been ordered back to Raleigh with several others once security was deemed sufficient. No one had expected the rapture, the disappearance of millions. That survivor's guilt sat in her chest like a weight she could not put down.

Perhaps it was guilt or perhaps it was the cold realization that there had been nothing she could have done to stop the erasure. Her days were now filled with the routine injuries of a stagnant occupation. She treated Marines cut by jagged debris, twisted ankles, and concussions from collapsing structures. It was the kind of work that made an assignment feel dull but manageable. Then there were the other times she lost a Marine altogether, but those were unpredictably rare. There was no trauma and no explanation, one moment they were there, and the next they weren't.

Camp Racetrack was a lethal assignment wrapped inside a boring one, and Six Parks had learned that those were the environments that claimed the most lives. She finished her coffee without tasting it as a voice crackled over the camp intercom. The voice coming through was low and showed little emotion.

"Recon elements, five-minute warning. Briefing at Command."

The camp shifted almost imperceptibly at the announcement, silencing conversations mid-sentence and drawing the raspy pull of zippers as helmets were lifted from crates and snapped into place. The Marines were already halfway through their next task before the order finished echoing. Six stepped away from the medical tent and crossed the packed dirt toward the command center. Her boots crunched softly over gravel and spent shell casings that no one bothered collecting anymore. Morning light crept over the grandstands to cast long shadows as the smell of diesel wafted across the infield.

Inside the command tent, a map of Uptown Charlotte filled the central display. Streets were ghosted out in gray while buildings were rendered in skeletal wireframes. Red exclusion zones pulsed faintly around the Convention Center and the surrounding blocks. Staff Sergeant Rourke stood at the table with his arms braced on either side of the display. He did not look up when the last Marine stepped inside. Colonel Brigham Mars stepped up to the podium.

"All right, folks," Brigham said with a southern accent. "Same mission as yesterday and the day before that." A few tired smirks flickered and vanished among the ranks.

"Two four-man teams," Mars continued. "East and south approach vectors. We stay outside the red, I don't want any heroics, and for God's sake if you find one of those puck things, don't touch it."

Staff Sergeant Rourke tapped the map, causing a yellow line to appear as it skirted the perimeter of the hot zone. "While you will be boots on the ground use your eyes only. Sensors ok, but caution required. You see something that does not belong, what do you do?"

"We do not touch it," a Marine finished automatically.

Rourke nodded. "You do not touch it. You do not poke it. You do not get closer to it than you absolutely have to. Mark it on the map and get the hell away from it."

Six leaned against a support pole with her arms crossed. She watched the faces instead of the map. She saw veterans, new transfers, and Marines who had been here long enough to stop asking questions. They were just long enough into the rotation to start worrying about the answers.

"Any changes?" one of them asked.

Rourke shook his head. "We haven't gotten new disappearances or signals in the last seven hours. Science says the area is stable, but remember, scientists aren't in the field."

A few snorts answered that claim. "Science also said the Convention Center was secure," another Marine muttered.

Lieutenant Taylor Mars stepped forward to address the dissent. "That is why we do not trust science alone."

Rourke glanced toward the doctor. "Doc."

Six pushed off the pole. "Vitals check before you roll. I want your comms to stay open. If anyone experiences disorientation, visual distortion, or auditory anomalies, you say something immediately."

A Marine raised a hand. "What if it is just nerves?"

Six met his eyes. "Then we will call it nerves from inside the wire instead of bravery from outside it."

A few heads nodded slowly as the briefing ended without ceremony. Marines filed out to break into their instinctive teams. Each respective team checked their rifles and ensured their packs were tightened. Final checks were performed with the same hands that had done them a hundred times before. Privates Three and Seven Parks lingered near the edge of the command tent with their helmets tucked under their arms. Their rifles were slung but not yet locked in. They stood a little straighter than the others, trying not to look as though they were waiting for special attention.

Lieutenant Taylor Mars noticed them immediately. "Parks," he said while glancing between them. "What is it?"

Three cleared his throat. "Sir. We were told to hold for you."

Mars nodded once and stepped aside, lowering his voice instinctively. "You are with Rourke today. South vector."

"Yes, sir," Seven said.

Mars studied them for a moment. He did not check their gear because he trusted that they were seasoned enough to have it all together. He looked at their faces instead. They were good Marines, and he knew exactly how long they had been stationed at this grave. "Doc already checked you?" he asked.

"Yes, sir," Three answered. "Cleared."

Mars hesitated before adding quietly, "Anything weird last night? Any strange dreams or gaps in memory?"

Seven shook his head. "No, sir."

Three hesitated just a fraction longer. "Just quiet, sir."

Mars almost smiled. "Quiet is good. We love quiet."

That earned a weak grin from Seven. Mars straightened his posture. "Rules are the same as always. You see something you do not understand, you back away and mark it. You do not try to be helpful and you do not try to be brave."

"Yes, sir."

"And you do not try to figure it out," Mars added. "That is someone else's job."

They nodded in unison. From across the infield, Six Parks watched the exchange without meaning to. She turned away before anyone noticed the look in her eyes. Rourke's voice cut through the morning air. "Mount up."

The teams moved. Engines started low and steady while radios chirped once before going quiet. Marines filed through the southern gate in staggered intervals to disappear into the city. Lieutenant Taylor Mars loaded into a Blackhawk with the two Privates and Staff Sergeant Rourke. The helicopter spun up and lifted off as the other Marines left through the access well in Humvees and Jeeps.

Six watched until everyone disappeared into the skyline. She checked her watch. It was 07:18 AM. It was another set of patrols into Charlotte and another day spent hoping the city stayed asleep. Dr. Six Parks turned back into her tent and sat at the table where her cooling coffee rested. Several of her medical staff appeared at the entry, laughing as they gossiped. To them, none of this even felt real. In a solemn place like the Charlotte Wastes where millions had vanished, she found it difficult to smile.

"Good morning, Dr. Parks," a young nurse said while walking past.

Six nodded shallowly as she took another sip of her coffee. "Ladies and gentlemen," she said quietly to the empty room. "We haven't seen anything yet. That does not mean we are done for the day."

Charlotte — Airspace over Uptown

The Black Hawk rode through the air, steady as it skimmed above Tryon Street with its lights cutting through the streets and alleys. Staff Sergeant Rourke leaned into the open door with his harness pulled tight across his chest. One hand wrapped around the frame while the city slid beneath them; he reached over with the other to tighten his glove. Charlotte looked intact from this height, resembling a preserved city where buildings stood exactly where they always had. Weeds and grass were slowly overtaking the asphalt while abandoned cars piled up in the roads and along the sidewalks in silent rows. Along the highway there were cars crashed all over the lanes, no signs of life. It was like everyone just walked out to never return.

"Movement," the pilot called quietly over the comms. "Southbound. Multiple heat signatures."

Rourke lifted his optics to scan the grid. A pack of dogs tore down Tryon Street. They were lean and fast with their ribs showing sharp beneath patchy fur. They moved in an organized pack, like wolves chasing prey.

"People," Rourke said as the shapes came into focus.

Three figures staggered into view. They were sprinting hard but moving badly, looking too slow and far too thin. One woman stumbled and nearly went down before the others hauled her upright to keep moving.

"They're not armed," Taylor Mars said from behind him. "And they don't look like us."

"The dogs will have them in thirty seconds," Rourke replied while signaling the cockpit. "Pilot, set us down now."

The Black Hawk flared and dropped into the street hard. Rotors kicked up a localized storm of dust and loose debris as the team spilled out before its wheels had even settled against the pavement.

"Taylor and Three, take the left. Seven, stay with me," Staff Sergeant Rourke ordered.

The dogs turned the moment the noise of the helicopter hit them. They bared their teeth with eyes locked on the new intruders, but Rourke did not hesitate. He fired short, controlled bursts. Three animals dropped instantly before the rest scattered with yelps to vanish into the deep shadows of alleys and doorways. Breath fogged the cold morning air as the men lowered their weapons and turned to face the people they had rushed to save.

The three civilians stood frozen where they were with their chests heaving as they gasped for air. Their hollow eyes were sunken deep into the bone, leaving their irises to appear unnaturally large against skin that was stretched tight. Their clothes hung loose over pale skin and matted hair. When they spoke, it was not English or any language Rourke recognized. The woman stepped forward with her hands raised while speaking quickly in a broken rush of syllables that felt dislocated and fundamentally wrong.

Seven shifted his weight beside him. "What language is that?"

"I have no idea," Rourke said.

Rourke's eyes settled on a thin cord hung around her neck. Dangling low against her chest was a smooth metallic puck of some sort. Rourke's eyes opened wide with sudden recognition, he'd seen the reports, and the pictures.

"Fall back. Now!"

"What is it, Sarge?" Taylor asked as they followed the order and began backing away.

Rourke pointed at the thing hanging from the woman's neck. "Just get back. That is an order."

It was the same shape and the same size. It possessed the same impossible lack of markings as the devices found in the reports. The woman reached up with trembling fingers and pulled it free from her neck.

"No," Rourke said sharply. "Do not—"

She stepped forward and pressed it into his palm. It was warm. Her large eyes locked onto his, and for just a second, he thought she understood exactly what she had done to him. Then she turned and ran. All three civilians vanished down an alleyway before anyone could move to stop them. Rourke stood there with the device in his hand, feeling a sudden and profound fear.

"What the hell, Sarge, drop it!" Taylor shouted.

Rourke did not argue, he let it fall. Once it hit the pavement it pulsed, and for Rourke everything went white.

Silence followed the flash as he blinked wildly. Rourke's vision collapsed inward as if someone had turned the bedroom lights off and then back on again. A bone-chilling cold slammed into him first followed instantly by a heat so intense it stole the air from his lungs. His knees buckled under the sensory assault.

Then the distortion vanished as abruptly as it had arrived, leaving the street standing cold against a mind that was still struggling to catch up.

"Rourke!" Taylor grabbed his tactical vest to steady him. "Talk to me!"

Rourke shoved him away with a force that was harder than he had intended. "Get the hell away from me," he snapped. His voice sounded raw and wrong even to his own ears.

Three stepped forward instinctively to help. Rourke rounded on him as his hand came up and his rifle barrel swung toward the Private without a second thought.

"Back up!" he roared. "I said back up!"

The words felt entirely justified and necessary to him. He felt as though they were too close and acting as a threat. Seven froze with his eyes wide while Taylor stayed perfectly still.

"Rourke," Taylor said evenly. "You are clear. You are with us. Look at my face."

Rourke's chest heaved as his hands shook. His head rang as if it had been struck from the inside by a heavy weight. For half a second, he could not remember where he was or who these men were. Then reality snapped back into place. He saw the street, the bodies of the dogs, and the dropped pendant which was now inert and ordinary. Rourke lowered his weapon slowly.

"I am fine," he said, though the words tasted wrong.

Taylor did not argue. "Back to the bird. Now."

No one disagreed. As they moved toward the waiting helicopter, Rourke glanced once over his shoulder. The metallic puck was gone.

Rourke's Quarters — 12.23.34

Rourke woke with a violent gasp while his lungs clawed for air in the suffocating quiet of the camper. The interior was dark and silent until the coughing hit him with a force that felt as if his internal organs were being shredded. The tearing spasms folded his body forward until his bare feet slammed into the far wall of the small living space. He braced a hand against the narrow partition to fumble for a light switch, but his trembling fingers found only smooth, unresponsive paneling. The air felt wrong, it was thin and smoky. Every time he tried to pull air in it was like he was sucking through a straw in a paper bag riddled with pinholes.

He finally began to settle but he found he still could not take a full breath. He sat on the edge of the bed while shaking uncontrollably. Cold sweat pooled along his hairline and soaked the back of his neck. His watch glowed a rhythmic green in the dark, marking the time at 03:00 AM. There were no alarms sounding outside and no voices crackling on the radio. He heard only the occasional sound of gravel crunching as a night guard walked past the unit. Rourke lay back slowly as his chest rose in shallow, painful increments. Tears burned at the corners of his eyes, uninvited and frustratingly weak. He closed his eyes and tried to force himself to sleep, but his heart refused to settle. It was not mere anxiety that kept him awake. It was a deep and primal fear.

Sleep never arrived. Rourke lay on his back staring at the ceiling while counting his breaths because the rhythm felt like the only thing keeping him tethered to the world. He inhaled through his nose and exhaled through his mouth, but he lost count somewhere in the teens and had to start over again. He blinked, and for a moment he was not entirely sure how long his eyes had remained closed. The camper was dark. He saw the familiar rectangle of the ceiling vent and the faint outline of the cabinet above the sink. Everything appeared to be exactly where it belonged, yet the sense that something was off persisted. He possessed a nagging feeling that something had happened, that somewhere he had failed or missed a vital step in a protocol he could no longer name.

He rolled onto his side and then paused, unsure of why he had made the movement. His body felt heavy and unresponsive, as if his muscles had not received the signals his mind was sending. When he reached for the edge of the mattress, his hand missed the target by an inch. He tumbled to the floor and pinned himself between the plastic wall divider and the mattress. He was slowly freeing himself from the cramped space when the second wave hit him.

The coughing did not return gradually. It arrived all at once with a raw, otherworldly sound that suggested his lungs might climb up through his throat. The hacking was so violent and the pain so harsh that he collapsed onto the floor, sputtering crimson onto the vinyl flooring. Rourke ran his arm across his mouth, leaving streaks of blood across his skin. He leaned against the frame of his bed while trying to catch his breath, and that was when he saw it.

On the floor in front of him sat the shiny metallic puck he thought had disappeared after the strange woman hung it around his neck. His eyes went wide as cold sweat poured in sheets off his brow. His mind scrambled to grasp if the device was actually present or if it was merely a nightmare peeking in from the forgotten corners of his memory. Auditory distortions began to crowd his hearing as he crawled forward toward the disk. He reached out to grab the metal, but his hand hit only bare floor. He jerked back and rubbed his eyes, the realization that the puck wasn't actually there caused a moment of relief.

The voices outside grew louder and seemingly urged him to come out of the camper. Rourke turned toward his radio, thinking that was the source of the mocking sounds. He held the device close to his lips. "Overwatch, overwatch, stop screwing around," he managed to say before coughing again. The voices only intensified. He grabbed the counter for leverage and braced himself as he stood. "I am serious. That is an order."

Rourke retched as more blood spilled from his lips. He slowly limped toward the door, unlatched the lock, and swung it open. He did not see the infield of the speedway. His camper sat in the middle of a city street with the bodies of the dead wild dogs piled neatly about twenty yards away.

"How did my camper get here?"

He shook his head in disbelief and stepped through the door. As he gingerly placed his foot on the ground of the ghost city, everything went black.

Camper Row Three — 12.23.34 — 6 AM

Plastic reindeer with faded red noses stood sentry along the gravel path, their power cords snaking through the dirt to silent generators. Corporal Jensen passed a camper festooned with a string of oversized, multi-colored bulbs that pulsed with a rhythmic, dying flicker, casting long, jerky shadows against the white siding. A tinsel wreath, missing half its silver, hung lopsided from a side-mirror, shivering in the biting December wind. It was almost Christmas, but the festive cheer felt like a thin veneer hiding the reason they were there.

The Marine almost missed him. Corporal Jensen was halfway through his perimeter check when his headlamp caught something wrong near the third row of campers. It was a shape where the walkway should have been. "Overwatch, this is Jensen," he said into his shoulder mic as he approached the shape and his light shone on Rourke's face. "I have a Marine down. Repeat, Marine down." He knelt beside the body and felt his stomach tighten. Staff Sergeant Rourke lay on his side in the gravel with one arm folded beneath him at an awkward angle. His face was streaked dark with dried blood, his lips were cracked, and his skin was pale beneath the grime. His chest moved, but barely.

"Hey, Sarge," Jensen said while tapping his shoulder. "Rourke." There was no response. Jensen rolled him carefully onto his back as he had been trained. Blood smeared across his glove as he checked Rourke's mouth and nose. The smell of blood and urine struck him as he pulled Rourke back slightly. Underneath the Sergeant, there was blood that was pooled and tacky. "Overwatch," Jensen said, his voice tightening despite his discipline. "We have a lot of blood. He is breathing but it is extremely shallow."

Rourke's chest rose again in an uneven manner. Jensen frowned. "That is not right." He leaned closer, trying to hear breath sounds over the hum of generators and the distant rotors of morning patrols warming up. He tilted his head to listen but heard nothing. He shifted to the other side. Air moved there, thin and strained, but present. Jensen pulled back slightly with confusion creeping in. He keyed his mic again. "Medical, this is Jensen. I need Doc Parks at Camper Row Three. Now."

"Copy," a voice chirped back. "Channel 5."

Jensen frantically adjusted his radio. "Doc Parks, do you copy?" Static answered him at first. Rourke's chest hitched again, moving too shallow and too fast. Jensen shifted closer and stripped off his glove to check the skin temperature. It was clammy and sticky, Rourke's lips started turning blue.

"Copy, Corporal. I am on my way. Tell me what you see," Dr. Six Parks spoke quickly through the radio.

"Doc," he said again, sharper now. "I have blood and respiratory distress with his lips turning blue. He is not responsive."

Static filled the channel for a few moments. "I am on my way," Six's voice came back, calm and clipped. "Do not move him unless his airway collapses. Stay with me."

Jensen exhaled through his nose. "Roger that." He looked down at Rourke again. The breathing did not sound any better. It felt like an eternity before the gravel crunched nearby and Dr. Six Parks jumped out of a golf cart. She ran to where Jensen was kneeling. Six dropped to her knees beside Rourke seconds later, already snapping on gloves as her eyes took everything in at once: the blood, the deathly color of his skin, and the way his chest moved incorrectly.

"How long?" she asked.

"I don't know," Jensen said. "I found him just like this."

Six checked Rourke's pulse. It was fast and weak. She leaned in to listen to his breathing while moving her stethoscope from one side of his chest to the other. Her brow furrowed. She listened again and then a third time. "That does not make sense," she muttered.

"What is it?" Jensen asked but Six didn't answer him right away. She pulled out her pulse oximeter and clipped it onto Rourke's finger. The number flashed, dropped, stabilized, and then dropped again. She stared at the reading.

"These numbers shouldn't exist," she said quietly. "He should be dead."

Jensen swallowed hard. "Ma'am?"

Six looked up at him. "When did you last have contact with him?"

"Yesterday afternoon. The patrol came back clean."

She nodded once. "Okay. We are moving him. Gently."

As they lifted Rourke onto the stretcher, Jensen's chest tightened unexpectedly. He coughed once into his elbow, a sound that was sharp and dry. He frowned. "Sorry. It's the dust."

Six's eyes flicked to him. "Are you good?" she asked.

"Yeah," he said while forcing a breath. "Just dry air."

She did not look convinced, but she nodded anyway. "Get him to Medical," she said. "And Jensen."

"Yes, ma'am?"

"After this," she said evenly, "you are checking in with me too."

Jensen opened his mouth to argue, but then he coughed again. It was harder this time. Six straightened slowly.

"Actually," she said, already reaching for her radio. "Scratch that." She keyed the mic. "Command, this is Medical. I am initiating containment procedures around Camper Row Three. Possible exposure event. I need isolation protocols enacted immediately."

A pause followed. "Say again, Medical?" Command replied.

Six looked down at Rourke's face, at the blood, and at the way his chest still refused to behave like a human chest should. "Containment," she repeated. "Now."

Around them, sirens began to blare. Floodlights snapped on along Camper Row Three washing the gravel in harsh white light. Marines moved fast but not frantically as they hauled rolled sheeting from storage crates and snapped PVC frames together. No one asked questions because they had drilled for this. Six stayed kneeling beside Rourke with one hand still on his wrist.

"Jensen," she said without looking up. "I need you to stay right here."

"Yes, ma'am."

She glanced at him now, his face was flushed. He was not panicked or visibly sick, he was just off. "Any dizziness?" she asked.

He shook his head. "No, ma'am."

"Nausea?"

"No."

She nodded once, filed the information in her head anyway, and turned back to Rourke. She pressed two fingers along his sternum to count his breaths again. One side of his chest barely moved while the other pulled too hard, acting as if it were compensating for something that was not there. Six swallowed hard. "That's not possible." She reached for the portable ultrasound from the med kit and snapped it on while a corpsman slid in beside her.

"Gel," she said.

The image flickered to life on the small screen as she pressed the probe to Rourke's ribs. There was an empty space where there should have been a rhythmic slide of tissue. She adjusted the angle, but found nothing. She frowned and shifted lower to try again, still nothing. Her own breathing shallowed.

"Ma'am?" the corpsman asked quietly.

Six did not answer. She moved the probe to the other side. The image jumped instantly to show the lung sliding and movement. It was imperfect but it was real.

She pulled the probe away and stared at the screen as if it had lied to her. "That is not," she started and then stopped. She tried again with the same result. One lung was present but the other was gone. She removed the probe. "Prep oxygen," she said a little too calmly. "Low flow."

The corpsman hesitated. "Saturation is holding at eighty-eight."

"I know," Six said. "Prep it anyway."

She stood and stepped back for the first time, giving the corpsmen room as they fitted the mask over Rourke's face. Jensen shifted on his knees while coughing again. He turned his head away this time, looking embarrassed. Six noticed anyway; she straightened fully now.

"Jensen," she said. "Stand up."

He stood while wobbling just slightly before catching himself.

"Walk to the light pole," she ordered, pointing. "Slowly."

He took three steps and then four. On the fifth, he stopped. "Doc," he said quietly. "Something is tight."

Six was already moving. "Sit," she ordered, guiding him down onto a crate. She checked his pulse. It was strong, fast, and normal. She stepped back again to scan the growing perimeter. Plastic walls were going up fast now, sealing the camper row in translucent white. Marines outside the cordon watched in silence with weapons slung and faces unreadable.

Six keyed her radio again. "Command," she said. "Upgrade containment to Level Two. Respiratory isolation. No one enters without a full barrier."

"Copy, Medical," came the reply. There was no argument or hesitation.

She looked back at Rourke. He coughed once under the mask and then stopped. For a terrible second, Six thought he had gone still. Then his chest moved again in an uneven, wrong rhythm. Six felt something cold settle behind her ribs. The feeling that something was fundamentally off began to circulate in her head as she stood looking toward Jensen.

"I need more tests. Full spectrum, spinal tap, and everything else." Deep concern crossed her features. "And I want everyone who had contact with Staff Sergeant Rourke in the last forty-eight hours identified. Primary, secondary, tertiary. No exceptions."

"That is a lot of people, Doc," Command said carefully.

"I know," Six replied. "That is why I am calling it now."

She ended the transmission and turned back to Jensen, who sat hunched on the crate with one hand braced on his knee as he worked through another shallow breath.

"Listen to me," she said, crouching in front of him so he had to meet her eyes. "You are not in trouble. You did not do anything wrong."

"Yes, ma'am," he said hoarsely.

"If you feel anything change," she went on, "any pressure, dizziness, or confusion, you tell me immediately. You do not push through it and you do not power on."

He nodded while swallowing. "Yes, ma'am."

Behind her, the corpsmen finished securing Rourke on the gurney. The oxygen hissed softly. His eyes fluttered once, unfocused, and then stilled again. Six stood up.

"Move him," she said. "Slowly. Keep him horizontal."

They wheeled Rourke toward the waiting isolation trailer, now half-swallowed by the rising white walls of the containment tent. The space felt smaller with every step. As the zipper sealed behind them, the sounds of the camp dulled and muted to a distant thrum. Six stopped just outside the barrier. She removed her gloves carefully, disposed of them, and reached for a fresh pair.

For the first time since she had arrived, she allowed herself to look at the scene as a whole. The floodlights, the plastic, and the Marines standing watch like sentries at the edge of something they could not see. She keyed her radio one last time.

"Log this as a suspected infectious event," Six said. "Unknown vector. Unknown incubation. Until proven otherwise."

"Understood," Command replied.

Six lowered the radio and took a steadying breath. She would find it. The cause, the mechanism, and the explanation that made this make sense. Because if this was not something that could be understood, she did not finish the thought. Instead, she turned, pulled on a respirator, and stepped into the white.

"We are going to get to the bottom of this."

22

THE ARTIFICIAL SUN ROSE on schedule while its pale light seeped through the smart-glass curtains of Jack's apartment. It was calibrated to feel warm; convincing. It was just bright enough to suggest morning without demanding it. Twelve was awake before it finished clearing the horizon. She lay still while listening to Jack breathe. His slow and even breath calmed her. Her body was tangled with his beneath the sheets with one of his arms draped over her waist. His leg was hooked around hers as if he were afraid she might disappear if he let go. The sheets were twisted and kicked loose sometime during the night. For a few seconds, she let herself pretend.

Then the communicator vibrated against the nightstand. It was not loud or urgent; it was just enough to get her attention. Her green eyes snapped open with every trace of sleep gone. She reached for it carefully while easing Jack's arm aside so she would not wake him. The screen lit her face in cold white text. Two words flashed across it: *It's time.*

Her pulse jumped with a mix of panic and timing. She knew the thirty days were over. She checked the timestamp automatically while running the math in her head. Phen would be moving with the HRT. They would already be suited up, and armed. Somewhere below them, the building's security systems were being quietly overwritten. This was the window. She swallowed and set the communicator face down. Jack shifted beside her while mumbling something she didn't catch. His grip tightened instinctively to pull her back against him. His face pressed into her shoulder.

"Twelve," he murmured while still half asleep. "You're up early."

"Yeah," she said softly. Her voice held steady because training held it there. "Couldn't sleep."

His familiar hand slid along her side, causing her skin to tingle. "Stay. We don't have anything today."

We. The word landed harder than it should have. The communicator vibrated again as a reminder; in case she missed the first one. Her heart picked up pace from the weight of inevitability. She rolled onto her back and reached for it without caution. Jack's eyes cracked open as the light shifted.

"Everything okay?" he asked.

She forced a smile and sat up while gathering the sheet around herself. "Yeah. Just ops."

He frowned slightly while waking. "We are on leave; ignore them."

I wish I could. "You don't ignore the Chairman." She laughed a little, but her heart beat sour in her chest.

She swung her legs over the side of the bed. "I need to shower."

She stood while allowing her silhouette to cast a shadow across his face.

"You are driving me crazy," he stretched while yawning, completely unconcerned. "Want me to come with?"

Yes, she thought immediately. The word came sharp and unfiltered to cut through everything else. She smiled instead. "I'd love you too," she said while reaching for her clothes, "I just need to get there early."

Jack pushed himself up on one elbow to watch her move through the room. She noticed the way his eyes tracked her automatically, as if this were still a life with continuity. As if this morning led to an afternoon or anything after for him.

"Early," he said with a faint smile tugging at the corner of his mouth. "You're never early unless something's wrong."

She paused at the foot of the bed with fingers resting on the edge of the chair where her clothes were draped. For half a heartbeat, she considered telling him something true. Not the truth but just enough to feel less alone. Instead, she smiled back. She knew this was the only way to save his life, even if it meant losing him.

"Since when is early a problem?" she asked. "You're the one who hates being late."

"Yeah," he said with eyes half-lidded and amused. "But I also hate when ops pretends leave is optional."

She turned toward the bathroom while keeping her pace unhurried. “You know how it is.”

“I do,” Jack said. “Which is why I’m saying ignore it.”

She stopped in the doorway and leaned her shoulder against the frame just long enough for him to notice. His lazy grin was confident as he looked at Twelve standing there, naked. “Come back to bed,” he added. “Five more minutes. Chairman won’t notice.”

The name landed wrong. Twelve felt her stomach tighten into a familiar coil she had learned to keep buried. The communicator vibrated again in her hand this time it was sharper and the warning more insistent.

Jack glanced at it then back at her. “See? Even the room’s annoyed.”

She laughed with a soft, controlled sound. It surprised her with how real it felt. “You know I don’t get to decide that,” she said. “You’re braver than I am.”

He shrugged. “I’m just better at priorities.”

She looked at him then with an uneasy smile crossing her lips. He was barefoot, unarmed, and his hair was a mess from sleep. The faint scar at his collarbone caught the light as he shifted. He was a man who had survived everything the world had thrown at him, yet he still believed the rules applied evenly.

“You should stay in bed,” she said.

Jack raised an eyebrow. “That sounded like an order.”

“Consider it advice.”

He chuckled and dropped back against the pillows. “Fine. I’ll make coffee. You owe me breakfast later.”

Later. Her chest tightened again. "I'll try," she said.

She turned into the bathroom and closed the door gently behind her while being careful not to let it click too loud. The mirror greeted her with a version of herself that looked calm, but underneath she felt cracks forming. The shower had not started yet, but she braced both hands on the sink anyway while breathing slowly until the tremor passed.

Thirty days were never just thirty days. They were a countdown. Behind the door, Jack hummed to himself while thinking about coffee and food and a morning that still belonged to him.

Twelve closed her eyes with tears welling as she heard the knock. Then she turned on the water to let the sound drown out the rest. She sat in the tub and cried while her chest sobbed uncontrollably. She heard a knock at the door and a moment later Jack open the door to whoever was there.

"Phen?" she heard Jack say through the bathroom door. "Why are you here?"

Shouts erupted in the apartment as Twelve sat in the shower flow with her mind swirling. She sobbed uncontrollably while her thoughts fractured: flashing suddenly to a sterile medical examination room. In the jagged memory, she saw a girl who possessed her own face being carried away by men in white. She did not know where the vision came from or if it was a memory at all, yet the image of the girl who looked like her being taken felt like the same moment. She gripped her knees as the water turned cold. She knew what she had done, even if she had convinced herself it was for his own good.

She betrayed the man she loved.

She would never forget, even when he does.

Jack smiled as he watched Twelve disappear into the bathroom. The shower kicked on a second later while steam already fogged the glass. He lay there for a moment longer than necessary to listen to the water and the muffled sounds of her moving around. It felt domestic in a way his life rarely allowed. A knock came at the door. Jack sighed while feeling more amused than annoyed. He slid out of bed and pulled on his shorts and a T-shirt while stretching as he stood. A yawn escaped as he crossed the apartment barefoot to rub sleep from his eyes. The knock came again, this time firmer.

"Yeah, yeah," he called. "I'm coming."

He unlatched the deadbolt and opened the door. Phen stood in the hallway. He was not in fatigues or relaxed; he was in full tactical kit with a plate carrier, sidearm, and gloves. Jack blinked once.

"Phen?"

Phen's expression did not change. He stood with a calm, and professional cadence. His face showed no emotion. "Morning, Jack," Phen said. His voice was even and almost friendly. "We need to talk."

Jack glanced past him instinctively. The corridor appeared empty, but he caught movement at the far end. He saw too many shadows. He frowned. "You guys really suck at respecting leave."

Phen did not smile. Jack felt the first pinch of something colder than irritation. He leaned casually against the doorframe anyway while blocking the entry without thinking about it.

"What's going on?" he asked. "If this is about last month, I already filed the report."

"This isn't about any report," Phen said.

Jack noticed then that Phen was not looking at him directly. His gaze kept flicking past Jack's shoulder toward the interior of the apartment and toward the bathroom. Jack followed his eyes. "Twelve's in the shower," he said. "If this is ops business, it can wait five minutes."

Phen's jaw tightened just slightly. "It can't," he said.

Jack straightened because something in Phen's tone had changed. There was a finality in his voice. The same one that Jack had delivered several times in his own career. Jack laughed once with a short and confused sound. "Okay. Then you'd better explain why you're standing in my hallway dressed like it's a breach."

Phen took a small step forward. He was not aggressive, but he was not retreating either. "Jack," he said while lowering his voice, "I need you to come with us."

The word landed wrong. "Us?" Jack repeated.

Phen glanced to his left. Two figures stepped into view then two more behind them with helmets on and visors up. Their weapons were slung but ready. HRT. Jack's smile faded. "This is a joke," he said. "Right?"

No one answered. The sound of the shower continued behind him. Jack's pulse picked up. "Phen," he said carefully, "if this is some kind of drill, you should probably loop me in."

Phen finally met his eyes. "I can't," he said. Jack searched his face for a tell or a crack, but he found none. "We are doing it this way because you deserve to be treated like a hero," Phen continued.

"Doing what?" Jack laughed as one of the other HRT operators pulled a large zip tie from his pack. Jack saw it. "Am I under arrest?"

"Turn around, Jack," Phen said bluntly. "Make this easy."

Jack stared at the zip tie as if it did not belong in the room. "Turn around?" he repeated. The laugh that followed came out sharper this time. "Phen, you're out of your damn mind."

No one moved. The operator holding the restraint did not step closer because he did not need to. The message was already delivered. Jack glanced past Phen again: this time deliberately. The hallway was no longer empty. The shadows he thought he had seen earlier had become more HRT operatives, too many to ignore.

"What are the charges?" Jack still believed in rules; he believed he was protected by them.

"National Security. That's all you need to know."

Jack turned toward the running shower. "Twelve!" he shouted, but the shower continued running. "Twelve!" Jack called again while louder now. "Hey—"

The water did not change. There was no pause or startled reply: just the steady rush of the shower hitting tile. Jack took a step back into the apartment. Phen moved with him. He was not fast or forceful, but he moved just enough to block the doorway with his body.

"Jack," Phen said quietly. "Don't."

Jack stopped short with disbelief flashing hot across his face. "Get out of my way."

Phen did not budge.

"This isn't how this goes," Jack said. His voice tightened despite his effort to keep it level. "You don't show up unannounced with a stack of operators and start throwing around 'national security' like it's a magic word."

Phen inhaled once through his nose. "I know."

Jack stared at him. "Then explain it."

Phen held his gaze for a long second then shook his head almost reluctantly. "I can't."

Behind Jack, the shower continued to run. Jack laughed again, but this time it was thin and edged with something close to panic. "You're seriously telling me I don't even get charges? No hearing? No counsel?"

"This isn't an arrest," Phen said.

Jack blinked. "You're holding restraints."

Phen did not argue the point. "Jack," he said again while softer now, "I need you to turn around."

Jack's jaw clenched. He looked past Phen one last time toward the bathroom door. Steam curled out from beneath it. "Twelve," he said again. He was not shouting this time; he was just saying her name.

No Response.

The realization came in a slow and sickening wave. It was not that she was not answering; it was that she was not coming. Jack looked back at Phen. "She knows," he said. It was not a question.

Phen did not confirm it, but he did not deny it either.

"That's enough," Jack said sharply. "Move. Now."

Phen raised one hand with the palm out: a signal. Two HRT operators stepped forward in unison to fill the space behind him. They were close enough now that Jack could hear their gear shift when they stopped. They were close enough to smell the polymer and oil. Jack exhaled hard through his nose while his eyes flicked between them.

"This is a mistake," he said. "And you know it."

Phen's voice dropped to a murmur meant only for Jack. "Maybe. But it's not mine to make."

Jack stared at him for another moment. Then, slowly and deliberately, he turned his back. The zip tie closed around his wrists with a sharp and final sound. Jack flinched despite himself. The restraint tightened while biting into skin and forcing his shoulders back. A hand settled briefly between his shoulder blades to guide him forward.

"Careful," Phen said. "Steps."

Jack was walked out of his own apartment barefoot with the tile cool under his feet and the air in the hallway colder than it should have been. As they moved, the bathroom door remained closed. The shower kept running. Jack twisted his head just enough to look back. For half a second, he thought he saw movement behind the fogged glass. Then the door shut. The deadbolt slid home.

Jack swallowed. As they turned him down the corridor, Phen leaned in one last time. "You're going to hear a lot of things," he said quietly. "Some promises. A few warnings. Keep your mouth shut.."

Jack did not look at him. "What am I being taken for?" he asked.

Phen hesitated. "Because you matter," he said. "And because that makes you dangerous."

Jack let out a breath that was almost a laugh. Outside, an HRT transport waited: it looked like a minivan but it hovered on the street. Everyone on the streets continued walking by as if what was happening was normal. Phen loaded him into the rear hatch.

"Wait!" Jack heard her voice.

"What the hell, Twelve?" he said as she loaded onto the transport. Her face was red and streaked, but her expression was unreadable.

"You don't have to be here, Twelve." Phen spoke as softly as he could over the sound of the transport's engine.

"I want to be here." She looked at Jack. "I need to be here."

The transport settled onto the roof of the George Bush Center for Intelligence with a muted thud while its stabilizers hummed as the ramp lowered into open air. Jack looked at the HRT as they lined up outside on the gray top of the building. There was no signage and no ceremony; it was a walk meant to be seen only by those who mattered. It was a perp walk. Jack remained seated. Twelve stayed beside him with her posture rigid, her hands folded neatly in her lap, and her eyes fixed forward. She did not look at him or the operators; she stared somewhere beyond the edge of the roof as if she had already left the moment behind. Jack tested the restraints instinctively: still tight.

Phen paused at the base of the ramp and turned with an unchanged expression. He looked businesslike and almost bored. "Up and at 'em, Jack," he said while sweeping one arm toward the exit. "We've got an appointment."

Jack did not move right away. "Twelve," he said quietly. She did not look at him.

Phen's jaw tightened just a fraction. "Let's go."

Jack stood because the restraints guided the motion rather than his legs. As he stepped onto the ramp, he glanced back once. Twelve finally turned her head. For a moment, their eyes met. There was no apology there and no reassurance. Only resolve stared back at him. It was the kind that does not bend, even when it hurts. Then Phen placed a hand lightly on Jack's shoulder to steer him forward. The ramp lifted behind them. Jack's eyes landed on Vannah who was fully kitted out next to the entrance. Her face lacked expression as she stared ahead. "What the hell is going on?" He shifted his hands to try and free himself, but the restraints felt like they only grew tighter.

Twelve stood and donned her helmet with the visor down. Stepping off the back of the transport, she watched the engines spin up as the craft lifted from the rooftop. She fell in line with the other members of HRT as they formed ranks. Jack tried to keep track of her, but she disappeared into the identical uniforms. The door opened as the Chairman and Board of Leadership stepped into the open. Their painted aluminum masks, which concealed their identities, caught the early sun to reflect light into his eyes. All of HRT immediately rendered the Consortium Salute and lowered to a knee. The Chairman stepped forward; Jack could feel the smugness radiating from behind the mask. The Chairman did not raise his voice because he did not need to.

"Jack Ashby."

The name was spoken like a designation being retired rather than a man being addressed. The aluminum mask hovered close enough that Jack could see his own distorted reflection. His hands bound, and barefoot on cold concrete decking.

"Why am I here?" Jack growled.

A ripple of amusement passed through the masked figures behind the Chairman. It was not laughter, but something quieter and more satisfied. "Not to die," the Chairman said. "That was discussed."

Jack's eyes flicked toward the ranks of HRT toward where Twelve had been, but he did not see her.

"But you are dead to us," the Chairman continued. "Which is rarer; and far more instructive."

Jack leaned forward as much as the restraints allowed. "You don't get to erase me because it's convenient."

The Chairman stepped back just enough to reclaim the space. "Oh, Jack. Convenience would have been your death, and that would be far simpler." He gestured once and sharply. Two members of HRT stepped forward to reposition Jack without force, turning him slightly so he faced the full semicircle of the Board. Their identical masks gleamed in the morning light. "This is not punishment," the Chairman said. "This is accounting."

Jack scanned them while cataloging everything instinctively. He looked for potential escape routes, but there were none. The roof edge loomed behind the Board, guarded by two more operators who had not knelt. "And what am I being accounted for?" Jack asked.

The Chairman tilted his head. "I question your loyalty. The risk of keeping you around." He paused then added casually, "You are becoming weak like your father!"

Jack stiffened. From the corner of his eye, he saw a movement in the ranks. Someone moved slightly. But he knew better than to look for too long.

"You served exceptionally," the Chairman continued. "Which made you visible. And visibility, as you know, is dangerous."

Jack exhaled slowly. "So what is this? Exile? Like what you did to my father?"

Silence lasted a moment before the Chairman laughed. It was a soft sound filtered through the mask that sounded almost kind. "No. Exile implies choice. Exile still means you can be a threat." He turned slightly to address the Board. "Jack Ashby is hereby retired from active operational status. Effective immediately."

The words landed heavier than any sentence before them. *Retired.* Jack's brows drew together. "You don't retire people like me."

"We do," the Chairman replied, "when they become liabilities we prefer alive."

Jack looked up sharply. "Alive for what?"

The Chairman stepped closer and lowered his voice so only Jack could hear. "To remind others what obedience buys and what it costs." He straightened. "By the authority of this Board, your identity is hereby terminated and your history archived, leaving you with neither the access to seek us nor the permission to be sought, effectively stripping the world of any memory that Jack Ashby ever existed."

Jack clenched his jaw. "And if I do come after you?"

The Chairman did not answer immediately. "You know what would happen, Jack." Pausing, he turned away. "You'll live, but you won't remember any of this. You won't remember Twelve. I know you love her, but she chose this for you."

"What do you mean she chose this?" Jack twisted.

"I guess you'll never know." The Chairman chuckled as he motioned for the scientist.

The scientist placed a pair of headphones on Jack. A resonant sound began swirling from all directions and he blacked out.

Darkness did not come all at once; it arrived in layers. Jack surfaced into awareness slowly, like a diver breaking through cold water. His body felt distant and uncooperative while his limbs remained heavy. The restraints were gone, but he could not move anyway. Not fully. He tried to open his eyes, but nothing changed. There was no light or dark: just absence. The air was still and musty. There was no hum, no echo, and no sense of space at all. He could not tell if the room was large or small, or if he was alone or surrounded. Sound did not travel here, and neither did time.

Isolation chamber, a voice in his mind supplied automatically. The thought startled him. *How do I know that?* The answer slipped away before it could form. Pressure built behind his eyes; it was not painful yet, but it was insistent. It felt like a thought trying to surface and being pushed back under. His breathing quickened then steadied as the chamber compensated automatically. Something began to hum. It did not hum through his ears; it vibrated inside his skull.

Images flickered at the edges of awareness: a firing range, steel targets ringing under gunfire, a briefing room, and a map with red circles. He saw Phen laughing over bad coffee. Jack reached for that last image instinctively, but it smeared and lost cohesion. Phen's face blurred then flattened before it vanished entirely.

Jack gasped. "No," he tried to say, but the word never reached his mouth. Another image surged forward, uninvited.

Twelve.

It was not a memory at first; it was a sensation of warmth. He felt the familiar weight of her body against his and the steady rise and fall of her breath as it slowed. Her arm was draped across his chest as if it belonged there, as if it always had. He felt the press of her forehead against his shoulder: the way she fit without effort. He saw the way her green eyes had searched his: unguarded and burning with something that asked to be believed.

"I love you, Jack." Her voice was not loud because it did not need to be. Then it faltered.

The warmth thinned and the weight lifted. Her eyes lost focus while draining of meaning as if someone were pulling the color out of them. The sound of her voice stretched, warped, and unraveled. He reached for her and found nothing but a pile of clothes. The space where she had been collapsed inward to leave only the ache of absence behind. *Zero Energy.* The thought terrified him.

Hold on to that. A muscular pain answered him. A deep, invasive pressure made his thoughts buckle. The harder he tried to focus, the worse it became, as if the chamber were correcting an error. Her face fractured. Her eyes were the last to go. Jack screamed. His hands curled somewhere he could not feel them while his mind clawed at itself to grasp for anchors: names, dates, and places. Each one dissolved the moment he touched it.

Jack Ashby. The name echoed once, hollow, then collapsed into meaninglessness. It was just a noise. Panic surged, pure and animal.

"*I am—*" The sentence never finished. Memories did not vanish cleanly; they degraded, skipped, and replayed out of order. A thousand moments were shredded into static. A voice, a hand on his shoulder, a rooftop, and masks. A decisive pain spiked again. Jack understood then that this was not death; it was erasure of everything he was. Everything he is.

Something brushed the surface of his thoughts: cool and clinical while evaluating resistance and adjusting parameters. He felt himself slipping, not into sleep, but into something thicker and heavier. A fog rolled in. He tried to remember why it mattered, or why any of it mattered at all. Somewhere deep inside, past the failing architecture of his mind, a single emotion remained intact: loss. It was not tied to a face or a name; it was just the certainty that something essential had been taken.

The fog thickened. His thoughts slowed then scattered before they stopped forming altogether. At the very end, one fragment surfaced unbidden: *At least I'm alive.* The thought barely completed before it, too, dissolved.

Darkness closed in: not sudden, but absolute. Everything that made him was gone. He was a man with only a name.

Jack Ashby.

25 Days Later

The first time Twelve returned to the isolation wing, she told herself it was procedural. Badge scan; clearance accepted; no questions asked. She had been coming every day for twenty-five days. No one knew, nor did they seem to care. The corridor lights came up in sequence as she walked the sterile white paneled hallway. Every footstep sounded too loud in the narrow space, even though she knew the sound dampeners would swallow the noise before it carried anywhere important.

Isolation chambers were buried deep with no windows, no external feeds, and no ambient noise. This was a place designed not just to contain someone, but to ensure nothing of them escaped. She stopped outside his door. The panel displayed vitals in a narrow column:

heart rate, respiration, and neural activity rendered into unreadable graphs meant for technicians rather than operators. Everything remained within acceptable parameters.

Alive.

She had not realized how tightly she had been holding her breath until she exhaled. Twelve did not touch the glass at first. She stood a step back with her helmet still on and visor down; her hands were clasped behind her back in the neutral observer posture she had been trained to maintain. Inside the chamber, Jack lay suspended in the restraint cradle with his head secured by the interface collar. His body looked wrong without tension or readiness. He was too still and too open. He did not react when she entered. There was no flicker or sign that he knew she was there.

Good, she told herself. *That's good.*

She stepped closer anyway. The glass was thick and layered to block sound, light, and electromagnetic leakage. He could not hear her, see her, or feel her presence. Twelve reached up and removed her helmet. The air felt colder without it. She stood there for a long moment while studying his face as if she were memorizing it for the first time or the last.

"I'm here," she said quietly.

The chamber did not respond. His vitals ticked on, indifferent. Twelve swallowed and sat down on the floor with her back against the glass and her knees drawn in. The posture was unprofessional, but she did not correct it. Her mind ran through exfiltration paths automatically while every route ended the same way. The sound of an alarm went off: a steady chyron that caused Twelve to shake from her reverie. The alarm cut off abruptly and voices replaced it.

Footsteps approached: multiple and unhurried. Twelve did not hesitate. She snatched her helmet from the floor and slid it on to seal the suit in one fluid motion. Her eyes scanned the room. There was no cover and no exits: just the terminal banks lining the far wall. She dropped to a crouch behind the main console. Her gloved fingers found the seam of the raised floor tile. With a sharp, controlled twist of her combat knife, she popped the vacuum seal. Beneath lay the sub-floor plenum: a narrow, dusty void of cabling and recycled air. She slid her body into the darkness while curling her legs tight to avoid the thick bundles of fiber optics. With her free hand, she guided the heavy composite tile back into place above her head. It clicked shut just as the observation door hissed open.

Twelve lay perfectly still in the crawlspace while the air smelled of ozone and dry dust. Her breathing slowed automatically as training overrode the spike of adrenaline. Whoever was coming was not security; security moved faster.

White coats appeared: two of them, joined by a third in a dark operations jacket with no insignia.

"Interface cycle complete," one of the scientists said while tapping a tablet. "Memory degradation is holding. No rebound signatures."

"Define holding," the man in the jacket replied.

"He retains motor function, learned behaviors, and tactical instincts," the other scientist said. "But autobiographical memory is gone. Emotional anchors are gone. Identity scaffolding collapsed cleanly."

"Good," the man said. "Then he's safe."

The first scientist hesitated. "Safe is relative."

That word made Twelve's fingers curl inside her gloves. The second scientist pulled up a neural readout to project it against the glass. "Even stripped, he's still highly adaptive. Pattern recognition remains elevated; threat anticipation too. You don't erase thirty years of survival conditioning."

"So he's still dangerous," the man said flatly.

"Yes," the scientist answered. "Just not loyal."

The man nodded once with his decision already made. "Then we proceed."

"Proceed how?" the first scientist asked.

The man gestured toward Jack's suspended body. "He's not an asset anymore. He's a variable."

"A variable where?" the second scientist asked.

"Maogon," the man said. "Behind the Wall. Deep enough that escape isn't an option. I don't see him climbing The Great Wall."

The word hit her like a physical blow. Maogon: the former state of Oregon, taken over during the Confederation Invasion ten years earlier. It was a dumping ground.

"We have a cabin set up there at Wallowa Lake. We promised not to kill him, not to make it easy," the operative said as the head scientist nodded.

"How does the Premier of Maogon feel about it?"

The operative shifted. "I am sure they love the idea of having our Most Wanted number one in their territory, but they don't have much of a choice." He lifted his visor just enough for Twelve to make out Phen's face through the slit in the vent.

Phen's visor slid back into place. "Timeline?" the first scientist asked.

"Five days remaining," Phen said. "Then transport."

"Five?" the second scientist frowned. "That's generous."

Phen shrugged. "The Chairman wants him stable. I have an HRT team standing by to drop him."

The word echoed in Twelve's head; she was certain it would give her away.

"Route?" the scientist pressed.

"Ghosthound," Phen replied without hesitation. "In and out. Veil edge river approach. Potomac to coastal corridor then handoff to our assets who will finish the journey west. Its clean, and guaranteed there is no Consortium signature."

Twelve's breath caught for a fraction of a second. Ghosthound. She forced her breathing steady again. A scientist nodded. "Containment until then?"

Phen glanced at Jack's vitals: unreadable through the glass. "Isolation continues. No visitors. No stimulation beyond baseline. He doesn't need reminders of what he's lost."

The first scientist hesitated. "There's still a risk of emotional reattachment or residual memory imprinting."

Phen's voice hardened. "I don't know what that means, but it doesn't change that we need to keep him alone."

Alone. Twelve felt the word settle somewhere deep.

"Fine," the man said. "Prep the transfer order. Flag it black. No audit trail beyond Board access."

The scientists complied immediately with fingers moving fast. The conversation shifted to the logistics, weights, tolerances, and neural stability thresholds. They spoke as if Jack were not there, as if he were already gone. Phen turned slightly while scanning the observation room out of habit. His gaze passed over the terminal banks where Twelve hid underneath. He did not stop or look twice.

Good, she thought distantly. That's good.

The group filed out moments later while the door slid shut behind them with a soft, airtight seal. Silence reclaimed the observation office. Twelve stayed where she was long after they were gone. Her pulse thundered in her ears with each beat syncing with a single truth: they were going to throw him away.

What did she expect? He was still dangerous to the New Dawn.

She pushed the tile up slowly while sliding it aside with agonizing care. The seal hissed softly; it was a sound that felt like a scream in the quiet room. She pulled herself up from the dark void with muscles tight then replaced the tile before standing. The glass awaited her, unchanged. Jack still floated there with eyes closed and a chest rising in a shallow, obedient rhythm.

Five days. That was the gift; that was the mistake. Twelve reached up and rested her forehead against the cold surface of the chamber. There were no cameras at this angle and no alarms triggered by proximity.

"I won't let them," she whispered.

The words were not a plan; they were a promise. Somewhere in the back of her mind, a route began to assemble. It was not a clean exit but it was all she had. She thought of Potomac access, the Veil edge, and a Ghosthound she knew better than anyone else. She considered the five days of isolation protocols she helped design. She only needed two.

She straightened while resolve locked into place with the same precision she brought to every kill and every impossible mission she had ever survived. They thought they were buying time. They were giving her one last chance. Twelve turned, replaced her helmet, and walked out of the isolation wing as if nothing had changed.

But everything had.

23

TWELVE COULD NOT SLEEP. A wadded sweatshirt was pressed to her face while the fabric, damp and twisted in her hands, tried to hold on to the last trace of him. The faint and familiar scent of skin and soap lingered as an indefinable reminder of the man who no longer existed and no longer remembered her. Bitter tears soaked into the cotton as she lay there with her shoulders shaking in silence. When the ache in her chest grew too tight to bear, she rolled onto her side and reached for her communicator.

The screen flared to life and washed the room in a pale, sickly light. She squinted at the time before letting the device fall back into her palm, realizing it was far too early to move yet far too late to find any meaningful rest. She closed her eyes and tried to pray, but the words would not come. The Consortium had outlawed religion years ago and classified faith as a destabilizing force while viewing hope as a gross inefficiency in their grand design. The only sanctioned prayer left was the Consortium Liturgy, a series of cold affirmations drilled into every operative until it replaced their natural instincts. Her prayers always started with the claim that the Board saw and heard everything, but the words tasted like bile. Anger flared within her, sharp and sudden, as she cut the liturgy off before it could finish forming. She let the silence rush back into the room. If she spoke those words aloud, she knew they would be listening, and she could not afford to be heard. Instead, she whispered to God, to her walls, and to herself. Her voice remained low enough to escape her throat but stayed barely audible in the stillness of her quarters.

"I don't know what I'm doing," she said.

The room offered no response. She turned her face into the sweatshirt again and breathed in what little was left of Jack, knowing the scent was fading even as she tried to trap it. Whatever she was about to do, she could not let it end before it had a chance to begin. She lay there and counted her breaths, focusing on the mechanical in and out just as she had been trained to do. It did not help settle her mind. Her thoughts kept circling back to Jack in the isolation chamber where he was suspended in a heavy, artificial silence. He had been stripped down to mere function and reflex. She told herself her exhaustion was playing tricks on her, or that this was just the inevitable adrenaline burn-off of a long deployment. She tried to convince herself that grief made the mind look for desperate exits that were not actually there. She told herself a lot of things, but none of them stopped her heart from hammering against her ribs.

Restlessness crept in next with a physical tension along her spine and a shallow tightness in her chest that came from being denied motion. She swung her legs over the side of the bed and sat with her shoulders hunched and her feet flat on the floor. Stillness felt like a slow death. That was the thought that finally broke through the static. She couldn't stay here. She knew the idea of trying to save Jack was objectively stupid and likely amounted to suicide. She stood with her bare feet on the cool tile, the word suicide echoing in her head with a sharp and clinical edge. It was a clean assessment, like a box checked in a mission brief, and she accepted it without hesitation. That was the part that should have scared her, but the certainty of it actually settled her nerves.

Twelve crossed the room and opened the narrow locker built into the wall. Inside, everything was arranged with the same precision she applied to everything else in her life. She reached for her running clothes without thinking, donning her black leggings and a lightweight top in the dark. She didn't slow down long enough to look in a mirror because she knew whatever she saw there would not stop what she was about to do. As she tied her shoes, her communicator chimed softly with a routine system ping. She ignored it entirely. She didn't care about permission or anyone's blessing, for she was planning. At the door, she hesitated for a fraction of a second, not because she expected someone to stop her, but because crossing that threshold meant something irreversible. If she returned, everything would be different.

This is just a jog, she told herself, clinging to the small and useful lie.

The lock disengaged with a muted click and she stepped into the corridor. The lights were dimmed to predawn levels, keeping Consortium City quiet in the way only controlled places ever were. There was no randomness or unpredictability in these halls. She started running, her strides measured and her breathing controlled enough to burn off the edge of her anxiety without drawing the attention of the patrols. Her body remembered what to do even if her mind refused to cooperate with the logic of it. The rhythm of her feet hitting the floor helped sharpen her thoughts. She passed the security nodes without slowing as her badge cleared the checkpoints automatically. Cameras tracked her movement, but she did not look up because she had helped map their blind spots months ago. With each step, something in her shifted. She stopped thinking about "saving" Jack. That word was too big and too close to a hope she couldn't afford. Instead, her mind reverted to its tactical training and began to assess the variables. Five days. Isolation protocols. Staffing rotations and shift fatigue. She knew which systems were truly redundant and which were merely assumed to be by the Board.

Her pace increased as the city around her began to resolve into tactical pathways instead of familiar scenery.

Routes replaced streets in her mind. She noticed the patrol timing without meaning to and noted the way certain corridors went dark for half a second when the local power cycled. She knew the access points near the Veil were monitored more loosely because no one in their right mind believed anyone would ever go out that way.

Her breath came faster now, not from the strain of the run, but from an excitement building for what she was about to do. *I'm not planning,* she told herself, which was another lie she had to tell to keep moving.

She crossed a bridge overlooking the Potomac and slowed just enough to glance at the water below. The facsimile of the real thing was eerie, almost as if the river was real and DC was never destroyed, just hidden from the outside world. It moved steadily and indifferent to the massive structures built around its banks. Something in her chest tightened at the thought of a Ghosthound. The word surfaced without thinking, and this time she did not push it away. She slowed to a walk and stopped near the railing, her hands resting on her hips as she bent forward to catch her breath. Anyone watching would see nothing unusual, just an operative keeping herself sharp.

Inside, everything locked into place with a sudden finality. She didn't have a full plan yet, but she knew she couldn't let them drop Jack behind the Great Wall in Maogon alone. Twelve straightened and turned back toward the city where the hangar depot sat with its long rows of aircraft. She saw the pilots lining up for their morning operations and stepped up to the security kiosk. Her picture lit up with an authorized status and the door slid open. She approached the elevator to descend to the Ghosthound bay.

"What in the hell am I doing?" she whispered to herself. The elevator door hissed open as warm air of the bay rushed in to meet her while carrying the smells of aviation fuel, heavy lubricants, and the sharp tang of ozone. The facility was already awake with technicians moving between the craft as if programmed perfectly. No one stopped her, and she heard no alarms because she was exactly where the system said she was allowed to be. She slowed her pace to match the environment as she passed the first row of dropships and couriers. At the far end of the hangar sat the UH-96 Ghosthound II that her team was assigned after Charlotte. It looked similar to the other Ghosthounds but featured a lower profile and a SuperBlack skin that drank the overhead hangar lights. The hull bore scoring along the intake edges from the test missions they had been flying. It was still a prototype, and it was the only one made so far.

She stopped without realizing it as her pulse jumped with recognition. Muscle memory stirred in her shoulders as she pictured the cockpit and remembered the slight drift in the left stabilizer. *You're just looking,* she told herself, yet another lie in a morning full of them.

A technician passed by and offered a casual nod. "Morning, Twelve."

“Morning,” she replied, her voice remaining perfectly steady.

She resumed walking and angled toward the Ghosthound II as her mind raced with security rotations and flight logs. This was a pathway assembling itself because she already knew every inch of the ground she was walking. She stopped beneath the craft’s wing and rested a hand against the cool composite skin of the fuselage. Five days. They would erase the last traces of Jack and then drop him like waste behind the Wall. Her jaw tightened with the realization that she didn’t want to save him as much as she wanted to ensure he wasn’t alone when the world started again. Twelve made her decision. She turned toward the operations desk with a neutral expression and then headed into the locker room. She pulled her flight suit from her locker and stepped into the trousers, inflating the air bladder slightly to ensure it was mission-ready. She pulled the zipper and attached the Velcro with a firm tug.

Twelve stepped back into the hangar as the noise of the morning rose around her. The operations desk was understaffed at this hour. A junior controller looked up as she approached. “Morning,” he said.

“Morning,” Twelve replied. “Requesting a systems check sortie.”

He did not question her. Her clearance populated the screen immediately. “Preflight window’s open,” he said. “You’re early.”

“I won’t be long,” she lied.

Twelve turned away before the weight of her thoughts could settle. *This isn't an extraction,* she told herself. She crossed the hangar with long strides and found the access ladder already in place. She rested one gloved hand against the hull while feeling the faint vibration of the standby power humming through the craft. It would not be long before the system started asking questions, and once she climbed into that cockpit, the clock would start for real. Twelve exhaled slowly. "I'm sorry," she whispered, though she wasn't sure who she was apologizing to. She grabbed the pull handle and started up into the personnel cabin. She slid the door shut and sat in a jump seat near the litter rack. *My God, Twelve!* The thought came too late to stop her now. She slid into the cockpit seat and buckled in before flipping the first bank of switches. The screens flickered to life and cast a green glow over her face as the diagnostic readouts scrolled by.

Systems Green. Ordnance Armed. Fuel: 3,260 lbs.

Pushing the cyclic control forward, she steered the Ghosthound II out of its slip. The nose tracked exactly where she pointed it as the wheels rolled over the hangar deck. The ground crew stepped aside without a second glance.

"Ghosthound One-Two, taxiing for systems check," Twelve radioed to control. "Refuel MAG requested while surfacing."

"MAG-Fuel system go. Copy, One-Two," came the response.

She rolled onto the helipad as the heavy bay doors parted to reveal the gray-blue light of the early morning. As the pad began to rise into the vertical launch tube, rows of induction lights flickered to life to illuminate her ascent. The MAG-Fueling system snapped into place from the floor with a series of heavy, metallic thuds that vibrated through the airframe. The digital totalizer on her primary display began to blur as the numbers spun upward. Beneath the tires, the induction pads hummed while pouring power back into the battery systems.

After a few minutes, the helipad leveled with the tarmac above. The airfield stretched wide and empty with a heavy fog hovering over the asphalt like a shroud. Twelve guided the Ghosthound II across the threshold while feeling the added mass of the fuel pulling at the suspension. The moment she cleared the helipad line, the echo of the enclosed tube fell away. Open air and a biting wind took its place, tugging at the fuselage as the city under the Veil flickered around her. She brought the craft to a brief stop on the tarmac for the last clean pause of her life. She keyed the throttle and the engines spooled with a rising whine that vibrated up through the seat and into her spine. Readouts scrolled across the displays while the rotor RPM stabilized and lift margins calculated in real time.

Systems Green. Ordnance Armed. Fuel: 6,400 lbs.

Cleared.

Twelve did not look back toward the facility. She gripped the collective and eased it upward, the engines deepening their growl as the rotor blades bit into the air to haul the heavy ship skyward. The tarmac dropped away in slow inches and then feet, the Ghosthound II finally breaking the suction of the earth. Her fingers adjusted the yaw to correct for the city's artificial crosswinds nudging at her flank. The craft rose with a weighted grace, climbing steadily above the perimeter lights and the security fencing until the hangar was nothing more than a dark shape in the fog.

Twelve reached out and cut the internal monitors to ensure that whoever might be listening on the sub-channels heard only static. She breathed slowly while looking out at the sprawling horizon of the City hidden by the Veil. "It's so peaceful up here," she whispered. She sighed once before pressing the pedals to swing the ship's nose toward the George Bush Center for Intelligence. With her target locked, she eased the cyclic forward and opened the throttle to full power. The turbines screamed in response as the heavy ship leaned into the wind. She took a deep breath, her eyes fixed on the distant building in Langley.

"I'm coming, Jack," she said, her voice finally loud enough to hear over the roar of the engines.

Phen and Vannah stepped into the corridor leading to the isolation wing. They walked slowly down the clinical hallway where the white panels were edged in a harsh, crimson glow of red LEDs. They wore their full tactical kit in preparation for their next deployment. A new team had already been formed with Phen as the commander; Vannah and Twelve remained on the roster, joined by a final member who had not yet been assigned. Twelve was absent from the formation. The Chairman had granted her a rare period of administrative leave to process the Jack situation, an act the Board touted as proof that the leader was harsh but ultimately fair and benevolent. To the rank and file, it was a gesture of mercy; to Phen, it felt like a tactical sidelining.

The corridor lights reflected dully off the composite walls and the scuffed armor that had seen too much use. At the observation glass, Phen stopped. He lifted one hand and pulled it free from the glove while setting the fabric aside before resting his bare palm against the cold surface. His head lowered slightly as his eyes remained fixed on the floor rather than what lay beyond the glass. Vannah stepped in beside him and placed her hand on his shoulder. She did not squeeze or speak. Neither of them did. Phen's hand stayed on the glass while for a long moment his breathing was the only sound in the room.

"I signed off on it," he said finally. His voice was low and measured. It was not shaken, but it was not rehearsed either. Vannah did not react. Her hand remained on his shoulder because she knew this was not about her; it was entirely about Phen.

"I told myself it wasn't my call," Phen continued. "I claimed it was coming whether I stood there or not." He leaned his forehead against the glass. "That was a lie."

He lifted his head just enough to look through the glass now at the shape suspended in the chamber. He stared at the man who had once stood at his back without needing to be asked.

"Twenty years," Phen said. "That's how long we worked together. You knew how I thought before I finished thinking it. You covered my blind spots and you trusted me when it mattered." His jaw tightened once. "And I walked you into a situation you could not escape from."

Vannah's fingers pressed into his shoulder then. It was not enough to stop him, but just enough to let him keep going.

"I won't pretend this changes anything," Phen said. "It doesn't balance out. It doesn't make it right." He swallowed loudly. "But it means I don't lie to myself about it anymore."

A long moment of silence unfolded while the machinery hummed with an indifferent vibration. Phen drew his hand back from the glass and flexed his fingers as if the cold had gone deeper than skin.

"Twelve went along with this because the Chairman agreed not to kill you, Jack." He sighed. "He wanted to kill you, and dammit Jack, I was okay with it. The longer you were in operation, the softer you got. That's why this—" his words trailed off for a moment before he slapped his hand against the observation glass, "—had to happen."

Vannah nodded once. She pulled his face toward her while looking deeply into Phen's eyes. "If they did this to Jack, Phen, you know they will do it to us if we step out of line." Her hand rested on his cheek.

"For all I know, they already have." Phen chuckled uncomfortably under his breath. He leaned forward and kissed Vannah, then turned back toward Jack behind the glass. "You have my word, Jack. I will protect Twelve."

He paused as the weight of his betrayal settled. "That's all I have left to give."

The Ghosthound II touched down on the roof of the George Bush Center for Intelligence. Twelve slid back into the cargo area to pull the litter down and check the straps. She ensured it was fastened properly in the loading system then pulled the wheeled carrier from its compartment and slid a secondary stretcher into place. She stood beside her chopper with the carrier and looked toward the door. She knew she couldn't pass through it, so she would have to find another way inside.

Twelve stepped away from the Ghosthound II. Her boots tapped softly against the composite rooftop as she moved toward the far edge of the structure. The roof was not flat like a civilian building; it was layered and segmented, built for industrial systems rather than people. She crouched and pressed a gloved palm to the deck. There was a low, constant vibration beneath the surface. It was too steady to be machinery cycling and too broad for power conduits. It was airflow. She followed the sensation while counting steps until she reached a recessed section of the roof marked with faded maintenance stenciling. It was not labeled HVAC or anything so obvious. It was just a sequence of numbers and a warning stripe worn thin by years of boots. Twelve gave a humorless smile. *Of course you're up here,* she thought as she knelt and traced the seam with her fingers.

The panel was secured with a series of bolts from the 1960s which were rusted shut from decades of exposure to the elements. She pulled her knife and tried to pry them open, but the metal did not budge. Frustration flared, but she remained determined. Twelve leaned back on her heels and looked at the panel again. The bolts were not just rusted; they were fused to the roof. Decades of oxidation had turned them into part of the frame itself. Whoever had installed them never expected them to be removed.

Good design but for her it was bad timing.

She sheathed her knife in her leg strap and reached into her pocket for a breaching kit. She fished out a Breachpen and struck the battle match to light the thermite. She slid the burning tip along the seams where the bolts were, working quickly because time was a luxury she didn't have. The metal hissed softly as it gave way. The seams glowed a dull orange before cooling almost immediately in the morning air. Twelve scraped the residue away with the spine of her knife and tested the panel. It finally shifted as her blade worked the edges.

She hooked her fingers under the edge and pulled. The hatch came free with a reluctant groan and released a breath of cold air from below. It was not wind, but merely the air circulation of a closed system. She shone her light down the duct and saw a straight drop. Twelve cursed under her breath as she lowered herself in while using her boots to brace against opposite walls of the shaft. The duct was narrower than it looked from above, forcing her shoulders in as she slid down inch by inch; her descent was slow and controlled. The metal was cold through her gloves and vibrated faintly with the constant movement of air.

She adjusted herself by shifting her weight so her legs took most of the load. Friction did the work. She continued slowly and as quietly as she could. Holding the flashlight in her teeth while the light reflected off the sheet metal all the way down. She counted floors as she worked her way into the dark. Jack was on the third floor. From the roof, she counted two floors down with two more to go.

Then the airflow changed. It was not abrupt, but it was enough that she noticed. The vibration softened and the hum flattened out as the shaft widened beneath her boots. She paused and braced herself in place to angle the light downward again. Her jaw tightened as she shifted her weight, and the flashlight slipped. It dropped from her teeth, bounced once, and then fell.

Clang.

A sharp and metallic sound rang through the duct, louder than she wanted it to be. Twelve froze. Every muscle locked as her pulse spiked hard enough to narrow her vision. She counted silently to five while waiting for alarms or boots. Nothing came. *Idiot,* she told herself while steadying her breathing. *Move.*

No alarms sounded and no voices rose. The duct continued its low, steady breath as if nothing had happened. Twelve exhaled slowly through her nose and reached for the ladder rungs welded into the shaft wall. This was old construction with actual metal rather than composite. Decades ago, someone had expected maintenance crews to come through here by hand. She resumed her descent. The flashlight lay below with its beam angled uselessly against the sheet metal to cast warped shadows. She passed it without stopping. Light was not worth the noise.

At the next junction, the shaft widened into a horizontal run. She swung her legs over and eased herself onto her stomach to crawl forward. The duct creaked faintly beneath her weight, but not enough to carry. She paused at the first grate and angled her head to listen. Distorted voices drifted up from below; they were muted but still loud enough for her to hear. They were likely technicians finishing a shift. She moved again. The second grate gave her a clearer view of a sterile corridor under white light. A security camera swept in a lazy arc. Twelve waited for the return sweep then slid past the grate and continued forward. Her shoulders burned and her forearms ached from keeping her weight controlled, but she ignored it. Pain meant she was still moving.

Looking through the second grate she saw the catwalk for a prison that was still being constructed. *We're gearing up for more arrests it seems,* she thought. Her mind swirled as she huffed silently. At the third grate, she slowed. She was at the right floor. Twelve dragged herself through the ductwork with agonizing care so the metal would not pop. More voices rose from below.

"You have my word, Jack. I'll protect Twelve." The voice paused. "That's all I have left to give."

Phen.

Twelve froze. Phen's voice carried upward through the angles of the ductwork. It was unmistakable. Ten years of shared operations had tuned her ear to it the way others recognized family. She did not move or breathe. She shifted her weight just enough to bring one eye level with the grate. Below, the observation wing glowed with red LEDs against the clinical white panels.

Phen stood at the glass with his back to her while one bare hand rested against the surface. Vannah was beside him. Twelve listened in the silence between the hum of machinery.

Phen stepped back from the glass. Twelve tensed instinctively, muscles coiling to retreat if he looked up. Phen pulled his glove back on in a slow and deliberate manner. Vannah leaned in and murmured something Twelve could not hear. Phen nodded once. That was it. There were no speeches or apologies. Just a promise given to a man who could not hear it.

Twelve swallowed hard. For the first time since the Ghosthound II touched down, doubt flared in her chest. *They know,* her mind whispered. *They can't know.* Vannah pulled her communicator out and heard her own voicemail play. "She must not be awake yet." Vannah hung up and pulled Phen closer for a kiss before they turned to walk down the hallway.

Twelve waited until their footsteps faded. Only then did she move. She eased herself forward and shifted her weight until she was positioned directly above the observation room. Her hands worked by feel to loosen the internal fasteners one by one. The grate gave just enough for her to slip through. She dropped the last few feet silently with knees bending to absorb the impact. She stayed low and listened. There was a mop and bucket in the corner. She lifted the mop to pull the grate closed; fortunately, the room was empty.

Jack floated in the cradle beyond the glass, unchanged. Twelve crossed the space quickly. Her hands moved over the console with fingers flying through manual overrides she had written years ago when this system was still theoretical. The locks disengaged with a muted hiss. She was there when the restraints released to brace his weight as he sagged forward. He was heavier than she expected.

"Easy," she murmured.

She guided him into a wheelchair and secured straps to his limbs. After checking his vitals, she nodded. That was enough. Twelve pivoted the wheelchair smoothly and pushed through the secondary access door before the system could finish recalibrating. She did not look back at the chamber; looking back wasted time.

The corridor beyond was empty. She kept to the service route where maintenance lighting and a lack of cameras provided a path. The wheelchair rolled quietly over the composite floor with bearings that barely whispered. When Jack's head lolled forward, she steadied it without breaking stride.

"I've got you, baby," she said under her breath.

The lift was where it should be. She thumbed the manual override and guided the chair inside. The doors slid shut with a soft seal. For half a second, the lift hesitated as if deciding whether to ask questions. Luckily, it didn't. The ascent was too slow for her comfort. Twelve stood behind the chair with one hand on the grip and the other on Jack's shoulder. She felt the faint vibration of the machinery through him. The doors opened onto the roof muster access. She pushed Jack toward the door with muscles burning and breath tight. The wheelchair grew heavier as she adjusted her grip and used momentum to clear the corridor. At the rooftop access panel, she keyed it open manually and pushed through.

The artificial wind hit her first, and her sweat caused her to shiver. In front of her sat the Ghosthound II with the litter waiting beside her ship, where she had left it. Twelve did not waste time feeling relief. She rolled Jack across the deck. Unlatching the safety straps, she hoisted his dead weight onto her back for the final few steps. She dumped him onto the stretcher, fastened the restraints, and slid the assembly into the cargo lock until it clicked. Throwing the wheelchair in, she secured it too. She knew she was running out of time.

She climbed into the cockpit and flipped the switches. The screens came to life to spill green light across her face.

Systems Green. Ordnance Armed. Fuel: 6,144 lbs.

The engine whine deepened as the Ghosthound II transitioned to live power. Twelve's hands moved without hesitation while muscle memory overrode her fatigue. She brought the engines up slowly. The Ghosthound II lifted cleanly and hovered just long enough to confirm stability. The building shrank into shadow and geometry below. She nudged the cyclic forward and the craft slid laterally to clear the structure before gaining altitude. Twelve pushed the nose toward the Potomac gatehouse rising over the horizon where floodlights cut through the dawn. She throttled back slightly and keyed the comm.

"Potomac Control, Ghosthound Six-Two-Nine requesting egress."

A pause followed, filled with static and the sound of keys. "State purpose."

"Flight exercise for prototype. Systems validation over Atlantic corridor."

"Transmit authorization."

She transmitted her active flight authorization. It was current and green across every field.

"Logged as training block and aircraft readiness," the voice came back.

The Ghosthound II held position over the river with rotors whispering against the cold air. The seconds seemed to take hours.

"Authorization confirmed," Potomac Control said. "Maintain river corridor. Veil boundary opening in three."

Ahead, the horizon began to part. A red light on her HUD acknowledged the countdown.

Three. Twelve eased the collective forward as her light turned yellow.

Two. The Ghosthound II responded smoothly with engines deepening in pitch.

One. The Veil parted fully and the Ghosthound II crossed through.

"Maintain heading," Potomac Control said. "Report return window upon completion."

"Copy," Twelve replied. It was the last truthful word she would give them.

She pushed the nose downriver and let the Ghosthound II settle into speed while skimming low over the Potomac. The Veil closed silently behind her to reseal the illusion of a destroyed Washington DC. Twelve did not slow. She knew Jack's disappearance would eventually raise alarms. She flew several miles out into the Atlantic corridor and set the aircraft into an auto-hover. The engines settled into a low hum over open water.

She unstrapped and stood. The transponder was mounted flush with the operations cluster. She slid her knife into the seam and twisted. There was a muted pop as the connection broke free. The Ghosthound II remained silent. Twelve held the transponder in her hand for a moment longer than necessary. Then she looked at Jack. He lay strapped into the litter, motionless, with a chest rising in a shallow rhythm.

"This should buy us some time," she said quietly.

She set it on the floor and crushed it under the hilt of her knife before opening the sliding door and letting the transponder fall. It vanished into the dark below, swallowed by the Atlantic. Twelve closed the door and returned to the cockpit. She strapped in, brought up the nav display, and entered new coordinates.

Charlotte.

The nose of the Ghosthound II dipped south as the engines deepened in pitch.

24

CHARLOTTE, CAROLINA — 03.20.35

Twelve set the Ghosthound II down on the hotel roof slowly while easing the collective until the wheels kissed concrete. The engines wound down into a low, patient hum. She unstrapped and moved aft. Jack lay where she had secured him. He remained unconscious. She checked the straps once more then slid the side door open and leaned out into the morning air. The city below was dead. She knew the reason; she and Jack were the cause. Weeds split the asphalt in the streets while small trees clawed through sidewalk seams. Somewhere nearby, loose sheet metal rattled softly in the wind. Pollen drifted through the air in thin yellow threads to catch the early light.

She stepped onto the roof. Near the far wall sat a half-unspooled coil of coaxial cable bleached by sun and rain. Someone had been here before the Accords while trying to reconnect something that no longer mattered. Twelve ran the cable briefly through her fingers before letting it fall. Her attention shifted to the roof access door. It stood ajar by a few inches. Something about it felt off.

She approached slowly with her hand near her sidearm. A chain lay slack at the base of the door; rusted links tangled where someone had dragged them aside. She nudged the door open with her boot. The smell hit first. It was not rot exactly, but something drier with a strong chemical odor. It was sickly-sweet underneath the decay. Inside, a body lay collapsed against the stairwell wall. It was emaciated; skin mottled in strange patterns with dark veins spidering beneath the surface. Lesions along the neck and forearms had crusted over in uneven patches like the aftermath of an untreated exposure.

Twelve did not step closer. She scanned the body to catalog details as she had been trained. There was no obvious trauma or blood spatter. Whatever had killed him had not been fast or clean. Infection, she decided. It was a threat she did not have time to diagnose and could not afford Jack encountering in his condition. She backed out and pulled the door shut. The rusted chain came next. She dragged it up and looped it through the handle and around the bar in the frame. She wrapped it tight enough to resist casual effort. There was a rusted lock in the pile; she shoved the shackle into the housing until she heard a click. She tested the weight until the door resisted without protest. It was not sealed forever, just strongly discouraged. She wanted Jack to leave this place on his own terms, but she wanted to curate the safest route; down the fire escape and into the open air. She wanted him away from confined spaces and whatever had taken root inside the building.

She stood for a moment looking at the door then turned back toward the Ghosthound II. That was as much protection as she could provide.

She returned to the aircraft where the cockpit lights looked dim against the gray morning. Jack lay strapped into the litter with his head turned slightly to one side. His brow looked relaxed in the deep stillness of sedation. She remembered the last time she had kissed him, the last time he held her, and the sound of his voice breaking as they took him. She reached out and brushed her fingers through his hair. The gesture was slow and careful as if she were afraid it might wake him or undo her work. His skin was warm and clammy to her touch.

"I don't know if this is mercy," she said quietly. Her voice caught on the word. "Or if I'm just choosing for you again."

He did not stir. She swallowed and leaned closer to rest her forehead briefly against his temple. The Ghosthound II shifted softly beneath her weight as she moved.

"I hope you find yourself," she whispered. "Even if it means that you don't remember me." Her lips pressed against his, but no reaction accompanied the touch. That hurt more than she expected. "I love you, Jack."

She pulled back before the feeling could spread and turn into something that would slow her down. Her hands moved automatically to check straps and secure the litter to ensure he would not shift. She pulled the litter from the wall unit and locked it into the carrier before pressing the switch to slide the ramp out.

Twelve rolled the carrier out onto the roof and lowered the hydraulics. She slid the litter free and stowed the carrier back inside the Ghosthound II. Behind her, Jack lay on the roof still strapped to the stretcher. She pulled the straps free and rolled him directly onto the concrete. She reached for the medical gown last. It was thin and utilitarian, marked with Consortium serial ink along the hem. It was not clothing; it was a label showing he was property.

Twelve's jaw tightened. She cut it away rather than pulling it over him. The blade whispered through the fabric so it would not tug at his skin. The gown fell open. She folded it twice before setting it aside like something that had already served its purpose. Jack looked wrong without it and wrong with it. He was bare and pale, scarred in places she knew by heart, and others that seemed new. She saw the collar marks where the interface had rested and the faint bruising along his wrists from the restraints.

She looked away long enough to steady herself then she dressed him. The white T-shirt went on first. She lifted his shoulders gently to guide the fabric down while being careful not to snag it. Her hands lingered as she smoothed the shirt flat against his chest as if the motion could make things normal. The jeans were harder. She worked one leg at a time by easing the denim over his feet and thighs. It was awkward and clumsy. Nothing could have prepared her for how heavy a person felt when they were a dead weight. She adjusted the waistband and zipped the fly slowly. These were ordinary actions she had never imagined doing for him.

The boots came last. She unlaced them fully, slipped them onto his feet, and tied them snug. She wanted them to stay on when he stood so he would not trip when he tried to walk. She sat back on her heels when she was done. He was a man again. She pulled a dissolving patch from her kit and pressed it beneath the hem of his shirt against his ribs. It adhered instantly. In a few hours, it would be gone. By the time he woke, it would leave nothing behind, but for now, it would keep him hydrated and deliver a small amount of calories. Her hand rested there a moment before she withdrew it. She gathered the remnants of the gown and folded them tightly to shove them into a compartment she would never open again.

She knelt beside him one last time. Her fingers brushed his hair back from his forehead. His breathing was steady and peaceful in a way that felt undeserved.

"I wish I could tell you who you are," she said softly. "But you wouldn't believe me. Not now."

She leaned in again. Her lips touched his; it was more a goodbye than a kiss. Then she stood. She knew if she did not stand now, she never would. She turned toward the Ghosthound II and started to gather the litter and anything out of place that could identify the

Consortium. Walking up the ramp, she sealed the door and stowed the equipment. Opening a compartment, she found a parachute. She took it into the cockpit and set it in the seat beside her.

Twelve strapped herself in and initiated the launch procedures.

Systems Green. Ordnance Armed. Fuel: 2,048 lbs.

The fuel had burned faster than she liked. She could not afford to be found by the UAA, so she had to leave. The engines whined loudly as the Ghosthound II flew straight into the air toward the Atlantic. It felt looser than on her trip to Charlotte; she knew she was running out of fuel. She had to hurry.

Hours slipped by as Twelve crossed the Outer Banks of Carolina. The Atlantic opened ahead of her in an endless expanse. She pushed the collective forward and yawned; the sound was hollow in the quiet cockpit.

Fuel Gauge: 1,600 lbs.

It was not enough to return, and going back would raise questions she could not afford to answer. The Ghosthound II hummed steadily beneath her with nominal systems and a smooth flight path. Every instinct screamed for her to turn around. She wanted to land somewhere forgotten. She wanted to take Jack with her to vanish into the Great Plains Nation or disappear south into Greater Mexizona; anywhere beyond the Consortium's reach. She knew no such place truly existed. Instinct was a liability. Acting on it would only draw attention, and attention would reach Phen and Vannah. She could not risk them being retired for her choices. Return meant interrogation rooms and enhanced methods. It meant flight logs torn apart frame by frame and questions designed to break her rather than be answered. Twelve stared out at the Atlantic where thousands of crests bloomed and collapsed in a repetitive cycle. She had made a contingency hours ago. Whether it would work was another matter.

She brought the Ghosthound II out of its cruise and began a steady climb. The nose lifted as the Atlantic widened beneath her into a cerulean blur. The sun had begun its descent while bright blades of light flashed into the cockpit as she pulled the stick back harder. Everything remained peaceful for the moment. The altitude warning chimed once. She silenced it.

The Ghosthound II was not built for this ceiling. The air thinned and the engines compensated automatically. But the ship still felt flighty and unstable. Pitch adjusted in smooth increments until the systems began to lag behind her demand. That was the point. She keyed in the destruct sequence, knowing the loaded ordnance would ensure the total destruction of the airframe. She reached over to grab the parachute from the co-pilot seat and disconnected her harness. Slinging the pack over her shoulders, she cinched the straps until they bit into her flight suit.

The cabin pressure warning chimed. Her breathing sharpened almost immediately. She did not panic but shifted her breathing patterns to smaller, shallower draws. A faint lightness crept in at the edges of her vision as the aircraft climbed well beyond its operational limits. She let it happen; this was her plausible deniability. She trimmed the Ghosthound II one last time into an attitude it resisted. The frame shuddered while rotors bit at thinning air. A heavy vibration crept through the cockpit like a final warning she chose to ignore.

"Enough," she said quietly as she stood. The aircraft wobbled as her weight shifted and the autopilot struggled to compensate. She did not steady herself. Instead, she reached up and pulled the manual release for the side hatch. The door tore outward. Air slammed into the cabin with immediate violence to rip the breath from her lungs. It hurled her sideways into the frame. Pain flared white-hot as her shoulder struck the metal with enough force to tear muscle deep beneath the skin. She barely registered the sensation. A crushing decompression hit next; she became disoriented. The sky became impossibly loud. The Atlantic flashed below through the open hatch. She caught the doorframe for a fraction of a second. It was long enough.

The Ghosthound II's engine stalled; its rotors stopping as its nose began to drop toward the earth. Then she let go and dropped away as the ship plummeted beneath her into the open sky. The aircraft began to yaw as systems unraveled without her input. Wind tore at her and spun her twice. The force knocked the remaining air from her lungs. She counted without sound. *One. Two.* She pulled the chute. The canopy snapped open with brutal force. The harness bit hard into her injured shoulder. Pain detonated down her arm with absolute power to tear a raw sound from her throat. It was done; now she hoped they would believe her. She toggled her chute to steer clear of the falling wreck as she drifted past it.

Below her, the Atlantic stretched out in rippling blues and gold as the sun stained the water with fire. Above, the Ghosthound II was already just a shape. A sudden bloom of light ignited the sky, followed heartbeats later by a blunt hammer of sound. The shockwave rolled through the air, shuddering through her harness and slapping the breath from her lungs. It spun her gently as debris vanished into the distance and clouds. There would be nothing left to find.

Twelve hung beneath the canopy with her arm useless at her side. Her breath was shallow and controlled by habit rather than comfort. Blood darkened her sleeve where the harness had torn skin. Between the altitude exposure, the decompression trauma, and the impact injuries, she knew exactly how the report would read. Mechanical failure during a test flight of the prototype. Emergency egress during decompression. Survivable loss, but back to the drawing board for R&D. She tilted her head back and stared at the sky. It was still blue, still beautiful, and still uncaring. Below, the Atlantic waited. She pulled her emergency transponder and pressed the SOS button. It flashed red as the blood loss and lack of oxygen caused her to lose consciousness.

The anomaly registered at 18:42 local time.

Potomac Gatehouse radar flagged a transient bloom east of Norfolk. It was high altitude with a rapid loss of mass and a thermal spike inconsistent with weather or civilian traffic. The system auto-tagged the event as an aviation incident. It pushed the data upstream before the watch officer finished reading the first line. Satellite confirmation followed five seconds later. There was a brief flash and fragmentation followed by nothing.

"No secondary signatures," the technician reported. "Detonation was contained over open water."

The Gatehouse commander stepped closer to the display. "Identify."

"Primary transponder lost prior to event," the tech replied. "Last known flight corridor matches Consortium military routing for a Ghosthound-class profile. We are picking up a secondary emergency beacon now. Weak signal. SOS pulse on a secure HRT frequency."

The room shifted from observation to response without comment. Launch clocks began counting down.

"Scramble recovery," the commander said. "HRT lead. Two birds. Pattern search, grid delta-seven through delta-nine."

The first Ghosthound reached the site twenty-six minutes later. Debris was minimal with no large wreckage or surface fires. Only scattered composite fragments drifted with the current. Then a beacon pinged.

"Signal lock," the pilot called. "Emergency transponder signal. Military-grade."

They adjusted course. A figure floated below while partially submerged. The flight suit remained intact with the inflation bladder deployed. Arms hung slack and the head stayed above water.

"Visual confirmation," the sensor operator said. "Single survivor."

They hovered low. A recovery swimmer jumped before the Ghosthound slowed to a full hover. He reached the parachute and noted the Consortium tags. She was unresponsive when he radioed for the basket. Pulse was present. Breathing remained shallow. Suit integrity was compromised along the left shoulder with signs of blunt trauma and possible dislocation. He noted mild hypothermia. There were no defensive wounds or signs of sabotage.

The basket dropped ten feet from the diver's position. He grabbed her harness and dragged her toward the lift.

Securing her into the frame, he gripped the cable as it hoisted them both from the Atlantic. The emergency beacon was silenced as soon as she crossed the threshold. Inside the cabin, a medic ran a rapid scan.

"Biometrics match," he said. "Operative Twelve Parks."

No one reacted.

"Condition?"

"Stable. Injured, I don't think critically."

"Cause?"

"Consistent with high-altitude bailout following catastrophic failure."

The pilot of the standard Ghosthound nodded once. "Log it."

The second Ghosthound joined the formation. "Any assist needed?"

"We are good, Captain," the pilot responded.

"Good. Return to base."

Deep in the Atlantic, a piece of fiberglass drifted briefly while bearing the Consortium seal. It lingered for a moment before the depths of the ocean swallowed it. The Ghosthound II was fully destroyed. Nothing remained on the surface except for a rainbow swirl of fuel mixing with the saltwater. The lapping waves continued to roll as the sun fully disappeared behind the horizon.

25

CHARLOTTE, CAROLINA — MARCH 2044

The bus rolled to a stop in front of the memorial wall at the Accord Memorial Center. The wall rose from polished stone where the Charlotte Convention Center had once stood. Thousands of names were carved into black granite; they stretched farther than the eye could comfortably follow. Above them, silent screens replayed archived footage from March 20, 2028. There was fanfare, applause, and leaders speaking over the roar of a crowd that no longer existed.

The doors folded open. Mr. Thaddeus Fad stepped down first while adjusting his jacket against the Carolina spring. His sophomore history class from Knoxville filed out behind him. Chatter replaced the hum of the engine. Parents followed more quietly.

"Remember," Mr. Fad called over his shoulder, "this isn't just a museum. It's a memorial. Stay with your groups."

The students scattered anyway. One student drifted from the group and stopped in front of a shadow box mounted along the outer wall. Inside was a Panther jersey, worn denim jeans, and a pair of Nike shoes. They were preserved, tagged, and recovered from the blast site.

Owner: Chad Wilson. Status: Unknown.

The student leaned closer. “Unknown?” she muttered.

Her friend joined her. “That just means they never found him.”

“They found his clothes.”

A parent standing nearby cleared her throat softly. “A lot of families never got confirmation.”

Farther down the wall, two boys traced their fingers just above the engraved names without touching. They read the names out loud the way people do when they are trying to make something real. There were entire families listed in sequence. There were single names with no duplicates. Some had their ages listed while others did not, depending on what information had been recovered.

Inside the Center, the doors slid open automatically. The main atrium was wide and bright; it was designed deliberately without shadows. Suspended above was a sculpted installation of fractured steel beams fused into a rising spiral to symbolize reconstruction. A guide met them near the entrance.

“Welcome to the Accord Memorial Center,” she said. “You’ll begin with the Great Unwinding Gallery to your left. You will then proceed chronologically through the UAA-Texan Wars and finally the Supranational Wing.”

The students moved in clusters. The Secession Gallery opened with maps. The United States had fractured into color-coded territories with their own national flags. The Remaining States were in red with white stripes. The Free States were in purple. The UAA was in blue. The Bluegrass States Republic was in green. Texas was shown in burnt orange. The Great Plains Nation was yellow. The Northwest Socialist States of America were in red. Deseret was in white. Greater Mexizona was gray. Alaska was blue with white stripes, and the Kingdom of Hawaii was yellow with red stripes.

Lines shifted across the interactive display to show the years from 2024 through 2038. A student tapped the Great Plains Nation. Pictures unfurled showing a man named Jeremiah Johnson along with several images of buffalo patches and a large wall.

"Why did they build a wall?" another student asked.

"Isolation doctrine," the guide replied. "After the Event that occurred here in Charlotte during the Accords and the disappearance of their president, Jeremiah Johnson, President Walt Ridley pushed for total border consolidation. There were to be no foreign entanglements and no supranational framework."

"They still don't trade?"

"It is limited and strategic only."

Another student had moved ahead to the Second War exhibit. Projected overhead was footage from the early days of the UAA–Texan conflict. Pictures of the missile barrages on Montgomery, Alabama played on loop. A proud man was pictured in a Naval uniform, underneath was his name, Admiral William Sentelle. Pictures of

Presidents of both the UAA and Texas and a replica of the signed Peace document between both nations after the end of the Second War. There were drone overlays, tactical maps, and grainy helmet-cam stills. There was no blood or bodies; there were only arrows and impact zones.

"Wasn't this after they signed the Mutual Defense Pact?" a girl asked.

"Yes," Mr. Fad answered. "The UAA and Bluegrass States Republic formalized their alliance in 2037. They established shared military command and citizen mobility across borders. Texas viewed it as encirclement. But it was also a second war. The first one ended in a stalemate, the second one ended with UAA Sanctions and blockades of The New Republic of Texas."

"And now Texas wants into the Mutual Defense Pact?" someone said.

The guide nodded. "As of last year, Texas formally petitioned to join the supranational governance structure."

"That's crazy," one boy muttered. "They just fought a war."

"History does that," Mr. Fad said. "It fights. Then it negotiates."

They moved into the Supranational Wing. The tone shifted here. Interactive kiosks showed projected shipping lanes pulsing between Charleston, Louisville, Wilmington, and Corpus Christi. Green lines thickened year by year. Trade tonnage ticked upward in the corner. Dual citizenship enrollment numbers rose steadily across the display. A boy tapped the Marine Corps insignia rotating above the kiosk.

"So who is actually in charge?" he asked.

The guide smiled faintly. "That depends on what you mean by charge."

"The military," he clarified.

"The UAA maintains naval and marine command," she said. "The Bluegrass States Republic administers the air guard and ground forces. It is a joint command structure for expeditionary deployments."

"Expeditionary where?" another student asked.

The guide paused for half a second. "Peacekeeping operations along the borders of our territories. Anti-piracy patrols in the Gulf. Border stabilization inside and around Greater Mexizona."

A quiet murmur moved through the group. Greater Mexizona appeared on the map again when someone tapped it. The gray region expanded while fractured by tribal governance overlays and autonomous zones. The city-state of Los Angeles was shown as a thriving entity established after being cut off following the Neutronium bomb of 2024.

"Is it still lawless?" a girl asked.

"Parts of it," Mr. Fad answered. "Parts of it are more stable than they have been in two decades."

"Who runs it?"

"Depends on which part," the guide said. "The Navajo Coalition controls the northern plateau. Several Cherokee bands relocated southwest after the 2039 migration. Independent councils operate under tribal charters. LA is independent."

On the screen, a photograph appeared of desert mesas at dusk. Wind turbines turned slowly along a ridgeline while solar arrays glinted beside adobe structures.

"How do we know all of this?" another student asked as others snickered.

"I need to know! How do we know all of this?" The student asked again, more insistent while he stared at the map.

The guide did not smile. "We know because borders do not stop satellites. We know because trade still leaves records. Because people still talk."

"And because history is written by the winners," someone added from the back.

Mr. Fad turned at that. "History is written by the survivors," he corrected. "There are no winners in war; there are only costs."

That quieted them more than the guide's answer had. The display shifted again. A timeline ribbon scrolled along the floor beneath their feet with a faint glow:

2038: Philadelphia Destroyed.

2039: Reconstruction and Supranational Accords Signed.

2042: Second UAA–Texan War Concludes.

2043: Texas Petitions for Entry.

Another student crouched to read a smaller plaque embedded in the wall to turn the conversation back to the Great Plains Nation.

"Who was Walt Ridley?" she asked.

"The second President of the Great Plains Nation," the guide said. "He succeeded Jeremiah Johnson after the disappearance."

"And Samantha Johnson?"

"Third President. Elected in 2038. She expanded the Wall Initiative and formalized isolation as constitutional doctrine."

"Why would people vote for that?" the girl asked.

Mr. Fad gestured toward the memorial wall visible through the atrium glass. "Fear," he said simply.

They moved deeper into the wing. A rotating hologram displayed the supranational charter between the UAA and the Bluegrass States Republic. Articles floated in clean text: *Shared Defense. Open Transit. Sovereign Retention.*

One boy squinted. "So it is like one country?"

"No," the guide said. "Two nations. A shared framework."

"That sounds like one country."

"It isn't," Mr. Fad said. "That distinction matters."

"Why?"

"Because the last time people thought it didn't," he said while nodding toward the Secession Gallery and pointing, "Everything fractured."

Silence followed. Near the end of the hall stood a final installation. It was not interactive or digital. It was a simple slab of concrete encased in glass. It had been recovered from the original foundation of the Convention Center. The inscription beneath it read:

March 20, 2028. The Accord Event. Charlotte. Below that, in smaller text: *Reconstruction began March 20, 2038.*

A girl tilted her head. "So was it worth it?" she asked.

The guide did not answer. Mr. Fad took a long breath before he did. "Worth is a dangerous word. People thought they were preventing something worse. Others thought they were creating something better."

"And what actually happened?" the boy pressed.

Mr. Fad looked around the room. He looked at the maps, the trade corridors, and the walls that rose because people were afraid. He looked at the alliances formed because people were tired of fighting.

"Everything," he said.

"What is the Consortium?" one of the students asked while pointing at a section under construction.

The panel was unfinished with temporary signage. A placeholder placard read: *The Consortium – Pending Archival Release.*

The guide hesitated. "It was a coordinating body," she said carefully. "It operated behind multiple governments during the early years of the Unwinding."

"Like a secret government?" the boy pressed.

Mr. Fad answered before she could. "Like people who believed they knew how to hold the world together," he said while looking at the guide, "by tearing it apart."

"Did they?" another student asked.

Mr. Fad looked back toward the scorched concrete slab. "This," he said while gesturing toward the slab, the maps, the trade corridors, and the memorial wall, "all of this traces back to decisions they made."

The students were quiet.

"But fault," he added, "does not travel alone."

The guide did not interrupt him.

"They believed the world was coming apart," Mr. Fad continued. "They believed strong hands could keep it from collapsing. Some of them thought they were saving it."

"And were they?" the girl asked again.

Mr. Fad looked at the memorial wall through the atrium glass. Sunlight caught the polished names and turned them briefly gold. "Sometimes when you hold something too tightly," he said, "you are the one who breaks it."

No one laughed. A boy pointed again at the unfinished Consortium exhibit. "So why isn't it open yet?"

"Because archives take time," the guide replied carefully. "Some records were sealed. Some people are still alive. Some truths are complicated."

Mr. Fad nodded. "History does not end when the war ends. It ends when the last person stops arguing about what happened."

A bell chimed softly through the wing as a timed signal marked the end of the rotation block. Parents began herding students toward the exit corridor. As they filed out, the unfinished placard remained: *The Consortium – Pending Archival Release.* Under it, in smaller lettering: *Full Declassification Scheduled: 2050.*

One of the students lingered behind. "Do you think they knew what would happen?" she asked quietly.

Mr. Fad considered that longer than the others. "I think they knew there would be a cost," he said.

"And they paid it?"

He looked at the names carved into black granite outside, his finger pointed to the myriad names. "No, they paid a lot of it. The others who fell during all the wars, all of the destruction, that was the cost that was paid in blood. But I hear the Consortium is still out there."

Mr. Fad seemed to know more than he was sharing. When the student looked at him puzzled, he simply smiled and moved into the afternoon light. Charlotte stood rebuilt with steel, glass, and green spaces where the rapture had once littered the ground with millions of piles of clothing. Trains moved by on the new tracks; Pristine and immaculate markets now opened. Children crossed streets without looking over their shoulders. Across the horizon, cranes still worked.

The bus doors folded open. Students climbed aboard while arguing about lunch. Mr. Fad paused at the bottom of the steps and looked back once more at the memorial wall.

Wind moved low across the high desert while bending scrub and carrying the dry scent of dust and cedar. Twelve stood at the edge of a shallow canyon to watch the late light settle across red stone and solar panels alike. The turbines along the ridge turned slowly with a patient and indifferent rhythm. Her left shoulder still had a chronic ache from years of her duty with the Consortium.

Below her, children ran between adobe structures painted in muted earth tones. Laughter carried upward in thin but real notes. A small flag bearing a Cherokee pattern, altered slightly to reflect the relocation into New Mexico, snapped softly from a wooden post. She was no longer called Twelve here. Her memory had returned years ago, but she told no one. She remained silent until the children found her bleeding in the trees. The name had been spoken once by an elder and then set aside. They had given her another. The elder had opened the Cherokee Bible and found her name in Genesis: Eden. ⊠⊠⊠. *Idani*. She wore the name proudly, as it was an escape from the identity where she had done so many evil things in service to The Chairman.

A teenage boy approached from behind while holding a small wooden carving that remained unfinished and rough along the edges.

"You said the grain runs this way," he said with uncertainty.

She took the piece from him and turned it in her hands. Her movements were precise and thoughtful. She adjusted his grip on the knife. "Don't fight it," she said. "If you force it, the wood splinters."

He nodded. She handed it back, but he lingered. "You used to be a soldier," he said quietly.

She didn't answer immediately. "I used to belong to people who thought they could fix everything," she said instead.

He waited for more, but she did not offer it. A girl called out from below, and the boy jogged away with the carving in hand. Twelve remained where she was. She reached into the pocket of her worn jacket and pulled out a small object wrapped in cloth. It was a metal dog tag with edges worn smooth by time. She did not look at it long. She had already said goodbye.

The wind lifted again. "I hope you found yourself," she murmured. She spoke not to the desert or the sky, but to a man who had once woken on a rooftop without remembering her name.

She remembered everything now. She remembered her mother, Troy Thomason's Vice President-elect, and her father, killed by the same Zero Energy technology she had later used alongside Jack, Phen, and Vannah to erase the Accords in Charlotte. She remembered the day she had seen Jack for the first time since abducting him from Camp Racetrack while she was still with the

Consortium. Most clearly, she remembered the love she had seen in his eyes when he looked at her identical twin, Eve—a doctor in the United Alliance of American Marines.

She remembered the attack on the cloning facility that had killed all of Zero Company, a slaughter she was lucky to survive. She remembered the young Cherokee children who had recovered her from the wilderness when she was seconds from death.

She closed her hand around Jack's dog tag and knelt, pulling her own tags off over her head. They dangled in her hand for a moment, cold metal catching the dying light, before she kissed his one last time. The desert soil was loose and dry beneath her fingers. She pressed the metal into the earth and covered it.

Below, someone laughed. Someone called her by her new name.

"Idani! Idani!"

She turned toward the sound and did not look back.

Destin, FL — 07.15.44

Late afternoon settled gently over Destin. The Gulf lay wide and flat beyond the dunes while the water turned a muted blue under a lowering sun. Sea oats bent in the breeze. The air carried salt and the faint hum of distant boat engines. Six stood barefoot in the sand just beyond the back deck with her arms folded loosely. She watched her children chase each other near the shoreline.

"Jack, not too far," she called.

The boy slowed but did not stop. He turned back with a grin that carried more confidence than caution. His little sister, Ashby, followed behind him, tripping and falling in the sand. Even though her steps were uneven, she laughed, trying to keep up with her big brother. Crashing waves drowned her laughter.

Behind Six, the screen door creaked. Jack Ashby Sr. stepped carefully onto the porch with one hand braced on the frame and the other gripping his cane. The movement cost him more than he liked to show. An oxygen concentrator hummed softly just inside the doorway while the line trailed discreetly beneath his shirt.

"You let him test the water," he said; his voice was roughened by age and weather. "That's good."

Six did not turn immediately. "He thinks he is invincible."

"All boys named Jack do."

That earned him a glance. He lowered himself into the chair beside the small table where a glass of iced tea sweated in the heat. His hands trembled slightly as he reached for it, though he steadied them before lifting the glass.

"You did not have to name him that," he said after a moment.

"I know."

The children's laughter rose again. Ashby had fallen in the sand and was protesting the injustice of gravity. Young Jack was already helping her up. Senior watched them quietly.

"You could have left all of it behind," he said. "The names. The history."

"I did not name him for the history," Six replied. "I named him because I wanted the name to mean something different."

He absorbed that. The wind shifted while carrying the sound of waves folding over themselves in patient repetition.

"You are a better Marine than I ever deserved," he said, almost to himself.

She gave him a sharp look at that. "I retired."

"Still."

Silence settled between them, though it was not uncomfortable. He studied the horizon where the water met the sky in a clean, unwavering line.

"We thought we could stabilize it," he said. "Control it. Pressure here, relief there. You build the right structure and you prevent collapse." His jaw tightened faintly. "Turns out people are not beams and rivets."

Six leaned her elbows on the porch railing. "You built something," she said.

"And it broke," he answered.

She watched her son pull a length of driftwood from the surf like it was treasure. "Everything breaks," she said. "The question is what you build after."

He looked at her then. "You sound like her," he said quietly.

Six did not ask who. The screen door opened again and her husband stepped out while wiping his hands on a towel. He'd lived his life as a civilian, a contrast to the life she had lived in the Marines. He nodded respectfully toward the older man before heading down the steps toward the kids. Senior followed him with his eyes.

"You chose well," he said.

"I did."

The children ran back up the beach. Jack held the driftwood above his head like a sword while Ashby trailed him, determined not to be left behind.

"Grandpa!" Jack called as he skidded to a stop near the porch. "Look what I found!"

The elder smiled; the lines around his eyes deepened. "Solid piece," he said. "You can carve that."

"Mom says I have to learn the grain first."

"Your mom is right."

Jack beamed and ran back toward the water. The old man leaned back in his chair with slow and measured movements. The breeze lifted the edge of the blanket folded beside him.

"You don't owe me anything," he said.

"I know."

"I do not expect forgiveness for what I helped create."

She considered that. "You are not the only one who lost people," she said gently. "We all carry it."

He nodded once. The sun lowered further to turn the Gulf into hammered gold. After a while, his breathing evened out. His chin dipped slightly toward his chest. The glass of tea rested untouched in his hand. Six stepped closer and eased the glass from his fingers before it could slip. She drew the blanket over his legs and adjusted the oxygen line where it had shifted. He stirred just enough to register her presence.

"You did good," he murmured.

"So did you," she replied.

His eyes closed again. Down by the shoreline, her children argued over who got to carry the driftwood. Her husband pretended to referee and failed on purpose. The tide moved in and out. Six stood there for a long moment while listening to the rhythm of it all: the waves, the wind, the rustle of sea oats, and the bright voices of children who had never known the world as it once was.

She looked at her son. She looked at her daughter. She looked at the old man resting in the porch chair. Then she turned back toward the water as the sun dipped lower to let the light settle over all of them without reaching for anything more.

Final Thoughts

What started as an idea in the 1990s was a simple question: what would happen if the United States fractured under its own weight? That question has now become the trilogy you have just finished.

The Lone introduced a world already broken. *Shadow Patriots* showed how it broke. *Broken Patriots* brought us to the true cost of those decisions and the people forced to live with them. The larger arc of *The Great Unwinding* is now complete. The wars were fought. The walls were built. The alliances were signed. The consequences remain.

History does not end when a treaty is signed. It continues in the lives of ordinary people who inherit the aftermath. It lives in rebuilt cities, uneasy alliances, and children growing up in a world shaped by decisions they did not make. There are still stories left to tell inside this world, but they will not be about how it unraveled. They will be about how people live within what remains. That was always the point.

This trilogy was never a prediction or a manifesto. It is a work of fiction built around questions that matter to me. It asks what holds a nation together and what tears it apart. It examines what loyalty costs, what memory means, and what love survives. If these books gave you something to think about, something to wrestle with, or even just a story that stayed with you for a while, then the journey was worth taking.

Thank you for walking through *The Great Unwinding* with me. There will be more stories, but this chapter is closed.

THANK YOU FOR READING

A Note from the Author

First and foremost, thank you for spending your valuable time inside this universe. As an independent author, nothing is more rewarding than knowing these stories have found a home with readers like you.

If you enjoyed your journey through these pages, would you consider taking a brief moment to leave a review on Amazon?

Reviews are the absolute lifeblood of independent publishing. They don't need to be long or deeply analytical. A single sentence sharing your honest thoughts helps other readers discover these books and allows me to keep writing them.

Your support makes all the difference. Thank you for being a vital part of the journey.

- JAMES C. EDWARDS -

LEAVE AN HONEST REVIEW

Scan the QR code to go directly to the Amazon review page

James C. Edwards is a novelist and publisher whose obsession with storytelling began in childhood. Long before entering the professional industry, he filled notebooks with hand-written narratives spanning political thrillers and speculative worlds. This early drive to build worlds reached a peak one summer when he compiled his stories into home-printed volumes bound in three-ring binders for friends and family. That fundamental passion has defined his career ever since.

In 2018, James released his debut devotional, The Song of You, highlighting a reflective and faith-centered dimension to his craft. He soon pivoted to fiction with The Lone, launching The Great Unwinding trilogy. The series expanded with the prequel, Shadow Patriots, and concluded its central arc with Broken Patriots. Together, these books trace the collapse and reconstruction of a fractured America across two decades of narrative history.

Alongside his political fiction, James has ventured into darker, speculative territory with the standalone novels Eden Unborn and Lost Coast — unsettling, character-driven stories in the tradition of Black Mirror and The Twilight Zone, where science fiction and horror converge to explore the fragile edges of humanity.

Through his imprint, Vanguard Patriot Press, James supports emerging authors and independent publishing initiatives. He also operates a printing and marketing business where he blends technical craftsmanship with creative vision. James lives in North Carolina with his wife, Amber. When not at his desk, he enjoys gaming, exploring new ideas, and constructing the next story waiting to be told.

THE WORKS OF JAMES C EDWARDS

THE GREAT UNWINDING UNIVERSE

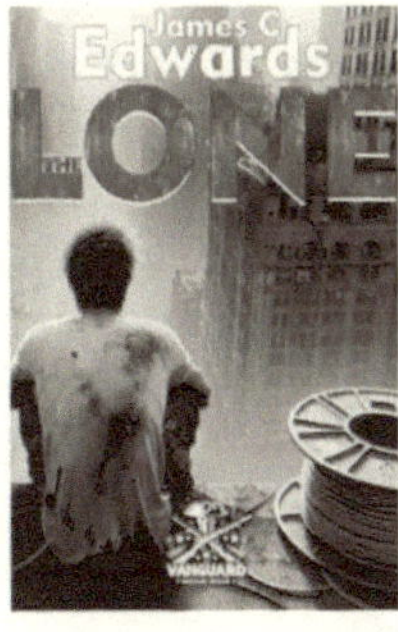

OTHER NOVELS

NON-FICTION

ALL BOOKS

www.ingramcontent.com/pod-product-compliance
Lightning Source LLC
LaVergne TN
LVHW100500110826
845146LV00002B/466

* 9 7 9 8 9 8 9 8 4 9 5 8 1 *